AIN'T
NO
BUM

DENNIS C. McCREIGHT

This is a work of fiction. The characters, incidents, and dialogue are the product of the author's imagination. Any resemblance to any living person is entirely coincidental

ISBN: 1466478004
ISBN 13: 9781466478008

"Ain't No Bum" is dedicated to my wife Linda, whose belief in me was the inspiration for this book. Without her encouragement this book would never have been started or finished.

My sincere appreciation is also owed to all my friends and family who offered me encouraging words during the writing and editing of the book, especially Bob Hartwig, John Vega, and my daughters, Mindy McCann and Renee Shelton.

I also would like to thank Linda Smith, my editor, who tried her best to convert me from a story-teller to a writer.

1

"Who that sad man, Mommy? Why he cry?" shouted little Butch, while pointing with the vigor only a curious rambunctious four year old could muster.

Vi, as she preferred to be called, turned towards the man who had captured her son's attention. *Oh my God! I think its Benny. I haven't seen him since he went off to war. If it's Benny, the war destroyed the most handsome boy in our class of '38.*

Butch tugged on her dress and yelled, "Mommy, mommy."

Hugging him, she said, "I'm sorry son, Mommy was thinking. I think that's Mommy's friend, Benny, and he's not crying because he's sad." *Or, I should say I'm pretty sure it's him. I can't believe how haggard and pale he's become. He used to dress like a movie star. Now, his dirty threadbare Army uniform just hangs on him. From the looks of all his medals and old body, he must have been through hell.*

Butch cocked his head at his mother's confusing reply. "He not sad? Why he cry, Mommy? He got owee?"

She smiled at her son's simplistic, but common sense, question. "He's happy the war is over. Sometimes people cry

1

when they're happy. Now, please stop your rude yelling and pointing!"

Butch turned his wandering attention towards a huge bonfire with sparks flying in all directions. "WOW!" he shouted as two men tossed another dilapidated outhouse on the town's end of the war celebratory bonfire.

Mom and Grandpa, like Butch, smiled and cheered at the ever increasing bonfire. As the flames peaked, so too did their joy and hope. Finally, the war is over! At last, Butch's father will be coming home.

Looking at Grandpa doting on young Butch, she wondered how her father would cope with her and Butch moving away. *I'm sure he'll relish the thought of a house and garden no longer terrorized by his grandson's boundless energy, but I know he'll miss him.*

"Penny for your thoughts," her father said. "You must have been dreaming about your husband finally gettin' home."

"A little. Mostly I was thinking about how you'll handle us moving out."

"Don't worry about me. I'll finally have time to nap and read," he said as he ruffled the hair of his grandson, "now that I won't have to be spending all my time chasing Butch out of the garden, or rescuing the cat."

Vi smiled. "I don't think I'll ever forget the look on that cat's face when Butch comes near him. Butch never did understand why you can't carry a cat by his neck."

Grandpa laughed at the thought of his poor tabby being held in a head lock that many a wrestler would be proud of. "Yeah, one year after Butch was old enough to catch the cat, it ended up with the longest neck in town."

"And the biggest eyes. I thought its eyes would pop out when he carried him around. Butch oughta be thankful that the cat was a mild-mannered one. He never once scratched him."

She watched Butch pester his grandfather to lift him up for a better view of the bonfire, and sighed at the thought of after four long years she would once again have the company of Butch's dad. She couldn't help but smile at the prospect of gaining an ally in facing the ever increasing complex challenge of raising their mischievous, energetic son. *Hopefully,* Mom prayed, *my husband's return will re-start the tender moments the war so abruptly interrupted.*

Before Mom's thoughts could run away to some of her fond pre-war memories and some painful disappointments, Butch interrupted with another of his seemingly endless questions. "Mommy, why Benny do that?"

Vi glanced at Benny, and noted that in response to the vigorous but slightly out-of-tune rendering of the National Anthem by the town's high school band, Benny was saluting the American flag so proudly displayed by a color guard comprised of well-beyond-their-prime members of the local chapter of the VFW. And, standing next to Benny was a disheveled old man—her notorious, and usually drunk, father-in-law.

After a moment to recover from the shock of the resurrection of her family's nemesis, she said, "The way Benny is touching his head is called a salute, and Benny's saluting the flag of our country."

"Why, Mommy?" asked Butch.

"Because the band's playing a song that makes soldiers salute the flag of our country."

"Him soldier like Daddy?" His wide eyes sparkled with the excitement of seeing someone like his dad. Even though his father had been gone for most of his life, Butch knew, thanks to all of Mom's stories, Dad was a soldier. To Butch's four year old mind all soldiers were alike, regardless of appearance.

"Yes," answered Mom. *Please God keep our soldier safe from the ravages of war that have so destroyed poor Benny, and aged him so beyond his years. And, please God, don't bring my husband home to more of his father's disturbing drunken behavior.*

Butch's attention, and the attention of the townspeople gathered around the dying bonfire, was interrupted.

"Stop! Stop! Don't throw my outhouse on the fire! Ma and I are still usin' it," cried a weather-beaten old man who was dressed in stained bib overalls and a faded red plaid flannel shirt.

"You've got to be kiddin' me," exclaimed one of the strapping farm hands who was preparing to feed the outhouse to the flames. "Your crapper looked like it was just waitin' for a puff of wind to blow it down."

"No, I'm not kiddin' ya. Please take it back to my farm," pleaded the farmer.

"Ah, come on. It's a piece of crap. Tell ya what, let me and my buddies stoke the fire with it, and we'll build ya a new one as soon as we can find enough lumber," offered the young, slightly tipsy, leader of the bonfire brigade.

Noting that the old farmer was wavering but not yet convinced, the bonfire leader sweetened the deal. "You let us feed your old crapper to the flames right now, and we'll open a bottle of Schnapps for you to celebrate its death."

After a moment to savor the thought of drinking the beloved alcoholic beverage of his Swedish forefathers, the old farmer agreed to the offer with a hearty, "Yah, yah, okay. But build it quick. Ma ain't gonna like doin' her business in the bushes."

"Fair enough—we'll start bangin' it together on Monday," the leader said as he and his cohorts lifted the outhouse in preparation for its flaming demise.

Butch, Mom, Grandpa and the other war weary citizens cheered as the last outhouse of Fulton County enhanced the flames while thousands of miles away the flames of the long war that stole away so many of their sons, brothers and husbands, finally diminished.

2

The night of celebration faded. Mom smiled as Butch snuggled tightly against her in deep slumber, while she too attempted to sleep. Her mind wandered back to what seemed like an eternity ago when war was "over there" and so meaningless.

Without direction or prompting, her thoughts of doubt once again arose. *What kind of a husband will return to me?*

Vi found her thoughts lingering on a memorable important moment of five years ago. Short years in measure of time, but years made long by the four year intercession of war. She fondly remembered the tall, handsome young man with a long angular face and oversized outward pointed ears who wandered into her life, and the Walgreens where she clerked. The vivid memory of her first meeting of her husband-to-be opened wider the floodgates of her memories and tears.

"May I help you?" Vi inquired in a manner not only in keeping with her Walgreens employee training, but also with a slight hint of a lilt that she hoped would draw his attention.

Pointing with his briar pipe at the tobacco display behind her, the slender, but muscular, young man asked, "Do you have Prince Albert in the can?"

"Why yes, we do," she replied, pointing to the cans of Prince Albert tobacco prominently displayed behind her.

With a small chuckle and barely visible grin, he said, "That's a mighty small can for a prince. You oughta let him out."

Despite feeling a bit foolish for falling for such a corny old joke, Vi couldn't help but smile at his humorous attempt to melt her "may-I-be-of-service" demeanor. Even though Vi was flattered by the man's desire to charm her, she, nonetheless was on guard. Being the five and dime, complete with soda fountain, nearest to the local Civilian Conservation Corp (CCC) encampment, Walgreens was from time to time full of strapping young bucks from the camp. Most were polite, friendly, and often shy young men who were only in Walgreens for fulfilling there toiletry needs and a welcome brief release from their hard labor. But, some of the young CCC workers visited Walgreens more in hope of female attention than the commercial offerings of a five and dime, as Vi wondered about the charming young man facing her.

Pushing her concerns aside, she asked, "Is there anything else I can interest you in?"

"Yes, you can get me a pouch of Sir Walter Raleigh pipe tobacco, and you could tell me your name," the young man confidently requested.

Normally, Vi would have gotten the requested pouch, demanded payment of a dime, noted receipt of the dime, and offered thanks for the business while encouraging a return visit for further shopping. But this time, Vi not only performed all the prescribed Walgreens transaction steps, she also added, "My name is Vi, what's yours'?"

He smiled, with a sense of achievement. "Pleased to meet you Vi. Friends call me Milt, Milt McCoy. Vi's an unusual but nice name. Is it short for Viola or Violet?"

She smiled. "Vi is the nickname I prefer. My real name is Violet, Violet Stewart, but I never liked the name my parents gave me."

"Why, not?" asked Milt.

"Because I want my own name; not some name that has been passed down in our family for generations. I want to be me instead of just someone continuing a tradition. Besides, Violet makes me sound like I am some fragile little flower that's good for only looking pretty and smelling nice."

An awkward silence descended for a moment.

Vi wondered why she had just revealed family history and her feelings to a seemingly interested young man she had only just met. *Either I am getting desperate for a beau or there is something more to this boy that only I can see.*

Milt tried, but failed, to think of some way to break the silence. A fear came over him that demanded him to come up with some way to further impress this young lady or the silent moments would end in only a sheepish good bye. Try as he might, his thoughts just kept dwelling on the pleasure of not having his clumsy advances rejected by such a pleasant young lady. Not just a pleasant young lady, but a very pretty one, even though she's a bit more buxom and robust then currently fashionable. As Milt gazed at her and continued his search for words, he was amazed that her smile wasn't only from her mouth but also from her sparkling hazel eyes. *I've got to come up with something. Good lookin' gals like her don't come along too often and they for sure don't often give me a smile like hers.*

Three short blasts of a shrill whistle broke the silence.

"Darn, my time's up. I have to go back to camp. Nice meetin' you, Vi, and I hope to see you next time they let us come to town," Milt blurted out with a smile as he quickly bolted for the CCC truck.

Flustered by his sudden departure Vi's voice almost departed with Milt but just in time she found voice enough to pleasantly reply, "Likewise, see you soon," and waved.

* * *

As the weeks passed since the CCC last visited Walgreens, Vi from time to time found her mind straying from her Walgreens duties as she remembered her brief but pleasant first encounter with the tall, handsome, somewhat humorous, Milt McCoy. Often, the brief remembrance would end with hope that Milt would again wander back into her life.

In the early spring, as the crops in the fertile fields and wild flowers of the meadows surrounding the Spoon River awakened, Vi's hopes also blossomed when one day a dusty stake-bed truck, labeled as property of the CCC, rumbled to a screeching stop in front of Walgreens. With no lack of chaotic hollering and youthful bravado, the truck's riders disembarked for their disorderly assault on Walgreens.

To Vi's pleasant surprise one of the CCC lads was Milt. Hoping Milt wouldn't notice, she quickly checked her appearance in a small mirror kept on the jewelry counter. Vi had just enough time to make minor cosmetic and hair adjustments.

"I was hopin' you'd be working today," Milt said in a soft blunt voice.

In a slightly nervous voice, Vi said, "I guess you picked the right day because tomorrow is my day off."

"Well fancy that. Tomorrow's also my day off. Maybe we could take in a matinee. I hear that new Clark Gable movie playin' at the Orpheum is pretty good," Milt nervously proposed, knowing full well he was being a bit forward, but hopefully not improper.

Vi was torn as to how to answer. She wanted to get to know Milt but not by starting off in a dark movie house where the temptation for hands to wander might arise.

"Excuse me Vi, could you help me?" Mr. Wilson, the town's Superior Court judge asked.

Thank goodness for the interruption. She signaled Milt that she would be back in one moment, and asked the tall, thin customer as to how she could be of service.

"Just buying some Burma Shave cream today, Vi", the judge said while he quickly sized up the young man who had been chatting with her.

"That will be twenty five cents, Judge Wilson."

Sliding a quarter over the counter to Vi, he gave a subtle, brief nod towards Milt, as he implored Vi to take care and departed.

The judge's nod worked. A subtle fear prompted Milt to warn himself. *Christ, that old coot, who looks like Lincoln without a beard, is a judge. Probably knows my folks. No wonder he gave me that skunk eye nod. I better watch myself.*

Vi returned her attention to Milt with a proposal of her own and a bit of a fib.

"You're right. The movie is quite good. I saw it last week. Why don't we go on a picnic instead? After a week of being cooped up in Walgreens, I like getting outside on my only day off."

Although he knew that after almost two years of serving with the CCC he'd had more than enough of the great outdoors, for the sake of being with Vi, he found himself agreeing that her preference was a great idea.

"Great, I'll fry some chicken, and –" Vi started to suggest other delicacies but was interrupted by three short blasts of the CCC whistle she was beginning to despise.

"Darn, gotta run. I'll see ya here at noon tomorrow, okay?" Milt said as he reluctantly scrambled for the CCC truck while sheepishly waving to Vi. *Hope the guys didn't see that wave or I'm in for a whole bunch of razzin' on the way back, but I sure as hell don't care.*

In a soft voice meant only for Milt, Vi agreed to a noon time rendezvous, and, in a state of anxiety bordering on panic, shifted her thoughts to how she would prepare a first date picnic for a young man whose tastes she knew nothing about. *I guess it will have to be fried chicken for starters followed by hope.*

3

Fried chicken and hope won the day. One successful picnic demanded another. Searching for suitable future picnic grounds amongst the parks, meadows and river banks of Fulton County seemed to now monopolize Vi and Milt's infrequent time off.

Privately they both sensed their numerous picnic ground searches were not solely for a perfect spot to picnic. Zero ants and smooth comfortable grounds were desired, but as summer neared the need for privacy surpassed the need for a comfortable pest free site.

Discovery of suitable private grounds inevitably led to picnics centered on not only food, but also idle conversation that raised questions meant for personal discovery. Not inquiries to assure themselves of their choice of whom they would pleasantly pass time with, but instead explorations of what made each other so unique and possibly desirable. "Tell me about yourself" questions were eventually exchanged and discovery, after a bit of stumbling hesitation, began.

"Milt, where are you from originally?"

Caught a bit off guard by the sudden question, Milt bought some time as he continued to cast their fishing poles. "Well, I'm kinda from Anderson County in Indiana and also from over in Knox County."

"Is Knox County where your folks live?"

He shrugged his shoulders. "Last I knew they were still there."

"What about your folks, do they live in Fulton County?"

"Yes, in fact I live with them on their small farm at the outskirts of Canton. We used to live on the edge of Farmington so that Dad could be close to his coal mine in Middle Grove."

"How come they moved to Canton? That's a bit of a stretch from Middle Grove."

"We didn't want to move, but when the bank went under Dad lost the mine. It kind of changed things. Dad didn't want to stay in Farmington because there were too many bad memories. He didn't want to live near the miners that used to work for him. I think he kind of felt he'd let them down."

"Hold on, I thought ya said he lost everything when the bank went under. How did he have money to move?"

"He only lost the money he had on deposit for his mine. Dad didn't completely trust banks. He still had some money he'd squirreled away. Actually, believe it or not, he buried the money in the back yard. He didn't have much, but at least he had enough cash to buy our small little farm."

"He must've got a good deal."

"Matter of fact, he really did, but we kind of felt sorry for the old couple that sold Dad the farm."

"Why's that?"

"They had to sell the farm, and we could tell they didn't want to sell. But the County was getting ready to take the farm for back taxes, and they didn't have any other offers or kids to take over the farm. They sold it really cheap and now they're living with relatives in Peoria. When they signed the deed over to Dad, you could see the pain on their faces. The old farmer's wife cried the whole time the sales papers were being signed. I felt so sorry for them."

"That must have been painful to watch."

"Yes it was. I'll never forget that day. I almost wish we hadn't bought it, but I'm glad Dad did because it sure has helped out during these tough times. It isn't much of a farm, just a few acres. We couldn't make a living off of it, but, thanks to Mom, we survive off that little bit of land."

"So your mom is the farmer in the family?"

"Actually she's the hunter in the family, but she also keeps the farm going. Thanks to Mom's canning and hunting, we never go hungry. Dad's gone quite a bit on business so coming up with food for all of us falls on Mom."

Milt raised his eyebrows. "Hunter? Your Mom's a hunter?"

"She sure is! Mom's been hunting with her old .22 rifle ever since her dad taught her to shoot when she was six. Grandpa says she's such a good shot because of the Sioux side of the family."

"Sioux! Your Mom's part Injun?"

"Yes, one half Sioux on her mom's side, and the other half Scotch."

"That's quite a mix. Bet that makes for quite a temper."

"Mom never shows a temper, but Grandma and Grandpa get going once in awhile. When they do, we all try to make ourselves scarce."

"Sounds like they live with y'all?"

"Yes they do, and believe me those two make it quite an interesting house when Grandpa and Grandma are fussin' at each other. When Grandma gets really upset at Grandpa, she pretends not to speak English and rattles off God knows what kind of Sioux hexes and curses. Grandpa just smiles and acts like he doesn't understand Sioux. Then Grandma clams up and once again all's well, or at least the house gets a bit more peaceful."

"There ain't no Injuns around here. How'd your Grandpa meet her?"

"When Grandpa was about eighteen he lit out for the Dakota gold rush. Gold panning didn't work out so he became a trapper. Turned out he didn't know as much about trapping as he thought he did."

"Sounds like he had quite a string of bad luck, what did he do about it?"

"Well lucky for him he met Grandma and she taught him the Indian way to hunt and trap. Next thing you know, he's back in Fulton County with a pretty young Indian bride fresh off the reservation."

"Sounds like huntin' comes natural to your mom, but what's there to hunt around here?"

"A lot of critters, you'd be surprised at the critters we have on the farm."

"Like what? All I've seen so far is rabbits."

"I guess that's why we have Mom's delicious rabbit stew quite a bit. She's also pretty good at shooting squab, turkey and, once in awhile, a deer."

"What the heck's squab?"

"It's what we had for our picnic. Did you like it?"

"Yeah, but what is it?"

"Well, my Dad says that when he was in France fighting the Kaiser he ate squab in one of their fancy restaurants. He thinks it's kind of funny because the Frenchies call 'em squab but in this country we call them what they are—pigeons."

Milt's face turned bright red. "Pigeon! You fed me pigeon?"

Milt's indignant shocked expression startled Vi. She stifled a laugh and attempted to soothe him. "Mom doesn't shoot just any old pigeons! She stays away from those pigeons you see in the city that do nothing but decorate statues. Country, grain fed pigeons are a lot cleaner and a whole lot tastier. I was almost a teenager before I realized fried chicken wasn't chicken. We can't afford to kill the chickens. Need their eggs. Mom's crack shooting keeps squab on the table so our chickens can keep laying eggs for breakfast."

"I reckon that makes sense. Breakfast without eggs once in awhile can be a bit hard to take. But ya gotta admit pigeon takes some gettin' use to."

She placed her hands on her hips, and said, "Only if you let it matter. I'll bet your family also has to eat a little different now days!"

"Yeah, the Depression sure has made me full of beans. And ring bologna when we can scrape some extra pennies together. I never thought I'd come to like boiled beans and boiled ring bologna. But it beats the heck out of goin' hungry."

"Nothing but beans and bologna, you must be a city boy. Don't your folks have a garden?"

"When I'm livin' with mom and dad I'm a city boy who lives on musical fruit and ring bologna. Or at least I do when we have a good week."

"Musical fruit – what's that?"

"You ain't never heard of musical fruit?"

"No. Really, what is it?"

Milt jumped to his feet and broke into what he believed to be a nimble Irish jig as he chanted, "Beans, beans the musical fruit the more you root the more you toot."

"Oh," Vi restrained her giggle as her slightly rounded rosy cheeks turned to a pale crimson blush.

She passed him a plate of deviled eggs, and started to ask him more about himself. But, before Vi could probe further into the mysteries of his life, he asked, "What kind of business is your dad in since he lost his mine? I'm guessin' he ain't mining cuz most all the mines around these parts are closed down. Probably glad he ain't still mining. That's tough work, but it sure is better than being out of work like the rest of us."

"I wouldn't say that he's glad to be out of mining. It is tough work but he always came home happy. He owned it, but he was right down there with the rest of them pecking away at the coal veins."

"Sounds like he's one of them bosses that treats his men like family."

"That's my dad. Over the years many of the miners, most of them Italians from the old country, became friends that were like a part of the family. Since he lost the mine, and many of his friends, he's a bit soured on mining."

"How'd he lose it?"

"Same reason most businesses around here failed – that damn Farmers and Mechanics Bank, pardon my French, went under, and the bank's creditors took all the local business pay-rolls that were on deposit."

"That must have been tough."

"That's not the half of it. When the bank went under, Dad couldn't make payroll so the miners took it out on him. Dad took their anger to heart. It especially hurt because most of the miners were not only his employees, but also friends and neighbors. Dad tried his best not to let it bother him, but when Mr. Signorelli shot himself he lost it."

"Who was Mr. Signorelli?"

"Mr. Signorelli was from a place in Italy that was famous for their quarries and mines. He claimed he was one of the best miners in that part of Italy, but he couldn't find work after the "Great War" because most of the mines were shut down. So in 1920 he wrote a letter to my dad. The letter was in Italian."

"Italian, does your Dad speak dago?"

She cringed at Milt's derogatory term for Italians but chose to ignore his slur. "No, after all the years of Italians working for him, Dad could speak a little bit of Italian, but not enough to read the letter. But Dad, with the help of our neighbor, Mrs. Procini, figured it out. He didn't even know Dad, but Mr. Signorelli wasn't afraid to ask Dad to sponsor him for coming to America. He promised to work for Dad "forever" and take a cut in pay for the first two years. Dad was a bit taken aback, but he figured that anyone that desperate was worth taking a chance on."

"Why did he shoot himself?"

Milt noticed a change in Vi. She looked bothered and was even starting to tear up. *Maybe I'd better change the subject. I ain't so good with bawlin' females.*

Choked with tears, she told Milt in a soft voice about the day she had, till now, kept private, "I don't think we'll ever really know. The day after the mine closed he showed up at our house rambling on in Italian. You could tell he had been drinking. He could barely walk straight – did more stumbling then walking. And, oh, did he reek of cheap wine. He was quite a site to behold. His hair, usually combed and greased, looked like it hadn't been touched, leave alone washed, since God knows when. He still had on his filthy, coal-dusted mining clothes, and his eyes looked more like pools of blood then eyes. You might say he looked like sin."

"He must have been a bit of a scary site to behold. What the heck was he doin' over at your house?"

"Oh, I was very scared. I had never seen him this way, and he kept rambling on about something that Dad didn't at first understand. Mr. Signorelli wasn't acting mean, but showing up with a pistol in one hand and a bottle of half drank grappa in the other made everyone a little nervous."

"A drunk with a pistol would make most anyone a bit on edge. What did y'all do?"

"Mom got out her .22, but Dad told her to get into the house with it. Mr. Signorelli kept babbling on in rapid Italian, punctuated in brief bursts of broken English, about his bambinos. He repeated himself quite a few times, and his demands for his pay got louder by the minute. Dad finally told Mr. Signorelli that he understood, but he explained that the bank took away all the money so he couldn't pay him. Dad offered to help him as much as he could to make sure that his bambinos were at least fed."

"Did that quiet him down?"

"No. Mr. Signorelli kept insisting his bambinos needed him to be paid. Dad's offering and Mr. Signorelli ignoring him went on for quite awhile. Eventually Mr. Signorelli got quieter so we thought all would be okay. We were wrong. All of a sudden Mr. Signorelli babbled something about life, and then he put his gun in his mouth and shot himself."

As happened on that awful day, a sudden silence descended.

Vi's usual smile disappeared as she told about that awful day. She began to cry and slumped into his shoulder. Soon, he felt Vi's tears on his shirt. Unprepared to handle female emotions, Milt lightly hugged her, offered his handkerchief, and said the only thing he had ever seen his gruff old man say when females cried –"I'm sorry."

She struggled to regain her composure. "No need to be sorry. I'm the one that should be sorry. I ruined our nice day with my blubbering and stained your shirt."

"Our day is still nice and my shirt will wash, so don't be sorry. I shouldn't of asked you about it. It wasn't any of my business."

"I don't mind that you asked. I never told anyone about it before. All my tears make me think I needed to tell someone. My whole family took that day hard. We were all shocked, but our day got a lot worse when we had to tell Mrs. Signorelli. Thank God for our neighbor Mrs. Procini. She helped us with the Italian when we told Mrs. Signorelli."

"What about his bambinos?"

"Mrs. Porcini took in the kids to give Mrs. Signorelli some time in private to grieve. Little did she know that she would end up raising the kids."

"Why did she end up raisin 'em?"

"Mrs. Signorelli went completely around the bend when she got the news. Last I heard she's still in the county loony bin. I hear tell that all she does is sit around babbling in Italian, staring into space, and trying to tear all her hair out. She used to be a pretty lady, but when I visited her last year she looked like a really old lady. What a shame for her and those kids."

"How did your dad take all that?"

"Dad really took it hard. He swore he wouldn't ever go near another mine. Dad said he was too old to mine anyway, but we all knew the real reason was that he was devastated by what happened to his miner friends. He stuck to his guns until the money got real tight for us."

"What'd he do then?"

"Just as it looked like he would have to go back to mining, out of the blue, he met a fella who introduced him to the head of the State Mining Board. Now he's a State of Illinois Mine Inspector. I know he misses the friendships of the mines, but we're all glad he isn't mining."

"Enough of my sad tales, tell me about your folks? What does your Dad do for a living?"

"I thought you'd had enough of sad memories." Milt said as he again turned his attention to their fishing poles that even an inexperienced fisherman, like Vi, could see needed no attention.

Why is Milt trying not to answer me? I hope he isn't hiding anything I should know about. I guess I'll just have to find another way to pry his mysteries out of him. "Okay, we can skip the sad parts. At least tell me something about where you come from."

"Knox is a lot like here. You know, lots of farms with corn as far as the eye can see. Land so flat you'd think it would go on forever, and pig farms you can smell for miles away. But we didn't live in the country. Dad's a baker so he kinda sticks close to towns with bakeries."

That's a surprise. I thought he didn't want to talk about his dad, but seeing how he brought him up I might as well ask about his dad one more time. "Is he still baking or did the Depression get him too?"

Without thinking, Milt blurted out, "Depends on whether the old damn fool isn't moon shinin', or getting stinkin' drunk and chasin' loose women."

Stunned by Milt's disdainful outburst, Vi decided to steer the conversation away from Knox and his folks. "Did you live in the country when you lived in Indiana?"

"Oh, yeah, my grandparents farmed about 60 acres."

"You and your folks lived with your grandparents?"

"Nah, I lived with 'em whenever my folks shipped me out to 'em. Times would get tough, or I would get in their way, and off to Indiana I'd go."

"Sorry, that must have been hard to take."

"No need to be sorry. It wasn't hard to take at all. Livin' with Grandma and Grandpa beat the heck out of dodgin' my drunken old man's belt and bailin' them out of jail. Besides I liked that old farm."

Jail—I'd love to know about that. Instead, she asked why he liked living with his grandparents.

"Lots of reasons, but one is that I never went hungry when I was with my grandparents. Grandpa brought in the vittles, and Grandma cooked 'em up real good. And, they were nice to me even when I got a bit too big for my britches."

"Sounds like you have nice grandparents."

"They are. Fact is, I probably love 'em more then I do my folks. They treated me real good, but they didn't take any guff off of me. Grandpa didn't break out the strap for every little bad thing I could find to do."

"I take it they weren't like your folks?"

"That's for darn sure. My grandparents were real Christian-like folks, but they weren't Bible-thumpin' softies. They just didn't think the same way as my folks. Grandma and Grandpa would thump the Bible once in awhile, but they didn't thump me with it."

"Did they make you help with the farming?"

"They didn't really have to make me. I liked it. Pestered them so much about helpin' out they decided to let me, but not before they showed me all the tricks and warned me about the critters' cantankerous ways. I ended up takin' care of most all the critters. Slopped the pigs and stunk to high heaven after I did. Kids teased me at school about stinking like a pig farmer, but I didn't much care. Every day, I collected eggs from about twenty ornery hens. Sounds easy, but unless you wear gloves and talk gentle to 'em it can be a painful job."

"Did you also milk the cows? I tried it once when we visited Uncle Harold's farm, but I couldn't do it right."

"Oh yeah, they showed me how to milk the cows, which I agree ain't easy, but I can do it. I gotta admit though it ain't my favorite thing to do. If those old heifers are in a bad mood there's no tellin' what they'll do. One kicked me so hard it almost broke a rib. I couldn't breathe right for weeks. "

"Ouch. That must have really hurt. Did you do any other chores besides taking care of the farm animals?"

"The last time I stayed with 'em Grandpa showed me how to drive the tractor and harvester. He thought I learned so good he let me harvest most of that year's corn. It was hard work, but I really liked it."

"Sounds like all you did was work. Didn't you get to have some fun?"

"Sure. Matter of fact, best fun I ever had. Almost every day after all the chores were done and the critters taken care of, Grandpa would break out the baseball gear. For an old guy he sure could play ball. That old man could throw a wicked curve ball that I had a heck of a time hittin', and he could catch dang near anything I threw him. We played catch sometimes till it got dark or Grandma got tired of waitin' dinner."

"Is that where you learned how to play ball, or did your dad teach you?"

"Are you kiddin'? Dad was never sober long enough to teach me anything. But thanks to Grandpa, I learned a lot about baseball. I even became a pretty darn good pitcher. He tried to show me how to hit, but I kept pulling my head."

"I don't understand what 'pulling my head' is. What is it?"

"That's what happens when you get so darn excited about where the ball's gonna go after you hit it that you forget to keep your head still so you can see the ball all the way to the bat. If I would've listened to him a bit more maybe that White Sox scout that came to town might of gave me a better offer. He liked my pitchin' and fieldin' just fine but not my hittin'."

"That's neat. You two must really love baseball."

"Yeah, we sure do. Grandpa and I listened to almost all the White Sox games. It was fun, but Grandma would get a bit perturbed with us. She wanted to listen to her radio soapy shows, but Grandpa always insisted on listenin' to the games. Only time he'd turn the radio over to her was when she threatened to not serve dessert. Grandpa would act all upset and storm out the door making a bee-line for the barn. Of course, he'd do his stomping out after he got his dessert."

"Your grandma's desserts must have been awfully good for you two to give up one of your precious games," she teased.

"They were delicious, but I didn't say we didn't listen to the games. See, we never told Grandma that Grandpa and I had hidden in the barn a crystal radio Grandpa and I built. It wasn't easy listenin' to the game on that thing. Signal kept fadin' in and out cuz it was hard to keep the tuning needle on the crystal just right. It wasn't the same as listenin' on the big Philco floor model radio, but it beat the heck out of missin' a game. "

"Didn't you do anything besides baseball for fun?"

"Kinda sounds like that's all, but truth is I had lot more to do for fun then play baseball," Milt said as he checked his bait.

"Like, what?"

"One of the things I really liked to do was tear the livin' heck out of the hayloft. Doesn't sound like much fun, but when you're doin' it with your three cousins that lived nearby it could he a hoot. We built forts out of hay, played hide and seek between the bales, and threw straw bombs at each other."

"I liked doing that too. My sisters and I used to terrorize my Uncle Earl's hay loft when we visited. Did you ever jump out of the hay loft?"

"Not all the time, but if we got real bored we'd throw a whole bunch of straw out the hay loft door and then jump out. Before we jumped, we made sure we had enough straw out the door to break our fall. The trick was to land on the pile. It was only about twelve feet off the ground, but we thought it was like jumpin' off the top of the world. Sure was fun, but I gotta admit it hurt like hell if ya missed the pile."

"When was the last time you were back there?"

"In the spring of my senior year. Mom and Dad didn't send me. I just went on my own. I knew I wasn't gonna graduate. I'd missed too much school. Kinda hard to attend when your folks are always screwin' you up."

"Why did you go?"

"I heard Grandpa was ailin' and worryin' about gettin' seeds in the ground, so I went back and helped him plant the corn. He'd started to slide, so it may've been the last time I'd get to see him. I knew it when I was there, so I tried to make it a good time for both of us. His ailments were givin' him so much trouble he couldn't play ball anymore, so I made sure we listened to all the White Sox games."

"Don't you mean you listened to all the games that didn't interfere with your grandma's soapy shows?"

"Nah, Grandma even gave up her soapy shows so that we could listen. I think she knew that Grandpa didn't have many more games left for him, and I think she knew the time with him meant a lot to me."

"That was awfully sweet of her. She must be quite a nice lady."

"Yeah, she is probably more of a mom to me than my real mom. She fussed over me and Grandpa quite a bit on this visit. She even got up early and did some of the chores so that me and Grandpa could go fishing."

"That was so nice of her, but wasn't it hard for your grandpa to go fishing?"

"It wasn't exactly easy for him, but we only fished at spots that were easy to get to and not too difficult to fish from. I had to do most of the castin' and haulin' the fish in, but I didn't mind at all cuz he really taught me a lot about fishin'. Probably will never be as good as him, but I enjoyed it and his company."

Milt suddenly stopped and shifted his attention to the present. "Vi, Vi ya have a bite!"

Mesmerized by Milt's first expansive revelation about his childhood, Vi completely lost her focus on today's excuse for another outing. Vi may have been distracted, but the fish weren't. Her fishing pole bounced along the river bank on a path straight for the river's muddy water. Quickly, she grabbed her pole just before it was about to go over the river bank.

Thank God! If it had made it over the bank Milt would have probably been upset. The thrashing fish on the end of Vi's line quickly drew her back to the present. *Now, what do I do? I'm not about to show Milt that I really don't have a clue when it comes to fishing.*

"Set the hook, Vi. Give it a big tug or it's gonna get away!"

"I think I've got a big one. I can barely move the pole," Vi groaned, as she strained to land the large creature struggling to free itself from her hook.

"Vi, don't pull too hard. Just keep a steady strain on the line. Let the critter get tuckered out and then you can pull him in real easy like."

"I think I might be the one that tuckers out first," Vi grunted again as she watched the big fish thrash and churn the water even more as she followed Milt's advice. *I hope Milt knows what he is talking about because that fish isn't budging.*

Just as she was about to ask Milt for help, the fish ceased to splash and stir up the muddy water. Encouraged, she increased her pull on the pole, and, as Milt predicted, her fishing line started to move towards the bank. Vi was proud as she turned and beamed a smile towards her fishing mentor. To her dismay, Milt didn't return the smile. Instead, he appeared shocked and perhaps even fearful.

"Cut the line, Vi. Cut the damn line," yelled Milt. "It's a damn snappin' turtle."

Knowing nothing about snapping turtles, Vi didn't fully understand Milt's urgent directions. That is, not until she turned her eyes towards her line. Expecting to see a large fish, instead she found at the end of her line something that appeared to have a large mossy green rock, instead of a fin, on its back. As she marveled at its incongruent lumpy, moss-green appearance, she noticed it didn't appear to be swimming. Instead, it slowly crawled on legs that resembled short hand-like claws, while it snapped its jaw and its interlocking sharp-ended hooked beak together so violently she could easily hear a loud snapping noise. One look at the beast as it climbed the river bank and snapped its jaws, spurred her into action. Vi shrieked, dropped her pole, and ran away as fast as she could.

Oh my God, she dropped her pole and that damn turtle is still coming.

Milt quickly stood with the intention of joining the fleeing Vi, but instead he launched himself into a not-so-graceful face first assault on the soft, grassy river bank. *Damn, I stumbled over my sittin' rock. I gotta get up and out of here.* As he started to rise, he was horrified to find the massive jaws of the turtle only inches away from his feet. *Damn! Those ugly bastards are quick once they get on land.*

As he drew his feet towards his waist with hope of jumping up, the turtle again lunged forward. Each rapid lunge of the turtle made Milt realize he might not get away before the turtle got hold of him. Milt desperately searched for any possible weapon that might stop those snapping jaws. Out of desperation, he rose to his knees, grabbed a nearby rock, and with all his might slammed the rock down towards the turtle. As the old saying goes, "Timing is everything", and for the turtle his time was up as his final lunge met with the timing of the downward violent trajectory of Milt's rock.

Milt stared at the suddenly still turtle and shook. *Man, am I ever lucky. If that rock hadn't got him I'd have been a soprano.*

Vi's voice quivered. "Milt, are you alright?"

Still shaken and momentarily beyond forethought, Milt attacked. "Yeah but no thanks to you! Why didn't you cut the line instead of droppin' the pole? If you'd cut the line, the turtle couldn't of kept climbin' and damn near castrate me. Sure as hell wouldn't have been any kids for us if he'd got to me."

Kids! He said kids, Vi noted, as her thoughts scrambled across a spectrum of emotions. At one end, her emotions dwelled on the lingering fear of the ugly, prehistoric beast lying dead at their feet, then progressed along the spectrum to the hurt of Milt's thoughtless rebuff, and then finally arrived at the other end delightfully focusing on the joy of knowing that Milt also was thinking of future marital bliss complete with their children.

Fighting back tears, Vi said, "I'm sorry. You had the knife and I didn't know what to do. I was so scared. You don't know how glad I am that you're okay."

Crap! She's right, I had the knife. Damn, I just chewed out the only lady besides my grandma that's ever gave a damn about me.

He wrapped his arm around her shoulder and gently squeezed. "No, I'm the one that oughta be sorry. Guess I got a bit scared too and took it out on ya."

"That's alright, I'm just glad that you're okay," she murmured as her soft sobs diminished.

Wow, what a gal! Most of 'em would've slapped me and high tailed it out of here. I kinda acted like an ass. I better do something to make it up to her. "After all that excitement I think we oughta get ourselves out of here. I'll pick up the fishin' gear if you'll gather up the picnic stuff. We'll be out of here in no time.

Maybe even in enough time for an ice cream sundae before I have to catch my ride back to camp."

"Okay, sounds yummy. Don't forget the turtle," she said as her usual smile returned.

"The turtle's fine right where he's at. Raccoons will have a good feast tonight."

"I'm not asking you to move him aside. I mean, let's take him home, so Mom can make her great turtle soup. You can come over for turtle soup dinner, and maybe some more delicious squab you're so fond of."

Milt smiled. "Boy, your mom sure cooks up most anything doesn't she? Next thing ya know you'll be inviting me for snake dinner."

Not to be outdone by another of Milt's humorous cracks that first attracted her to him, Vi smiled and joked right back. "Well, if you'd rather have snake than squab, or turtle, I'm sure Mom knows where some of them slippery critters are in the holler."

Milt declined with as much false sincerity as he could muster. "That there turtle will spoil by the time I get off again, but thanks for askin'."

"No, it won't. Mom will get our neighbor to put it in his ice house. It'll keep for quite a while in there."

Crap! Looks like I ain't gonna get out of this one, Milt thought as he reluctantly agreed to Sunday dinner at her folks' house. *God, I hope Vi's folks don't know about my folks. I wonder what that old asshole of a pa is doin' these days that will embarrass me and scare off Vi's folks.*

4

Milt wondered, but Frank, his father, confirmed; drunk again and caring less whom he embarrassed or offended.

The murmur of the late afternoon drinkers crowded into the dusty, dimly lit bar room of Jake's Tavern and Pool Parlor was raised by the almost understandable drunken slurred request of Ned, Frank's long time drinking buddy. "How 'bout fixin' me up with a shot and a brew, Frank," Ned mumbled as he struggled to maintain his short, skinny body upright by leaning on Frank's broad shoulder.

Interrupting his short drink induced nap, Frank picked his large, angular head up off the bar and demanded, "What the hell did ya just ask me? And what the shit are ya doing sittin' on the floor?"

Recovered from the disruption of his balance by Frank's sudden awakening, Ned spiced the cigar and booze aroma of Jake's with a series of stale beer and pickled pigs feet belches.

"I said, wake your drunken old fool ass up and buy me another round!"

Lifting one bushy eyebrow and the middle finger of his large, perpetually dirty right hand, Frank growled, "Screw you, ya old drunk! I ain't got squat. Get your own, and one for me too while you're at it!"

Ned wobbled in place and pointed a crooked bony index finger at Frank. "Don't give me that crap! You're rollin' in it, so buy me a round."

"How ya figure? Sheriff raided my last delivery."

"Too bad about that, but I know ya got all that dough your boy's been sendin'."

Now fully awake at the mention of his son, he stared in disbelief. "You're drunk outta your mind. Milt ain't gave me nothin' his whole life but a load of crap."

"Maybe he gave ya some hard times, but I know he's been givin' ya his CCC pay."

After downing his boilermaker in one fast swallow, Frank scratched his head and asked, "What the hell are ya babblin' about? What CCC pay?"

"Frank, I've known you forever and a day so don't try to bullshit me. Ya know I'm talkin' about the $25 a month the CCC makes their boys send home to their folks."

Shaking his head in disbelief, Frank leaped off his bar stool and jabbed his rigid index finger at the long, bony, pock-marked face of his friend, and yelled, "That's bullshit! I ain't seen a dime since that bum of a son joined up."

"Well, then your boy done screwed ya but good. I know cuz my brother has a son in the CCC, and he gets his $25 first of every month since his boy joined."

Stumbling towards the back door of the tavern, Frank yelled, "Ya gotta be shittin' me! I guess I better go pay that no good bum a visit and get my money. First I gotta go take care of some out-house business. Order us another one, will ya?"

"What can I get ya?" the bartender asked.

"Two boilermakers, right snappy like, before I die of thirst."

"You want rye or bourbon with your beer? And, that'll be a dollar."

"Rye! Ain't no other way to make a boilermaker. Put it on Frank's tab."

"Cash only! He doesn't have a tab."

"Well he oughta, cuz he's gonna be rolling in dough when he gets done with the CCC and his boy."

"In the meantime, it'll be cash!" the bartender said.

"Frank will pay ya when he gets back from visitin' your Sears Roebuck readin' center, and gets his business taken care of."

Slamming his huge hands on the bar, the bartender leaned his massive broken nosed, multiple-scarred face that sat atop a six foot, two-hundred-fifty-pound muscular frame to within inches of the old drunk's rummy nose and growled, "Call me when he gets back and has some cash ready for me."

Grumbling, the skinny old drunk slammed down his last dollar and told the bartender, "Serve 'em up right quick like, I'm thirsty. Ya know, I never thought I'd see a boy screw over Frank McCoy, but his boy sure done did."

* * *

"What the hell ya tappin' me on my shoulder for while I'm doin' my business? This better be good or I'm gonna put some whuppin' on your ass," Frank snarled as he drained away the gallon of beer he'd drunk over the past few hours.

"Oh it's damn good, Frank, because you're under arrest. And if you think you're gonna whup my ass you better think twice and then some," Sheriff Ben Foster said from deep within his six foot four, two hundred fifty pound stout muscular physique.

As he turned towards the Sheriff, while continuing to drain his bladder, Frank yelled, "Ya ain't arrestin' me—I got business to do."

Looking at his wet steaming shoes, Sheriff Foster removed his night stick from his belt and said through clenched teeth, "Frank, I'm gonna let that piss on my shoes pass, but your business is over. One more problem from you and this club will end the problem. Now git your ass marchin' to the jail! You know where it's at."

Extending his palms-up hands, Frank pleaded, "I'm sorry about your shoes Sheriff. I'll clean and shine 'em real good, but ya can't arrest me cuz I still got some business to take care of."

"Not in the town square fountain you're not. We got a perfectly good toilet in the jail for your business."

"How the hell did I get in the town square? I was headin' for Jake's out-house."

"I have no idea, but the citizens don't take kindly to you addin' to the fountain, so let's get to marchin'."

"I can't, Sheriff. I just found out my boy, Milt, done screwed me and his ma out of our CCC pay, so I need to go visit him and get it back."

"That's not any concern of mine. After you visit our jail for awhile you're free to do whatever you want. Meantime, get to walkin'."

Walking away from the sheriff in the direction opposite of the jail, Frank yelled, "Damn it, Sheriff, I said I can't, and I meant, I can't. I'll clean up my mess, but not until I get my money!"

As Frank's stumbled departure picked up its pace, the sheriff yelled, "Frank, get your ass turned around. Now! I don't want to have to carry your drunken ass to the jail, but I will."

Frank raised his middle finger to the Sheriff, and yelled, "Screw you, Sheriff!"

"Crap, now I gotta carry the old coot," he muttered to himself as he chased the drunken Frank McCoy.

Once the sheriff had closed the gap between them, Frank turned and kicked the sheriff's left inner thigh as he screamed in a voice laced with beer spittle, "Damn it Sheriff, I said I can't, and I meant I can't!"

Grimacing from Frank's kick to his groin, the Sheriff hovered over the incapacitated Frank McCoy, whom he had just laid low with a well placed blow from the night stick, and said, "Damn it! I said you were goin' to jail, and I meant it."

As he lifted the dead weighted drunken Frank onto his shoulders for the short hike to the jail, the Sheriff couldn't help but think, *What an embarrassment this old drunk is. I hope no one that might hold Milt in high regard saw this, or hears about it.*

5

"Mc Coy . . . McCoy, where do I know that name from? Seems I've heard or read that name somewhere," Vi's dad, Denny Stewart, wondered aloud as he ran his calloused, age spotted hand through his thin gray hair.

"I don't know where from, but I think you'll like him. You two both like to fish. Besides, I like him, so I'm hoping you do," Vi said as she passed the green beans to her mother, Sarah.

"Besides fishing, which by the looks of it he ain't that good at, if all he got was that turtle you drug home, what do you know about him?"

"He's from Knox County, and works for the CCC. He's always polite and nice to me. I've only been seeing him for a couple of months."

Vi knew that if she let him, her dad would find some reason to cancel the turtle dinner. It wouldn't be the first boy her father ran off. The last one was probably still running. One look at that boy trying for a good night peck convinced Dad that the only appropriate thing to do was to see if their dog

39

Wolf wanted a piece of that boy's butt. Not for the first time, Vi thought, *I know he loves me and wants to protect me, but I wish he would realize that I'm not a little girl anymore.*

"What church does he attend? He ain't one of those Irish mackerel snappers is he?" Denny said as he wagged his thin right index finger at Vi.

"Dad . . ." Vi once again gently chided him for another of his derogatory titles he used with such ease.

"He doesn't cross himself before meals so I don't think he's Catholic, but I'm not sure. Truth is, I don't know much about his church preference. I'm sure there are at least a few more things I don't know about him that I probably should."

In a voice tinged with aggravation, Denny agreed, "I guess you should know a whole lot more. Can't expect me to give permission to continue to court if you don't know much about him, now can you?"

"I agree, Dad. I just hope you're a bit gentler then you are with most of the boys I bring home. Especially that boy I brought home last summer."

Denny raised his slender six foot frame from his chair and said, "What do you mean? I couldn't help that the boy didn't seem to know much about how to address elders. I'll be damned if any young'n is gonna call me by my given name before I give him permission to."

"Please calm down Dad, Milt's not like Robert."

"I am calm! That Robert boy was so damn dense that he even kept calling me Denny after I told him more than once that I preferred Mr. Stewart or Sir. He's lucky I was gentle for your sake, or he would've got some flying lessons as I booted his tail out the door."

"Like I said Dad, Milt isn't like that. He's very polite. Treats me with respect and never has got out of line with me. I hope you like him and let me keep seeing him."

"We'll see ... we'll see."

6

Vi's mom widened her stance, slammed her hands to the hips of her bony body, thinned by the recent onslaught of cancer, as she gently confronted her husband.

"Denny, you know Vi seems to like that young man she's seeing a whole lot. It seems every time I turn around she's singin' his praises to her sisters. Milt this and Milt that, Milt said and Milt did. As much as she is smitten by him, I hope for her sake you'll give him a chance. With all the disappointin' beaus she's had she could use someone that makes her feel good. I know you love her, but we need to give her a chance to find her way. This boy may not be all we'd like him to be, but we gotta trust her judgment."

Denny looked surprised. *What got into Sarah? Can't believe she's poisin' like a lion tamer and spittin' out more words then I hear out of her in a week. Ain't like her at all.*

"You got something there, Sarah. I'll give him a chance, but I think I'll poke around a bit before she drags him home. Knox

43

ain't that far away, so somebody's liable to know something about this boy."

"Just don't go stretchin' what loose tongues wag at you."

"Why, Sarah how can you say such a thing? You know I wouldn't do that," Denny said in that mischievous tone he had become famous for in family circles.

"Now don't you go tryin' your charms on me," Sarah said suppressing a giggle. "Now get yourself on to work, Denny Stewart. I got too much to do to be standin' here listenin' to you not really listenin' to me."

"Love you too, Sarah. See you about sundown."

* * *

Well, the sun ain't down quite yet, so I guess I can stop at the tavern for a game of pool and still make it home on time.

Two steps into the tavern, Denny found who he'd hoped to find. "Hello, Judge. I see you still like to shoot a game after a hard day of listenin' to those snakes that call themselves lawyers."

Without turning to look, a grinning Judge Wilson growled at his old boyhood friend. "Fancy seein' you here, Denny, I thought Sarah regarded pool halls and taverns as the devil's playground."

"Nice to see you too, Judge. What you been up to lately? How's the family?"

"I haven't had time lately for much of anything except work. Ever since the Sheriff's deputies got their schedules mixed up and didn't show up to escort Mrs. Roosevelt when she toured the county, the District Attorney— a duly-elected Democrat I might add— keeps bringing me requests for warrants against Sheriff Randall."

Denny chuckled. "Why don't you just show that slimy-weasel-of-a-DA the door? The way I figure it, he's trying to push some Democrat politics on ya."

After missing another of his shots, the Judge smiled and scratched his five o'clock shadow beard. "You're right. I'd love to show him the door, but I'm sure he'd make my next election a real pain in the neck. On the bright side, my family is doing great. How about yours?"

"Not too bad. But it could be better if the doctors weren't so glum about Sarah."

"My secretary told me she saw Sarah at Dr. Pritchard's last week. I hope she wasn't there for anything serious."

"Afraid it might be serious. Doctor says she has cancer but he's not too certain how bad it is. He said not to worry, because it might just be one of those mild cancers. I never heard of such a thing as a mild cancer, but then again I ain't no doctor."

"I'm sorry to hear that, Denny. If there is anything me and the missus can do please make sure to let us know."

"Thanks, Judge. I really do appreciate it."

"Think nothing of it. We've been friends for way too long for me not to be there in your time of need."

"Yeah, it has been awhile, but even long time friends aren't there like you are for me."

Uncomfortable discussing personal feelings, Judge Wilson decided a new subject was in order. "Oh, by the way, I dropped in at Walgreens the other day and I'll be darned if I didn't see that CCC lad again chatting with Vi. Is she getting serious about that boy?"

"Don't know for certain, but she goes around the house a lot yackin' about how wonderful this Milt McCoy is. She even invited him over for dinner next Sunday."

"Did you say, McCoy? Is he related to the McCoys over in Knox County?"

"I know he claims to be from Knox, but I don't know if any of his relatives are over that way. Why do you ask?"

"Well there's a McCoy family over there that the Knox County Sheriff, and my friend the Knox County Superior Court Judge, know quite well."

"How so?"

"The old gal of the family, I think her name is Bess, winked at Prohibition, and a couple of times lately she's been charged for running a string of girls. Served a little bit of time for one of the charges, but it didn't seem to faze her."

"She sounds like quite a piece of work."

As he attempted an easy shot, the Judge continued, "Yeah she is, but the old man, name is Frank, if I recall, isn't much better. He's a likable guy, but he can't hold his liquor or a job. Though I understand he's a real good baker when he gets his nose out of the bottle. Heard tell he might also be runnin' a still in the holler out by the lake. Sheriff Foster can't prove it but he has his suspicions."

The Judge once again jerked his stick as he shot and sent the cue ball somewhere besides where it needed to go. "Nice shot." Denny grinned. "While you're recoverin' from not makin' another easy one, tell me what you think I oughta do."

"First thing you ought to do is quit giving me advice on my shootin'. Memory serves me, your shootin' isn't much better."

Lifting his hands in surrender, Denny grinned. "Okay, okay, I guess you can only polish a cow paddy so much cuz all that polishin' never makes it a diamond. Seriously though, what should I do about this McCoy fella?"

"Well, if it were me, I'd look into this McCoy family before I made any decision. If it turns out that Milt is related to them you might want to think twice about letting Vi get mixed up with that bunch."

"Thanks for the advice, Judge. I'm supposed to inspect a mine in Knox County, so when I do I think I'll find some time to drop in on Sheriff Foster. Mind if I tell him we chatted and you sent me his way?"

"No, of course I don't. You know the Missus and I think the world of your girls, so if droppin' my name helps you, then it's fine by me."

"Thanks, I'll do that. Take care, Judge, and oh by the way, if you'd smooth out your stroke you might have a snowball's chance in July of makin' that eight ball."

"Git, you ornery old cuss, and good luck."

7

Thrusting his hand out to the short stocky man striding toward him, Denny greeted the man the miners nearby hailed as "Boss". "Hello there, my name is Denny Stewart."

He shook Denny's outstretched hand, and said, "Nice to meet you Mr. Stewart, I'm Bill Paddington, owner and operator of this here mine."

"Nice to meet you too, Bill. Starting about now, I'd appreciate it if you'd just call me Denny."

"Not a problem, Denny. What can I do for ya?"

Denny removed his Mine Inspector badge from his shirt pocket and held it out for Bill's review. "The State of Illinois assigned me the task of inspectin' your mine, and all the others in my district, for compliance to recent revisions to the Mine Safety Act. If you'd be kind enough to show me around, I'll make my visit as short as possible."

"Oh, so you're the inspector we were told to expect. We got all the documents together we figured you might want to see. If there's anything in particular you want to inspect, please let

DENNIS C. McCREIGHT

me know and I'll get right on it. Is there anything you need right now?"

As he chatted with Bill, Denny noticed how unusually clean and organized the Paddington Mine's above ground operation appeared. Hoping to shorten his inspection and put Bill at ease, Denny said, "Your mine looks like one of the more orderly ones I've visited. Can't believe how neat and tidy your slag heaps are. Most of the other mines look like some kid had a hissy fit and threw the slag in every direction he could. My experience is that a good above ground operation means it's a mine that doesn't need much inspectin'."

"Thank you for the kind words. Is there anything in particular you want to inspect?"

"Well, Bill, if you'd show me the controls for your mine sprinkler system we can get started towards getting me out of your hair."

Seems to be a nice fella, but I wonder if he knows that I'm not officially scheduled to be at his mine for at least another six months or so. If he's as sharp as his mine is orderly, he's probably got all sorts of questions about this inspection.

"Just wonderin', but how come your inspection of my mine got moved up to now? I thought I wasn't due to be inspected for another six months."

That man is sharp, so I better be on my toes. "Like I said earlier, there have been some minor revisions to the Mine Safety Act."

"What kinda changes? I don't recall any."

You don't recall any cuz there ain't been any, but I'll be damned if I'll admit it, Denny thought as he quickly searched his mind for

50

some little-known regulation that would cover his tail and put away Paddington doubts.

Eyeing a manifold apparatus that looked only months old, Denny asked a question he already knew the answer to, but he hoped might deter further questions and doubts Paddington might have. "Is this here the main control station for the sprinklers or the secondary station?"

"Oh, no sir, this here is the main control station. We have several secondary stations, one right over by the entrance of the mine, and also one secondary station on each level of the mine."

"How come so many? You know the law only calls for one secondary."

"After that fire down in Kentucky a few years ago, I decided to put a secondary on each main level of the mine. I had a cousin involved in that fire, and if they would've had a secondary on his level he would probably still be with us today."

"I'm sorry to hear that. Good to hear that you're thinkin' of your miners instead of your pocket book. Before the Depression took it away, I owned a mine, so I understand how you feel about lookin' after your boys."

"Thank you, sir. Didn't mean to get so personal, but truth is it's personal for me. Most of these boys have been with me for a good long time, and I don't want to have to tell any of their wives we lost their man because I got cheap."

"Think nothing of it, I totally understand." He pointed down the elevator shaft. "Now, if you'll show me one of the secondary stations and the test records, I think we can wrap my visit up."

"Sure thing, let me get you a hard hat and a lamp and we can get going."

Waiting for Bill to return, Denny poked around the grounds and once again got the old itch to mine. Mining was still in his blood, and he still longed for it, even if he could still remember how he felt after a day in the mine. You gotta either love or hate something that makes your muscles ache after a day of swinging a pick against a vein, and makes grabbing a deep breath almost impossible. Heat down under can deplete your body after a day of sweating till you swear your body has no more fluid to offer. Denny shook his head in disbelief that he actually missed all those body-destroying and low paying days.

"There you are. I've got your hat and lantern if you're ready."

"Ready if you are. Sooner we get this goin' the sooner you can get back to more important business." *And I can get to the real reason for being over here in Knox.*

"Thank you, Denny. I'll help you any way I can to keep it short."

"You've already been a big help. Not all the mines I visit are this prepared. But I've got to admit I'm not certain what to make of this lantern you want me to use. I heard some miners were shiftin' over to the electric lanterns but this is the first one I've come across. Do the fellas like 'em?"

"Most of my men are okay with 'em, but some still prefer the old kerosene lanterns. They worry about the new kind runnin' out of juice and leaving 'em in the dark. I've convinced most of 'em to use the new ones by remindin' 'em of all the times a draft would blow out the flame of their old kerosene lamps.

Believe it or not, I still have one old miner that uses the candle lantern. You know, the type they used to use back around the turn of the century. I guess change comes hard for some folks."

"Yeah, believe me; I do understand fear of the new."

As they silently descended into the mine, Denny found himself descending into his mind as he questioned whether his fear of the new was about things in general or the change in Vi since she met that McCoy boy. *I wish things could just stay the same he thought. My daughters have always been the joy of my life, and now they're changing into women who might be the joy of some boy's life.*

Denny was jolted back to the present by the abrupt halt of the elevator's descent.

Bill Paddington broke the silence. "This here is the first level that has a secondary sprinkler station. Will you want to go on down to the other levels?"

"Let's take a look at this one, and then I'll let you know."

As they walked to the secondary station, Denny mentioned that Bill's mine was well within standards. "From the looks of the sprinkler piping, it looks like you upgraded the size of the pipes beyond standards."

"Would ya like a demonstration of the system?" Paddington offered, even though he hoped the answer would be no. He knew what a waste of time a demonstration would be. Mining would have to come to a halt or the boys would get mighty wet and ticked.

"No, that won't be necessary. In fact we can head back up. I'm impressed. We get up top, let me take a gander at your test records and I'll be on my way"

"No problem. In fact, I have the results of our latest test with me if you want to take a look at it as we head up."

Denny reached for the report. "Might as well test out how good this here new lantern is. If I can read your report in this dark, I'd say it's a pretty good lantern."

After a quick review of the recent tests, Denny decided he didn't need to waste any more of Paddington's time. As the late afternoon sunlight suddenly illuminated the ascending elevator, Denny shook Paddington's strong knarled hand. "Looks good, I've seen all I need to see."

"Well, you said it would be a short visit. Good time to end it cuz it's about quittin' time anyway. Would you like to join me and the boys over at the Lake Tavern for a cool one before you head out?"

"Thanks for the offer. I think I'll take you up on it, but only for one cuz I've got one more stop before I head back."

"Great. I have a couple of things to do, and then we can head over. Or, if you want, you can give one of the fellas a ride and I'll join you shortly."

"If you don't mind, I think I'll head over with one of your men."

"Fine by me," Paddington signaled for one of the miners to join him. "I'll get Roy, the young man headin' our way, to show you the way to the Lake Tavern."

Denny shook Roy's coal-dust-crusted hand. "Nice to meet you Roy. When you're ready to go I'll be over in my old Tin Lizzy waitin' on ya."

"I'm ready to go now, sir."

"Sounds good, and, oh by the way, you can call me Mr. Stewart. Calling me sir don't make me too comfy."

"Yes, sir, I mean Mr. Stewart," Roy stumbled over the words as he climbed into Denny's old Model T Ford. "Thanks for driving me over. I'm a bit thirsty today, but I wasn't lookin' forward to the hike no matter how good the beer is at the Lake."

"No problem, which way to the Lake? Probably can just follow my nose. I can already smell the liquor, but your directions would be faster."

"Nah, that ain't the tavern you smell. I hear tell old man McCoy brewed up a new batch of corn liquor lately, and when he first starts his brew you can smell it for miles.

"Isn't he afraid that the Sheriff can smell it?"

"I don't know if he's afraid, but I know the sheriff can't seem to find it, so instead he gets old man McCoy on everything and anything else he can. Matter of fact, he's got him locked up right now cuz I hear tell the old man got a bit more drunk than usual and thought the town square was an out-house."

Pulling up to the Lake Tavern, Denny was torn. Should he have a beer with Paddington, or should he leap at the opportunity to visit the sheriff and maybe get some time with his prisoner, Mc Coy. Can't pass up this opportunity Denny thought as he shook Roy's hand and told him to tell Paddington that he had to change his plans.

* * *

Denny held his Illinois State Mine Inspector badge up, as close as polite standards allowed, to the pudgy face of the coke-bottle-thick-eyeglass-wearing Knox County Sheriff Deputy manning the front desk. Denny officially identified himself and requested to see the Sheriff.

"What's your business with the sheriff, sir?"

"Tell him I'm here on behalf of Fulton County Superior Court Justice Wilson in regards to his prisoner McCoy."

Satisfied he wouldn't be wasting the Sheriff's time with the demands of just any old fool off the street, the Deputy asked Denny to take a seat while he delivered Denny's request. After a short struggle to get out of his chair, the Deputy walked towards the door labeled Sheriff. Denny watched and let his judgemental mind take over. *It's no wonder the Deputy was manning the desk as blind and fat as he is. The man can't even walk. It's more like a waddle.* Shaking his head, he thought of what Sarah might say, *Denny Stewart, shame on you! You're not thinkin' like a Christian. For all you know, that poor fella may have been beat up pretty bad by some criminal. Now shake yourself real good and be respectful to that man.*

Denny returned to the present just in time to notice the Deputy returning with a uniformed, tall, stocky but not fat, man who looked the picture of fine health and conditioning. The uniformed man introduced himself as he offered his huge hand. "Howdy, Mr. Stewart. I'm Sheriff Ben Foster. I understand Judge Wilson asked you to see me about that McCoy character we have visiting our fine establishment."

"Yes sir. Would you mind if we chatted in your office?"

Pointing to an office at the other end of the Sheriff station, the Sheriff agreed, "Wouldn't mind at all. In fact, I think it would be best. Make yourself comfortable in my office, and

I'll be in right after I help this here Deputy Rheinholt with a report the state is beatin' us up about."

Denny was certain he heard right about the Sheriff's office – it was the Deputy Rheinholt part he was uncertain about. He resolved that as soon as the Sheriff joined him, he would temporarily detour from his quest for knowledge of McCoy. The name Rheinholt was haunting him.

"Sorry about the delay, Mr. Stewart. That report's overdue and doin' reports ain't Rheinholt's cup of tea. Now, how can I help ya?" the Sheriff said as he strode towards his oversized, cane-backed, swivel chair.

"Before helpin' me with McCoy, would you tell me if that Deputy out there is the same one that got in a gun fight with Dillinger back in '34?"

"You've got a good memory. Deputy Rheinholt took three bullets from Dillinger when that jackass criminal roared through these parts after he busted out of jail over in Indiana. He damn near captured Dillinger, but he lost so much blood he couldn't hold him down 'til help came. Rheinholt just about bought the farm that day, and he ain't been the same since. About all he can do now is man the desk."

Wait till I tell Sarah about that one, but I sure ain't telling her about my non-Christian judgment of the Deputy.

"Wow! I remember that like it was yesterday. As I recollect, if it wasn't for the Deputy's quick thinkin' and heroic acts, a lot of folks, includin' a Sunday school class, would've probably got killed. You got yourself quite a hero working for ya."

"Yeah, I do, but I'm sure you're not here just to wander down Memory Lane. So, how can I help ya?"

"I'm interested in knowin' a bit more about that McCoy fella. Judge Wilson thinks he has a son by the name of Milt that's workin' over in Fulton County with the CCC. Several folks in Fulton County have asked about the son's character. The Judge knew I was headin' this way, so he asked me to see if I could learn a bit more about the dad. He's lookin' to see how far the Milt apple fell from the tree."

Sheriff Foster tipped back in his chair, propped his size fourteen feet up on the desk, stared up at the ceiling and gave the appearance of a man who was uncomfortable.

The silence made Denny squirm.

The Sheriff suddenly took his feet off the table, righted his chair, pointed at Denny and in a blunt deep bass voice said, "Before I answer you Mr. Stewart, first I'll ask you a question. What's the real reason you're askin' about the McCoys?"

"You got me Sheriff. Judge Wilson did point me to you, but not for official reasons."

As his voice became louder and blunter with every spoken word, the Sheriff said, "If it's not official, you better have a good reason for takin' up my precious time."

Denny coughed. "Uh . . . well, you see, my daughter Vi, who the Judge has known since she was a toddler, is seeing the McCoy boy, and we don't know anything about him other than the fact that he's from Knox and so is a notorious McCoy family. The Judge and I want to know what my daughter might be getting herself into."

"I thank you for your honesty, and, believe me, if it wasn't for me knowin' Judge Wilson, you'd be on your way out of here about now. I can understand you wantin' to protect your daughter. Two of my daughters are at that age, so I do understand. You say the boy you're askin' about is named Milt?"

"Yes sir, he claims to be from Knox County and he's about twenty years old."

"Sounds like it might be the Milt I know. Is he about six foot two, 175 pounds or so, with thick black hair, and smokes a pipe?"

"Honestly, I don't know. I believe Vi said he smokes a pipe. The rest of it I don't know because we haven't met him yet. He's supposed to come over for dinner Sunday to request permission to court Vi, and I wanted to find out a bit more about him before he shows up."

"Let's say it's the Milt I know. That Milt's really a pretty good kid in spite of his crummy parents. The mom's nothin' more than a law-breakin' hussy, and the father's an old drunk that can be meaner then a cornered coon. Matter of fact, that's one of the reasons why that nasty old cuss is residin' in our jail house right now."

"I take it this visit ain't his first?"

"No sir, it's not. Both of Milt's folks have been the County's guest from time to time."

"What about Milt?"

"Nah. Like I said, he's a good kid. Milt's never been in trouble with us. But, I've heard he's constantly havin' problems with his parents. He didn't graduate from high school because his worthless parents shipped him out to his grandparents whenever they got tired of bein' parents. It's really a shame. He seems to be a smart young man, and most everyone likes him. Baseball coach sure wishes he could've stayed in school cuz I hear tell he's quite the pitcher."

"I'm surprised he didn't try playin' ball for a livin' if he was that good. Kinda hard to believe he'd go into the CCC instead of playing ball."

"Truth is, he was scouted by the Sox, but they didn't sign him."

"That explains baseball, but how come the CCC?"

"I've heard he went into the CCC just to get away from his folks. No one can really blame him. Lots of stories goin' around about how they treated him, but I can't lock 'em up just on stories. Wish to God, I could."

"If you don't mind me askin', what kind of stories have you heard?"

"Actually more like gossip. He's shown up in town more than a few times with some bruises and black eyes. He always claimed it was because he fell down, walked into a door, or got in a fight with other kids. Don't particularly believe him, but I can't prove otherwise. If it's the parents beatin' on him, as I think it is, they're gettin' by with somethin' that makes my blood boil. Haven't seen Milt lately, but unfortunately I see the folks too damn often."

"Sounds like quite a family. What little Vi has told us, doesn't sound like Milt's anything like his folks. After all I've heard, I guess as a father I should ask you if you would let your daughters see him."

The Sheriff stroked his lantern jaw with his huge hands for a short while before he answered. "Like I said, he's not a bad kid. He didn't get much of a break growin' up, but I think he'll probably do okay in life. But I gotta tell ya, only way I'd let him court one of my daughters is if I could make sure his parents weren't around. You bein' over in Fulton County, and if he doesn't come back to Knox, I'd say it might make it okay for Milt to court your daughter. Of course, that decision's up to you."

Rising from his chair, Denny said, "Thanks for your honesty and time. I best be gettin' on my way, but before I do would you mind if I chatted with old man McCoy?"

"If you got the time, I'll do better than that. Frank McCoy is due to be released this afternoon. County policy, which I don't agree with much, is that we're supposed to give our guests a ride home when they get out. If you want, I could let you give him a ride home. Would save my deputies time for doin' more important law keepin' stuff, and you could get a good chance to talk to the old coot."

After a brief glance at his watch, Denny grinned. "If you'll let me use your phone to let my wife know I'll be a little late, I'd be honored to help out the Sheriff of Knox County."

* * *

"Thanks for givin' me a ride home. If I had to wait for those damn lawmen ain't no tellin' when I'd get home," the old man said. His gravely, smoker's voice not only conveyed gratitude, but also turned the interior of the Model T into the smell of a smoke filled tavern.

"Not a problem. Glad to help. I know a McCoy over in Fulton County that helped me out a bit, so I figured I was due for helpin' a McCoy. Besides, your place is right off the road I take to get home."

"Fulton County? Only McCoy I know of over that way is that disrespectful, lazy, no good, bum of a son of mine. His name wouldn't be Milt, would it?"

"Well you got the name right, but it must be another fella named Milt cuz the one I know is a polite fella that sure ain't lazy. He's been with the CCC for awhile, and if he was lazy they would've booted him shortly after signin' on. From what I hear, they also don't put up with much lip."

"If he's with the CCC then he's my bum of a son."

"Must be another side of him I ain't aware of. What makes you say that about your boy?"

"I'll tell you what, you pull over at the tavern up ahead, and I'll tell you all about that bum that has the nerve enough to call me Dad."

Denny found himself in a quandary. He wanted to keep the old reprobate enlightening him about Milt, but, on the other hand, he didn't want to be seen with such a vile, unkempt person. *I may not get back here too often, but I still have some reputation I'd like to maintain.*

As they drew closer to the tavern, Denny said, "Tell you what Frank, I need to get home, so I don't really have time to hang around a tavern, but I think I've got enough time to get you some beer for the road."

"I guess that'll have to do. Three days in the clink gave me a thirst for liquor, but I'll settle for beer. Besides, you don't need to waste your money on liquor cuz I got all I need at home. I'll just tap my still when I get there."

"Did I hear you say you've got a still? I thought that was illegal."

He looked at Denny in disbelief. "Only if you get caught."

Parking his car, Denny almost couldn't restrain himself from leaping away from the despicable old drunk, but somehow he mustered up the restraint. "Sit tight, I'll be right back." *Why am I doing this? I sure hope this beer and puttin' up with him is worth it. Maybe one day Vi will thank me.*

"Here you go, Frank. Hope you like Pabst Blue Ribbon cuz that's all they had."

"Beer is beer. Thanks. I was thinkin' while you were gone about how best to tell you 'bout Milt. I could go on for quite some time about that bum of a son, but I think I'll just tell about what he did the first time that made me think he's a bum, and what he done did lately."

"That would be fine cuz I'm gonna have to get headin' home soon anyway."

"I guess the first time I knew he was nothing but a lazy bum was when the Sheriff locked up his ma, Bess, cuz the Sheriff caught one of her girls charging for what she'd might be givin' if the man was lucky, if you know what I mean."

"No, what do you mean?"

Cocking his head in disbelief, Frank said, "You're pullin' my leg, right? In case you aren't, I'll tell you straight out – she was one of Bess's whores!"

"I thought that's what you meant, but you caught me a bit off guard. Anyway, what's his ma gettin' arrested got to do with Milt?"

"Well, shortly after she was arrested I heard tell the Sheriff was headin' our way with a search warrant. I wasn't certain what he was after, but I figured I'd better hide a bunch of things right quick like. I needed some help, but I couldn't ask just anyone to help me or otherwise word might get back to the Sheriff. Wasn't anyone around that I could trust, so I had to get Milt to help me."

"How old was he at the time? Did he know why his mom was in jail?"

"I reckon he was about ten. I didn't tell him why she was in jail. In fact, he didn't know much about how Ma and I put food on the table. But, when I told him what I needed him to help me with, he figured out where our livin' money came from."

"That must've been a bit of a shock for a ten-year-old. How'd he take it?"

"Didn't set well with him at all, He turned his nose up and promptly started preachin'. Told me what we were doin' was sinful. Really pissed me off! Who the hell did he think he was giving me a talkin' to about righteous livin'?"

"I imagine he was just passin' along some of his church learnin'."

"Could be, but after I educated him with a little strap, he finally got to work."

"Did that work?"

"Sorta, I had to constantly keep my eye on him and boot his ass now and again or he didn't do diddly. He complained about everything. I ain't never seen anyone so worthless in all my life, except one of them bums layin' around the town square."

"Aren't you being a might bit harsh, Frank? Seems to me it's kinda hard to figure the character of a young fella when he's only ten and after just one disappointin' time?"

"No sir, I expected out of him the same as my pa did me. Hell, by ten I damn sure knew what the birds and bees and the money for the honey was all about. He just got high and mighty on me."

"He was fairly young so I imagine he changed as he got older, didn't he?"

"No sir, He only got worse. In fact, after he learned how to pitch real well and what girls were good for he got even lazier. That bum would rather play ball or chase a girl then do any kind of useful work. We shipped him off a few times thinkin' it might help, but it didn't."

"What do you mean shipped him off?"

"Sent him over to live with Bess's folks a couple of times hopin' that farm livin' would shape him up. They got a nice farm over in Indiana, but they're kinda churchy.

"Sounds like a good idea. Did it help?"

"Nah, he'd get back and in no time a ball game or a skirt would turn him into a lazy bum. Ma thought a little time with one of her girls might cure him of chasin' skirts, but it didn't."

"Did I understand you right? She fixed her son up with a floozy? From what I know of Milt, I'll bet that probably didn't help. Like I said Frank, you may have forgot that he was just a boy, and you just mighta been askin' him to be more than what he was ready for."

"No sir. That weren't the problem at all. The problem was he got uppity. Now I hear tell the bum lately done went and screwed me and ma over, but good."

"What do you mean?"

"I'll tell ya here shortly. I might as well tell Bess at the same time I tell you. We're just about there. You need to take a right at the road about 100 feet ahead."

No wonder the Sheriff can't find his still. These woods are so thick and the brush so dense you could hide an army in here with room left over for another one.

"How much further in is your place, Frank?"

"Not far, just around the next bend. In fact there's ol' Bess waitin' on us. Don't worry about that shotgun she's packin'. We don't get many strangers back this way, so when she sees one the shotgun comes out real smart like." He stuck his head out the window and told Bess not to worry it was just him coming home.

The large hipped, buxom, cheaply-painted woman sashayed towards his car. *Good Lord, if this old hussy ain't a madam, she sure looks like one.*

"Who's the stranger, Frank? Don't look like none of the Sheriff's deputies I know. He looks a bit like that Jimmy Stewart, but he sure as hell don't drive a movie star car. That old '26 Model T he's driving sure hell ain't anything one of them there high and mighty sheriff boys would be caught dead in," Bess yelled.

"This here's Mr. Denny Stewart, a State of Illinois Mine Inspector, and friend of Milt's, that gave me a ride home."

Bess looked Denny over. "Friend of Milt, you say? No disrespect intended mister, but you look a bit long in the tooth to be a friend of Milt's."

Hiding his growing agitation with the McCoys, Denny said, "Actually, he's a friend of my daughter's"

Bess cocked her head to one side and scratched her temple. "Milt ain't much good at havin' girls for friends. Kinda chases 'em off right after he gets a bit too friendly. If you know what I mean."

"Can't say that I do, but I trust my daughter so I'm sure she chooses her friends carefully." *Boy, the Sheriff wasn't wrong about this old hussy. I better git before I unload on these two.*

Bess grabbed Frank and gave him a loud, wet kiss. "Welcome home, Frank. Did you tell the Sheriff to go screw himself? Besides sleepin' with the drunks, what the shit have you been up to?"

My God, she has a mouth on her like a sailor.

"Sleepin' ain't all I been doin'. The Sheriff gave me a whole three days to figure out how I can get that bum of a son to pay up."

Bess scratched her dirty, disheveled reddish-brown hair as her look of bewilderment grew. "What're you talkin' about? You didn't loan him money did ya?"

"Hell no! Where the hell you think I'd get money to loan him?"

"How the hell should I know, but it sounds like one of your dumb ass stunts."

"Come on Bess, you know I wouldn't do shit for that little bum."

"Alright, alright, but what do you mean by him payin' up?"

"After I talked to Ned, before the Sheriff drug me to his jail, I come to find out that Milt was supposed to be sendin' most of his CCC pay home to us."

"You're not shittin' me are ya Frank?"

"Nope, Ned told me his brother's boy is in the CCC, and they make him send his folks twenty five dollars of his pay every month. Way Ned tells it, the reason his boy sends it is because it's the law."

"By God, Frank, we're gonna be rich! Milt's been in CCC for pert near two years so he must owe us damn near five hundred dollars."

"Your figurin' is about the same as mine. I got one of the jail keeps to check my numbers, and he agreed that twenty five dollars times the twenty two months the CCC's been puttin' up with Milt comes out to be five hundred and fifty bucks."

"Holy cow! That's a load of money. I hope you figured out how you're gonna get that cash cuz we could use it. Your truck is on its last legs, and that kind of money could almost buy a brand spankin' new one. Anything left over I'm gonna use to buy a few fancy woman things. I can't believe that little bum held out on us."

"Don't worry I got it all figured out. As soon as I get some gas, I'm gonna find his CCC camp and pay him and his boss a visit. That little asshole thievin' bum of a son is gonna pay up."

Stunned, Denny said, "Don't you think there might be an explanation for why you're not getting' the payment? Maybe he figured you'd rather get it in one big payment when he gets out of CCC."

"No, I don't need no explanation. He's just tryin' to screw us."

Holding back the anger that was welling up in him, Denny, as calmly as possible, said to Frank, "Sounds like we aren't gonna see eye-to-eye on this. Ain't no sense tryin' to change your mind cuzz I hardly know Milt. Besides, I doubt if we'll be seein' much of each other down the road."

"Got that right," Frank said with a sneer.

"Sorry about dumpin' Frank and runnin', but I got supper waiting for me and quite a few miles still to go," Denny said as he climbed back into his car without shaking any hands or uttering any customary departure pleasantries. *Lord, I've investigated these McCoys enough. Please deliver me out of this hell hole.*

8

Sarah waved from the porch as Denny drove into the drive-way. At the sight of her, Denny beamed a contented smile. *I sure am a lucky guy. Sarah ain't nothin' like that McCoy woman. Thank God I'm home!*

Inspired and still smitten after all these years, Denny leaped from his Model T and embraced Sarah in a hug that lifted her off the ground.

"Welcome home, dear," Sarah said as she slowly disentangled herself from Denny's affectionate hug. "Not in front of the children," she softly implored while she pointed to their youngest daughter, ten year old Barbara.

"Sorry, I was so excited to see you I forgot myself," Denny whispered.

Hiding a blush she turned away to depart for her kitchen. "Supper's almost ready."

"Great, I'm starved and the aroma from your kitchen is hard to resist," Denny said as he snuck a quick, soft pat on Sarah's departing derriere.

"Stop that, you old hound, before the children see."

"You're right, I'll save it for later," Denny promised.

Ignoring Denny, Sarah smiled. "Get washed up and seated. Supper's ready and it would be nice to eat while it's still warm."

* * *

"Sure am glad to be home. Pass the spuds, would ya, Sarah?" Denny sighed. *Nothing like one of Sarah's pork chop dinners, complete with mashed potatoes, greens, and cornbread to soothe a man.*

"I'm glad you're home too. Sounds like you had a rough day."

"Most of the day was pretty good, but the end of the day was kinda hard to take."

"Why's that?"

"Well, I had an easy inspection at a mine that reminded me a lot of my old one."

Sarah frowned and stared at Denny.

"Now don't get me wrong. That mine I inspected and its organized owner didn't make me wish I was still minin'. You can put away any fears you might have about me going back to minin'."

"I know you won't worry the family by doin' that," a relieved Sarah said as she patted Denny's hand.

"You're right. I won't put us through that again, but what turned my day sour was meetin' up with the Knox County Sheriff."

Sarah's eyes widened. "You didn't get another of those expensive traffic tickets did you?"

"No, no, nothin' like that. Judge Wilson asked me to give the Sheriff his regards, and when I did the Sheriff mentioned he had a McCoy in his jail that he needed to let out before we could chat."

"No, not Milt, please say it wasn't Milt," Vi said as she started to tear up.

Patting Vi's hand, Denny reassured her. "Not Milt. It was his dad."

"His dad? What was he in jail for?"

"Sheriff said it was for the same thing he's been in for several times over the years – drunk and nasty in public. To hear the Sheriff tell it, old man McCoy and his bride ain't exactly what you'd call upstandin' citizens."

"Oh. Milt has a couple times kind of hinted that they aren't like him," Vi softly said.

"According to the Sheriff, Milt isn't like them at all. I'll be interested to hear what young Mr. McCoy has to say about them when he comes to dinner. Both of his folks are really something, but his old man isn't like anyone I ever knew. I got a hunch there's no tellin' what that old fool might do."

* * *

After standing in front of the Fulton County CCC's administrative building for what Frank believed to be a disrespectful long time without any attention directed at him, Frank took a swig of corn liquor from his ever present quart jar and bellowed at the entrance of the building. "Where in the hell is the son-of-a-bitch that's in charge of this here crap hole? He's got business to see to with me, so get his ass out here right now!"

Before Frank made any further profane demands, the screen door of the administrative building swung open from the violent push of two men quickly exiting through it. Both men wore Army uniforms with CCC insignias prominently displayed on the upper part of the left shirt sleeve. But, the uniform attire was all that was the same. The first one out was a short, stocky, barrel-chested man of about thirty years, whose beet red face failed to hide the anger generated by Frank's outburst. The second man, quite the opposite—tall, thin, pale and well over 40 years old, appeared quite calm despite Frank's slurs and demands.

In three fast, long strides, the first man drew within inches of Frank, and answered in an agitated tone, "My name is Supervisor Merrill, and if you'd tell me why you interrupted our lunch with your loud unnecessary profanity, I just might help you."

"Like I said, I want to talk to the son of . . ."

Before Frank could finish repeating his slurs, Supervisor Merrill jabbed his index finger, protruding from his clenched, white-knuckled fist, at Frank and warned, "Finish that curse and it will be the last bit of scum language you utter at this camp. Now, act like a gentleman, if you can, and tell us what you want."

After a hard swallow, Frank stammered, "I – I – I – um want to talk to the son of, I mean – I mean – um – man, in charge about my son's pay. Are you the – um – um – man in charge?"

"That's better. I'm not the man in charge, but I am the man you got off on the wrong foot with. The man in charge is Supervisor Haney." He pointed to the tall thin man standing nearby.

Stepping forward, the tall, stiff-postured man introduced himself and offered his hand. "I'm Supervisor Haney, and I'm in charge of the Fulton County CCC camp, and you are?"

Accepting Supervisor Haney's hand, Frank replied, "I'm Frank McCoy. I hear tell my boy, Milt, is one of your CCC boys."

"Yes, he is. He's one of our senior volunteers. You must be quite proud of him."

Frank pulled his head back with a look of dismay, and said, "Are we talking about the same Milt McCoy? He's about six foot two, 175 pounds or so, thick wavy black hair, and smokes a pipe? I don't know if it's the same fella, but I sure as hell ain't proud of my Milt. That bum ain't been sending his pay home like he's supposed to."

"Milt fits your description, but the behavior doesn't sound like him at all. Besides, the boys don't send the money home. Headquarters sends it to the address the boys provide us. Have you moved since he volunteered?"

"No, sir, we ain't moved in the last eight years. Knowin' that bum, he gave you the wrong address. Bet he's sendin' it to himself instead of helpin' his folks like he's supposed to."

"Like I said, Mr. McCoy, the serious charge you're making just doesn't sound like Milt. However, I'll check into it and get back to you real soon. If you'll leave your phone number, I'll call you as soon as I can with an answer."

"I ain't got no phone! Why don't you just figure it out right now?"

"I wish I could, sir, but unfortunately Milt is working in the field until about sundown tomorrow. I'll need to talk to him and review his payment forms before I can give you an answer. Tell you what, come back in a week at about noon and I should have your answer."

Frank's anger once again began to show. "Come back in a week?" he yelled. "That ain't gonna work! I can't afford another trip. Hells bells! Gas costs twelve cents a gallon, and I ain't had a job since them there politicians screwed this country up."

Supervisor Merrill stepped towards Frank and started to speak, only to be restrained and interrupted by Supervisor Haney. "I understand, but without first talking to Milt and reviewing the forms, which are in Washington, I can't begin to give you an answer that I can be certain is correct. If you want, I can give you a voucher for one dollar of gas that you can use at any Sinclair gas station for your return trip."

Frank lunged at Supervisor Haney and shouted, "I want an answer not a goddamn government run around."

"That's enough! I told you no more profanity! And, I sure won't put up with any violent behavior out of you or any other visitor. Now get your tail out of here!" Supervisor Merrill bellowed.

Frank launched a sloppy roundhouse right at Supervisor Merrill and screamed, "Screw you, you ain't the boss and I . . ."

Frank never finished as Supervisor Merrill deflected Frank's wild roundhouse and kicked Frank's feet out from under him. A surprised and disheveled Frank attempted to rise as an angry

Supervisor Merrill hovered over him. "Get your tail out of here, now! We don't tolerate your kind of behavior!"

Haney pulled Supervisor Merrill away from Frank. "I hope when you come back you keep a civil tongue and an even temperament. I think it is best that you leave and let us investigate your charge," Supervisor Haney said and handed Frank the promised voucher.

A now vertical Frank weaved towards his vehicle as he grumbled in a voice searching for air, "You damn right I'll be back and you best have my money!"

* * *

"Civilian Conservation Corps, Fulton County, Supervisor Merrill speaking, how may I help you?"

"I would like to speak with Milt McCoy, if that is possible. This is his Aunt Vi calling."

"What is your request in regards to, ma'am?"

Vi glanced around the room to assure herself that her mom or dad were not within range to hear her obvious, but necessary, lie. "A family matter. I'm afraid it may require his immediate attention. It's a bit of a sensitive matter, so, if you don't mind, I would rather not go into much detail."

"I understand, ma'am, no need for an explanation of the matter, but I must tell you that personal calls are not encouraged. I'll pass your request to his supervisor, and if he approves your request Milt will call you after he gets in from the field."

"Oh, I hope he approves it. When do you expect that I might hear from Milt?"

"I hope this matter isn't too urgent cuz he won't get back in from the field much before six or so."

"Six or so will be fine, and please give my appreciation to his supervisor when he does approve the request."

"I have a hunch he'll approve your request. I'll put in a good word for ya."

"Thank you so very much. Please tell Milt that he can reach me at the Stewart family, whom I am visiting, and their number is CAN 4421."

"Will do, ma'am, anything else I can help you with?"

"No thank you, you have been very kind and quite helpful. Good bye and God bless."

"Bless you too, and I'll make sure that Milt gets to call his Vi that he tells me about every chance he gets."

Oh my goodness. I guess I didn't fool him one bit. Vi fumbled the phone as if it was suddenly on fire. The line died. But, Vi's thoughts and spirits soared by the revelation that Milt thought of her so often, and, like herself, he couldn't keep his feelings to himself.

* * *

As the Friday afternoon sun began to fade, the tired and dusty young men of the Fulton County CCC troop tumbled from their work truck and shuffled about in an attempt to fall into ranks that would prompt Supervisor Harris to announce the much anticipated release from their duties.

"Now listen up!" Supervisor Harris barked.

"You boys did a decent bit of work this past week. It could have been better, but I guess it was good enough for weekend passes. Behave yourselves, and I'll see y'all back at the camp before sundown on Sunday. Y'all are released."

Over the din and racket of the boys celebrating their release, a barely audible request came from Supervisor Merrill standing in the open front doorway of the administrative building. "Supervisor Harris, can I see you as soon as possible?"

Dusting himself off as he trotted towards the admin building, Supervisor Harris asked, "What's up Merrill. Hope it's important. After a week in the boonies I ain't much in the mood for some admin stuff."

"Got two things Supervisor Haney wanted me to talk to you about, and both of 'em are about McCoy."

"McCoy? What's he done to grab the boss's attention? McCoy can be a bit sassy at times, but he's one of my better ones."

"He didn't do anything, but his Aunt requested him to call her on the camp phone. She says it's about some family matter."

Furrowing his brow, Supervisor Harris asked, "What kinda family matter?"

"She said it's a bit of a sensitive matter she would rather not discuss. But she did sound like it was serious. I told her we don't normally allow personal calls, but I think just this once we need to let him call. He can use my phone if it's okay with you."

"Guess it wouldn't hurt. I'll get him in here right soon. You said there were two things. What's the other one?

"Milt's drunken old man showed up the other day and accused the CCC of not sendin' Milt's pay to him. Supervisor Haney wants to talk to Milt about his pa's accusation as soon as possible."

"I'll fetch him right now if the Super's available."

"Oh yeah, he's in and real anxious to talk to him"

* * *

Slicking down his just showered wet hair with his left hand, Milt knocked on Supervisor Haney's open door and asked, "You wanted to see me, sir?"

"Yes ...Yes, come in McCoy."

Standing in a rigid posture that somewhat resembled a military attention, Milt waited as Supervisor Haney completed processing a form he was working on when Milt entered. *I thought he was in a big hurry to see me. If I'd known he was gonna pull the old make-'em-sweat routine I would of finished my shower. He just wants to remind me who's boss. After a week of bein' in the holler with that hard ass Harris I don't need any more reminders.*

Laying his pen down, Supervisor Haney told Milt, "Your father visited the camp yesterday. He seemed rather upset. I must say, he quite profanely brought to our attention a matter of concern."

"Sorry if he was out of line. I'll bet he was drinkin' and actin' like a fool."

"As a matter of fact, he seemed intoxicated, and, yes, he did get out of line. However, he also raised questions about a discrepancy that needs to be addressed. Has your father chatted with you lately?"

"No sir. I ain't talked with my father in well over two years."

"I see. Well, regardless of that gap in communication, it seems you might need to chat with him in the near future."

"About what, sir?"

"According to your father, he has never received the monthly twenty five dollar allotment that he's entitled to. I'm sure there is a logical explanation for this discrepancy. I assume you submitted the forms for the allotment. True?"

"Yes, sir, I did."

"Then, I am a bit confused. Your father seems to think that you found a way to send the money to yourself. Is that true?"

No, I didn't send it to myself, but I did find a way to keep it out of the hands of that old drunk. "No sir."

"You confirmed what I suspected. I'm sure that the payment forms were submitted properly. Our paymaster probably made an error in sending the payments. Headquarters is sending me a copy of your forms and they are looking into your father's accusation. I'm sure this problem will be resolved soon. In the meantime, I suggest you chat with him, and assure him that his concerns will be put to rest soon."

"Yes sir." *Crap! I'll probably have to leave the CCC after they get those records, but I'll be damned if I'll talk with that old drunk.*

* * *

Please ring, please ring, Vi pleaded to the phone while she twirled her long dark hair around her finger and paced back and forth in front of the phone. Six o'clock had come and gone without a call from Milt. *I hope, oh how I hope, he calls before Mom and Dad get home from dinner at the Procini's. I need to talk to him in private.*

As her pacing continued, her little ten year old sister, Barb, couldn't pass up the opportunity to tease her older sister. "What ya doin' sis? Trying to wear out the carpet? Your pacin' and hair stylin' won't make it ring. Are you waitin' to hear from sweety Milty?"

"Go away you little pest. I know you have better things to do besides pester me. I'm sure you still need to finish your homework before Mom and Dad get home."

"No I don't. It's all done, so there! Besides, I don't think Mom and Dad said you could use the phone. I think I'll stick around and watch, Dad will get all over you for being on the phone alone."

"More like, he'll get all over you because right over there on the table sets your homework and it's for sure not finished. You know Mom and Dad aren't happy that you have to take summer school. If you'd done your homework during the regular school year you wouldn't have any now. "

"Yeah, yeah, but I'll have it done before they get home, miss smarty pants that so luvs Mr. Milty."

"Stop calling him that and git. Tell you what, you take your homework out back on the porch and give me some privacy, and I'll give you a dime."

"A dime? What a cheapskate! Make it a quarter and I'll be gone lickety split"

What a little brat. She's trying to hold me up for almost an hour's worth of work at the Walgreens. Some private time with Milt will be worth it though. She reluctantly paid off the brat, and shooed her out the door just as the phone rang.

"Hello. Stewart residence," Vi, said.

"Hi, sweetheart. It's Milt. Supervisor Merrill said you needed to talk with me. Are you all right?"

Stunned by Milt's first utterance of an endearment, Vi just stared at the phone.

"Vi? Are you still there?"

"I'm still here. I was just surprised you were able to call."

"You got lucky when Supervisor Merrill answered the phone. He's a good egg. Merrill put in a good word for me. He told my supervisor that my Aunt Vi needed to talk to me about some kind of family emergency. Good thing you said you were my aunt, or old do-it-by-the-rules Harris would of never let me call."

"I figured that might work. I wish I wouldn't have had to tell that little fib, but I'm glad it got you on the phone. We do have a bit of an emergency, but it's not the kind I told him. Guess I'll need to ask the Lord's forgiveness for stretching the truth."

"What kind of emergency? Your folks didn't give you a hard time about seein' me, did they?

"Not really. But Dad did some poking around when he was over in Knox, and he really wants to meet you before he lets me see you again."

"What kind of pokin' around?"

How do I tell Milt this without scaring him away? I guess I might as well just say it. "He met the Sheriff and your folks."

"Oh, I guess that does it. I really like you, Vi, but I'm afraid my folks once again screwed up my life. I appreciate you callin'."

Vi choked back tears. "Wait, wait, wait . . . please don't hang up! I love you, and I don't care about your folks. They aren't you, and I know you aren't them. When Dad gets to spend some time with you he'll know you're different from them."

Now it was Milt's turn for silence. *Oh my Lord, she said she loves me. I like her a lot, but I don't know if I'm ready for all that.*

"Milt . . . are you still there?"

"I'm still hangin' on. I just got a bit flustered and caught without words."

"What words got you so silent, sweetheart?" Vi cooed.

"Well, well ah–um, all of 'em. Uh, uh, uh . . . What are we gonna do? You want me to cancel out on Sunday and give you a chance to feel your dad out?"

"No, I think you coming over Sunday would be the best thing. Dad seems a bit confused because the sheriff said some nice things about you. But, your parents kinda stunned him. I think he wants to give you a chance, and he wants to size you up."

"What all does he want to ask me? I'll bet my parents really threw him for a loop. Probably wonders how far I fell from that rotten old apple tree."

"I'm not certain what he wants to ask you. He didn't say much about the details. He did say that your dad gave a lot different description of you then the good one that the sheriff gave. My dad really is a fair man, so I think if you are honest with him and tell him about your childhood he won't judge you by your parents."

"I hope you're right. I'd like to keep seeing you. What time is dinner on Sunday?"

"Dinner is at about three— we eat a late dinner/early supper on Sunday. I'll get Dad to pick you up at the Walgreens on the way home from church."

"That ain't necessary. I can get a ride to your house—just tell me your address."

"You sure you don't want a ride?"

"Nah, I can get a ride. I can't see makin' your folks go out of their way. Especially on the first time they meet me. I'm sure your dad would prefer that I come a courtin' instead of him bringin' me to court."

"Alright, I think I see your point. We live on the east side of Canton. Our address is 3450 Lincoln Rural Road. Ask most anybody and they can tell you how to get here. Oh, before I forget, don't come straight into the yard until Wolf gives you permission."

"Wolf? Who the heck is Wolf?"

"Wolf is the dog that grandpa brought back from the Dakotas. He claims that Wolf is a dog, but truth is most of us think he's a sort of tamed wolf. He's a really friendly dog, once you get to know him, but until you do, he takes protecting the family very seriously."

"You sure know how to scare a fella off. What should I do when I get there to get on that dog's good side?"

"Just stand real still and let him bark and sniff you. We'll hear him barking and come running. When we come out, he'll settle down, if we tell him to."

"Sure hope you do. Any other dangers I oughta know about? You don't have a moat I gotta swim, do ya?"

"You don't have to worry about the moat—we haven't finished digging it yet. But you might have to look out for some of them snakes Mom brought up from the holler."

"That's okay, as long as she ain't feedin' 'em to me. I'll see you about two on Sunday."

9

"Sure do appreciate you givin' me a ride into town, Mr. Merrill," Milt said as they traveled over one of the many endless straight dusty rural roads that cut through the flattest, but greenest, as the inhabitants like to brag, places on earth.

The warm June day and leisurely Sunday pace, put Milt in a reflective mood. *I am so lucky to even be on this ride. Doubt if I'd be going to meet her father, if Vi hadn't of believed in me. Sure glad she was workin' that day the CCC dumped us at Walgreens. I hope Vi's old man takes to me. I'd hate to have to quit seeing her.*

Jolted back to the present by the trucks' journey across another of the numerous pot holes and worn ruts, Milt heard Merrill say, "You're welcome. Least I could do for a young man goin' to see such a nice young lady. Wish I could take you all the way to her house, but I gotta get back before they miss the truck."

"Don't worry about it. I understand. I'm just glad you could get me this far. With all the church traffic in town I'm bound to get my thumb answered. Besides, it's only noon, so I got plenty time even if I gotta walk."

"You're right about that – plenty of traffic for thumbing a ride. I ain't never seen this town on Sunday before. From the looks of it, they take Sunday church goin' pretty serious. Well anyway, here we are." Merrill pulled over to the curb in front of Walgreens'. "Good luck to ya, and tell Vi hello for me. See you tomorrow."

"Once again, thanks for the ride. See you tomorrow," Denny said as he tipped his hat to the departing Supervisor Merrill.

Man, has this town ever got a lot of Sunday drivers. Hope they're paying attention enough to see my thumb. Milt crossed the street to get directions from a fella standing near a Sinclair station, and dodged out of the way of a huge, black, 1935 open air Cadillac. *Damn, there sure are some drivers with their heads ringin' from sermons cuz that idiot Bible-thumper damn near hit me. That sure was one hell of a big car. If he'd got me I'd been squished like a bug. Maybe some day I'll have a fancy car like that and dress in Sunday fine clothes. Hope I ain't dressed too shabby for today.*

Milt approached a short, stout, scruffy dressed, older man standing in front of the Sinclair station. "Sir, would you be so kind to give me directions to Lincoln Rural Road?"

Pointing to the east, the old man said, "Sure thing. It's over that away, but it's a far piece. If you're walkin' it'll take you about an hour or so."

"Thanks, mister. I guess I'd better get movin' if it's that far."

"Welcome, but if you can wait a minute or so while I get some gas I'll be glad to give you a ride most of the way."

"Sure, I can wait. Ridin' beats the heck out of wearin' off some shoe leather. But how you gonna get some gas? Ain't everything closed on Sunday?"

The man removed a large key ring from his pocket. "Yeah, but I know the owner of this here Sinclair station. He doesn't pay too close a mind to those damn Blue Laws. Closes up on Sunday like he's supposed to but he'll open now and again for me when the Sheriff ain't around."

Milt watched the old man enter the Sinclair station. "Boy, your friend must really be a good friend to trust you with the keys to the station."

The old man smiled, and then chuckled as he offered his hand to Milt. "Truth be told, I'm my own best friend. I own this here station. Name's Felix Steinberg. And, you are?"

Milt smiled and shook his hand. "I wondered how you knew your way around the station. Pleased to meet you, sir, I'm Milt, Milt McCoy."

* * *

This Steinberg fella wasn't stretchin' it when he said it was a far piece to walk. I sure am glad I ran into him. It's a bit toasty today, and I don't want to show up at Vi's smellin' like a sweaty boar hog. I'll have enough to concern me when her Dad's grillin' starts.

"Sure do appreciate the ride, sir."

"You're welcome. Glad I could help. Mind if I ask you why you're heading over to Lincoln Road? I can't recall ever seeing you over that way before."

"I ain't from these parts so I've never been there before. I'm headin' over to have dinner with the Stewart family."

"Are you talkin' about Denny Stewart's family?"

"I believe that's the dad's name. I've never met him. I'm actually goin' to see his daughter, Vi, and ask for her dad's permission to court her."

Felix cocked his head cocked and showed a mischievous grin. "Now that's a term you don't hear much anymore."

"Yes sir, you're right. I was a bit surprised that I had to ask permission."

"Well it sounds a lot like Denny. He tends to be a bit old fashioned. I'll warn you young man—you just might be headin' for some kind of interestin' dinner."

As he tried hard to hide a sudden flush sweat, Milt calmly asked, "Why's that, sir?"

"Well, Denny's down right protective of his daughters. Don't get me wrong. He's a mighty fine fella, but he has some mighty high standards when it comes to his daughters. Don't be surprised if he says no. You won't be the first fella he found not worthy of his daughter."

Not the kinda news I wanted to hear. I wonder if he's just blowin' smoke up my butt. "How come you know so much about Mr. Stewart? Is he a friend or neighbor?"

"He's sorta both. I used to live near him when I lived in Farmington, and we became friends. I've known him for some number of years. Ever since we got to jawin' about him buying the Sinclair station I own over in Farmington we got to know each other pretty good."

"You got me a bit confused, sir. I thought the Depression pretty much wiped the Stewarts out. How's he gonna buy your station?"

"Don't really know, and it's not really any of my business. I think he may be hopin' that bankin' law Mr. Roosevelt is pushin' will help out folks that got screwed by the banks. I don't know or much care where he's gonna get the dough, but I'm hopin' he does. I'm gettin' too damn old to run two stations, and I know his family is gettin' a bit tired of his wanderin' around the state doing mine inspectin'."

After a short period of silence, Milt realized that sitting right next to him was the perfect source for forming his courting strategy.

In hope of completing his strategy, Milt asked, "Mr. Steinberg, seein' how you know Mr. Stewart pretty well, you got any advice you might give me for when I ask Mr. Stewart for permission to court his daughter?"

Felix pulled off to the side of the road and looked quizzically at Milt. "We got plenty of time. Let's sit here a piece while I think over your question. Don't like drivin' when I'm thinkin' hard. You're welcome to get out and stretch your legs if you want."

Startled by the quick stop, Milt hesitated to move. *I'll bet if I get out he'll be gone like a scalded cat straight for the Stewarts with plenty of words I wouldn't want said.*

As if reading Milt's mind, Felix patted Milt on the back. "Don't worry I ain't takin' off on ya. I might even get out myself. I can't hold my water like I used to."

Sounds like he ain't gonna be leavin' me out here in the middle of nowhere, so I might as well take a stretch. Besides stretchin' is better then sittin' here fidgetin' and worryin' over whatever that old man's contemplatin'. Milt stepped out of the car.

Stretching his legs and diverting his eyes from Felix doing his business, Milt once again was struck by what a beautiful day it was. *I'm on my way to see a beautiful young lady, and mother-nature sure is tryin' her best to match Vi's beauty. The pale blue sky has only a few wispy, feathery clouds and a gentle breeze. Barely enough wind to sway the tops of the corn growin' in the fields. Heck, there ain't even a bug to be heard leave alone seen. Let's hope my visit is as good as this day is.*

"Ready to get movin' if you are Milt"

"Sure thing, it's such a pretty day I can't see wastin' it standin' around here."

"Now that I had some time to think about your question, I think I can give you two pieces of advice, even though I don't really know much about ya."

"Any advice you can give me would be appreciated. I can understand you hesitatin', but all I can say is that I do have nothin' but the best of intentions when it comes to Vi."

"I figure any young man that was willin' to walk to the Stewarts probably does have some pretty good character and intentions. So, here's my advice you'd do well to remember. First, don't ever call him by his given name. He hates it when young folks call him anything but Sir or Mr. Stewart—unless he gives them permission first."

"No problem with that, I wouldn't do that anyway. What else?"

"The other thing, and probably the most important thing, is don't try to bull shit him. Mr. Stewart hates bull shitters. And, believe me, he is a walkin', breathin' bull shit detector, so don't think you can sneak any tall tales by him."

"Sounds like a man I can respect," Milt said as Felix turned on to another rutted, dirt road.

Slowing to a stop, Felix informed Milt, "This here's as close as I can get ya. The Stewart's place is about a five to ten minute walk up the road I just turned off of. Good luck to ya, and tell Denny, Mr. Stewart to you, that I said hello."

"Thanks a lot, Mr. Steinberg. Hope to re-pay your kindness some day."

10

Not *much of a fancy house, I'll bet it's one of those Sears comes-in-a-kit-ready-for-you-to-build-homes.* Milt speculated as he approached the Stewarts' gray colored, probably once white, multiple-level-home, complete with a shaded front porch. And on the front porch was living proof of some of Vi's tales. A faded red rocking chair held a slumped over, perhaps sleeping, body, wrapped in a faded blue and red plaid blanket that wasn't necessary for such a warm day. *Probably Vi's Injun grandma. Even from a distance the person looks weather beaten, wrinkled, and darker than Vi.*

Near the rocking chair lay a large gray and brown haired dog that stared without blinking at Milt. As he drew nearer to the house, the dog rose.

Whoa, that ain't no dog! This must be Wolf that Vi warned me about. Milt stood stock still, as Vi had advised, and hoped Vi, or someone in the house would soon hear the loud, deep barks of the slobbering, lunging dog. Beads of worry sweat trickled down Milt's back and forehead. *Damn, I wish someone would hurry up and get this monster away from me. Don't know how much longer I can stand here without wettin' my pants.*

The screen door banged open, and Milt sighed with relief when he heard Vi command, "Wolf, Wolf! Come here boy! Good boy. Good boy, Wolf. Now hush and go lay down by Grandma."

"Is it all right to move, or will that beast rip my head off if I do? You warned me, but I thought you were jokin'."

"Wolf greets all strangers that way. Don't know if he'll bite, but he sure gets their attention. We never have to worry about unwelcome visitors. You want to pet him?"

"Pet him, are you crazy? I'd like to keep all my parts."

"Well, if you're planning on courtin' you best git to know Wolf or you'll never make it to my door."

Milt smiled, "You sure have figured out how to get your way with me, ain't ya? Bring the beast over and I'll let him sniff all he wants, but make sure you bring your mom's .22 in case he decides to like me a little too much."

Ignoring Milt's apprehension and request for a .22 backup, Vi called Wolf to her. Ruffling Wolf's hair and loosely clutching his mane, Vi, said calmly, "Wolf, this is Milt. Now you be real nice to him. He won't hurt us, so treat him like family."

Wolf stared at Vi, a stare from the pits of his yellow-brown eyes that lasted such a long time it left all uncomfortable. It was as if he was deciding to believe her—or not. To the relief of all, Wolf lowered his massive head and slowly began to sniff Milt for any offending odors that reeked of danger to him or the family he so loyally defended. Vi and Milt's noticeable sigh of relief was only surpassed by their deflating body tension.

Standing as still as one can as a wolf dog slowly sniffs every inch of your legs, including areas you'd rather not think of as fair game for a sniffing dog, is challenge enough. But when it jumps up, lands its heavy paws on your shoulders and stares you in the eyes the challenge becomes almost unbearable.

"Wolf, Wolf get off Milt right this instant," yelled Vi as she tugged at Wolf's mane.

Milt's eyes grew wider by the second, especially when Wolf seemed to object to Vi's tugs and loud commands. Visions of gory mutilations sprung to his mind. Forcing himself to push away his fear and maintain what little control he still had, Milt whispered while staring straight into Wolf's intense eyes, "Easy Vi, don't get him mad. I'll be okay, won't I, boy? He's about done, aren't ya, boy?"

Suddenly Wolf dropped off of Milt's shoulder and began to lick the back of Milt's left hand. *Thank God that's over.* Milt carefully bent down to Wolf's level and began to pet him under his neck.

"Wow! I've never seen Wolf let someone pet him after such a short time. He tested you more than he usually does. The only time I've seen him jump up like that is when he's mad. He has run off quite a few bill collectors by jumping up like that. Don't know what you did, or said, but he seems to like you."

"I don't know what I did either, but I'm glad I passed his inspection. Hate to have to fight that dog every time I come a courtin'."

Vi smiled at the acceptance of her dog and the prospect of courting that Milt had mentioned more that once in the last few weeks. She took his hand. "Come on, let me introduce you to everyone."

"Good idea, but let's wait to hold hands until after I've talked to your dad." *Her dad might not approve of hand holdin' before grantin' his consent to court. I ain't takin' any chances of screwin' this up.*

* * *

They climbed up the front porch steps, just in time for Grandma to wake up and spit.

"I ain't believin' she just spit tobacco on my shoes!" Milt said with dismay. "I'm guessin' she ain't the best shot cuz that pretty brass spittoon wasn't too far from me."

After a short breath, Milt broke into a grin and blurted out, "Wait a minute. I get it. I got past that thing you call a dog, and now I gotta get past Grandma. Is that what's goin' on? How many suitors did you say got ran off before I was crazy enough to give it a try?"

Staring in disbelief at Milt's shoes, Vi searched for some soothing explanation. *Oh my God, Grandma's having another one of her ornery days. When is she ever going to spit in that spittoon, and why in God's name did she have to pick now to shower the porch floor?*

Vi attempted to buy some more time by instead sternly scolding Grandma. "Shame on you! That's no way to treat a guest."

Grandma stared quizzically and cocked her head to her left then slowly to her right. She mumbled incoherent sounds at Vi and shrugged her shoulders.

Leaning in close, Vi shook her finger at Grandma. "Don't you act like you don't understand me! I know you know what I'm saying. You know you're supposed to use the spittoon we gave you last Christmas. We're all getting tired of cleaning up your spits, and I'm pretty certain you know how to treat guests better than you just did."

Oh brother, I haven't been here but a few minutes and already I got the family stirred up. I gotta admit I don't much like tobacco spit on my shoes, but I think I best let this spittin' pass or who knows how much more this family might get stirred up. "Don't worry about me, Vi. I think I just walked up on her spittin' spot at the wrong time. I'm sure she didn't mean anything by it."

Grandma's subtle nod of acceptance told Milt that Grandma understood his offer of peace. Patting her chest with her arthritic, tobacco stained right hand, Grandma slowly stammered a few words from her tooth barren mouth. Milt took the string of discordant sounds to be either an apology or a don't-worry-about-it statement.

He nodded back to Grandma while patting his own chest. He hoped that was the right way to answer an Injun Grandma. "See? Everything's fine with me and Grandma."

Vi crossed her arms, frowned, and leaned in close to Grandma's face. "It may be okay between you two, but she needs to know that I'm not happy with her. I'm so sorry that she greeted you so rudely."

"As long as that is the last test, I'm fine with it," Milt grinned.

"Oh, that wasn't a test. That was just Grandma being Grandma. I wish I could tell you it was the last test, but there's no telling what test my dad has waiting for you."

Suddenly the screen door creaked open and a tall, gray haired man joined them. In a deep baritone voice tinged with a mischievous chuckle, he said, "Vi, are you tryin' to scare the boy off before I get a crack at him?"

Blushing, Vi smiled, and in her best manipulating daughter voice said, "Of course not, Daddy. You know I wouldn't dream of spoiling your fun. Daddy, please greet our guest, Mr. Milt McCoy."

He extended his hand to the young man. "Welcome to our home, Mr. McCoy. I am Vi's father, Mr. Denny Stewart."

Milt shook his hand. "Thank you, sir, for inviting me to your home. If you prefer, you may call me Milt."

Surprised by Milt's formal response, but not ready for granting informality, Denny squeezed Milt's hand a bit more than considered polite. "Until we get to know each other, I think Mr. Stewart and Mr. McCoy would be appropriate. Please come in and make yourself comfortable."

Relieved to release Mr. Stewart's strong grip, he nodded to him. *Oh boy, I'll come in, but comfortable I sure ain't.*

He entered the Stewart home, and the aroma of a delicious meal simmering on the old wood stove directed his attention to a thin, yet sturdy, salt-and-peppered haired lady, whom he guessed was Vi's mom. *If whatever she's cookin' on that old stove is half as good as it smells, I'd say that Vi wasn't joshin' about her mom knowin' her way around a kitchen. As busy as that lady is, I'd say she puts a lot of sweat and love into her cookin'.*

"Mom, if you have a moment, I'd like to introduce you to Mr. Milt McCoy."

She turned away from her cooking. Wiping her hands on her apron, she flashed a smile that explained where Vi got hers, and said in a soft, melodious voice, "So this is the Milt McCoy that Vi speaks so highly of. I am so pleased to finally meet you. I'd give you a hug but I'm still in my cookin' clothes, and I wouldn't want to dirty yours."

Milt tried to hide his surprise at the difference in the greeting he'd received from Vi's dad. "Pleased to meet you too, Mrs. Stewart. Something sure does smell good. Now I know why your daughter brags about your cookin' so much."

She waved away the compliment. "Well I hope it tastes as good as you say it smells. It's been a while since I made turtle soup. I appreciate you lettin' me have the turtle, and I'm awfully pleased that you could join us for our Sunday dinner."

"You're welcome, ma'am, and I appreciate you folks invitin' me."

She pulled Milt closer and whispered, "When Vi's dad's not around you don't need to call me Ma'am or Mrs. Stewart. My name is Sarah, and I'm very pleased to finally meet you."

As she whispered into his ear, Milt's view beyond Sarah was expanded to bring a cute, pig-tailed, freckle-faced young girl into his field of vision. Drawing back from Sarah, Milt asked, "And who is your pretty young helper that is hidin' behind you?"

Sarah gently took the little girl's hand. "This is my youngest daughter, Barbara. She's a bit shy till she gets to know you."

Milt offered his hand. "Pleased to meet you, Barbara. How old are you?"

With eyes down cast and head gently swaying back and forth, Barbara delicately placed her hand in Milt's and attempted to curtsy. "Pleased to meet you, sir. I'll be ten years old next month."

Denny entered the kitchen with a confidence befitting lord of the manor. "Sarah, how close are we to dinner? Do I have enough time to show young Mr. McCoy your fine garden?"

"Vi still has to set the table while I finish fixin' our dinner, so you have more than enough time to show off my puny little garden. As warm as it's gettin', a nice cold iced tea might be good to take with you. Can I get you and Mr. McCoy one?"

"Fine idea, Sarah. Iced tea sound good to you Mr. McCoy?"

"If it's not too much bother, I sure would like one. Thanks for askin', ma'am."

Sarah poured two iced teas as the men chatted. Handing the ice teas to her husband and the guarded young Mr. McCoy, Sarah suggested, "Here you go. Now why don't you two get yourselves out from under foot so we can have our dinner before it gets over cooked?"

As Denny exited the kitchen for the back porch, he decided to spring his first test on Milt. "Sorry I can't offer you anything stronger then ice tea, but we don't abide by alcohol on the Sabbath. In fact, we don't much abide by alcohol at all. I might have one with my friend Judge Wilson over a game of pool, but that's once in a blue moon."

"No need for apology, I understand and agree with you. Truth be told, I don't drink alcohol at all."

Before Denny could delve deeper into Milt's abstinence, a large, elderly man, whose body appeared to still be formidable in spite of his slumped back and slow movements, opened the screen door. In a booming voice that caught Milt by surprise, the man said, "Mind if I join you two young fellers?"

Denny rose from his chair. "Sit yourself in my chair, Grandpa. I've been sittin' long enough."

Grandpa slowly lowered himself into the offered chair and extended his hand to Milt. He winked and spoke in a voice that seemed almost depleted of breath. "Everyone calls me Grandpa. I'd tell ya my given name, but I can't recollect it cuz I ain't heard it in quite awhile. What's your name?"

Milt shook Grandpa's hand. "Pleased to meet you, sir. I'm Milt McCoy."

Grandpa cupped his hand to his ear. "Come again? My ears ain't workin' of late."

In a raised voice, Milt repeated himself. "Pleased to meet you, sir. I'm Milt McCoy."

After several deep breaths, Grandpa wheezed as he said, "Nice to meet you, Milt. What brings you," Grandpa stopped and gasped for air, "to our neck of the woods?"

Before Milt could answer, Denny said, "Vi invited Milt to share Sunday dinner with us. We're havin' iced tea while the women are finishin' dinner. Would you like some?"

Grandpa's eyes sparkled and his voice rose. "Nope, but I'd take some 'Old Crow' if the ladies ain't watchin'."

"Grandpa, you know hard drink on the Sabbath ain't allowed!"

"I know ... I know, but we gotta treat our guest proper!"

"That's okay, sir. Besides, I don't drink alcohol," Milt said.

Grandpa reared his massive, scraggly-bearded head back in disbelief. "Huh? Mind if I ask why?"

Yeah, I do mind. But, I got a hunch Mr. Stewart already knows, so I might as well lay it all out there. "I figure my old man, I mean my father, drank enough for the whole town while he was raisin' me. I watched liquor make a fool of him. Far as I'm concerned, liquor just ain't worth drinkin'."

Sounds of heavy snoring drowned out the sounds of nature. *Damn, I just opened myself wide to a sleepin' old fart. Hope those words ain't gonna bite me on the butt.*

Denny patted Milt on his shoulder. "Good for you. I'm glad to hear you don't have the taste for the devil's brew like your pa does."

Milt tensed up, as if he'd just grabbed the wrong end of a snake. "Mind me askin' how you know about my dad?"

"Word gets around, and besides I met your folks earlier this week."

"How did that happen, sir? That must have been quite a shock."

"I was over in Knox on business, and Judge Wilson, the judge you met when you were in Walgreens, asked me to call on the sheriff while I was there. Sheriff seems to be a nice fella. Might be pleased to hear he had some kind words to say about you."

"I'm glad to hear someone over in Knox has something good to say about me, but I'm still a little stumped on how you met my folks."

"Sheriff asked me to do him a favor. His deputies were too busy to give your dad a ride home after he got out of jail, so he asked me to do it. All I can say is it was quite a ride. I won't sugarcoat it, your folks are a bit of a shock to a fella."

"Wish I could do somethin' besides apologize for their behavior, but I guess all I can do is tell you that I ain't nothin' like 'em. I don't approve of their sinful ways, and I sure don't want to be anything like 'em."

Don't really know this kid, but he sure sounds like a good kid that got stuck with some nasty characters for parents. "If it means anything to ya, like I said, Sheriff said you were a pretty good fella in spite of your folks."

A deep silence, broken only by the sounds of nature and Grandpa's snoring, fell over the porch. Both men slumped further into their chairs and their minds as their glazed, perplexed eyes stared off into the garden. Neither wanted the uncomfortable silence, nor the words that might be uttered should the silence be broken. Denny wasn't ready to offer solace or quarter, and Milt wasn't ready to gamble that further words might thwart his quest for courting Vi.

Eavesdropping, Vi and Sarah noted the silence. No words passed between them, but both traded looks of concern. Sarah knew that silence too well after so many years with Denny. In the past, Sarah would've let the silence linger until Denny was ready to break it. But now, as if she sensed this silence was different, she lowered her hands below her waist and pushed her hands, palms up, towards the back door hoping that Vi would understand her message.

Vi understood, and poked her head out of the door to intrude on the silence. "Dinner's ready, Daddy. Hope you and Milt are hungry."

Denny rose slowly from his chair. "Guess we better get in there and grab it while it's still hot."

Almost jumping from the chair, Milt agreed. *Thank God! If dinner wasn't ready I don't know how much deeper a hole I would've dug with my answers to that crafty old man.*

"Should we wake Grandpa?" Milt said as he walked through the door Denny was holding open.

"Nah, we'll let the old fella sleep. He gets a bit uncomfortable eatin' with the family. He needs false teeth, but he won't get 'em, so his eatin' ain't exactly pretty."

"I don't mind if y'all don't. I'll bet he's hungry."

"It's okay. The older he gets, the less he eats. Besides, he prefers we make a plate for him to eat later on."

* * *

Wow! Look at that spread. There ain't much room on that table for any more food. "I can't believe my eyes, Mrs. Stewart. You surely didn't conjure up all those delicious smellin' vittles from just that old turtle I gave Vi."

Sarah smiled and stifled a giggle. "No, that turtle only goes so far. I'm not a kitchen magician, so I had to add a few things from our farm. I figured you two grown men might like a bit more than just turtle soup."

"I am a bit hungry after a week of CCC grub, so I truly appreciate all you set on the table, ma'am. I haven't seen such a fine lookin' dinner table in a long time. You must have been workin' on it since sun-up."

Sarah smiled. "Don't be silly, I had two girls that were more than willin' to help. You can thank Vi for the green beans. She cooked them the way you said your grandmother cooks them—simmered with bacon and onions."

"Thanks, Vi. Hope they taste as good as they smell. Those spuds look real creamy and buttery. Barb, did you mash 'em?"

"Uh huh, and I peeled 'em too," Barb said as she blushed.

"From the looks of all those vegetables, I'd say the garden must look as if it was raided by a horde of locusts. And, if my eyes aren't mistaken, it looks like you shot a few squabs."

Giggling openly now, Sarah assured Milt that the garden had plenty more left in it. "I'm sorry to disappoint you Mr. McCoy but we won't be havin' any of those squabs you're so fond of. We were getting too many hens in the chicken coup, so I thought you might like a break from squab. Now if everybody would be seated, I'll get the biscuits and we can say grace."

Excited at partaking in another of Sarah's fine meals, Denny spoke in a booming voice. "Good idea, Sarah. I'm starved and I can't wait to dig in to all this fine food you've fussed over since we got home. Barb you sit next to me, and, Vi, you can sit to the left of Mom. Mr. McCoy, please be seated to the right of Mrs. Stewart, and when she gets back with the biscuits, would you be so kind as to say grace?"

Oh crud, I'm not any good at this. I hope I can remember how Grandpa used to say it. I don't think they'd be pleased with the CCC way. Got a hunch they don't want to hear: 'Ru-dub-dub, bless this here grub'. "Thank you, Sir. I'd be honored to say grace."

Returning to the table with one of the biggest baskets of fluffy buttermilk biscuits Milt had ever seen, Sarah said, "Sorry that took so long. Let's say grace and eat before it cools off."

Here goes nothin'. Help me, Lord. In what he hoped to be a voice solemn enough for the occasion, Milt said, "Thank you Lord for your bounty, and the hands that prepared it. Please bless us, and watch over us in the days to come. Amen."

"Well said, Mr. McCoy. Is that how you say grace at home?"

"No sir, I learned that off my grandparents."

"How did your folks say it," Sarah asked?

"Honestly, Mrs. Stewart, it's been awhile since we had Sunday dinner together, so I can't remember real well how we used to say it. One thing's for certain – our Sunday dinners sure weren't this good. Please pass the potatoes."

"Must be hard not having Sunday dinner with your folks. Do you get to see them much?"

I gotta get her off these family questions before I'm booted outta here. "CCC doesn't give me a whole lot of time off, and when they do I'm all the way over here in Fulton County without a jalopy. So, it's been a while since I seen 'em. Please pass me that delicious lookin' squab, I mean chicken."

Chuckling, Sarah passed the chicken. "I hope you like it as much as my squab."

"I'm sure I will ma'am. But, I'll bet this here chicken was a whole lot easier to get then the squab Vi's been feedin' me. Gotta admit, I've a hard time believin' you can shoot one of them there squabs with nothin' but a .22. You must be some kinda sharpshooter, Mrs. Stewart."

Blushing a bit from his compliment and not used to being the center of a young stranger's attention, Sarah took a second to compose herself. "I'm not really that good of a shot, but my dad was a pretty good teacher."

Milt turned his head towards Vi's grandma. *Is that old Injun upset at what her daughter just said? Hard to tell cause all I'm hearin' is gibberish, grunts and groans. The way she's kinda smilin' and wavin' her arms around I think she sayin' she's proud of her.*

Leaning towards Sarah, Milt spoke in a quiet voice. "What did she say, ma'am? I hope I didn't say anything to upset her."

"No, of course you didn't. I'm not certain what she said. My dad never did teach me enough Sioux to hold a conversation. What little I understood, I think she's braggin' about how her husband, my dad, taught me."

Remembering how unsettling it was the first time he met Sarah's mom, Denny couldn't help but console Milt. "Nothin' to worry yourself about. Grandma lives in her own world. You didn't do anything. Now pass me that chicken before it gets cold."

As he passed the chicken to Denny, he heard a shy child voice say, "Mr. Milt, when Daddy is done, may I have some chicken, too?"

"Of course you can, Barbara. Do you like your mom's fried chicken?"

"Uh huh. Me and my sisters like it a lot more than Mommy's squab."

"My sisters and I, not me and my sisters," Barbara's mother corrected.

"Sisters? I thought Vi was your only sister."

In a voice that rose in volume and excitement, Barbara said, "I got me two other sisters. My sister Joan, and my other sister, Rose."

"I think you're pullin' my leg. I only see your sister Vi."

"Nah uh, I got two more but they don't live with us. My sister Joan got hitched, and my sister Rose is at school for nurses."

After a brief stern look at Barbara, Denny changed the subject. "Milt, tell me a little bit of what you do in the CCC. I've heard a lot of nice things about the CCC, but I don't know much about them."

"Well, sir, I probably don't know a whole lot more about it than you. It's one of them there Roosevelt programs for makin' work for young folks. The Army is in charge of it, and believe me they sure let us fellas know they are."

"What kind of work does the CCC do?"

"Mostly we go around clearing brush and planting trees. Army don't tell us much why, we just go where they tell us and do what we're told."

Denny sensed Milt was hiding some thoughts about the CCC, so he asked, "Sounds like you don't much like the work and the way the Army runs it."

"Don't mind the work at all. Hard work never hurt anyone. I just wish the Army didn't boss us around so much. I'd already had enough bossin' in my life before I joined up." *Oops, I shouldn't of said that about bossin'. I better get off that subject right quick like.* "We also build our own camps and take care of our own vehicles and work gear. Woodworkin' and mechanical stuff is right up my alley."

I'll let that problem of bossing he has pass for now. "When I was your age I liked woodworking and vehicle work too. Of course in those days there weren't too many jalopies around. What kinda wood and mechanical work do they have you doin'?"

"Well, sir, we just do the simple woodworkin' we need for buildin' our cabins. Mostly we just lay the foundations, put up the framin', and raise the roofs of our cabins. I also get to make most of the cabinets and inside stuff."

"Buildin' a cabin ain't exactly what I call easy," Denny said.

"No, sir, but it ain't something that most anybody can't learn. CCC keeps it pretty simple, so I don't get to build any of the fancy stuff I learned in high school."

"Like, what?"

"If I see you folks again, I'll try to remember to bring the smoke stand I built in high school. That's the kind of wood-workin' I like to do. Can't bring any example of my mechanical stuff, but you got any vehicles that need fixin' I'd sure be glad to fix 'em for you."

"Milt, it sounds like you picked up some good skills in high school. I'll be lookin' forward to findin' out what the heck a smoke stand is when you join us again."

If I'm hearing right, old man Stewart is saying I can come callin', but maybe I'm gettin' ahead of myself. "Well, sir, it's really nothin' more than an ashtray that has a fancy stand attached to it. I'll be glad to bring it with me on my next visit, and if you got any car fixin' to do, I'll be glad to do it if you have the tools."

"Appreciate that. My Tin Lizzy actually runs pretty good. Its been overheatin' a bit more than it used too, but I'm not real good at car fixin' so I'm not certain why."

"Knowin' the Tin Lizzy, either the water pump seal is leakin' a bit or the radiator needs to be flushed. If you got the tools, I can fix it. If ya want, I can take a look at it before I leave."

"I may not have the tools, but I know where I can get 'em."

"Besides industrial courses, what else did you like in high school?" Sarah said.

"Truthfully, ma'am, I didn't get a chance to find out what else. I couldn't attend as much as I needed too, so I'm ashamed to admit I never finished high school. I woulda liked to have attended more. Sure did want to play on the baseball team."

"I'm sorry, Milt. I wouldn't be ashamed though. Nowadays lots of young men seem to have to work instead of finishing school."

"Yes ma'am, I heard tell that's happenin' to a lot of fellas. I could've probably gone to school when I was living with my grandparents in Indiana, but it would have been hard to do."

"Didn't they have a school nearby?"

"They had a school, but my grandparents farm was so far out in the sticks it would've took me half the day to walk to it, and the other half to walk back. I wouldn't of had any time for chores. Besides, I was havin' too much fun. When I wasn't farmin', I was playin' ball with my grandpa."

"Was your grandpa a pretty good ball player?"

"Yes ma'am, he taught me all about the game. My dad was kinda interested in the game but my grandpa was nuts about it. He taught me so good that the White Soxs took a look at me."

Denny raised his eyebrows. "You must've been pretty good for the Soxs to take a look. How did they hear about you?"

"My grandpa was real excited about my playin', so he sent a letter to the owner of the Soxs, old man Comiskey. I guess his dad, my great grandpa, had known him at one time or another. Comiskey surprised us with a scout that showed up at our door one day."

"Wow! Sarah we got a baseball star at our table. Did they try to sign you up?"

"Scout worked me out till I darn near dropped. He sorta tried to sign me. He liked my pitchin' enough to offer me a spot on one of their C League teams."

"Did you sign?"

"No sir. Grandpa and I decided that startin' at the C level didn't have much of a future. We were a bit disappointed, but we figured it just wasn't meant to be. We still rooted for our Sox. They'd been our team since way back."

Sarah's eyes widened and her hand patted her cheek. With mock horror, she said, "Oh my, this might be a bit uncomfortable. We've got a devoted Cub and Sox fan at the same table."

"I wouldn't worry none, Sarah. Both of our teams aren't gonna set the world on fire this year. If they both end up in the World Series then we might have a problem."

"That's for sure. Your Cubs have got a few good hitters, like that Stan Hack and that second baseman Billy Herman, but your pitchin' is horrible. Shoot, they're still tryin' to get some more games out of that old Dizzy Dean."

"I gotta agree with you Mr. McCoy, but your Sox aren't a whole lot better. Most of their good players are gettin' pretty long in the tooth. Luke Appling is thirty-eight and sure as heck ain't a shortstop anymore. He was great in his day, but not now."

"Guess we're both in for a long losin' season, sir. One thing you can be thankful for though is that your Cubs won't have to face them damn Yankees."

A brief stunned silence fell over the table. Vi and her mother's eyes widened.

Gripping the edge of the table, Denny told Milt in a soft, yet blunt, voice, "We don't cotton to cursin' in our home."

Milt drew back into his chair, took a breath, and started to apologize.

Before he could get his words out, Denny spoke. "Except when it's part of a name—like damn Yankees. We may not play 'em but I'm like most folks —I despise that team. They don't develop players. They just buy 'em from teams down on their luck. I gotta admit all that money they got gets 'em some good ones, but they aren't choosy about how their players behave. That big, old, fat drunken Ruth sure wasn't much of an example for young folks. Only one I had any respect for was that Gehrig fella. Shame what happened to him at such a young age."

"Sorry about that slip of the tongue, sir. I'll remember to watch it in the future. But I will say I agree with you on the Yankees."

"We all make slips once in awhile. What say we head out to the back porch for coffee and a pipe? Mrs. Stewart brews a mighty fine pot of chicory coffee."

"Sounds like a good idea sir, but what's chicory coffee?"

"You'll like it. At the start of the Depression we had an old neighbor that was originally from Louisiana. He showed us how to add a little chicory to our coffee so we wouldn't have to use so much of the expensive coffee grounds. He said that's how they drink it down there. Got to likin' it so much we just kept drinkin' it that way."

"If Mrs. Stewart makes it, I'm sure it's good. Everything was delicious, ma'am. Never had turtle soup before, but I really liked it."

"Thank you, Milt, I'm glad you liked it. It's been awhile since I had one to turn into soup so I'm glad it turned out well."

Raising his right hand as if taking an oath, Milt promised. "Ma'am, if you'll make soup every time I find me a turtle, I'll be keepin' my eyes out for 'em."

"Milt, as much as you like her cookin' you sure are gettin' on her good side. Let's get ourselves out to the porch and let these ladies take care of the dishes."

Holding the door ajar, Milt motioned Denny towards the door, but Denny grabbed it. "No, no, guests go first in this house, so after you young man. And, oh by the way Vi, would you fetch me my pipe and tobacco."

"I'll be glad to, Daddy."

"Have a seat Milt, or would you rather first stretch your legs a bit?"

I must be doing something right. He just called me by my given name. "A stretch sounds invitin'. Besides, I don't want to wake Grandpa."

"Eh … Eh, did someone call me?" a confused, suddenly awake Grandpa said.

"No, Grandpa. Milt and I were tryin' to have our after supper coffee and a smoke without disturbin' you."

"Well, I'm awake now! Think Sarah might fetch me a coffee and my pipe?"

"Coffee she'll probably get you, but you know you aren't supposed to be smokin' no more."

"Maybe cuz we got a guest she'll be nice to her Pa. You think?"

"Don't know, but I'll ask."

"Sarah … Sarah, Grandpa wants to know if you'll fetch him a coffee and his corncob pipe?"

"I'll get him a coffee, but he knows he's not supposed to be smokin'."

"When you bring his coffee, would you also bring a chair? With Grandpa entertainin' us we're short one chair."

Milt opened the screen door for Sarah as she passed through with the requested chair and coffee. "Thanks for the coffee and the chair, ma'am. After a great meal like that one, a good cup of coffee and a good pipe sure hits the spot."

"What meal? Did I sleep through supper again? Hope Sarah saved me some," Grandpa said.

"Don't worry, Grandpa. Sarah saved you a bowl of that delicious turtle soup she made," Denny said.

"Turtle soup … where the heck did she get the turtle?"

"Milt caught it last weekend when he was fishin' down on the Spoon."

Stroking his scruffy beard, Grandpa said, "Caught it on a fishin' pole? Ain't never heard of such a thing. What kinda bait was ya usin'?"

Milt chuckled. "I'd never heard of catchin' one on a pole either. I was fishin' for catfish with my secret stink bait. Next thing I know an ugly old snappin' turtle was on Vi's pole."

"Stink bait, huh? That's how I used to fish for catfish. I'll bet your stink bait is a bloody chicken back ya buried for a week in a gunny sack full of rotten cheese. Tell the truth now, that's your secret bait, ain't it?" Grandpa challenged as he leaned towards Milt.

"Like I said, it's a secret bait. I ain't sayin' your wrong, but I ain't saying your right," Milt smiled.

Vi opened the screen door and saved Milt from what she sensed was the start of another of Grandpa's ramblings about his wilderness experiences. "Here's your pipe and tobacco, Daddy."

"Thanks, Vi." Denny sat down. "Like you said, Milt, good food followed by coffee, and a good pipe sure is hard to beat."

"Yes sir, I notice you have Prince Albert in the can."

"Yeah I do, and before you try that old worn out joke on me, I assure you I do intend to let him out and smoke him."

Milt chuckled. "Guess you got me on that one. It's a bit of an old corny joke, but you gotta admit sir it never fails to bring out a chuckle."

Denny smiled. "You're right. It does bring out a chuckle, and it seems to break the ice when told to a pretty young lady."

"On that note, I think I'll leave you two to your men talk," Vi said as she slipped through the open screen door before her blush became obvious.

"Sounds like Vi told you all about how we met. Hope she's had nothin' but good to tell ya."

"Must admit, she, and the folks my friend Judge Wilson steered me towards, like the Sheriff of Knox County, had lots of good things to say about ya. Now your pa, on the other hand, didn't have much good to say."

"My dad never will have much good to say about me. We both have different ideas on how to get through life."

"What little time I spent with him, I got the feelin' most folks view righteous livin' quite a bit different than you pa does."

"You got that right, sir. To him, as long as you don't get caught and can make yourself feel good, then you can do pretty much anything you want."

"I'm guessin' your grandparents must've taught you different."

Yes, sir. Thank God! I'm glad for my grandparents' Bible lessons. Thanks to them, I ain't nothin' like my ma and pa, and I don't intend to ever be. I probably shouldn't say this, but I could care less if I ever lay eyes on 'em again."

Sounds like Milt's folks really did wrong by him. Can't imagine what it must've been like bein' raised by that old drunk and his hussy. Thank God for his grandparents.

Denny patted Milt's forearm and lowered his voice to a gentle murmur. "I can see the ways of your folks really bothers you. Hope you know I didn't bring them up to hurt your feelings or blame you. I looked into 'em only so I could know a bit more about who will be a courtin' my daughter."

I hope I heard him right. Guess it's time for me to take a gamble. "Sir, did I just hear you give me permission to court your daughter?"

"Well, I guess I did. Now let's finish our coffee and I'll give you a ride back to camp. It wouldn't be right for my daughter's beau to be hitch hikin', when I could be drivin' him instead."

Milt offered his hand and in a rising voice said, "Thank you sir, I won't make you regret your decision. Believe me, sir; I'll do right by your daughter."

Inside the kitchen, the eavesdropping mother and daughter silently hugged each other. Both wanted to say so much, but both also wished to keep their joy private. Neither would chance breaking the silence, and perhaps be the cause of another potential beau to be denied.

"I know you will, Milt. Now let's finish that coffee and get you back to camp before it gets dark."

"Appreciate it, sir, but before we go, let me take a look at why your Model T's over heatin'."

11

Good thing I checked out Denny's car before we left. His water pump was really leakin'. I'd say his gasket is shot. Wish I coulda fixed it right, but it looks like I got lucky with my jury-riggin'. Two miles to camp and no steam risin' from the radiator sure is a good sign.

"Looks like you did a pretty good job on my old Lizzy. Sure is a relief to not see steam after all these miles we've traveled."

"Sure is, but to fix it right I need to change the water pump gasket. I'll be glad to do it next Saturday, if you can get the tools and gasket material."

"I'll take you up on that kind offer. Pretty sure I can get the material off my old friend Felix."

"That wouldn't be Mr. Steinberg that owns a Sinclair station in Canton, would it?"

Denny cocked his head and raised his right eyebrow. "That's the same Felix, but how do you know him?"

"I just met him today when I asked for directions to your house. He was kind enough to give me a ride. He said to give you and your family his best."

121

"Well I'll be darned," Denny said as he slapped his knee. "What a small world. He's a fine fella for a Jew. Of course, he's the only Jew I've ever known. For all I know, they might all be good people like him."

"I don't even know what a Jew is, but I sure liked him. Got the feelin' he ain't shy about helpin' folks in need. Sounds like you two have known each other for awhile."

"Sure have. You might do well to get to know him. When you get out of CCC, he might have a spot at one of his stations for a good mechanic, like yourself."

"I hadn't really thought of it. Guess I should though, cuz I may be gittin' out sooner then I thought."

"Why's that?"

"When I signed on with the CCC, I was told I had to send twenty-five dollars a month of my pay to my parents. I signed the papers for sendin' the money, but I wrote down my grand-parents address."

"Did you do that cuz you didn't want your mom and dad to get it?"

"You hit that nail on the head! I couldn't cotton to the idea of sendin' them more drinkin' money. Besides, the CCC said I had to send the money home. And to me, my grandparents were really the ones that raised me and gave me a home."

As the last rays of the day withdrew, Denny and Milt withdrew into their inner world of thoughts and doubts.

I wonder if I should tell him all the truth. Would he think less of me if he knew that I sent it to my grandparents for safe keeping?

Rounding the bend in the road that lead to the entrance of the CCC camp, Milt and Denny were jolted back to the present by the unexpected appearance of Frank's rusty, mud-encrusted old Ford truck parked haphazardly near the camp entrance. Nearby, Frank and Supervisor Haney were engaged in a conversation. Not an adult, calm conversation, but instead an exchange of contrasts. Frank's arms flailed wildly and his angry contorted face flushed into a rummy red. As Frank spewed his venomous verbal assault, a calm and collected Supervisor Haney set his jaw and ducked Frank's flailing punctuation.

Frank stumbled towards Denny's Model T, and yelled at him in a drunken slurred voice. "Well, look what the cat just drug in. Surprise, surprise, it's that high and mighty inspector chauffeurin' my thievin' bum."

"Mr. Stewart, why don't you let me out right here. I better take care of this."

Denny continued to drive towards the camp. "No, I ain't lettin' you out here alone. From the looks of it you might need some help."

"Appreciate it sir, but you've already done a lot and you don't need to see this. Knowin' my dad, it could get ugly."

Denny climbed out of his parked car and attempted to dissuade the charging Frank. "Good to see you too, Frank. I think your boy might be willin' to talk with you if you'd just kindly calm down."

"Calm down my ass! I ain't doin' no calmin' till I git my money!"

Supervisor Haney added, "As I said Mr. McCoy, we still haven't determined why the family allotment hasn't been sent to you as it should have. If you will come back later this week, we should have the information from headquarters that will clear this up."

"Ain't gonna happen, we're clearin' this up here and now! This little thievin' bum knows why I ain't gittin' it," Frank yelled as he took a wild swing at Milt.

Milt took one quick step to the left to avoid Frank's wild right roundhouse punch. His sloppy drunken swing not only missed Milt, but also launched him into a stumbling lurch that carried him past Milt.

Spitting dust as he attempted to rise from his head-first plunge into the hard-packed dusty road, Frank glared at Milt. "You're gonna pay for this, you little good-for-nothing asshole bum!"

Concerned by Supervisor Haney's lack of response to the escalated situation, Denny said, "Frank, before you get up, why don't ya take a few moments to collect yourself so we can calmly sort this out."

Frank stared up at him then jumped to his feet, pulled a knife from his pocket and yelled, "The only collectin' that's gonna be done today is me collectin' from that –"

Thanks to a vicious right cross from a fast-charging Supervisor Merrill, the unconscious Frank never finished his outburst. "Sorry about that folks. I would've put a stop to this sooner, but I didn't hear it goin' on till old man McCoy started yellin'. I called the sheriff. If you want to press charges, I'll be glad to be a witness."

Milt shook with anger. "As much as I despise his behavior, I can't sic the law on my own father. I appreciate your offer, but I just can't."

"I understand. Sheriff will at least keep him until we can sort this situation out."

Kicking away Frank's knife, Milt shook his head. "No – we can sort it out right now! I filled the family payment forms out, but I gave my grandparents address."

"That is unfortunate," Supervisor Haney said as he slowly shook his head, "because the forms clearly requested the address of the parents."

"No disrespect intended sir, but your form asked for my *home* address."

"Young man, I caution you not to attempt to twist words on the form for your own benefit."

"I'm not, sir. My grandparents were the ones that raised me for the better part of my life, so I figured they really are my parents and my home. Besides, I wasn't about to give money to my mom and dad. You've seen what kind of a man my father is, and, believe me, my mom ain't much better."

"Nonetheless, the CCC clearly intended to assist your parents, not the persons you considered worthy of payment. I will need to consult with headquarters about this. I suggest you bid your companion good-bye, and return to your barracks. We will chat after I hear from headquarters."

Milt joined Denny at the back of his car. "I'm sorry you had to see and hear all that. Appreciate your help. If you want to change your mind about my courtin' your daughter, I wouldn't blame ya."

Denny offered his hand as he clasped Milt's right shoulder with his left hand. "No need for apology. You don't get to choose your parents. Expect to see ya next Saturday. If something comes up, call us at CAN 4421."

12

"Hello. Stewart residence," Denny said as he answered the family phone.

"Sorry to disturb you, Mr. Stewart. I hope I didn't catch you at a bad time."

"Not at all, not at all Milt. Glad to hear from ya. Your ears must have been twitching. We were just talking about ya."

"Good things, I hope?"

"Mostly me braggin' about how my water pump is holdin' up since you fixed it. The women were doin' a bit of worryin' about that Haney fella. Is he still chewin' on ya?"

"The ladies must have been readin' my mind. That's why I'm callin'," Milt said.

"Sounds like things aren't quite right for ya. Anything we can do to help?"

"I'm hopin' you can. You might say, Supervisor Haney is bein' down right difficult."

"Going by the book, is he?"

"Yep."

"Does headquarters agree with him?"

"Don't rightly know, but they seem to. Ever since he got their letter, he's been grindin' me pretty good. Ain't exactly said what he's gonna do, but he sorta hinted I'd have to pay my dad or leave camp."

"I imagine you don't have the money, so when's he gonna make ya leave?"

"Don't rightly know, but I'm hopin' he just lets me go. Yesterday, he strutted around like a banty rooster. He rattled on about chargin' me for lyin' to the government."

"Oh come on, he ain't gonna charge ya, is he?"

"Really don't rightly know. He darn near blew a gasket when I showed him that all his form asked for was who and where to send my family payments," Milt said.

Denny chuckled at the thought of Haney's discomfort. "I'll bet he wasn't mister calm and cool after that. I would've gave a chunk of change to see him get his by-the-book knickers in a knot."

"Nope, he sure wasn't, and that's why I'm callin' ya. Right after I gave him my view of things, he raised his hand up and started countin' off three things he might do to me. After he got done, I figured I might need your help with a couple of 'em."

"Be glad to, but I thought you said three, not just a couple."

"Only two I'm worried about. I ain't worried about paying Dad. Got no money, and I'm pretty sure he can't force me to. What I'm worried about is him chargin' me or kickin' me out of the CCC."

"Like I said, how can we help?"

"Depends on what Haney does. If he charges me, I might need a lawyer, but I got a hunch he won't. What I said about the forms ticked him off, but his eyes said 'Oh crap, the boy's right'."

"If he charges ya, I know a fella over in Peoria that does lots of lawyer work for free. Especially if it lets him twist the tail of those Roosevelt government boys and helps his runnin' for Congress."

"Good. Like I said, I ain't got a lot of dough. But, I'm really worried more about Haney's other threat."

"Are you talkin' about him tossin' ya out of the CCC?"

"Yes sir, I am. The way he's carryin' on, Haney will probably make me leave camp early. My time is up in about four months so I've been preparin'. But if I leave all of sudden like I'm in trouble—I've got no job waitin' for me and no place to stay."

"We might be able to help if push comes to shove. We got lots of relatives in the area. I'm sure one of 'em has got some room for ya. Jobs are a bit scarcer, but I'll see if Felix Steinberg might have need for a fine mechanic."

"I really appreciate that, sir. I don't want to feeload off of 'em. Once I find a job, I'll pay 'em rent. It might help if you'd tell Mr. Steinberg about my water pump fixin'."

"Way ahead of ya, I saw him last week and bragged about it. He was down right impressed. Spoke highly of ya, and said to say hello. If Felix's got a job for ya, when can you start?"

"Way things are goin' I might be ready to start next Monday. Hope it'll be okay if I show up at your door before Saturday."

"You do what you need to do. I'll get the ball rollin' over on our end. Take care, and don't do anything that'll cause you any more grief. See ya Saturday," Denny said and hung up.

Or sooner, Milt thought.

* * *

"Thanks for giving me my last ride," Milt said as he offered his hand to Supervisor Merrill. "I hope I didn't get ya in trouble."

"Don't worry about me. I was scheduled to pick up supplies today, and I made sure that Haney didn't see ya load up your gear. But, I wish it wasn't your last ride in this beaten up old piece of crap."

"I wish it wasn't too. Woulda been leavin' in a few months anyway. But, I sure woulda liked to had those months to plan. Thanks to old by-the-book Haney, here I am four months early, and no job."

"I know, but, believe me, a good hard-working, smart fella like you will find a job right quick like."

"Sure do hope so. I appreciate all you've done for me. Heard about how you tried to talk some sense into Haney. Guess he had his mind set, so here I am. You take care, Mr. Merrill, and don't forget to check this old crate's oil and water every chance you get," Milt said as he shook hands and smiled.

"You take care too, and I'll try to keep this old piece of crap runnin'. It'll probably fall apart now that you ain't jerry-rigging it every time it decides it needs some coaxin'," Merrill said as they shook hands.

* * *

Crossing the street, Milt took a deep breath. *Here goes nothin'. Walgreens doesn't look too busy. Hope Vi still thinks highly of me now that the CCC booted me early.*

Milt approached Vi from the side and was overcome with doubt when he saw her. *What did I do to deserve such a beautiful lady?*

Even though he didn't want to, Milt waited patiently as she assisted her demanding customer. *Damn, that old lady sure can ask a lot of questions. Just buy the damn bracelet, lady! I need to talk to Vi before I get cold feet. The old bat musta read my mind. She finally bought that ugly jewelry.*

Doubts and customer distractions casted aside, Milt tapped the very busy, focused Vi on the back of her shoulder.

Vi turned towards the intrusion. "May I help . . . oh, Milt it's you! I'm so glad you're here! But what are you doing here on a Wednesday?"

"Same thing I'll be doing for quite a few days to come, if I can find a job."

"What do you mean?"

"I don't know if your dad told ya, but, thanks to my old man, me and the CCC had a partin' of ways."

"Dad mentioned something about your father making some trouble for you. He didn't tell us what it was, though."

"Oh yeah, he made quite a bit of trouble for me. So, here I am." Milt smiled and spread his arms out wide. "Hope you're glad to see me. If Mr. Steinberg takes me on, you'll be seein' a lot more of me."

"That would be wonderful! Maybe that's what Dad is talking to Mr. Steinberg about right now."

Surprised, Milt said, "You mean he's over at Mr. Steinberg's station right now?"

"Uh huh. He gave me a ride to work today because he said he had to chat with Mr. Steinberg. He's probably still there."

"You think he'd mind if I dropped in on 'em?"

"Can't see why he'd mind. Why don't you go on over. Afterwards, maybe you and Dad can join me for lunch."

"Think I will join 'em. Wish me luck."

Vi leaned in as close to Milt as she dared without offending her boss, and whispered, "Good luck, sweetheart. See you soon."

* * *

Felix turned towards the tinkle of the door bell. Surprised, he thrust his hand towards Milt and said, "Why look who the angels delivered! How are you, Milt? Me and Mr. Stewart were just jawin' about you."

Milt grinned and shook Felix's hand. "So that's why my ears were twitchin'. Hope y'all had a few kind words to say."

"Good to see you Milt. Matter of fact we just said enough good words that we decided you oughta work for me."

Confused, Milt shook Denny's hand and asked, "Don't you mean work for Mr. Steinberg?"

"Guess that was the plan when I walked in here today, but Felix up and offered me a deal I couldn't refuse. As of now you are lookin' at the new owner of the Farmington Sinclair station that's in dire need of a good mechanic. Job's yours when you've had enough of that Supervisor Haney."

Milt broke into a wide smile and wildly pumped Denny's hand. "I can start right now! I've definitely had enough of Haney."

"I had a feelin' that's why you're here on a Wednesday. Come on. Let's go celebrate and have some lunch with Vi. Felix, you're welcome to join us, if you'd like."

"Wish I could, but that mechanic of mine can service cars, but he can't service customers. See you at your place tonight to finish signin' the paperwork."

* * *

The country road from Canton to Farmington cuts through gentle rolling fields that usually are abuzz with the sounds of nature. As expected on a hot July day, the chirping of the birds, croaking of the frogs and the buzzing of the insects were present, but they, as well as the rattling of Denny's old Model T, were overwhelmed by the incessant questions of an excited Milt McCoy.

"How big a station is the one ya just bought?"

"If I recollect right, it's about the same size as Felix's Canton station."

"Has it got all the tools, or are ya gonna have to buy 'em?"

"Good question, Milt. I'm supposin' they come with the station. I better ask Felix tonight when he comes with the papers to sign."

"Has it got a grease pit? Hope so. A pit makes workin' under cars a whole lot easier. "

"Don't recall one. Tell you what. We probably got time, so let's stop at the station before I take you over to meet Punch."

"Who's Punch?"

"He's Sarah's uncle, and he's the head of the Campbell family you'll be living with till you get your feet under ya."

"Oh. What kinda name is Punch?"

"I reckon it's Scottish. He was born on the ship that brought the Campbells from Scotland to America. Sarah says no one knows where he got the handle of Punch. No one seems to know his given name because no one's ever called him by it."

"Ain't cuz he goes around beatin' on folks is it?"

"No, no. It ain't nothin' like that. He's a big fella that could put some lumps on ya if he got a mind to, but truth is he's a gentle man who's as kind as the day is long."

Denny pulled into the driveway of Farmington's Sinclair station, as he said, "Well, let's give my new station the once over."

"It looks closed. Where's the pump jockey?"

"It's closed. Felix fired the last fella when he caught him stuffin' some of the cash in his pocket. I'd been talkin' to Felix for quite awhile about buyin' this station. After he fired the fella it got too hard for Felix to run two stations, so he got serious about selling it," Denny said as he unlocked the front door.

After a brief inspection of the garage and the store, Milt said, "Well the garage is okay, but it would be better if it had a grease pit. One good thing, it's got all the tools we might need. Don't worry about the pit. I can dig one in no time at all."

"You're the mechanic. If you think we need a pit then we need a pit. When I talk to Felix tonight, I'll make sure the tools are in the deal."

"I gotta hunch the station was at one time a bit more than a station. From the looks of that pot belly stove and the chairs it was the town meetin' place."

"Felix said the old boy that owned it before him liked to jaw with folks, so I ain't surprised by the stove and chairs. From the looks of those shelves and some of the old cans on them, at one time this station might have been like a general store."

"Sure does, but I'll bet the A&P and Walgreens over in Canton took away a lot of that business."

"You're probably right, Milt. I know a lot of these old small-town stations used to be a little bit of everything. I ain't gonna try and compete with them big city stores, but maybe we can put in a few things that'll save folks a trip to Canton. At least it's worth thinking about."

Milt nodded. "Yeah, like ice cold soda-pop and candy. I might even be your best soda-pop customer. Ain't nothin' like a cold pop on a hot day."

Denny smiled as he turned on the gas pumps. "We'll see. Now, let's check out the pumps before we get you over to the Campbells."

"Thank God, the pumps work," Denny said as he began to fill his car's fuel tank, "I was getting' a bit low on gas."

"Good thing they still work. I'd hated to have to push your Lizzy home," Milt chuckled.

"Me too. Looks like everything's in order, so I better get you settled in with the Campbell's right quick like before Felix shows up. Unless you hear different from me tonight, plan on meetin' me here at seven tomorrow mornin'."

13

Denny forced himself to smile as he drove into the driveway of his newly acquired Sinclair station. *First day of a new adventure, it oughta be interestin'. I don't have the foggiest idea about runnin' a gas station. Hope Milt does.*

"Mornin', Milt." Denny greeted his pacing mechanic. "All set for our first day?" Denny unlocked the station door.

"Yes sir. What do you want me to do first? Maybe I oughta stoke the pot-belly stove so we can get some coffee brewin'?"

"Good idea. The smell of fresh brewed coffee oughta bring in customers," Denny said as he picked up the old blackened coffee pot.

"Or folks that just want to chew the fat and drink some free coffee," Milt said.

"Either way, we win. Drinkin' coffee with folks is a good way to introduce ourselves. Who knows, might even get a few customers out of all that jawin'."

"I sure hope so. If it doesn't, we might have ourselves a problem." Milt muttered.

As the warmth of the stove drove away the cool of the morning, cold reality crept into Milt's mind. *I don't think Mr. Stewart knows how much I want this station to work out. If it doesn't, his family will be hurtin', and I'll be out of a job. Wonder what he's gonna pay me?*

Noting Milt's look of concern, he said, "Don't worry, the customers will be beatin' our door down. Me and you are gonna make this station work. Can't let my family down, and, with the ways thing are nowadays, I don't want you to have to look for a job."

"I don't want to have to look either, sir." Milt placed his hand a few inches over the top of the stove and said, "I think the stove is hot enough for the coffee."

Denny placed the coffee pot on the stove. "You know, I think we never did get around to chattin' about your pay. I don't know exactly what to pay you cuz I don't know how much business we'll have. Got any ideas?"

"Not really. But I'm okay if I get a little less until business comes in. How much do ya figure?"

"Sad truth is I can't pay you what you're probably worth. Your idea is kinda what I hoped you'd think is fair. What would ya say to twenty percent of the profit until the station brings in enough to pay you fifty cents an hour?"

Even though Milt trusted Denny, he couldn't help but be skeptical. "That's a right fine idea that makes sense, but I imagine the customers ain't gonna be beatin' a path to the door right away. What happens if the station doesn't make much profit?"

"Good question. I wouldn't worry too much. This station was profitable when Felix owned it, so I think it will be just as profitable soon enough."

"I reckon you're right, but how long you think it'll take to get it profitable enough?"

"Tell you what, if it ain't profitable enough in two months from now to pay you fifty cents an hour, I'll call some of my friends in Peoria. I'm sure they'll know of a job over there that can pay you a steady wage. Fair enough?" Denny offered his hand to seal the deal.

"Fair enough. Rest assured, sir, I'll work my butt off for ya. I ain't too partial to big cities."

Denny smiled and shook his hand. "Glad that's over. We've done enough hard work for awhile. Negotiatin' is hard on the jaw. I think the coffee is ready, so let's have our first coffee break."

"Sounds good, I'll wash us out some cups, and a couple extra ones for those fellas walkin' up the driveway," Milt nodded towards the station's front window.

Denny watched the two older, un-kempt, overall-clad men shuffle up to the smell of brewing coffee. *Bet these two old coots are some of Felix's regular coffee moochers. Doubt those fellas are payin' customers. They don't look like they can afford gas; leave alone a car to put it in. Still though, gotta treat 'em good or they're apt to do some bad mouthin' that'll scare off the payin' customers.*

Denny opened the door for the men. "Morning gents, what brings you out on this fine early morn?"

The first man to enter offered his dirty, arthritic deformed hand to Denny. "Howdy, name is Earl Freeman. Thought me and Ed would drop over and see if ya knew how to make coffee better than that Jew did."

Before Denny could answer, the second man extended his tobacco stained hand. "Like Earl said, I'm Ed, Ed Herrman. Coffee sure smells good."

"Nice to meet you fellas. I'm Denny Stewart, the new owner, and that fella over by the stove is my mechanic, Milt McCoy. Coffee's ready. Help yourself. Cups are over that away, but we don't have any sugar or cream."

"Don't worry about sugar and cream. We drink it black. Besides, we're used to doin'without. The Jew always said he couldn't afford coffee fixins," Earl said with a scowl.

Got a hunch these two are the town's haters. Don't remember them when I lived here before. Hope they knock off that Jew talk. Running his fingers through his hair, he chuckled. "I can understand Felix not affordin' the fixins. If this here station was rakin' in the dough he wouldn't have sold it to me. Why don't you fellas make yourself comfy while I take care of my first customer that just drove up?"

My Lord looks who's my first customer. Good old Ron Parker. We started minin' together right after the Great War, and I'll be darned if he ain't startin' off my gas station business. Ain't that fittin'.

"What can I do for ya Ron?" Denny said to the tall, handsome man, who was the same age as Denny – but didn't look it.

"Not much Denny. My mine's been inspected from one end to the other and then back again. Could get me Felix if ya know where he's hidin'. I gotta get some gas. I'm runnin' on fumes."

"Can't get you Felix, but I can get you the new owner, which just happens to be me," Denny smiled and pointed to his chest with his thumb.

"Ya pullin' my leg, Denny?" Ron said as he cocked his head to the side.

"Nope, I bought out Felix, and you're my first customer."

"Well I'll be damn. Guess its only right I'm your first customer. Hell, I started you off in minin', so I might as well start you off in the gas business," Ron said as he shook his head and smiled.

"Funny you mentioned that, I was thinkin' that as I walked up to your car."

Ron looked towards the station and said, "I see you've met the local chapter of the American Bund. As much as Earl and Ed carried on about Jews, I always wondered how they could drink Felix's coffee without chokin'."

"Never heard of the American Bund, but they started Jew bashin' shortly after they came in. That kinda thinkin' is beyond me."

"Sounds like 'em. Thank God we ain't got many around these parts that think their way."

"Amen to that, but what in the heck is that Bund thing you say they belong too?"

"Truthfully, I don't know if they belong to it or not, but they run their mouths like them there Bund fellas over in Lewiston."

"No wonder I ain't heard of 'em. Lewiston's quite a ways from Canton."

"Believe me, if you were in Lewiston when they meet you'd sure hear 'em. When they get to carryin' on about how right that Hitler fella is you can hear 'em all over town," Ron said.

"Ain't he that German fella who blames all the troubles of the world on the Jews?"

"Yep, that's the jackass Earl and Ed thinks the sun rises and sets on. I wouldn't mind chewin' some more fat, but I gotta git 'fore my men beat me to work. Good luck with those two," Ron handed Denny the fifty cents he owed him for the fill up.

* * *

Denny smiled as he returned to the garage after pumping gas for their latest customer. *I swear it ain't even noon yet and Milt and I must of filled half of the Farmington's cars.* "Milt where are ya? Back down in that grease pit again?"

"Yes sir. I ain't made much progress today cuz of all the customers we've had. But, I ain't complainin'. The more we have, the better."

Denny looked down into the pit. "I agree, but you need to take a break. Day ain't half done, but ya look a bit done in. You need to have a seat and a bottle of cold soda from our new ice box." *This boy said he'd work his tail off to make us profitable, but I can't let him overdo it. Sarah and Vi would never let me hear the end of it. Besides I need a live mechanic not one that's dead on his feet.*

Denny handed Milt an ice cold soda and sat down next to him. "Here. Time to cool off before you drop. Take a break and I'll man the pump for awhile."

"Thank ya, sir. It's a bit warm today. Got a feelin' this is gonna be a hot August."

"Yeah, it seems that way. Heat keeps up, you and Vi might want to take a dip in that new pool they dug over in Canton," Denny said and grinned.

Milt tried not to squirm while he considered an appropriate response. Meanwhile, the station's screen door creaked open as a welcome visitor entered. "Well, I see business is so good that all you have to do is rest on your duffs and drink cold soda-pops."

Denny jumped to his feet, and dramatically gestured to Milt. "Quick Milt, jump to it. That nasty old Steinberg inspector's here to check up on us."

Felix laughed as he shook Denny's hand. "Glad to see the customers ain't beat your sense of humor out of ya just yet."

"Nah. Not yet. But some of 'em, like that Earl and Ed sure are tryin' too."

"You mean Earl and Ed are finally payin' customers? Never thought I'd see the day they'd do anything besides mooch coffee and gripe about most everything and anything."

"Still ain't seen the day, and doubt if you ever will."

Felix gave a soft whistle and wiped his brow. "Whew! I thought you might have to call a doctor. Don't think my old heart could take the thought of them two payin'."

Denny grinned and patted him on the back. "Your heart's safe for now, and probably for a whole lot more days. I got a hunch they'll always find someone to mooch off of and somethin' to complain about."

"Probably so, what's their latest ax to grind?"

Denny and Milt drew a long draft off their sodas and grew silent.

Felix noted the delay. "You fellas are acting like they got so many gripes it's hard to know where to start."

"Actually they only have one burr under their saddle, but it's a bit embarrassin'."

"Are they still carryin' on about Jews this and Jews that?"

"How'd ya know?"

"You think they didn't pull that crap on me? They muttered amongst themselves and thought I couldn't hear, but I heard every damn despicable slur they had to offer."

"Why didn't you kick 'em out?"

"Probably for about the same reason Denny doesn't. If I kicked them out they would of bad-mouthed me from one end of this town to the other."

"Yes, sir, I understand. But you'd been here for a good long while. The town folks would of just thought it was bull. They know what kind of no-goods Earl and Ed are. Mr. Stewart just opened, so he needs to still butter folks up."

"Milt, for a young fella you seem to think things through, but you're forgettin' one thing."

"What's that?"

"You're forgettin' that I'm Jewish," Felix said in a proud voice, but with a shrug that spoke more of acceptance of prejudice then it did his pride of heritage.

"What's that got to do with it? I don't even know what a Jew is, but I do know good people and ya sure have been good to me and Mr. Stewart."

Wish this was the time and place to answer Milt's question. It is so good to find a young man that the world hasn't tainted. "Thank you for the kind words Milt, but I didn't come here to upset you two. I was just passin' by and thought I'd drop in and give my regards. So how's business, Denny?"

"Can't complain, but I must admit it could be better." Denny poured himself a cup of coffee. "Now pull up a chair and fill me in on what I could be doin' better."

"Wish I could, but I gotta get back and close up my station. That mechanic of mine isn't like yours. He's a fine fella, but I don't dare leave him alone for too long. Can't imagine how the station would fare if I let him close up," Felix said as he turned towards the door.

Denny shook Felix's hand. "I understand. You're right. I'm lucky to have Milt. Come back and see us when you have some time."

"God only knows when that will be," Felix said.

"Well when you do, coffee's free and company's pretty darn good – or so I've been told."

Felix grinned and started his car. "Must have been someone butterin' ya up for somethin'."

As he drove off, Milt asked, "What do folks have against Jews?"

"Good question. I don't rightly know, but some folks, like that Hitler fella, seem to down right hate 'em. Next time the Professor comes in we'll have to ask him. He was Vi's Bible school teacher, so he oughta know why."

* * *

"Fill 'er up sir?" Denny asked the thin, slovenly stranger, who looked and smelled as if he had drank the local tavern dry.

"Nah sir. Only gots me two bits. That oughta get me back to Monmouth," the drunken man said.

"Milt …Milt, answer the phone, would ya?" Denny yelled as he pumped gas for the stranger.

Milt dashed from the grease pit to the phone, and answered, "Hello, Sinclair station, how can I help you?"

"Hello Milt, would you ask Mr. Stewart to call home as soon as he can?" Sarah asked.

"Sure will, ma'am. *She doesn't sound her usual happy self. I hope it ain't her sickness gettin' worse. I better tell Mr. Stewart right away.*

Milt hung up the phone, and yelled towards Denny. "Mrs. Stewart asked ya to call her right away."

Before Denny could answer, Milt recognized the customer Denny was helping. *Crap, that's my dad's drinking buddy, Ned. Hope like hell he didn't see me.*

"Thanks Milt, come out and finish pumpin' this fella's gas, and I'll call Sarah." Silence and no appearance by Milt prompted him to repeat his request. "Milt …Milt, where are you?"

More silence, and still no Milt.

Withdrawing back to the grease pit, Milt worried. *Damn! He called me by my name. Hope that old coot's pickled mind didn't pick up on it.*

Denny turned back to the customer. "Sorry about the interruption. You're all set to go. That'll be a quarter."

The customer flipped a quarter to Denny and mumbled as he drove away, "It's all right."

After four long, quick strides to the station door, Denny yelled. "Milt …Milt, where are you?"

From the grease pit he answered, "Right here, sir."

Denny peered down into the nearly finished grease pit, and said in a quiet, but stern tone, "Wondered where you got off to. Let's talk after I call Sarah!"

Uh-oh, he doesn't sound real upset, but he doesn't sound happy either.

"Hello Sara, Milt said you called. Are you all right?" Denny asked. After a brief pause, Denny continued. "Oh, I see. Do you want me to come home?"

Denny took a deep breath as Sarah tried to convince him that he wasn't needed at home. "Don't worry about the station. Milt can run it till I get back."

Once again, Sarah insisted he should worry more about the station than her. "Okay, okay! You know what's best, but at least tell me what they said."

Sarah told him, and Denny turned his head to hide the tears that were starting to well up in his eyes. "Did they say how long we have?"

Sarah's tearful response convinced Denny that he had heard enough. "It's okay sweetheart, I'll be home as fast as I can."

Denny hung up the phone and yelled. "Milt, I gotta get home. Take care of things, and don't be workin' the grease pit. I'll be back to close up."

* * *

147

Seconds after Milt wished for a lack of customers during Denny's unexpected absence, he heard a car drive up to the gas pump. As he approached the car, the driver said, "Well hello there Mr. McCoy. I'm Judge Wilson, remember me?"

"Nice to see ya again, sir, how can I help you?"

"Fill 'er up and rustle up your boss. Where's he hidin'?"

"I can fill your car sir, but Mr. Stewart ain't here."

Surprised Judge Wilson stroked his chin and exclaimed, "My, my. He must think pretty highly of you. Already lettin' you run things."

"Nothin' like that, sir. Mrs. Stewart called and asked him to come home."

"Oh! I hope she's okay. Not ailing is she?"

"Don't know, sir. He didn't say. Hope not. She's a mighty nice lady," Milt said as he finished filling the Judge's car.

"Yes she certainly is. How much do I owe you?"

"That'll be seventy two cents sir."

"Seventy two! Last week it was sixty cents."

"Yes sir, it was, but Mr. Stewart had to raise the price to twelve cents a gallon."

"Why's that? He must be tryin' to get rich quick," the Judge said with a slight grin.

"Mr. Stewart said the Army's gobblin' up so much gas now days that it's makin' the price he pays climb."

"Hmph. Doesn't surprise me. That foolishness in Europe is bound to bump prices up. Hope we stay out of this European fracas. Got enough problems to solve here at home; we don't need to solve theirs."

"I hope so too. Can I get anything else for ya Judge?"

"No, I'm fine. Just tell Denny hello for me, and ask him to give me a call," the Judge said as he departed.

The Judge stopped his car parallel to a very old, but well kept, black Model T entering the station's driveway. With a wave to the driver of the vintage Ford, the Judge smiled. "Well hello there, Professor. I see you survived another day of attempting to pound knowledge into the hard heads of our local resistant youths."

The meticulously groomed, white haired driver smiled and said, "And a good afternoon to you, Judge. I see you survived another day of imparting justice to the unjust."

Judge Wilson chuckled. "Milt, you take good care of the Professor. He taught Vi in high school and Sunday school. You don't treat him special, I'm sure she'll make your ears ring."

One look at the Professor convinced Milt that this definitely was a man of authority. *Even if the Judge hadn't called him Professor, I woulda pegged him to be one. He's got a sharp angled face that would get the attention of most any student. His eyes look like two steel marbles peerin' out from under bushy eyebrows. But that sharply-trimmed full mustache makes him look more like Wyatt Earp then a Professor.*

"Afternoon sir, how can I help ya?"

"I only need fifty cents worth today. And would you please wash my back window. It appears to be a bit hazy for some reason."

"Yes sir." Milt stepped around the corner of the Professor's car, and said, "Sir. Ya might want to come back here and look at your car."

As he disembarked from his cramped front seat, the tall, trim man spoke. "Why do you suggest that my presence is required? Is something wrong with my car?"

"Nothin' really wrong, sir, but someone painted some words I don't understand and a crooked looking cross on the back of your car."

The Professor took in the defiling of his car and stroked his dimpled chin. "Oh my, it looks like the Bund is at it again. Did they use paint or whitewash?"

Milt wiped the Professors window with a damp cloth. "It's coming off fairly easy, so I'd say it's probably whitewash."

"Thank goodness for that. If I pulled my car off to the side; would you wash it for me and get these vile words and symbol off of it?"

"Be glad to sir, but before I do would ya tell me what that word Juden and that crooked cross mean?"

The Professor extended his hand to Milt. "I'll be glad to explain these despicable words, but first let me introduce myself. I'm Mr. Harmon, and like the Judge said, I was Vi's high school and Sunday school teacher. What is your name, son, and how do you know Vi?"

"I'm Milt McCoy, Mr. Stewart's mechanic, and I'm also Vi's boyfriend."

"Nice to meet you. I must say you picked a fine upstanding young lady to court. I appreciate you taking the time away from your work to wash off the Bund's vile vandalism."

"Not a problem sir. I'm glad that I can help, but what's this paintwork all about? I take it this ain't the first time your car's been painted."

"It's the first time for the car. Up untill now they've only whitewashed my house and fence, but always in the dead of night. Anyway, you asked about the words. The word Juden is German for Jew, and the crooked cross is called a swastika. It's the symbol that the American Bund and the new leader of Germany, Adolf Hitler, use for their Nazi movement."

"Why did they paint 'Juden lover' on your car?"

"That is most likely a longer story then you have time for, but the short story is it's because I spoke out in church against hatred of Jews. Consequently, they decided I was a lover of Jews."

"What's wrong with lovin' Jews? Mr. Steinberg, who used to own this station, is a Jew and a mighty nice fella."

"Yes he is, but in hard times, some people, like Hitler and his Bund followers like to blame the hard times on other people. Unfortunately, down through the ages a lot of misinformed people have blamed any and all of their troubles on the Jews."

"That sounds downright stupid and hard to figure. Anyway, I did manage to get the whitewash off your car."

"You're right. It is a rather complicated subject. Thanks for washing my car. What do I owe you?"

"Nothing at all, sir. I'm glad I could help ya. Next time you're passing by, and we all got the time, me and Mr. Stewart would sure like to hear more about these hateful Bund folks and this Hitler."

"Thank you, Milt. Give Mr. Stewart and Vi my best wishes."

* * *

Denny trudged through the station's front door. "I'm back! Sorry about leavin' so sudden-like. Everything go okay while I was gone?"

Oh my Lord! Denny looks like he aged a good ten years since he left for home. He looks like he's been cryin' a bit, and his hair is all messed up. I ain't never seen him like this. "Everything's fine here. We weren't too busy. Only two customers while you were gone. Judge Wilson dropped in and said to say hello, and Vi's old teacher, Mr. Harmon, came in. I hope ya don't mind me askin', but is everything okay at home?"

Denny fell into one of the cane backed chairs and answered in a barely audible voice. "Everything's fine for now. Sarah needed me right quick like. The folks we been talkin' to about our farm came out with cash in hand. She didn't know quite what to do."

I ain't believin' that. Got a hunch he ain't tellin' everything. He ain't one to cry over sellin' a farm. I'll bet they got some bad news from the doctors, but I sure ain't askin'. Got a hunch he'll tell me in due time. He handed Denny a cup of coffee. "Glad to hear that's all it was. If ya need to go on back home I can close up."

Denny looked up from the coffee cup he had been staring into. "That's okay. I took care of what I needed too. But I might need ya to mind the station when we move into the place we been dickerin' over."

Milt smiled. *Heck yeah, I'll help! After they move, Vi will be livin' less than a block from where I'm staying.* "Be glad to, and if I can lend a hand with the move, all ya gotta do is whistle."

"Thanks! I'll keep that in mind," Denny said. "You say the Judge came in for his weekly fill up? I'll bet he banged on your ears about me raisin' the price of gas."

"Not really. But he sure did tell me what he thought about why the price went up. He didn't sound too pleased about the Army and the mess in Europe."

"You got that right, and neither am I. The Judge and I were both in the Great War. That war was such a screwed up bickerin' of rich European kings that it left a bit of a sour taste in our mouths. We shoulda never been in that war."

"Why were we?"

"Cause that damn high and mighty President Wilson decided he wanted to make a name for himself like Teddy Roosevelt did. That war was none of our concern. Germans weren't doin' a thing to us till they sank the *Lusitania.*"

"Why did they sink it?"

"Some folks say the Brits cooked up a deal with Wilson to intentionally send that ship where the Germans warned against sailin' through. Don't know if they cooked it up or not. But to me it didn't matter because we didn't lose enough American lives on that ship to go gettin' into a war. That war took the lives of over a hundred thousand fine American soldiers, and there ain't no good reason why."

"Wow, I didn't know so many of our boys were killed."

"Yeah, that's why the Judge and I aren't too interested in getting' us into another European fight," Denny paused to light his pipe. "You say the Professor also came in?"

"Yes sir, he came in right as the Judge was leavin'."

"Good thing he was leavin'. They got a disagreement goin' on now days."

"Why's that? They seemed friendly to each other."

"Oh they've been friends from way back. They just don't see eye-to-eye about this Hitler's campaign against the Jews. Judge doesn't like it any less than the Professor does, but they disagree on what to do about it. Professor had his way we'd already be over there lockin' horns with Hitler."

"I kinda figured that, cuz he told me he spoke in church about how it was wrong to hate Jews."

"That's amazin', usually the Professor doesn't say much. He musta took a likin' to you."

"Don't know about that. He just told me that when I asked about why someone whitewashed his car."

"What? You're kidding – the whole car?" Denny said as his eyes widened.

"No sir, just the back. Someone whitewashed on the words Jew lover and a crooked cross the Professor called a swastika. I asked him why they did it, and he gave me an earful."

"I'm sure he did. He thinks we need to stop Hitler before that little peacock-struttin'-short-ass wipes out the Jews in Europe. Don't know if he's doin' that, but that's what some people say."

"I think the Professor wanted to talk some more, but he had to go. Said he'd drop by some time when we weren't busy and tell us all about why some folks hate Jews."

"Oh boy, here comes a sermon. Hope Earl and Ed aren't around when he comes. They could make it down right interestin'. We sure have had our share of interestin' customers today, ain't we?" Denny said as he shook his head and rolled his eyes.

"Sure did, includin' Ned, my dad's drinking buddy."

"You mean that old drunk from Monmouth that got a quarter's worth?"

"That's the one."

"Is that why you made yourself scarce?"

"Yes sir. I'm sorry. I didn't want Ned seeing me, cuz he would of made a bee line to my dad. My dad doesn't even know I left the CCC, and he sure don't know I'm here. I hope to keep it that way."

"Amen to that, we got enough problems without him comin' around makin' more," Denny patted Milt's sagging shoulders.

14

A red faced Frank yelled loud enough to momentarily silence the usual murmur of the crowded Jake's Tavern and Pool Hall. "You're shittin' me, Ned. Milt ain't over in Farmington. Last I knew the CCC was still puttin' up with his shit,"

"Well, if they're puttin' up with him, then their doin' it by long distance. I'm tellin' ya he's workin' in the Farmington Sinclair station!" Ned insisted.

"Are ya sure? Did ya see him? Were you sober?"

"I was about as sober as I can get."

"About as sober? What the hell does that mean? Hell, you were probably drunk on your ass."

"Nah uh, I was damn sure sober enough to drive, and hear that old fart fillin' my car yell for Milt to get out there and finish the pumpin'."

Frank ignored Ned and yelled, "Barkeep! Draw me and this lyin' sack of shit another beer."

Ned slapped the bar with his bony hand. "I ain't lyin'. I might not saw him real good like, but I swear it was Milt."

"Ya know Ned, for once I think ya might be shootin' straight with me."

"I am, Frank! Hell, I know better not too cuz you'd kick the shit out of me."

"Ya got that right. Guess the only way I'll find out if he's workin' there is to pay that station a visit. Ya better hope he's workin' there. If he ain't you're gonna owe me some gas money and a whole lotta beer, or your ass will be grass and I'll be the lawn mower," Frank said as he poked his rigid index finger into Ned's chest so forcefully that he almost knocked him down.

* * *

What a great time to be alive. The weather is perfect for August, not near as hot and sticky as it could be for this time of the year. Our picnic spot is perfect— ain't got an ant or a human within miles. I sure am a lucky guy to be lyin' on this blanket next to a lady that I gotta admit I'm thinkin' about marryin'.

"You look deep in thought, sweetheart. Hope its nice thoughts about me," Vi teased as she ran her fingers through his hair.

Milt reached out to embrace her, and his hand accidentally brushed against her breast. With a quick withdraw of his hand, Milt stammered, "I'm, I'm, I'm sorry. I need to watch where my hands wander."

Vi gently kissed him and said, "It's okay, sweetheart. I know you weren't trying to get fresh. Maybe some day you won't need to apologize."

Stunned and flustered, Milt was without appropriate words, so he did what he often did when he was uncomfortable—changed the subject. Pointing to the nearly empty picnic bowls and plates, he said, "This is one of the best picnics we've had. Did ya make the potato salad? I've never had any that good."

She smiled and said, "I not only made the salad, I also baked the bread for our ham sandwiches, and made the deviled eggs. I thought I'd show you how good a cook you might be getting."

"Glad ya did cuz I was wonderin' if I'd starve," he said in a mock serious voice.

"Oh, you won't starve, now or later," she cooed as she reached out to tickle him.

"You tease. Ya know I'm ticklish. Keep it up, and I'll have to see if you're ticklish too."

"Maybe I am, but you'll never find where."

"Oh yeah? I'll bet I will," he said as he tickled the acceptable areas of her voluptuous body.

"Stop, stop. You found the spot," she giggled as she squirmed closer and closer to Milt.

As their bodies intertwined he lost all restraints as he enjoyed her wiggling. "What ya gonna do if I don't stop?"

Her cheeks flushed red as she lied. "If you don't stop soon, I'll probably pee myself."

"No ya won't," he said in a lecherous voice that even he didn't recognize.

"Really, you must stop!" she said as she broke free from him and stumbled off the picnic blanket.

"Sorry," he said as he watched her attempt to regain her balance. "I got a little carried away. Are ya upset with me?"

"Not really, I got a bit carried away too, I should of . . . . ," she said as she tripped over a rock and fell backwards into the river.

"Milt! Milt! Oh Milt, I can't swim!" Vi violently splashed about terror-stricken.

"Don't worry, sweetheart, I'm coming," Milt said as he made several desperate, awkward attempts to remove his shoes.

"Hurry, hurry," she pleaded.

One clumsy belly flop into the muddy water, and two strokes quickly closed the distance between them. He lifted a struggling, panicked Vi, and said, "I've got you sweetheart. Are ya all right?"

"I'm better now, but our clothes are all wet. What are we gonna do?"

"First thing we're gonna do is get out of this current. We get a little closer to shore, we can walk back to our picnic ground. But, you need to quit squirming. Just relax. I've got ya," he said as he blushed from an erection that was growing as each wiggle of her wet body brought them closer and closer.

She matched his blush as she felt her breasts swell and Milt's erection grow. Disturbed that this feeling brought her so much pleasure, Vi stood, now that they were closer to the river bank, and quickly disentangled from him. With a heavy sigh, she clutched his hand as they slowly walked towards the river bank. Vi stumbled over a submerged rock and looked down at her dress. *Oh my Lord, no wonder Milt is growing. He can see every thing through my wet dress. I shouldn't think this way, but I'm glad he likes what he sees.* "Oh my, we need to get our clothes dry! You have any ideas?"

A devilish smile broke over his face as he hugged her. "They won't get dry with us in 'em."

Vi giggled and smiled her own non-angelic smile. "I know! I could take off my clothes and wrap up in the blanket till they dry. If I did that, would you peek?"

"I admit I'd be mighty tempted to, but ya know I wouldn't. I love ya and respect ya too much to do that," Milt said.

Her eyes widened as she caught her breath. *He said he loves me! I thought he did, but I wondered if he'd ever tell me.*

"I love you, too," she said leaping into his arms and kissed him. "I love you so much! I've loved you from the start! I kinda thought you loved me too, but why did you take so long to tell me?"

As his lust, as well as his love, became more apparent, Milt pondered whether he should pry himself away from Vi. He enjoyed the effects of her body so close to his, but he knew the pressing of her body would only make it harder to explain his hesitancy. He drew slightly apart from her. "You wowed me from the start, but I knew that love leads to marriage, so I was afraid."

With tenderness, she lifted his downcast face. "Afraid of what, sweetheart?"

"My family makes me wonder if I could be a good husband. So, I've been afraid of marryin'. That is, until I met you."

Vi gave him a light embrace, and said, "Don't be afraid, it's not your family I'd be marrying. It's you! You're a wonderful caring man that any woman would be honored to marry and raise a family with."

"Children scare me too, but the way I feel right now they might be comin' sooner than later."

She blushed and slipped out of his arms to pick up the picnic blanket. She wrapped it around her still fully clothed, wet body. "I know sweetheart, but not quite yet."

Embarrassed, he attempted to hide his erection with his clasped hands held over his groin. "I'm sorry. It's just that you're drivin' me crazy. I want ya so much I can hardly stand it."

Torn by her adherence to chastity and her love for Milt, she drew a quick calming breath. "I understand, but we must wait. I want to wear white at my wedding."

As his raging hormones began to be tempered by love and respect, Milt said, "You're right! Let's get dried off as best we can, so we can get back and I can ask for your hand."

She smiled and spoke in a playful, mischievous tone, "Aren't you forgetting something?"

Puzzled, he glanced around the picnic grounds for overlooked items. "What?"

She smiled and reached her hand out to his. "You haven't asked me."

Embarrassed, he murmured, "I'm sorry. You do want to marry me, don't you?"

Like a school girl who'd just been asked to go on her first date, Vi struggled to stop giggling. "Oh Milt, of course I do. Now let's go talk to my dad."

Taking her hand, he rolled his eyes and grinned as he placed his other hand over his heart. "Thank God! You gave me a fright. I thought ya might turn me down."

They kissed gently and embraced, with care to avoid once again arousing each other's passion. "Don't be silly. I wanted you to be my husband from the moment I first met you." Breaking off the embrace, Vi dropped the picnic blanket and began to run to the car. "Let's catch my dad before you change your mind. I'll race you to the car."

Milt picked up the picnic blanket and basket, and admired her beauty. *What a great day we've had. I sure hope Mr. Stewart had a good day. I hope he's in a good mood when we get back cuz I'm nervous about asking for Vi's hand.*

* * *

Denny sighed and rolled his eyes as he watched a disheveled, red faced Frank McCoy, in his rusted, dented truck, drive into the station's driveway.

Well there goes that fine day. Frank looks drunk and loaded for bear.

Denny approached his unwelcome customer and forced himself to be cordial. "What can I do for ya Frank?"

"Ya can't do shit for me. I don't own no coal mine so ya ain't exactly any use to me unless ya know where the owner of this shit hole is," Frank said in a drunken slur, punctuated by wild flailing hand gestures.

"I don't exactly consider it to be what you said it is, but, anyway, I happen to be the new owner. Now what can I do for ya?"

"Fetch me that no-good-thief-of-a-son ya got working for ya," Frank demanded as he thrust his head out of his truck.

"Can't do that, Frank," Denny answered truthfully. *I had better be careful with what I say. I may have to fib a bit, but I need to protect my family and Milt.*

"What do ya mean ya can't? I know he's workin' for ya, so get that bum out here," Frank said as he got out of his truck in a clumsy drunken hurry.

"I mean I can't cuz he ain't working for me," Denny said. *At least he's not on his day off.*

As Fulton County Deputy Sheriff Gary Clark pulled in for gas, Frank lunged at Denny. "Ya lying sack of shit! Ned saw him last week, and heard ya yell at him like a boss man. Now get that bum out here before I kick your ass!"

Deputy Clark quickly got out of his patrol car and approached Frank in a confident bow-legged gait. "Is everything all right here, Denny?"

Before Denny could answer, Frank made a quick turn towards the Deputy and yelled, "No! Everything ain't all right. This old fart's hiding my son from me. That boy owes me a passel of money, and this here boss of his won't fetch him for me."

"Before I ask Mr. Stewart what he knows about this, I advise you to calm down a bit," Deputy Clark said as he drew back from Frank's drunken breath.

"I ain't the one that's hiding anyone, so why should I calm down?" Frank bellowed while he closed the gap between him and the Deputy.

"Cuz if you don't, I'll have to calm you down. Either you do, or I'll do it for you. Which way's it gonna be?" Deputy Clark said as his hand moved towards his night stick.

Much calmer, but still belligerent, Frank said, "Alright, I'll do the calming down, but ya tell this Stewart asshole to fetch my son."

"What's this all about, Denny?"

"Frank seems to think that his boy is here, but the truth is he isn't and I don't know where he's at."

"Okay, sounds like if you let him take a look around your station we can solve this real easy like. Mind if he looks?"

"No, that'll be fine. I'll even open up the garage so he can look in there. I don't usually have that open unless we're fixing a customer's car," Denny said.

"Well, mister … what did you say your name is?" Deputy Clark asked.

"McCoy, Frank McCoy!"

"Well, Mr. McCoy, it looks like Mr. Stewart is willing to let you look around his station. I'd say that should answer your question about whether your boy is here or not."

"I'll take a look around! Even if I don't find that boy, I'll still have some questions."

"Let's cross that bridge after you have a look, okay?"

"Okay," Frank grumbled as he entered the station and tripped over the lip of the door.

"Watch yourself, Mr. McCoy," the deputy said as he reached out to the unsteady Frank.

"Are you all right?"

"I'm fine. Now goddammit, let go of me, and let me finish my lookin'."

Concerned by Frank's alcohol spiced breath, the Deputy said, "Before you get on with your tour of the station maybe you oughta take a seat and have some of Mr. Stewart's coffee."

Frank pointed his finger at Denny. "Don't want none of his coffee! If I do some sittin' it'll just give him time to hide that bum of mine."

"That's fine, but before you get back on the road, I'll want you to get some coffee in ya. If you don't want any of his coffee, there's a diner just down the street. Can't let you be driving around all liquored up," Deputy Clark said.

"Sure, sure," Frank grumbled as he poked his head through the garage entrance and yelled, "Milt . . . Milt, get your no-good ass out here!"

After Frank's search failed to produce his son, Deputy Clark said, "Looks like your boy ain't here, so let's get you some coffee at the diner that's a short walk from here."

"He ain't here right now, but that don't mean squat."

"How do you figure? You didn't see him, and this here station is a bit small to be hidin' folks."

"My boy not being here don't explain what my friend Ned saw and heard last week," Frank said as his agitated voice rose once again.

"Is that why you came here today?"

"Yes sir, cuz Ned said he saw this Stewart fella bossin' Milt around last week like he worked for him," Frank said as he pointed at Denny.

"Who is this Ned? The only stranger we had in here last week was a short, skinny little feller that needed gas to get back to Monmouth."

"That's him, and he said that you even called Milt by his name."

"As I recall it, Ned was drunk as a skunk! I'm surprised he even remembered bein' here."

Deputy Clark gently took hold of Frank's arm and said, "Looks like Mr. Stewart has helped you as much as he could. Let's go get that coffee. It's on the Fulton County Sheriff."

Frank wrenched and pointed a rigid index finger at Denny. "This ain't over! If I find out ya snookered me, ya can damn well believe I'll be back, and I won't leave till I get that thievin' son of mine."

"Okay, but for now let's get that coffee."

"Guess I gotta get some coffee or ya might get all fired up, so let's go. But I ain't walkin'! Don't wanna have to come back to this shit hole for my truck after you drown me in java."

"Alright Frank, you drive to the diner and I'll follow. But if ya don't stop at the diner, you'll be stayin' in our jail for a stretch."

As they drove away, Denny wiped the tension sweat from his brow. *Boy, dancin' around the truth sure can be hard work. Good thing Milt was off today. He gets back I gotta talk with him and the family. Can't tolerate visits from Frank, and as long as Milt's here I think we'll see more of Frank.*

* * *

Relaxed in his favorite chair, with one foot propped up on the pot belly stove rail; Denny savored his coffee. *Frank McCoy sure knows how to spoil a day. Hope Vi and Milt are havin' a better time then I just had.*

Deep in thought, Denny was startled by the rattle of his old Model T that he had loaned Milt for the day. Soon after, he heard Vi's cheerful greeting. "Hi Dad, how was your day? Hope it was as good as ours."

My God, those two are soaked. "From the the way you two are drippin' wet, I'd say y'all fell in the Spoon, so how can you say your day was good?"

Hand-in hand they beamed. "I sure did fall in, but Milt rescued me. But that's not really why our day was so good."

"I kinda figured that. A dunkin' in that muddy Spoon ain't exactly fun. So what made your day?"

After several nervous seconds of silence, Milt said in a trembling voice, "I don't know how to say it, so forgive me if I stumble over the words. Sir, would you please grant me permission to marry your daughter?"

Silence, an uncomfortable silence, enveloped the room. *How should I answer? Before Frank showed up I would have been pumpin' his hand and welcoming him into our family. I want to answer them, but my mind is clouded by Frank. I wish Sarah was here.*

Denny scratched his head. "Milt, I ain't sayin' no, but before I answer you I'd like to talk to Sarah."

Before Vi could speak, Milt gave her hand a tender squeeze. "I understand sir. Would ya like for me to take over so ya can go home and talk it over with her?

"Good idea. After you close up, come on over and I'll give you my answer. Vi, why don't you stick around and keep Milt company."

* * *

"You did what? How could you, Denny Stewart? Those two are so in love with each other. You makin' 'em wait for an answer is terrible," a red-faced Sarah said as she shook her finger within inches of Denny's nose.

"Sounds horrible, but wait till you hear what happened shortly before they came drivin' up with marriage on their minds."

"What, Satan gave you a visit?" Sarah said as she slammed the meat cleaver down on the chicken she was preparing for supper.

"Not the devil himself, but one of his apostles sure did. Somehow Frank McCoy found me and Milt."

"Oh no! Why in the world is that old drunk bothering us?"

After he gave Sarah a condensed version of Frank's exasperating visit, Denny asked, "Now do you see why I decided to delay my answer until I spoke with you?"

"Not really! Frank is a rotten no-good, but that ain't who Vi is wantin' to marry."

"True, but she would be marryin' into that family, and I doubt if Milt's father is gonna stay away."

"Why? Milt's a grown man. Frank has no hold on him."

"Wish that were true. He seems to think Milt owes him his CCC money. So far he's raised cane with about everyone and anyone about that money."

"I, for one, don't care if Frank's in the picture or not. Vi knows full well what she's getting into. As much as they love each other they will figure out a way to handle Frank. Now quit frettin' and give them your blessin'. I sure would love to have a grandchild before I pass."

Seeing the tears in Sarah's eyes, Denny hugged her. "I'm sorry, dear. I forgot about your worries, but what if they can't handle his family? I don't want to see Vi drug down by those reprobates."

"I have faith in them, but if you want to do anything to feel better about it, call Judge Wilson and ask him what the law can do for us."

"Good idea. Now, how can I help you get ready for supper?"

Sarah smiled and shook her head. "Denny Stewart, you never were much good at women things, so don't start now. Only way you can help me, is get these two married as soon as we can."

* * *

Vi and Milt strolled, hand-in-hand, fingers intertwined. The world seemed to stand still in a calm that only those in love could experience. But, Milt's mind was anything but calm. Instead, it raced from worry to worry. *Why didn't Mr. Stewart just say yes? Did I do something to cast doubt on him and Mrs. Stewart? God, I hope he says yes. I love Vi so much.*

A sudden tense squeeze of her hand prompted Vi to stop and take hold of both of Milt's hands. She stared into his eyes and softly said, "Don't worry, Daddy always talks to mom before he says yes."

"I hope you're right. I'm probably just worrying cuz I've never asked for someone's hand before."

She laughed. "Well that's good to know! Now come on, we're almost there."

As they approached the Stewart home, Wolf walked towards Milt. *I can't believe it. They let the beast loose. Maybe they're trying to run me off. Wait a minute. Wolf's waggin' his tail. He never does that unless he's happy. Hope that's a good sign.*

"Look, Milt, even Wolf's happy to see us."

Before Milt could answer, Denny poked his head out the front door and hailed them. "Come on you two, supper's about ready."

Milt stumbled up the front porch. Denny caught Milt before he could fall, and said, "Easy, Milt, can't have our future son-in-law walking down the aisle with a broken neck."

Did I just hear him right? Sounds like the answer's gonna be yes. "Thank ya, sir, I almost tripped over myself."

"Glad you didn't. Now get yourself in here. We got some talkin' to do while the women finish getting supper on."

"Yes sir."

"Sarah, do me and Milt have time to chat before supper?"

"Gracious, yes, Vi and I still have to get the spuds going. Do you want an ice tea to enjoy while you're chattin'?"

"Good idea. Son, would you join me out on the back porch?"

"Yes sir," Milt mumbled as he followed Denny outside.

Denny settled into his chair and gestured to the other. "Have a seat, Milt. If I was in your shoes I'd be shaking like one of them crazy tetched ones at a tent revival. I remember how nervous I was when I asked for Sarah's hand, so I ain't gonna beat around the bush."

"Appreciate it, sir."

"I'll bet you're wonderin' why I didn't give you an answer right away?"

"Yes sir, but Vi said ya always ask Mrs. Stewart before ya give an answer on important things."

"She's right, but that isn't why. You see, about one hour before you asked me for Vi's hand, your dad paid me a visit."

Milt looked down and shook his head. "I'm sorry, sir. I guess I shoulda known better then to ask for the hand of a nice lady. My folks kinda do scare nice people away."

Denny smiled and put his hand on Milt's shoulder. "Well, he didn't scare us away. Sarah and I chatted, and we decided to ask you two to do a few things before we say yes."

Milt snapped his head up and broke into a wide smile. "You don't know how happy I am that you're givin' me a chance. I promise, I won't disappoint ya. I love Vi and I'll take good care of her."

Denny slapped Milt on his back. "I know you will, son, but like I said you need to do some things before you stand before the preacher."

"What do we need to do? I'm ready to do 'em right now if I need to," Milt said as his voice grew louder.

"First thing you gotta do is talk to Judge Wilson."

"About what? Is he gonna marry us?"

"No, but you are gonna talk to him about a restrainin' order against your dad."

"What's a restrainin' order?"

"We chatted with the Judge before you came over, because we wanted to know what the law can do to keep Frank from pesterin' you and Vi. He said that we can get a legal order that says he'll go to jail if he comes near you, or my family."

"Sounds good to me. I'll see the Judge first thing tomorrow if that will get my old man off my back."

"I kinda figured you'd say that, so I made us an appointment with the Judge for tomorrow at noon."

"Thank you, sir. What are the other things ya want me to do?"

Denny leaned in closer to Milt and whispered. "Milt, you probably know that Sarah is ailin', so she wants you two to get married as fast as we can get the preacher. She wants grandbabies while she's still got some time to spoil 'em. That be all right with you two?"

"Fine by me, but I'll have to check with Vi. We both want children, so I'd say grandchildren will be coming right soon like."

15

We musta picked the hottest day of 1941 to get married. I'm sweatin' like a dog that forgot to shed his winter coat. Hope I don't ruin the wool suit Punch loaned me for the wedding.

"Quit your fidgetin', Milt. It won't make the weather cooler or you any more comfortable," his best man, Punch Campbell, said.

"I know, I know, I'm just nervous. I ain't never done this before."

Punch chuckled. "From what I hear, it don't matter how many times you've walked down the aisle. If you were a drinkin' man, I know the cure that worked for me."

Attempting for the third time with trembling hands to knot his tie, Milt stopped and said, "If ever there was a day to start drinking, this would be the day. I'm shaking like a leaf in a tornado."

Patting Milt on the back in an attempt to console him, Punch said, "Don't get too worried about it. I'll bet Vi isn't doing much better then you."

* * *

"Mom, you're dress is so beautiful, but I'm having a hard time fitting into it. I hope I don't tear it," a distressed Vi said as she sniffled. "I think I gained some weight since you tailored it last month."

Sarah embraced her daughter. "Now, now, don't fret. I'm sure I can let it out a little more. Now, step out of the dress, and let me work some magic with my needle."

"I hope so, Mom. Ever since you showed me your beautiful dress when I was nine, I've wanted to wear it for my wedding."

Her eyes misted with joy as she let the seam out of the dress. "I remember that day like it was yesterday. The look in your eyes thrilled me to no end. Since then, I always hoped that someday I'd see my daughter marchin' down the aisle in my dress."

"I really want to Mom. I just hope it can be let out enough."

Sarah examined the seam, and said, "There isn't a lot of material left, but I think there is room enough to let it out a bit. It might be a little tight, but you'll only have it on for a short while."

"Mom! I know you're in a hurry for grandbabies, but let us get the wedding over first."

Sarah chuckled as she sewed the dress back together, and Vi turned her face to hide her blush.

Finished, Sarah held the dress up for examination. "What do you think? I can't even see where I let it out."

Vi gently squeezed her mother's hand. "Oh, Mom, it's perfect. I love you so much."

"I know, my dear daughter, and I love you too. Now, try on the dress," Sarah said.

With a joyful sigh, Vi said, "Thank goodness, it fits. Mom, you are a genius with your needle."

Not being used to compliments, Sarah blushed. "See, I told you everything would be all right."

Vi hugged her mother again. "I know, Mom. I'm so nervous that I'm trembling inside and out. I love Milt so much! I just want this day to be perfect."

"It will be, and you'll remember it forever. Now let's finish your dressing so you can join the man you will spend the rest of your life with."

* * *

Facing the pews of the Stewart family's church as he awaited Vi's company, Milt felt overwhelmed. *I swear half of Fulton County is here. Not surprised to see Mr. Steinberg, Judge Wilson and Professor Harmon, but I am a bit surprised to see Supervisor Merrill sitting in the back pew. Glad he could make it. Even Fulton County Deputy Sheriff Clark is standin' back there by the door.*

Milt returned to the moment when a quiet, gentle voice from behind him spoke in a slight Scottish brogue. "And how be you, Mr. McCoy, on this fine day that the good Lord has granted?"

Milt turned toward the soft, accented voice coming from the tall, silver haired Pastor Brown who would perform the marriage. "A bit nervous, but fine, sir."

"'Tis to be expected my son, but grant you it tis a fine day for such a glorious event." Pastor Brown smiled and shook hands with Milt and Punch.

A murmur suddenly rising from the wedding attendees and the sound of the wedding march directed Milt's attention to the back of the church, just in time to capture the moment as Vi joined her father for their march down the aisle. *Wow! I can't believe she's marryin' me. What a lucky guy I am.* Milt's gaze was riveted on the beautiful lady in white that would soon be his companion and partner for life. *She is so beautiful. I wonder if she is as happy and nervous as I am?*

* * *

"You look so beautiful my dear daughter, but I hope you don't shake apart before we get to Milt," Denny said with a smile and a gentle pat on her hand.

She smiled a smile reminiscent of her young childhood. "I am so happy and nervous Daddy. Mom tried to calm me down, but I can't seem to stop shaking."

"What's to be nervous about? You are marryin' a fine young man that loves you very much," Denny whispered to her.

"I know, but I just hope I can be a good wife."

"Don't be silly. When you love someone you can only be good to them—and for them. Now quit your worryin' and let's join Milt before he shakes apart."

AIN'T NO BUM

* * *

Pastor Brown gazied down upon Milt and Vi and smiled. *Oh my Lord, tis a wee miracle that with all the world's troubles, two young people still can find each other.* "Today, we are gathered in the presence of friends and the love of Christ, to join Milt McCoy and the lovely Violet Stewart in the honorable and solemn estate of holy matrimony. As the Lord has instructed, joining into this estate of these two fine young persons is not to be taken lightly, but instead reverently and soberly. Therefore, if any one present can show just cause for not joining these two persons in holy matrimony speak now, or forever hold your peace."

From the back of the church a familiar drunken voice yelled, "I sure as hell can show ya why these two pups …"

"Say another word, damn you, and I swear you'll eat it!" a red faced Supervisor Merrill quietly hissed as he clamped his massive hand over Frank's mouth. "Now let's you and me take this outside."

"Can I help you take care of this?" Deputy Clark quietly asked.

"Appreciate it if you'd open the door, so I can drag this old reprobate out of here," Merrill whispered.

"Gladly. Then I'll take him off your hands."

"Good idea, before I beat the crap out of him. Then, you'd have to take me in. Ain't the first time this old coot's caused problems," Merrill said as he roughly pushed Frank out of the church.

"I know. He ain't even supposed to be here. He has a restrainin' order against him."

"Bullshit, I can be anywhere I damn well want to" Frank said as he stumbled while he recoved from his abrupt expulsion from the church.

Ignoring Frank, Merrill asked, "What's a restrainin' order?"

"It's an order from a Judge that says you can't be seein' or callin' a person. Judge Wilson issued one against Frank to protect Milt and Mr. Stewart's family."

"Lot of good it did."

"Yeah, sometimes they get ignored—like they were today. Anyway, turn him over to me, and then get back in there and tell everyone that things are okay."

"Sounds good, but what do I tell 'em?"

"Don't rightly know. Ya might tell 'em he was at the wrong weddin'."

Merrill chuckled. "Good one, thought I was gonna have to lie in the Lord's house. He sure did pick on the wrong one to interrupt. Lock that old son-of-a-bitch up and throw away the key. See you around, Deputy."

Merrill slid quietly through the doors of the church, and found wedding guests in an uproar, Vi crying, Milt confused, and all eyes on him. With as much confidence as he could muster, he said, "Good news folks. The old gent was confused. He thought he was objectin' to another weddin'. So let's get these two fine young folks hitched."

Pastor Brown smiled. "As I was saying …"

16

"**W**elcome home sweetheart. How was your day?" Vi said as she wrapped her arms around Milt's neck and drew him closer.

After giving her a kiss she so warmly returned, Milt whispered, "Good, but it's a whole lot better now that I'm home. You look so good I can't believe I'm married to ya."

"I hope we're married because if we aren't, my news won't be so great," she giggled and ran her fingers through his dark, wavy hair.

Sliding his hand slowly down her back, Milt teased, "What news can top that great pork chop dinner I smell? Or, maybe you have a new perfume you'll let me get a whiff of real close like for a late dessert."

In spite of the past month of marital bliss spent mostly in their comfortable goose down bed, Vi blushed and struggled to reply in a serious tone. "No, it's a lot bigger news than that."

"What is it?"

Vi fidgeted and curled her hair with her finger. "I hope you are as happy as I am."

"You're killin' me sweetheart. Tell me quick before I drop from suspense."

Her eyes twinkled. "We're gonna have a baby."

Milt opened his mouth, but no words escaped. His eyebrows threatened to join his hair line before he stammered, "Are, are, are ya, ya sure?"

"I hoped it would be good news, but you look like it's not," she said as a lone tear trickled down her cheek.

Milt wiped away her tear and kissed her gently. "I'm sorry, sweetheart. You just surprised me. Of course, it's good news. The best news a man could ask for. I love you so much."

Tears of joy now streamed down her face, as she kissed Milt repeatedly in ever increasing intensity. "Oh, I'm so glad. I wanted so bad to give you a child. I so hope it's a boy."

Milt smiled. "Thank ya for givin' us a baby. Boy or girl, I just hope I'm up to it."

Her arms loosely encircled Milt in a tender embrace. She looked directly into his eyes. "Sweetheart, I know you'll be a good father to our children. Otherwise, I wouldn't have married you! You're not your father, so put your worries away."

"I know you're right, but I'm scared that I might copy some of his bad examples," Milt said as he held on to Vi as if she were his safe haven.

"Quit worrying about that. Let's celebrate our growing family."

"Before we do, I've got a question. How'd ya find out? Are ya sure?"

"That's two questions, not one," she grinned. "But, because I love you, I'll answer both."

"Picky, picky. Who's counting?" Milt smiled and wagged his finger. "Answer me, woman, or I'll tickle you into bed!"

"Huh, what a dilemma," she smiled and batted her eyelashes. "Answer, so you don't die of curiosity, or be quiet and have some marital fun before your croak. Umh, let me see . . ."

"Wife, you best be answerin' me!" Milt leered as his hands began to explore areas of her body that before their marriage were off-limits.

"Oh my, you just might die of curiosity," she said and squirmed in reaction to his tickles. "I wouldn't want that to happen, so I guess I'd better tell you. My time of the month is overdue by about two weeks. I never miss, so I'm pretty certain."

Milt hugged her again. "Guess all we need to make it official is for that cottontail to croak."

"Uh-huh, and poor Peter Rabbit's days are numbered. I have an appointment next week with Dr. Morgan."

Milt, the now lecherous husband, hugged Vi close enough for her to feel his excitement. "Talk about a dilemma," he said as he pulled her towards the bedroom. "Celebrate there or at the dinner table?"

Vi resisted his tug. "Don't be silly. Let's eat while it's still warm."

He patted his wife on the derriere as he followed her to the kitchen table. "What a spoil sport. Good thing I love you soooo much."

* * *

Vi ducked her head through the front door of her mother's home. Surprised to not find her preparing the bread for the day, she once more hailed her mother. "Yoohoo, Mom, where are you?"

Sarah's slight voice called from her bedroom. "I'm in here, sweetie. I'll be out in just a minute."

The minute dragged on into several minutes. Concerned, Vi looked into her parents' bedroom and found her mother sitting on the bed. *Oh my! The way she's slumped over, she looks as if she's bearing the weight of the world.* "Mom, are you all right?"

"I'm fine," Sarah said even though her appearance said different. "I was just resting a bit. I'm glad you came over. Making bread today seems to be a challenge. Will you help me?"

"Of course I will. What do you want me to do?"

"I've already got it started, but I just don't seem to have the oomph to knead it. Would you mind?"

"I'd be glad to. Why don't I get started, and you can join me as soon as you feel up to it," Vi left the room as her tears threatened to flow.

"Thank you, sweetheart. I'll be out right after I make myself presentable."

"Don't hurry, Mom, I remember all the tricks you showed me. I might not do it as good as you, but I'm sure Dad will understand."

Sarah smiled as she joined Vi. "You were a good pupil, so I'm sure it will be as good if not better."

"It might be close to as good as yours, but never better."

"Well, I'm just glad you're here. But, I'll bet you didn't come over to bake my bread. How are things with you and Milt?"

"We're fine. It's you I'm worried about."

Sarah turned to avoid revealing her true feelings. "I'm fine. I just get tired a bit now and then."

"Maybe so, but you need to take better care of yourself. Things like this bread aren't near as important as you are Mom," Vi said as she reached out to her mother.

Sarah squeezed her daughter's hand. "I love you too, sweetheart," she said, as she gazed at her daughter's rose tinted complexion. "Oh my Lord, you're going to have a baby, aren't you?"

Flustered, Vi said, "How did you know? I wanted to surprise you!"

Tears of joy streamed down her cheeks as she embraced her daughter. Her words of joy gushed forth. "You can't surprise me - - I had you four girls. My dear daughter, you just made my day. I am so happy. I can't wait to spoil my grandson."

"Why are you so sure it's a boy? What if it's a girl? Will you still spoil your grandbaby if it's a girl?"

Sarah smiled. "Women just know. Believe me, it will be a boy. If it's not, I'll love my granddaughter, and spoil her as much as the Lord will give me time to."

* * *

"You look mighty chipper today. Marriage must be agreein' with ya." Denny told Milt.

"Guess I don't do much of a good job at hidin' it, do I? Marriage is a lot more than I thought it would be."

Denny chuckled. "It always is son, it always is."

He smiled. "Yeah, I sure did find that out yesterday when Vi told me we got a young'n on the way."

"Well I'll be darn!" Denny said as he slapped Milt's shoulder. "Congratulations son. When's it due?"

"Don't know just yet, Vi hasn't visited the doctor."

"I gotta call Sarah, and give her the good news," Denny said as he picked up the phone.

"If it's alright with you, I'd rather ya didn't call her. Vi's droppin' over this mornin' to tell her. She's so darn excited I had to stop her from wakin' y'all up with the news."

"That's alright, let the women have their moment. Vi will make her day. You sure did make my day."

"Crap! There goes that good day," Milt said as he pointed out the window at his dad's rusty old truck.

"Damn, that man sure knows how to show up at all the wrong times. Stay inside and let me handle him."

"If it's all the same to you, I'd like to be out there with ya," Milt said through clenched teeth.

"Got a bad feelin' about this. No tellin' what Frank's gonna pull. You stay here with the phone handy. If you even think Frank's gonna get out of hand, you call the Sheriff."

"What the hell's a body got to do to get some goddamn gas-o-leen? Get your old ass out here Stewart, and pump me some gas! Or send out that no-good Milt you got working fer ya," Frank yelled and pointed at Milt.

"Call the Sheriff, and then you might as well join me. Looks like he's seen ya, and I might need some help. He sounds drunk and itchin' for a tussle."

"Yes, sir, be careful! I'll be there in a minute," Milt said as he picked up the phone.

In a determined gait, Denny approached Frank. "What can I do for you, Frank?"

"Fill 'er up and get that damn shit-head son of mine out here!"

"I'll pump you some gas, but I'd appreciate it if you'd keep your voice down and civil. Folks around here don't much like cussin' and carryin' on."

Frank ignored his request and pointed at the station door. "Well, well. Look who the cat drug in. If it ain't the Milt that old man Stewart said didn't work for him."

After he whispered to Denny that the Sheriff was on his way, Milt crossed his arms and said, "What are you doing here, Dad? You know we've got a restrainin' order against ya."

"So? That's just a damn piece of paper that ain't worth as much as a Sears Roebuck catalog page," Frank said as he pretended to wipe himself.

"I'll ask you again Frank. Keep yourself civil," Denny said in a low stern tone.

"Screw that! The only thing that'll keep me quiet is that goddamn bum forkin' over the five hundred and fifty bucks he owes me."

"You know I don't owe you anything, Dad. The CCC doesn't agree with ya, and I'll bet you'd lose if you took me to court."

Frank lunged at Milt, and yelled as he struggled to maintain his balance. "I don't give a good fiddler's shit what the CCC says! Ya owe me and ya know it!"

While Frank ranted, a police car turned into the driveway. Deputy Clark got out of the car, and barked in a commanding tone that caught the attention of all. "Alright, that's enough! Looks like you're gonna stay with us till you learn to stay away from 'em," The deputy turned towards Denny and said, "Sorry I took so long to get here."

"No need to apologize. I'm glad you made it when you did."

"Yeah, it's about goddamn time ya got here. Milt ain't forkin' over the dough, so I could use me some lawman help," Frank yelled.

"Sorry, Frank, I don't have orders from a judge to help you. But, they have a restrainin' order against ya, so I'm gonna have to haul ya outta here. Now, get in the patrol car."

"Bullshit, I ain't gettin' in 'til I get my money." Frank shook his fist.

Deputy Clark grabbed Frank's fist, and, in a blur of action, handcuffed Frank. "I'll get him out of here, but first I gotta know if you'll be pressin' charges?"

"I doubt if it'll do any good. All I want him to do is to go home and leave us alone," Milt said.

"You're probably right. Tell you what. I'll call Sheriff Foster over there in Knox, and see if he can meet me at the county line. That way I know Frank will go home."

"Sounds good, and thanks for the help," Denny said.

"That's what I'm here for. Y'all take care," Deputy Clark said as he marched the handcuffed Frank to his police car.

"Wait, just a goddamn minute! What about my truck? I ain't leavin' it here!" Frank yelled as the deputy pushed him into the police car.

"Yes you are! We'll deliver it to the Knox County Sheriff sometime next week."

"That don't get it for me, goddamit!"

"Hush up Frank! You got bigger problems right now then that beat-up old piece of junk," Deputy Clark said as he drove away.

After a long sigh of relief left his body, Milt said, "Got a hunch we ain't seen the last of him."

"I think you're right, but we gotta figure out a way to get him to leave us alone. Can't have him upsettin' my Sarah, as sick as she is, and Vi don't need his crap now that's she's pregnant."

"I know, but what are we gonna do?"

"We need to get him out of here. Any ideas?"

"If he wasn't my dad, I'd say send him to jail and throw away the key. Lord knows he's done enough to deserve it. But I can't do that to him."

"I think I'll call Sheriff Foster tomorrow and see what he can do."

* * *

"Bess, Bess, wake up, wake up! Goddamn it git your ass movin', we got company, lots of company! Get me the sawed-off real quick like," Frank yelled as he roughly shook her awake.

"What? What? Go away. I'm sleepin'. Leave me alone," Bess mumbled as she was forced awake. "Why do you want the shotgun? Wait a minute! What in the world is all that grumblin' and rattlin'? Sounds like all the cars of Knox County comin' to visit."

"Goddammit woman! That's what I'm tryin' to get through that thick head of yours."

Confused, Bess asked, "Why are they comin' to our place?"

"I don't know, but it looks like the Sheriff is leadin' the parade. Now give me that gun and join me on the porch," Frank said, as he snatched the shotgun from her and departed.

As the Sheriff got out of his patrol car, he unsnapped his holster and commanded, "Put down your gun, Frank! Hate to ruin everyone's day with an early mornin' shoot out."

Noting every Knox County patrol car, and twenty some other cars, in his front yard, Frank placed the shotgun on the floor of the front porch. "Mornin' Sheriff, what brings ya out my way?"

"Got me a search warrant I intend to execute, so just stand out of the way and let us do our job."

Frank sneered. "Ya ain't lookin' fer that still again are ya?"

"Nope, not lookin, we're findin'!"

"Good luck. Ya ain't findin' no still on my property. Bring all the deputies ya want, but it ain't gonna do ya no good."

"Bet me! I got a secret weapon this time."

Frank laughed as he pointed to a shriveled old man with a long white cane. "Yeah right, next thing ya know you'll say that blind-ass, old man Erickson is gonna find it."

"Laugh all you want Frank, but that's whose gonna find it. He may be blind but he can sniff things out better than a bloodhound."

Holy shit, Erickson's walkin' right for it. "Even if ya find it ya can't do anythin' about it. You know that only them there revenue boys can lock my ass up for havin' a still."

"You're right, but we can damn sure sit here 'til they come. In the meantime, let's take a walk, Frank." Sheriff Foster beckoned for him to join him.

"Might as well. Could use to get the mornin' kinks out." Frank stepped down the steps that creaked almost as much as his knees did.

Out of earshot of the rest of his search party, Sheriff Foster stopped and said in an almost pleasant voice, "You know Frank, if we find it, and I have no doubt that we will this time, you are going to the federal pen for a good long stretch."

"Yeah, but first ya gotta find it."

"Quit kiddin' yourself Frank. Just before we started this walk one of my deputies signaled to me that they'd found it. But if you're willin' to work with me, I'll ignore that signal."

"How much ya want?" a solemn Frank asked.

"I'm gonna forget you just tried to bribe me," Sheriff Foster growled.

"Well, then what the hell do ya want?" a confused Frank asked.

"Gone! I want you gone."

"Whoa, Sheriff, ya can't shoot me for havin' a still."

"Nope, and I don't intend to."

"Then what the hell ya mean? That iron you're showin' makes me wonder if I'll be seein' daylight much longer."

"I mean that later on today, in the company of one of my fine strapping, young deputies, you're gonna get on a bus that's headed on a one way trip to Inez, Kentucky."

"You're shittin' me, right? What the hell's in Inez?"

"I'm dead serious. You're gonna join all the other McCoys that roost in Inez. You'll be right at home with all your feudin' kin," the Sheriff said as he fought to suppress his 'I-got-you-you-old-reprobate' grin.

"What if I don't take you up on it?" Frank defiantly asked.

"Then your ass is goin' to prison. You'll be an old man when you get out. Of course, Bess will be a bit younger when she gets out."

"Hold on there, ya can't charge Bess with any thing!"

"Oh yes I can! She's an accessory. Of course, that's only a one to three year sentence, which is a whole lot shorter then you'll get. Think about it," Sheriff Foster said as he started to get out his handcuffs.

"Alright, alright, ya win. I ain't crazy about the choices, but I sure as hell don't want Bess havin' to go to jail cuz of me. Can I take Bess with me?"

"Only if you pay for it, and agree that this is a one way trip."

"How much is it? How long do I have to stay?"

"Five dollars and forty two cents. You might even talk me into payin' for it if you agree to stay out of Knox and Fulton County for at least ten years."

"What happens if I don't stay?"

"You better have a damn good reason for showin' up or you're goin' to prison."

"Okay, but I want to leave tomorrow. Bess and I got a few things we'll need to do," Frank said as he began to walk back to Bess, who was waiting on the porch.

"Bess, pack your bags. Courtesy of the county, we're headin' to Kentucky," Frank yelled to Bess.

Bess scratched her head in dismay. "What the hell ya talkin' about? You get drunk durin' that short walk?"

"Didn't have time to get drunk, but I did have time to figure out that livin' in Kentucky beats hell out of a federal pen. Now come on."

"I ain't goin' nowhere! Ain't my still!"

Drawing close enough to Bess to keep their conversation private, Frank hissed, "Yes ya are! If you don't they're gonna put you in jail for a long stretch for bein' an accessory."

"That's bullshit! They can't do that!"

"Oh yeah they can, and they are dead serious. Get to packin'. We're leavin' tomorrow."

* * *

"Hello, Stewart residence," Denny said.

"Denny, it worked like a charm! Those McCoys just got on the bus for Kentucky."

"Both of 'em? Did I give you enough money for tickets for both?"

"Don't worry about it. It was worth the extra five bucks to get rid of both of my biggest repeat residents."

"Did ya find the still?"

"Hell yeah. Your idea of usin' a blind person to sniff it out was down right brilliant. Old man Erickson had it sniffed out in five minutes. Ever decide to quit pump jockeyin' I'm sure I can find you a detective job."

Denny chuckled. "Thanks for the offer, but I'm gonna stick with my station, I don't think I could handle constantly puttin' up with characters like the McCoys."

"Believe me, there are a lot of days I'd trade places with ya. If you hear of the McCoys comin' back, give me a call and I'll fix their wagons."

"Will do. And thanks a lot for helpin' us. Take care, Sheriff."

"You too, and I'll make sure to drop in when I get over your way."

"Look forward to it."

17

For an early January day, it was beautiful. The snow glistened as it reflected the bright winter sun that turned Fulton County into a chilled, but not frigid, winter wonderland. Even the ever present winter wind blowing off the prairie had ceased to stir the path between Denny's station and Milt's home.

Wish my day was as calm as this weather. What a day! Weren't too busy, but we sure had a hot time in the station. The way the Professor and the Judge got into it over the war in Europe, I probably coulda quit stokin' the stove and those two still would of kept the station heated. They both made some sense, but all they did was make me more confused. Oh well, I got a family to think about. Smarter folks then me are gonna have to solve this Hitler problem, without me.

From the other side of the street, a large middle aged man hailed Milt. "What a beautiful eve it is for a walk. Home to the missus, are ya?"

"Good evening Mr. Campbell," Milt replied. "Yeah, I'm headin' home after a long day. How are you today, sir?"

Mr. Campbell, in his winter attire, resembled a bear, more than a man. He crossed the street smiling through a full reddish-brown beard. "Couldn't be better, but, please man, as I've asked so many times, call me Punch."

"Sorry sir. I mean Punch," Milt said. "Punch, would you mind if I asked you how you got the name of Punch? Is it an old Scottish name?"

Punch chuckled and spoke in a Scottish brogue. "Would like to say yes, but I would be tellin' a wee bit of a tale. Wouldn't want that, now would we?"

"No, but, seriously, how did you get that name?"

"Truth to be told, tis me mum gave it to me. After me birthin', me gran asked mum if she was happy. She said she was glad that I'd now be punchin' air instead of her tummy. So Punch was me name, then and forever."

Milt chuckled. "I thought us Irish could tell a tale."

With mock indignation, Punch said, "'Tis true man, 'tis true. Now tell me, 'tis Denny workin' your soul to an early departure?"

"No. He's a good man to work for, but puttin' up with some of the coffee drinkers sometimes makes me wish I could depart."

"Ah, yes, I've contributed a time or two meself."

"Oh, you're always welcome. Your stories make me smile, but the war worries from some of the others are another story. Today was one of those days."

"Bein' Saturday, I'll bet the Professor and the Judge were on their soap boxes."

"Oh, yeah. Truth is, I almost didn't hear you when you said hello. My mind was still stuck on what they ranted on about."

"Let me guess. The Judge, with Denny probably chimin' in, went on a bit about how America comes first, and the Europeans need to solve Hitler without us."

"Yep, and the Professor fired right back."

"Were I a sportin' man, I'd wager he preached about our Christian duty to stop Hitler's slaughter of the innocents. Now, do tell, would I be right?"

"You sure are. I listened and made coffee. I decided it was their job to figure it out, not mine."

Punch smiled. "True, true, raisin' your wee baby 'tis what you needs to do. Not listenin' to old sods solvin' nothin'. Home with ya, lad, and give your lovely lass our love."

* * *

"Honey, I'm home. Where are you?" Milt called out, surprised to not find Vi attending to their supper.

Vi entered the kitchen and mumbled as if she had been sleeping. "Sorry, I was in the bedroom. I didn't hear you."

"What's wrong?" He hugged Vi and gently rubbed her growing stomach. "Is the baby kickin' a lot today? You look like you had a rough day."

"No, nothing like that," she said as she handed him a letter from the government.

Milt quickly scanned the letter. "They gotta be kidding! I thought married men with families weren't supposed to be drafted."

Flustered, she said, "I don't know. I thought the same thing. There must be a mistake. What are we going to do?"

"I guess the only thing we can do is visit the Draft Board over in Lewiston. I'm sure it's just a mistake. We'll get it straightened out." Milt hoped it would allay Vi's concerns, even though he feared the visit would be futile.

"Good idea. Let's call on them first thing Monday. I'll call Dad and see if he'll loan us the car." Vi said as some of her usual optimistic glow returned to her cheeks.

* * *

Milt parked the car in front of the Fulton County Courthouse as questions of doubt and dread kept coming to the fore. *What if, they're draftin' married men with families? How will Vi survive? Will they make me go in before our son's born?*

"Milt, are you all right?" Vi suspected her husband was somewhere else besides next to her.

"What? Oh yeah. Sorry, my mind was wandering."

"Don't worry, sweetheart. I'm sure everything will be fine. Now, let's go get this straightened out."

A man dressed like a lawyer passed them as they approached the Court House. "Sir, could ya tell us where the Draft Board is at?"

"Third floor, room 311, but they don't open until ten. Stairs are to the right of the Court House entrance."

"Thank you, sir. By the time we get there it will be ten," Milt subtly tilted his head towards Vi, whose gait had slowed considerably with the advancement of her pregnancy.

"Sweetheart, are ya up to climbin' those stairs, or would you rather wait in the car?"

"No, I'm going with you. You need me there. Besides, maybe as big as I am they might think twice about taking you."

"Let's hope so."

Two stories of stairs later, Vi sat down on the next step to rest. "Can we take a little break?"

"Okay, do you want me to get you a drink of water?"

"No, I'll be fine. I just need a short rest, and a big hug from you."

"I'll give you more than one hug if it'll help," Milt said as he hugged her.

"One is plenty. I'm fine now, so let's push on," Vi said as she stood up for the final assault of the stairs.

To the left of the third floor landing Milt saw room 311. "We made it, sweetie. Let me get the door. You go in first. Your growin' baby belly just might get their attention enough to let me stay with ya."

She entered the open door and whispered, "I sure hope so, dear."

"May I help you?" the receptionist said in a pleasant but formal voice.

"We hope so, ma'am. We would like to talk to someone about this notice," Milt said as he handed her his Draft Notification letter.

"Perhaps, I can help you. What's unclear in the letter?"

"The letter is clear, but we think it may have been a mistake," Milt said as he gestured towards Vi.

"I see. Let me check my files." Her search completed, she extracted a carbon copy of the letter from her files. After a brief review of the letter, she said, "No, it was sent as the Board directed me to."

"I think my husband means it shouldn't have been sent because we are married and soon to be a family of three," Vi suggested.

"Oh, well, in that case, I think you will need to speak with the Head of the Draft Board. Let me see if he can see you now." The receptionist said as she knocked on the office door behind her desk.

Following a brief conversaition with the office occupant, she returned to her desk, and said, "Mr. Haney, will see you now."

Haney! I hope he isn't related to Supervisor Haney, Milt thought as he opened the door for Vi.

About to follow Vi through the door, he heard a familiar voice ask, "How may I help you young lady?"

"Supervisor Haney, what are you doing here?" Milt said before Vi could respond.

"Well, well, if it isn't Mr. McCoy. As you can see, I am no longer associated with the CCC. The Army retired me and put me in charge of the Fulton County Draft Board."

Milt managed a feeble, "Oh."

"Please, have a seat. Now, how may I help you? I understand you have a question about your notice."

"Yes, sir, I think it wasn't supposed to be sent to me. I'm married now and soon we are to have a child."

"I don't understand why you believe the notice is in error. The law clearly states that all men between twenty one and forty five are subject to selection for service for a term of one year. You are over twenty one, aren't you?"

Milt's neck instantly reddened, so Vi interrupted Milt before he could answer. "Yes sir, he is. But our understanding is that family men are exempt from the draft."

As he made a temple in front of his face with his hands, he sternly said, "I'm afraid you are misinformed. Family men are not exempt. However, those with children, which you are not, as of yet, may defer the date of their entry into service for up to six months. Of course, such a deferment is subject to the decision of the local draft board."

Before Vi could stop him, Milt blurted out, "This is bull! We aren't even at war, so why should I be taken from my family?"

With a stern stare firmly affixed on Milt, Haney calmly asked, "Don't you want to be there for your country in time of need?"

Still fuming, but with a bit of regained self-control, Milt said. "What need? We're not in a war. Time comes that we are, I'll be first in line. Ya won't have to draft me."

"We may not be in a war, but one is coming. We must prepare, and thus this draft. Do the honorable thing and answer this call to arms that you were issued, and report for duty," Haney said.

"A war may be comin', but so is my child. That's why I am fightin' this here draft notice," Milt said as once again his face reddened.

"Mr. McCoy, you cannot fight the draft notice! Now report for duty, or face the consequences!" Haney said as his face also began to redden.

After a moment to digest Haney's threat, Milt said, "Alright, I know when I'm whupped, but how about one of those family deferments?"

"Mr. McCoy, either you did not hear me or you are not thinking. You do not have a child, but, instead, a child is on the way, that may or may not survive its coming into this world. Therefore, you are not eligible for a family deferment," Haney said as he impatiently gazed over Milt and Vi's heads.

"No, you're the one that's not thinkin'. You're just hidin' behind the rule book. The war ain't here either. It may not ever be, so why should I be apart from my family?"

"As I said before, because your country is preparing for a war, and the regulations governing family deferments quite specifically state that such deferment pertains only to a family man with children."

Milt jumped from his chair and sneered as he said, "If ya think about it, our child not being here yet don't mean I ain't got a family I need to worry about!"

"Don't attempt to escape the draft with sympathy and con-voluted logic. This isn't a badly worded CCC pay form. You twisted that around, but you can't argue your way out of the draft. Unlike the CCC form, the law governing service is quite clear. The board will consider your request for deferment and notify you of our decision within two weeks. Good day, sir," Haney stood up to open his door and gestured for Milt and Vi to exit.

* * *

"Hello. Sinclair Station. How may I help you," Denny said.

"Hi Dad, is Milt available?"

"Not right this moment, can he call you back?"

"Yes, please, but ask him to call me as soon as he can. It's sorta important," Vi said in a voice that, to Denny, seemed to lack her usual cheerfulness.

"What's the matter Vi? Are you alright? Is it the baby?"

"No, I'm fine. But, we got a letter I think he'll want to know about."

"I can take over if you really need to talk with him right away."

"That's okay Dad. I know Milt doesn't like to be bothered at work. Just have him call as soon as he can."

"Okay, I'll let him know." *I've got a hunch this ain't good news. Hope it isn't about Frank. Of course it's not, how could I be so stupid? I'll bet it's a draft notice. They don't need that. The baby is just around the corner. If he's drafted, Sarah and I will have to figure out some way to help.* Denny opened the station's screen door, and said, "Milt, when you get done pumpin' Mr. Ryan's gas, would you please come see me? Repairin' that Buick can wait."

"Be there in a jiffy." Milt said as he turned towards the station.

One look at Denny prompted him to quicken his step. *Something's up, Denny looks worried. I hope it's not about that call. Got a hunch this ain't gonna be good.*

"Who called?" Milt asked as he entered the station.

"Vi. She asked you to call."

"Did she say why?"

"Somethin' about a letter she thought you'd want to know about. She didn't sound too good."

"Oh crap, it's probably from the draft board."

"Oh! A draft notice ain't exactly what you need right now. I thought they weren't draftin' family men?"

"That's what I thought too, but I got my notice a couple weeks ago. Remember when we borrowed your car awhile back?"

"Yeah, you said you two needed to go to Lewiston."

"Well we went over there to fight my draft notice. Don't think it did much good though, cuz, low and behold, the head of the draft board turned out to be Supervisor Haney."

Denny rubbed his cheeks and scratched his chin. "Wasn't he the fella that was after you about not sendin' home your CCC pay?"

"Yep, and he remembered me real good."

"Bet he wasn't too ready to listen to your take on the draft."

"You'd win that bet! The letter Vi called about is probably Haney's answer to our request for deferment."

"Deferment? You mean exemption, don't you?"

"Wish it was exemption. Good old by-the-book Haney read us the law. Guess all we can hope for is a six month delay in me going into the Army."

Denny patted Milt on the shoulder. "That is a damn shame. Why don't you and Vi come over for supper tonight. We'll put our heads together, and see how Sarah and I can help. Meanwhile, call your wife."

* * *

Denny looked out the front door window. "Sarah, they're just about here."

Sarah stirred the vegetable soup she had made for the unexpected, guests. "How do they look?"

"Not too good. Vi looks like she has been cryin', and Milt looks like he's boilin' mad. He's got a death grip on that letter."

Sarah joined her husband at the front door. "Let me have some time alone with Vi. You and Milt gather the wood for the stove while we chat."

"Okay, but I can't say how long our gatherin' is gonna take. It's only twenty degrees out and the wind is pickin' up."

"We won't be long. She needs a chance to talk woman-to-woman with her mom, and I need to tell her what you and I talked about. Don't forget to also tell Milt."

Denny opened the door. "Get on in here you two before Jack Frost finds his way inside."

One step inside, Vi threw her arms around her mother's neck and softly blubbered, "Hi Mom, I love you. I'm so scared."

Before Sarah could answer, Denny said, "Milt, we need some wood. Would you help me get some from the wood shed?"

"Yes sir."

"Vi, while the men are gone, please help me with supper."

"Okay, Mom," Vi said as she sniffled and fought to hold back her tears.

When Milt and Denny were out of earshot, Sarah asked, "What are you so scared about?"

The simple direct question opened Vi's emotional spigot. Events, perspectives, shattered understandings, and Vi's raw fear engulfed the room. "What are …we going …to … do?" Vi said between her body racking sobs.

Sarah embraced her daughter. "Now, now, let's talk about it over supper. Dad and I can help. We can't keep Milt home, but we can help."

"I so hope you can. We need to do so much before he leaves."

"I know, but the first thing you need to do is pull yourself together before the men come back." Sarah peered out the window and said, "Look at those two, you'd think they had nothing better to do then smoke before work."

Denny finally got his pipe lit despite the gusting prairie wind. "I take it from the looks of you two that you didn't get good news in the letter."

"That's for darn sure. That damn Haney denied our request for deferment. His letter says I'm supposed to report to the induction center in Peoria on Monday, February 10th. Boy, what a hell of a way to start 1941."

"That rotten S.O.B.! That's only a few weeks from now, and only two months before the baby is due. Will they let you come home for the baby?"

"Don't know. But, I kinda doubt it. I'll still be in basic trainin' down in Georgia."

"That stinks. What about after basic? Any idea where you'll be stationed? Maybe it'll be close enough to come home once in awhile."

"Hope so, but if they are anything like the CCC, they'll find a way to make my life difficult."

"Won't be the same as you being home, but we can make things a little less difficult. Sarah and I will help as much as we can. Now, let's get this wood in and talk about it over supper."

Sarah yelled, "Supper's ready, let's eat while it's still warm."

"Be there in a few shakes," Denny said as they carried the wood to the back porch.

The flavorful aroma from Sarah's kitchen escaped through the open backdoor, Milt smiled. "Something sure does smell good. What kind of critter did you cook up? Can't be snake, cuz their all bedded down for the winter."

Sarah chuckled, "No snake today, but I'll be lookin' for 'em as soon as we get the first thaw. You'll have to make do with plain old vegetable soup today."

After she served everyone and assured herself that all were comfortably seated, Sarah asked Denny to say grace.

"Thank you Lord for delivering us safely through another blessed day. Thank you for this bounty and the hands that lovingly prepared it. Thank you for the many blessings we often fail to notice, and please watch over us in the days to come. Especially, keep safe these two fine young persons that have blessed us with their presence today. Amen"

"A fine blessin' Denny, but, as always, a fine Scottish ramblin'. Let's eat before it gets cold." Sarah said as she winked at her husband.

"Ramblin'? I wasn't ramblin'. A lot needed to be said," Denny said as his trademark subtle grin began to appear.

"You're right, and a lot more needs to be said. Milt, would you explain to us why that letter got you two so upset?"

"Yes, ma'am," Milt said as he looked to Vi for support. "I won't dance around it. I gotta report to the Army for one year of service startin' the tenth of next month."

"Oh my goodness! Now I know why Vi was so upset. She told me about your draft notice, but I thought if you had to go it would be after the baby was born."

"We hoped so, but the letter we received today turned down my request for a six month delay in going," Milt said.

"Milt, I think you know my feelings about the stupidity of this draft, but if you have to go, you can go knowin' we'll keep Vi safe in our embrace," Denny said in a soft, serious voice.

"I know, and believe me, that means a lot to both of us," Milt said as he took Vi's hand into his.

"That's what families are for. Now eat up. We've got a few weeks before you leave to figure things out, and get Vi moved back in," Denny said. Noting the surprised look on his daughter's face he added, "I mean if that's what you two want. It would help Sarah if she did stay with us, and Sarah would be close when the baby decides to come into this crazy world."

"I'm okay with moving back in, if it's okay with Milt. You just surprised me."

"Sounds great, living with family might make the year go quicker."

Sarah smiled at the prospect of having her daughter and grandchild so close. "Good! Now let's eat, and don't forget to save some room for dessert."

18

"**M**ommy, mommy, why you sad?" Butch asked as he rubbed the sand of sleep from his awakening, big-brown eyes.

Vi gently embraced her son and kissed his chubby pink cheeks. "Don't worry, I'm not sad."

Butch patted his mother's face with his small, young-boy hands and asked, "Why you cry?"

"I'm crying because I'm happy. Daddy is coming home soon. All the bad guys are gone, so he is coming home."

"Did daddy shoot them all, bang, bang?"

Smiling at her son's innocence she said, "No but he helped make them quit fighting. Now go back to sleep."

"I don't wanna!" Butch said as he squirmed closer to her.

"I'll make scrambled eggs for breakfast if you'll stay in bed while I do. Will you do that for mommy?"

"Eggies, eggies. Oh boy, eggies," said Butch, the only young child she ever knew to love scrambled eggs, which, in spite of her teaching, he still called them what he did when he was two.

As she got out of the bed and dressed to collect the eggs from the hens, Vi said, "Mommy will call you when breakfast is ready. Now you stay in bed, okay?"

"Okay," Butch said as he snuggled under the covers.

Although she was tired from a sleepless night of vivid memories she could not, and would not, even if she could, turn them off. Vi cooked their breakfast while her mind once again wandered. Not to long ago precious events, but this time to thousands of miles away to her loving husband. *Hurry home dear. We need to share breakfast with you for all the years the good Lord will give us. You have a baby boy who really wants to know his daddy.*

19

Milt smiled while his fellow jubilant 1st Division brothers-in-arms danced awkwardly about their Czechoslovakia mountain bivouac as if some drunken god of war was pulling their invisible puppet strings. *Thank God this war is over, and I'm still in one piece.*

"Hey, Mac, get your paddy nose out of that picture and join us," Milt's buddy, who he'd served with since boot camp, shouted.

"In a minute, Joey, I owe this lady and little boy a good long look. They got me through this damn war."

Short, wiry Joey of Brooklyn shouted and gestured with a bottle of recently liberated champagne held high. "Yeah, Yeah, you'll get to see 'em up close real soon. Now get over here and hoist a glass."

"I'll join ya, but I'll let you fellas do the hoisting. Hitler bitin' the dust deserves a toast, but for me it'll have to be with coffee."

"Come on! Just once! We won't tell anyone."

"I ain't worried about that. It's me I gotta live with."

"You know, Milt, you are the goddamndest hero in this crazy-ass Army. You got through damn near four shitty years of combat without even a drop of alcohol. Shit, man, you even got yourself a Silver Star. You are some crazy, sober sonbitch."

Either I was crazy, or the good Lord was lookin' out for me. I still can't believe I caught those kraut grenades and tossed 'em back. "Silver Star was just some general needin' to pin some medals on somebody for the cameras. I was the only one who'd shaved that day so he picked me."

"Bull! You forget, I was there and saw the whole damn thing. Still can't believe you caught those suckers and didn't blow your hand off. Got more balls then I got. I saw you catch the first grenade, and then all I did was bend over and kiss my sweet Italian, made- in-America, ass goodbye."

"I just got lucky, I guess."

Joey wildly gestured to the other members of Milt's squad and yelled, "Yous guys believe this goombah? No way, he was just lucky! Crazy I'll buy, but not just lucky. Hell, after he threw them babies back he shot the shit out of those krauts. Milt saved our ass that day."

In an attempt to deflect Joey's gratification and attention, Milt said "I just didn't wanna go home in a steel box."

As the rest of Milt's squad nodded in agreement, Joey said, "I can buy that, but I still don't know how the hell you got through this FUBAR war?"

"Same as you, I just kept my wits about me every day and prayed for luck."

"Yeah, me too, but I was also shit-faced or scared out of my mind most of the time."

* * *

Another day of damn trainin', I haven't done bayonet drills since boot camp. General must think the war is still on. Milt shook his head in disbelief as he waited for his name to be called at mail call.

"McCoy, you got one," the long necked, pimple faced company clerk yelled in his high pitched effeminate voice that no one joked about in fear that the skinny little weasel would get even by forgetting to call their name.

Thank God, I could use some of Vi's sweet words. Let's see what good news she has for me. I could use some about now. This damn trainin' is getting old.

Hi Sweetheart. I'm so glad you're coming home soon. Do you have any idea when you'll return to us? Paper has confused all of us. It said you'd be coming home when you have enough points. Do you have enough points? I sure hope so. We miss you so very much. Little Butch keeps bragging about you coming home. He'll be crushed if you have to stay over there. Did you guys celebrate war's end? We had a big town bonfire celebration. I saw Benny Sheely at the bonfire. He looked worse then when he came back. He looked like he wasn't all there and twenty years older than his age. The war must have been horrible for Benny. I'm so thankful you didn't have a war like Benny. Running out of room to write. These V letters seem to get shorter and shorter. Write soon. All our love, Vi and Butch

If Vi knew what Benny went through, she would know that for Benny war was a trip through hell. I knew when I saw that look on Benny's face after I dug him out of his foxhole that he would never be the same. Before he was buried, Benny was full of life. Joked about skinny dippin' in the Spoon, and teased me about that snappin' turtle I killed. He thought it was pretty damn odd that I got so scared of a little ugly turtle. Then those damn German 88's started firing. Friggin' Nazis used those anti-tank guns on us ground pounders instead of our tanks. Every time one of those 88 millimeter shells landed, trees fell everywhere and huge walls of dirt were thrown in the air. Guys were duckin' into every crook and cranny they could find. Some weren't lucky. A direct hit didn't even leave enough parts of 'em to know who the poor fella used to be. A lot of us, like Benny, got buried by the walls of dirt and the felled trees. Most of us dug ourselves out, but on the second day of the battle Benny was buried and couldn't move. We could hear his soft cries, but it took us hours to dig him out. He lived, but after that any loud noise would set him off. He'd scream like a banshee, shake as if he was comin' apart, and sweat buckets full. Sometimes he'd even mess himself. Last I saw him they had to strap him to his bed at the field hospital. From what Vi just wrote, I'd say Benny is around the bend for good. Thank God the war didn't do me in like it did Benny.

"Hey Mac, my girl says rumor has it we're goin' home. Hope so, cuz her letters are drivin' me crazy," Joey said as he loudly sniffed his girl's perfumed letter while he grabbed his crotch.

"Yeah, my wife says the paper has us goin' home if we have the points."

"How the shit they figurin' those goddamn points?"

AIN'T NO BUM

"Don't exactly know. Heard ya get points for time served and time in combat. I guess ya also get points for other stuff, but I don't know what stuff. Way I hear it is if you have enough points you get to go home. I just hope I got enough."

"Trust me, we're going home. You and me damn sure got the points," Joey said as he departed for chow call.

Hope that crazy Brooklyn wop is right. I miss Vi so much, and I've missed so much. Thanks to that son-of-a-bitch Haney, I even missed being home for my son's birth. Four years, and I've only seen him once. I got lucky or I wouldn't have seen him then. I hope Vi knows how thankful I am that she took a bus to my base in Georgia when the little guy was only a couple of months old. I know Vi tells my boy about me, but I'll bet I'll scare the crap out of him when I get home. Hope not. I want a chance to be the dad my dad wasn't. This friggin' war damn near did me in. Somehow I dodged most of the bullets, but I missed so many family things that sure screwed my spirits up. I not only missed my family, but I also missed a lot of good-byes. Sarah passed without me getting a chance to thank her for helpin' Vi and me. I'm sure Vi could of used me to be there for her when her mom went to her reward. I damn sure wanted to be there for my grandpa's funeral. If it weren't for that man there is no tellin' how I woulda survived that useless father of mine. This Army crap can't end too soon. I know I had to do my duty for my country, but now it's damn sure the time for me to start takin' care of my family.

* * *

"Sergeant McCoy, the Lieutenant wants to see you, sir," a barely-ready-to-shave, fresh out of boot camp Private said.

215

Milt smiled. "How many times do I have to tell you not to call me sir? Remember, you only call officers sir."

"Yes sir. Sorry, I mean, I mean, I'll try to remember, Sarge."

"Okay, Private, just try harder. Is the Lieutenant in his office?"

"No sir, I mean, no Sergeant, he's in his tent," the Lieutenant's nervous runner said.

"Thanks. Tell the Lieutenant, I'll be there in a couple of minutes," Milt said as he grabbed his helmet and departed.

Be glad when I don't have to wear this damn tin pot. Wish those die hard Hitler idiots would get it through their thick skulls that the war is over.

"You wanted to see me, sir?" Milt asked as he poked his head into the Lieutenant's tent.

"Come on in, Milt. Take a load off," Lieutenant Merrill pointed to a camp chair. "Probably wonderin' what you did to deserve my attention?"

Milt looked down at his dirty boots. "A little bit, but I imagine it's about my uniform. I heard the General's crackin' down. He must be gettin' us ready for a big welcome home parade in the states."

Not returning Milt's smile, Merrill said, "Yeah, he's crackin' down, but goin' home ain't the reason."

"Did you just say we're not goin' home?"

"Yep, but keep it in this tent."

"That really stinks! Why not?"

"Couple of reasons you probably aren't gonna like."

"Try me."

"For starters, General Patton says so."

216

"What's he got to do with it? He ain't in charge of 1st Division."

"Nope, but our General sure as hell answers to him."

"Oh, I forgot about that. So what's Patton got planned for us?"

"If he had his way, we'd be kickin' the Russkies all the way back to Moscow."

"Whoa . . . aren't they on the same side as us?"

"Yeah, but he's convinced that if we don't fight 'em now, we'll have to fight 'em later."

"Sounds like old Blood and Guts. What's the other reason?"

"Secretary of War wants us to be ready in case we're needed when we invade Japan."

"Wait a minute. I thought beatin' the Japs was up to the Marines?"

"They're doing most of the fightin', but General McArthur is makin' sure the Army gets its share of the glory. Old Dugout Doug loves his medals."

"Crap, that ain't gonna sit well with the guys. I thought we were supposed to get out if we had enough points?"

"Some will and some won't. Draftees, like yourself, might get out if they have eighty five points."

"So let's start countin' them points," Milt said as he held up his fingers to aid in the calculations.

"Before you start countin' chickens, I mean points, you need to remember what the draft law says."

"What about it?"

"Remember, it says the Army can hold you for up to six months after the war's over."

"What! Are you sayin' they can hang on to us till damn near Christmas?"

"Yep, but it might be even longer then that."

"How ya figure? War was over last month."

"Not hardly. We're still fightin' the Japs. But before you get all down in the mouth, remember the Army can turn you loose if they don't need you and you have the eighty-five points."

"How ya get those points?"

"They give you one point for each month in the Army, another point for each month in combat, and five points for each combat medal earned."

"Sounds like I got my eighty five."

"Don't worry. After you get your third combat medal you got more than enough points."

"Great. So that's why you wanted to see me." Saluting and then extending his hand, Milt said, "Been great servin' with ya, Mr. Merrill. Where do I go for musterin' out?"

"Whoa, whoa . . . slow down. You're not headin' home just yet."

"Uh . . . why not - - sir?"

"If you were listenin' you might of heard me mention you're gettin' another medal."

"Fine! Give it to me, and I'll be on my way home," Milt said as he extended his hand, palm up for receipt of his medal.

"Wish I could, but the General wants to pin it on during tomorrow's parade."

"Oh, come on, sir. My medal ain't that big of a deal."

"You're wrong, Milt. The Distinguished Service Cross is the second highest medal you can get."

"What! You're kiddin', right? What the heck did I do to get it?"

"If I had my way, you'd be gettin' the Medal of Honor I recommended you for. General turned it down cuz you're still breathin'. Remember that first day of the Battle of the Bulge when you carried me on your back to the aid station, even though you were wounded yourself?"

"Yeah, but I was just doing what you woulda done for me."

"You can bet you're ass I sure as hell would of, but that ain't why you're gettin' the medal."

"Huh, then why am I getting' it?"

"Don't you remember those prisoners we passed on our way to the aid station?"

Like it was yesterday! The day started off cold but quiet, and ended up like something from hell. Germans were everywhere. No one even heard 'em coming. Heard they snuck into our front lines by wearin' U.S. uniforms. Not surprised. I caught a couple of spies the week before dressed in our uniforms. Didn't know our password, but tried to bluff me by talking baseball. That was a mistake. They didn't even know that his nickname was Babe. I almost busted a gut laughing when one of 'em kept ravin' on about how great a ball player Baby Ruth was. That first day of the battle, the krauts wiped out our whole platoon in less than ten minutes, except me, Joey and Sergeant Merrill. It was a miracle we survived. We fought like crazy men. I guess we did all right because they promoted all three of us. When it got down to just the three of us we took off. Joey got separated from us cuz he thought we were headed for the platoon to the rear of us. I grabbed the Sarge, who was shot up real bad, and headed for the field hospital. We'd only went a few hundred yards, and I heard some of our guys on the other side of the field surrender. Couldn't blame 'em cuz the krauts were everywhere. Wasn't seconds later, and I saw one of the krauts shoot one of our guys in the face. That Nazi bastard made me so goddamm mad that everything after that shot is just a blur.

Merrill watched Milt's eyes glaze over. After giving him a moment, he gently returned Milt to the present. "I know, Milt. That day still haunts me too. If you hadn't charged those krauts, they woulda wiped out that whole squad."

Tears began to trickle down his cheeks. "I just did what anyone else woulda done."

"I wish it were true, but it's not. Most guys, maybe includin' me, woulda protected their ass and laid low. Hells bells, all you had was your forty five and mine against eight krauts with Lugers and sub machine guns. I still can't believe you nailed four of 'em and sent the other four runnin' like hell for the woods."

"I remember after they turned tail, I looked all over myself for holes. They must have been pretty piss-poor shots, cuz I didn't even have a scratch."

"They could shoot straight enough to kill two of the prisoners before you took 'em on. It's easy to hit someone standing still, but it's hard as hell to shoot straight when you got a crazy man chargin' ya."

'Yeah, I did get a bit crazy, but I couldn't let them get by with murder. Goddamn it, our boys had surrendered!" Milt sniffled and attempted to regain his composure.

Merrill patted Milt on his arm. "Believe me, you damn well deserve that medal. Those guys wouldn't be going home if it weren't for you." He slapped Milt on his back, and said, "Now you ready for some good news?"

"Hell yeah! Damn sure ain't much of that around here."

"If you'll volunteer to help the Army out, you'll be home by the 4th of July."

"Hot damn!" Milt said, but froze as the word volunteer registered. Oh how Milt and his buddies hated that word. Four years of the Army taught him to be quite skeptical of that word. "Wait a minute. Wait just a galldurn minute. What am I volunteerin' for?"

"Not a whole lot. Just help the War Department sell War Bonds at a rally at Chicago's Navy Pier on July 4th, and at a rally in Peoria on Saturday the 14th of July."

"I don't know a thing about selling War Bonds. How do I do that?"

"Easy, all you gotta do is get all spiffed up in your dress uniform, and flash a smile and your medals at the crowd."

"Hell, I can do that in my sleep. Looks like Chicago here I come."

"Slow down. You still gotta get your medal tomorrow. Before you do that you better write Vi real quick like and tell her you're on your way home. Tell her "hi" for me."

"Will do, sir. See you at the parade tomorrow."

* * *

"First Division, attention!" barked the division's Master Sergeant.

Boots snapped together, followed by the sudden silence of soldiers at attention. On his way to the raised podium directly in front of the troops, the General wandered through their ranks, stopping from time-to-time to inspect the appearance of some of them.

"First Division, parade rest!" the Division Master Sergeant commanded as the General reached the podium.

Prompted by a nod from the General, the Master Sergeant said, "Sergeant McCoy, attention!" As Milt came to rigid attention, the Master Sergeant commanded, "Sergeant McCoy, front and center!"

Milt approached the podium as the General said, "Good morning men. Today is a glorious day. It is the first day that we all can assemble knowin' that enemy action is not imminent. Let's us give thanks to God, and remember our brothers-in-arms that could not share this fine day with us. Amen."

Following a murmur of "Amen" from the assembled 1st Division, the General continued. "Today is also a day that we give thanks for those that are still with us due to the courageous act of valor of Staff Sergeant Milt McCoy. Without his blatant disregard for his own safety, there are eight of you out there that would not be here today." Tears streamed down the faces of the eight survivors as they nodded agreement and gratitude. As he moved with military precision towards Milt, the general received a box from the Master Sergeant.

"Staff Sergeant McCoy, by the power invested in me by the Congress of the United States of America, it gives me great pleasure and honor to present to you, in gratitude for your meritorious and courageous actions on December 16, 1944, the Distinguished Service Cross. It's getting a bit warm out so I won't read the whole citation. I'm sure everyone by now knows what you did to deserve this."

"Thank you, sir," Milt said as he crisply saluted the General.

The General returned Milt's salute and smiled. "It is also my duty to inform you that you are out of uniform. You will report to me tomorrow mornin' at 0800 with the proper stripes on your uniform. Dismissed. Return to ranks."

The General pivoted to face the ranks of 1st Division. "This parade was not only called for recognizing the valor of one of our own. It was also called to inform all of you of pending orders for 1st Division. You men must be commended for your dedication to your duty. The past three years have tested the mettle of 1st Division. All of you have fought hard and deserve all accolades and gratification this country of ours can afford you. In the comin' days you will once again be given another opportunity to stand up for your country. I have been informed by CENCOM headquarters that we are to remain ready for possible use of 1st Division in future actions against the Empire of Japan. Division Master Sergeant, dismiss the troops."

* * *

"Morning Sergeant, Staff Sergeant McCoy is ready to report as ordered," Milt told the Division Clerk.

"Go ahead and knock on his door. He told me you'd be reporting."

"Staff Sergeant McCoy, reportin' as ordered, sir," Milt said as he rapped on the General's door.

"Enter and report."

Coming to attention in front of the General's desk, Milt saluted and once again said, "Staff Sergeant McCoy, reporting as ordered, sir,"

"At ease. I see you are finally in the correct uniform." The General said as he smiled and directed Milt to take a seat in the chair at the side of the desk.

"Yes, sir, thank you, sir."

"No . . . thank *you!* What you did was not only courageous but served as a shining example of comradeship that hopefully will inspire the rest of the troops."

"You're welcome, sir," a blushing Milt replied.

"Speaking of inspiration, the War Department is hopin' that you'll agree to inspire some of our citizens back home to dig deep."

"I'm not certain how I can do that, sir."

The General smiled. "I understand. Like you, I'm just a simple soldier from the prairies of Illinois. Don't know exactly how you'll do it, but as of tomorrow, you'll be detached from 1st Division and assigned to the War Department office that works with the U.S. Treasury on the War Bond drives. My understandin' is they'll be showin' you off at Chicago's July 4th celebration and War Bond rally, and at another rally in Peoria on the 14th of July. I guess heroes like you make folks a bit more generous. Sound good to you?"

"Yes sir. Where do I report?"

"My office. Tomorrow, at 1100. Any other questions?"

"Yes sir. Can I tell my wife? Can she come to the rally? I haven't seen her in almost four years."

AIN'T NO BUM

"Of course you can tell her! In fact, bring your V letter with you tomorrow. I'll make sure my clerk get's it off right away. Wish I could say that she'll be at the rally, but I can't because it's up to the War Department folks. But, I'll put a good word in for you."

* * *

"Where the hell you think you're goin', goombah? Don't need to pack all your shit for a weekend pass," Joey said.

"Ya ain't gonna believe this, but I ain't goin' on a pass."

"Oh! You musta really pissed off the General. I'll bet he chewed your ass but good for bein' out of uniform."

"Nope. That was just his joke. He made me report so he could give me a new assignment. I'm headin' for the States."

"You're shittin' me, right?"

"Nah, I ain't kiddin' ya. General gave me the best damn orders anyone could ask for. I'm gonna be in Chicago on the 4th to help sell War Bonds so you guys can get paid."

Pumping Milt's hand as if it would render water, he yelled, "Guys, guys this lucky friggin' hero is headin' to the States."

To a man, a general disbelief sounded in a chorus that turned the barracks into a bedlam of happy, but envious, soldiers. Every Army-inspired profane adjective and adverb could be heard intermingled with hoots of joy.

"Wish I could take you guys with me, but my barracks bag is full. I'll miss you guys, but not enough to stick around for some more of this Army stuff," Milt said as he departed. "Maybe, I'll see you later on in Brooklyn, Joey, or at my place."

225

Joey waved from the barracks door. "Make it Brooklyn. There ain't no delis in the sticks. Good luck, goombah!"

Can't believe I'm finally goin' home. Wish those guys could go too. They've been through plenty. Cake walk in North Africa followed by a surprise in Italy. Damn Anzio turned out a lot tougher then we thought. Then, we got the shit kicked out of us in Normandy. I thought nothing was as scary as that landing, but the Battle of the Bulge was a whole lot worse. What a trip though hell! I'm lucky to still be standing. Only three of us from our original platoon left: Joey, the crazy dago from Brooklyn, Merrill the rock, and lucky me. We lost a lot of buddies along the way. I'll miss 'em, but I miss my family a whole lot more.

"Lieutenant Merrill, you in there?" Milt yelled out as he approached Merrill's office.

"Come on in Milt, and take a load off. I'm just finishin' up my daily report. "

Milt saluted and thrust his hand out. "I can't stay, sir. I'm on my way to Division for my transfer to the War Bond folks. Just stopped by to tell ya how much I appreciate all you've done for me. On my way over I was thinking of all three of us survivors, and I thought of you as the rock of Gibraltar. If it wasn't for you I wouldn't be here."

Merrill pulled Milt in and gave him a bear hug. "You got that wrong. If it weren't for you, I'd just be a stiff lyin' in the Ardennes forest."

"Maybe so, but you did a hell lot more for me. Tamed me enough to get me through the CCC, went to bat for me against Haney, and helped me get together with Vi. Thanks to your nerves of steel, we all got through the hedges of Normandy without buyin' the farm. Hell, I could go on and on, but I gotta get to Division before 1100."

"Milt, I think the world of you and Vi, but I was mostly just doin' my job."

"I don't believe that for a minute. You went way beyond what you had to. You take care, Mr. Merrill. If you ever get our way, remember we will always have a place at the table for you. I'm gonna miss ya, sir."

"I'll miss you too Milt, but get the hell out of here before both of us start doing some unmanly bawling."

* * *

The General pointed at Milt and told the bespectacled, thin man sitting on the corner of the General's desk. "There's the man you're looking for."

"Good morning, sir. Staff Sergeant McCoy reportin' as ordered," Milt said as he saluted the General.

The General returned Milt's salute. "Good morning, Staff Sergeant. Stand at ease, and allow me to introduce you to War Department Under-Secretary Powell."

Milt offered his hand to the short, expensively-attired, Under-Secretary. "Pleased to meet you, sir."

"Mr. Powell will escort you back to the States, and will be in charge of the upcomin' War Bond rallies."

"Yes, well, in truth, I will not be in charge of the rallies themselves. My role is limited to only being the Liaison Officer between the War Department and the Treasury Department.

However, in all matters related to the rallies, Sergeant, you will report to me. Is that clear? Do you have any questions?"

Boy, I got a hunch this guy's a stuffed shirt. The short little prick is probably related to Haney, or took lessons off the old asshole. General doesn't seem comfortable with this fella. Wonder why. This Powell fella seems a bit full of himself. Maybe he's just as nervous about this as I am.

"Yes sir. I do have one question. Will it be okay for my wife to join me at the rallies?"

"You will be representing the U.S. Army at the rallies. I understand your desire to be with your family. However, the best interest of the Army must be paramount. Consequently, your family will not be allowed on the rally stage."

"I understand, sir. I meant is it okay for her to attend the rallies?"

"The rallies are, of course, open to the general public. However, the rally itself is only part of your duties. I'm sure that after you review the itinerary for the Chicago rally you will realize that little of your time will be available for other engagements."

"Oh! I was hopin' to spend some time with my wife and son. I haven't seen them in almost four years."

"I understand, but do keep in mind that fulfillment of your duties comes first." The Under-Secretary said as he jutted his clenched jaw up towards Milt as if he were delivering a silent message of domination.

What a prick! I'll bet this is the first time he's been away from his family during this damn war. "No problem, sir. I'll make sure my family doesn't get in the way."

"You two will have plenty of time on the plane to go over plans. Right now we better hustle you two out of here. Plane is waitin'. Go with God, Sergeant." The General extended his hand to Milt. "See the Division Clerk before you leave for your official orders. Also, don't forget to give him your letter to your wife. Got a hunch you might beat the letter home, but in case you don't, you best be mailin' that letter."

20

"**G**randpa, Grandpa, wake up, wake up. We're home. Daddy coming home." Butch squealed as he jumped on the bed that his grandpa was lying on.

Hope for an afternoon nap gone, Denny tickled his excited grandson. "I'm glad you're home you little rascal. Where's your Mom?"

Vi leaned her head into his bedroom, and smiled. "Sorry about interrupting your nap. He got away from me when I opened the front door. He's so wound up."

"I can see that." Denny hugged his wiggling grandson. "What's this about his Daddy coming home? Did you get a letter?"

"No, but everyone in town knew he was coming home."

"Oh, how did everyone find out before you?"

"Looks like the Army contacts the newspapers before they do the families," Vi handed her father the latest Peoria newspaper.

"I'm sure Milt sent you a letter. Anyway, I'm glad he's coming home. Wow, he got another medal. A big, important one. No wonder they're gonna show him off at the War Bond rallies. But, I wish the paper wouldn't have used the front page to tell about Milt comin' home."

"Why?"

"I'm hopin' his dad doesn't see the paper."

"I doubt if the Peoria paper is delivered to Kentucky."

"It doesn't have to go that far for him to see this big headline. I'm surprised it's on the front page and so big. He won't miss that headline even if he's in his usual drunken state."

"Are you saying he's back?"

"I hate to say it, but that old reprobate has come back to haunt us."

"I don't understand. I thought he couldn't come back to Illinois for ten years?"

"No, not the whole state, just Knox and Fulton Counties. He's not in either one, so he hasn't went back on his agreement with Sheriff Foster. I heard Frank's workin' in a bakery over in Pekin, and, so far, he's stayin'over that way."

Vi pointed to the paper. "Oh no, I hope he doesn't see this and start pestering us again. That restraining order didn't seem to keep him away."

"He's been back for awhile without botherin' us so maybe he's keepin' his nose clean."

"Let's hope." Vi ran for the house phone that was incessantly ringing. "I better get that."

"Hello, Stewart residence."

"Hello sweetheart, I'm comin' …"

"Oh my God! Oh my Lord, it's you, it's really you! We were just reading about you. Where are you?"

"We just got into New York. I'm headin' to Chicago in a couple of hours. Did you say you read about me? You got my letter?"

"No, we didn't get your letter, but you are all over the front page of the Peoria paper. It said that you would be appearing at War Bond rallies."

"Sorry you had to learn about my comin' home from the newspaper. I thought my letter would beat me home."

"As long as you are home, I don't care how I learned about it. Are you home for good? When will we see you?"

"Wish I knew. All I know right now is I'm in the Chicago rally on the 4th and the Peoria rally on the 14th. Lieutenant Merrill seems to think I won't be goin' back overseas. By the way, he said to tell ya hi."

"Who is Lieutenant Merrill? Oh, I remember he was one of your bosses in the CCC that ended up in the Army with you. I sure hope you are home for good."

"Me too. I missed you so much, but I'm not certain how soon I'll see you. The War Department guy I'm workin' for is kinda like Haney. He didn't seem too keen on havin' my family at the Chicago rally."

"We probably would have a hard time making the Chicago rally. We haven't got our gas ration stamps for July yet, so driving up there might be a problem. If you want, I can see if I can get Butch and me on the bus."

"I would be in heaven if you could. Let me ask my War Department boss again, but don't get your hopes too high.

First time I asked, he got all stuffed-shirt about it, but he said okay for the Peoria rally so we probably should just plan for meetin' then."

"It probably would be best. I want to hold you right now and never let you go, but to get to Chicago in four days might be hard. I can wait till Peoria if you can."

"I don't want to, but we've waited four years. Another two weeks is a piece of cake. Only have a minute or so left on this call. Is Butch there? I really would like to talk to him."

I hope I don't scare the crap out of the little guy, Milt thought as he heard Vi call Butch to the phone.

"Hi, Daddy," Butch murmured.

Tears of joy streamed down his face as Milt softly said, "How's my boy? Daddy's comin' home. I missed you. Did you miss me?"

Hope for a robust childish outburst of joy was quickly dashed by a prolonged silence followed by a soft cry of, "Mommy, Mommy."

"Sorry, sweetheart. He's a bit shy. He'll be all over you when he sees you. All he does is talk about you. We miss you so very much."

"I had a feelin' I might scare him. Soon, we'll have lots of time to get to know each other." *Damn, that prick from the War Department is signaling for me to join him. He's waiving his arms like a crazy man so I'd better get off the phone.* "I hate to, but I've got to go. I love you very much. I'll call you when we get to Chicago."

"I love you too, sweetheart. We'll see you soon. Call me from Chicago, and let me know when and where to meet you in Peoria."

AIN'T NO BUM

"Will do. Love ya sweety. Gotta go."

* * *

Christ, I'm dead on my feet. Three days of traveling, and then straight to this shindig. This War Bond selling crap is almost as bad as the Army. Oh well, at least I'm not gettin' shot at.

"Milt, straighten your tie and follow me. Several dignitaries are awaiting your presence," the little pain-in-the-ass-war-department-twerp hissed.

This little shit is a bigger asshole then Haney. I wouldn't be so tired if the sawed-off little bastard woulda let me get some sleep. All the way from Prague to London he drilled me on what I was supposed to do. Kinda figured he would. I had no idea how to sell these damn bonds. Should have been able to grab some zzz's on the way to New York, but he never shut up. Got a few winks on the way to Chicago, but I needed a whole lot more.

Milt was in awe as he floated in a sleep deprived haze across the floor of the Drake Hotel's mirrored, crystal-chandelier-lit ballroom. *From a drafty barracks to a palace in three days, I must be dreamin'.*

"There he is. The man of the hour," a portly, formally-attired man boomed as he heartedly shook Milt's hand. "We are honored to host you and tomorrow's rally in our windy city."

"Thank you, sir. I'm Staff Sergeant Milt McCoy, but please just call me Milt. Sorry sir, but I didn't catch your name?"

With a chuckle from deep within his barreled chest, the distinguished, grey haired man said, "That's because I didn't throw it. Allow me to introduce myself. I have the good fortune to be known as the Mayor of Chicago." He lowered hi voice. "In private, please call me Cy."

Crap! That dirty look from my twerp of a boss tells me I screwed up. Too late now, I might as well act like I know what I'm doin'. "Please to meet you Mr. Mayor. Thanks for invitin' us to your fine city. Sure found out quick why they call it the windy city. Two seconds off the plane, and I ended up chasin' my hat half way across Midway airport."

Cy laughed and slapped Milt on the back. "Looks like you've been properly introduced to our fair city. Of course, you being from Galesburg, I imagine you already know all about our town."

"Afraid not sir, this is my first visit to Chicago."

"No, no, I meant you being from the same town as Chicago's poet laureate, Carl Sandburg, you'd be well versed in the glory and warts of our home."

"Wish I could say that I am sir, but truth is I've only read Sandburg's books about Abe Lincoln. The Depression kinda took away my reading time."

"In that case, we'll have to make sure to introduce you to our beautiful city by the lake. But, first, allow me to introduce my friends and family."

Twenty some introductions later, Milt's tired hand and fading smile were relieved to hear the Mayor say, "And last, but not least, allow me to introduce you to my niece and your dinner partner for this evening, Miss Monica Wilder."

Wow! This babe is a knockout. Niece? I thought she was a movie star. Hope nobody takes a picture for the paper. Vi sees me with her, and I'll be explainin' till hell freezes over. If the picture shows me below my belt, I'm dead!

"Pleased to meet you, Miss Wilder."

"The pleasure is all mine, Sergeant," she said in a sugar-sweet purr as her million dollar smile and dark flapping eyelashes provided punctuation.

God, I hope this woman is just being polite. If she has any designs I'm in trouble. The Devil sure knows how to tempt a fella. After almost four years, why in God's name does the first female to cross my path have to be so damn good lookin'.

Monica asked as she lightly slipped her well manicured, red tipped hand into the crook of Milt's arm. "Shall we join the others for dinner?"

Wow! Even her touch gets my attention. Her long legs and coke-bottle-figure is temptation enough. I don't think her dress could get any tighter. That dress sure shows off every little wiggle.

"Um . . ., yes, I . . . I, suppose we should," Milt stammered as he felt himself being led to one of the longest tables he'd ever seen.

"Is this your first time in Chicago, Sergeant?"

"Ma'am," he said as he held out her chair.

"Please, call me Monica," she said as she slowly glided into her chair.

Holy cow! She even gets a rise out of me when she takes her seat. I better sit down quick before someone sees how much this gorgeous blonde is gettin' a rise out of me.

"Yes ma'am, I mean Monica, this is my first visit to your city."

"Oh, this isn't my hometown. I'm actually from Peoria."

"Peoria? Are you by any chance related to a Bill Wilder?"

"He's my brother. My family will never forget what you did for him." Her deep blue eyes gazed into his while her right hand disappeared from view. "I hope you will allow me to show you our gratitude."

Oh my God! She's got ahold of my thigh and her hand is wanderin' higher. I better do something quick before this gets out of control. I'm ready to pop! Four years away from Vi's pleasure is tough enough, but her light touch rubbin' me up ain't makin' it easier.

He lifted her hand and directed it away from his upper thigh. "Bill returning home safely is all the thanks I need."

Monica cast her eyes down to Milt's hand, and for the first time noticed his wedding ring. Blushing, she said, "I understand. I apologize for any discomfort I may have caused you. You must love your wife very much."

"No need to apologize. I must admit I was flattered. You are a very beautiful young lady, but, like you said, I love my wife very much."

* * *

"What a grand day for being an American," the Mayor of Chicago shouted as he flung his arms in a wide lift to the heavens. "Even our famous winds agree." The Mayor continued as he raised a finger as if testing the strength of the usually present gales. "Tonight is a perfect night for the rockets red glare.

This old boy sure knows how to stir up the crowd. I thought we made a hell of a ruckus when we got our weekend passes. Sounds like this crowd is tryin' to wake the heavens above.

The Marine Corps band struck up another patriotic Sousa marching song, and the Mayor shouted into the microphone, "Before we light the fuses to our rockets, let me introduce to Chicago an Illinois hero we are honored to have with us tonight. Chicago, please welcome, Staff Sergeant Milt McCoy."

As he waved his hat to the crowd and followed the Under-Secretary's instructions, Milt's ears detected a faint, familiar voice that barely rose above the cheers of the crowd. *It's been awhile, but I'd swear I just heard my old man booing me and callin' me a bum. What the hell is he doin' here? Hope my tired brain is just imagining things.*

"This fine young man is not only a hero to the United States Army, but he is also responsible for saving the lives of several other sons of Illinois," the Mayor shouted over the cheers of the crowd. Holding on to Milt's shoulder, the Mayor said, "One of those fine young soldiers that is lucky to be alive, thanks to Sergeant McCoy, is very near and dear to my heart, my nephew Private Bill Wilder, who is at this moment in his home in Peoria recuperating from his wounds."

Before the crowd could resume their wild cheering, a lone voice at the back of the crowd could be heard to say, "Ain't no hero, my son is just a goddamn thievin' bum."

Oh, shit, it is him. I sure hell didn't want to come home to his crap.

"Sergeant McCoy, you need to explain this disruption when the rally is over," the red-faced Under-Secretary whispered into Milt's ear.

"Yes, sir," Milt said through his smile. *I ain't smiling for the crowd, but watchin' the cops beat the crap out of my old man does bring out a smile. They are really wailin' the tar out of him. Maybe he'll finally get the message.*

* * *

239

"Hello, Stewart residence," Vi said as she picked up the phone.

"Hi, sweetheart, I'm on my way home."

"Oh. Hi."

Boy that sure doesn't sound like Vi. "Did you hear what I said? I'm done with Chicago and headin' home."

"I heard you! Are you sure you want to come home?"

"Of course, I'm sure! Why would you ask such a silly question?"

"Talk about silly questions! I'm surprised you even called me. You looked awfully cozy with that blonde man-stealer hanging all over you."

Oh shoot! I was afraid that some damn newspaper jockey would snap a picture.

"Sweetheart, that picture wasn't what it looked like."

"Don't you sweetheart me, and don't tell me what I didn't see!" Vi said as her volume rose to punctuate her increasingly curt tone.

"The picture is of me and the lady the Mayor of Chicago ordered me to accompany to the rally dinner. I just met her. You got nothing to worry about."

"Nothing to worry about! She was all over you!"

"Well, I gotta admit I wasn't happy that she latched on to my arm, but I guess that's how high-falutten folks escort ladies."

"Lady? She sure didn't look like one to me!"

"No, you got it all wrong. She was just all dolled up for a fancy dinner. Believe me, that picture doesn't show it all."

"I'm sure it doesn't! She looked like she couldn't wait for dinner, and you were the dessert!"

"I didn't mean that. After we got to the table, I untangled myself and told her I was married."

"From the looks of her, I don't think that much mattered to her!"

"You're wrong, Vi. After I told her, she was mighty embarrassed."

"Well, she should have been! Why was she all over you in the first place? What did you do to encourage her?"

"I saved her brother's life, and she wanted to thank me. Someone told her I was single, so she got all dolled up for me. When I told her I loved my wife very much, she turned beet red and apologized a whole bunch."

After a short period of silence Milt heard Vi softly utter a long "Ohhhh," followed by another prolonged silence.

"Vi, Vi, are you still there?"

"I'm still here, sweetheart. I'm sorry I doubted you.

"I understand. I probably woulda wondered if I'd seen you in the paper on the arm of some handsome fella."

"I can't wait to get my hands on you. You think she was holding on. I'm going to hold on tight and never let go. When will you be home?"

"We're fixin' to get on a plane later on today. We should be in Peoria at 4 PM. Do you think your dad can drive you over to meet me?"

"I'll have to ask him, but don't worry, I'll be there. Would you mind if I left Butch with Mrs. Procini?"

"I miss the little fella, but I sure do like your idea. See you at four," Milt said.

"I love you sweetheart, see you soon. Bye, bye," Vi cooed.

241

* * *

"Sergeant, now that we both have some time on our hands, I insist you tell me the meaning of that disturbance during the Chicago rally!" Under-Secretary Powell asked through clenched teeth shortly after take-off from Midway Airport en-route for Peoria.

Doesn't this guy believe in sleep? I was just about to nod off. Soon as I'm free of this pencil pusher I'm gonna sleep for a week.

"Did you hear me Sergeant?" Powell said as he shook the drowsy Milt.

"No, sir. I was trying to grab a few winks."

"I asked you to explain the disturbance at the Chicago rally. The man said you were his son. Is that true?"

"Yes sir. I wish I could say different."

"He didn't seem too proud of you. Is there something between you two I should know about? We can't have a repeat of such a disturbance."

Oh boy, how much should I tell this prick? If I tell him anything, he'll probably want to know everything. But if I don't tell him and the old man acts up again, I got a hunch the War Department folks won't be to pleased with me.

"Sergeant, I asked you to explain yourself. Please promptly do so. I don't wish to raise my voice and embarrass us in front of our fellow travelers, but your conduct may not leave me any choice."

"Sorry, sir, I wasn't trying to not answer you. I was just tryin' to figure out where to begin. This answer may be a bit more than what you want to hear."

"Let me be the judge of that. Now, please tell me, and start from the beginning."

"Started when I was a kid. Long and the short of it is we didn't see eye-to-eye on most anything, so we we never much cared for each other."

"I appreciate your brevity. However, your answer doesn't explain why he called you a thief and a bum."

Twenty minutes later, the Under-Secretary slumped back in his chair, overwhelmed by Milt's explanation.

"Believe it or not Sergeant, I understand. I also had a difficult relationship with my father. However, my father never would publicly embarrass me like your father did."

"I imagine most fathers wouldn't, but my old man is different. Most folks try to live a Christian life, but not him. He only follows the righteous and legal path when he thinks God or the law is watchin'. Trouble is they can't watch often enough."

"I thought I had a difficult childhood. It must have been tough growing up with a father like him."

"It wasn't easy, but I had grandparents that made sure I grew up different than him and my ma."

"Did your grandparents live . . .," Powell asked but was interrupted by the plane's sudden change in altitude.

Whoa we musa hit some bumpy clouds. Hate it when planes I'm on get thrown all over the sky. That was a good bump. I stayed in my seat, but that little twerp damn near landed in my lap. Good thing I caught him or he woulda banged his head against the ceiling.

Settling himself back into his seat, Under-Secretary Powell said, "Thanks for grabbing me before I crashed."

"You're welcome, sir." Milt hoped the bumpy ride would kill all the questions.

"Just before we hit that turbulence, I was thinking that perhaps I haven't been honest with you. I'm new at this rally stuff myself, so I've probably been a bit too stuffy and hard on you. Allow me to properly introduce myself. I'm Gerald. Please call me, Jerry when we are in private." The Undersecretary extended his hand. "Would you mind if I addressed you as Milt?"

"I'd rather you did, and nice to meet you Jerry. Glad you came clean with me."

"Me too. I was probably more scared of these rallies then you. When I heard your dad carrying on, I almost had a heart attack."

"You and me both. That old fool has a way of makin' ya worry. He's screwed up a whole bunch of times for me. He even tried to screw up my weddin'."

"My dad made things hard for me, but he would have never acted like yours did the other night. I was scared of the repercussions, and I was embarrassed for you."

"Don't be. I hate to say it, but I'm used to it. I just hope he didn't cause a problem for ya."

"Not yet, but if he continues his antics at the rallies it may cause a problem. We'll cross that bridge when, and if, we get to it."

"Thank you, sir. I'm glad we cleared the air. I was startin' to think you and I were gonna have a miserable time together."

"Me too! Now let's get ourselves ready for Peoria. There's the airport right below us."

* * *

Sure is funny that I've never been to Peoria seein' how it's so close to Knox and Fulton County. I guess I just didn't want to smell it. Heard tell you can get drunk by just breathing. I can believe it. Hell, they got three beer breweries and one liquor distillery. It's bad enough sniffin' my old man's still. Town sure looks pretty though. At least from up here it does. It's kinda puny compared to Chicago, but it's got a lot more green fields and trees than Chicago. They even got a river runnin' through the town that's a whole lot prettier than the Mississippi. Enough gawkin'. The only thing I want to see out this window is Vi. God, I hope she's there!

"Will your family be waiting for you at the airport?" Jerry asked in a much more friendly tone.

"I sure hope so. Will I get any time with her before the rally?"

"Nothing is planned before the rally. No reception dinner like we had in Chicago. I'm sure they'll have some speeches at the airport, but nothing else that I know of."

"Hope they don't, cuz all I want to do is spend time with Vi."

"Is Vi your wife?"

"Yep, and I intend to remind her!" Milt said as he smiled.

"Well . . . well, I'll remember to knock."

As the plane approached the runway the pilot spoke. "Hold on folks, we are getting some nasty cross winds. The landing might be a bit rough."

Within seconds of the warning, the DC-3 made its first jarring impact with the runway. Although many of the passengers knew the DC-3 had proven it's mettle in many military and civilian flights since Douglass Aircraft put them in service in 1936, all of the passengers sucked in their breath. On the second, and even harder impact, they screamed or gasped in horror. As the pilot attempted to get the struggling plane under control, the right wing dipped and scraped along the runway. All, except the seasoned fliers and the pilot, were now showing signs of fear and near-panic.

Aw come on, this can't be the way it all ends. I've been through hell in this damn war. Please God, don't let this be my time. Vi is probably out there watchin'. She doesn't need to see this!

After a small lift off the ground followed by one more blunt impact, the screech of brakes gave the passengers a large sigh of relief. "Sorry about the rough landin' folks. Crosswinds in the summer are sometimes quite a challenge. Hope your time in Peoria is better than my landing."

Relieved passengers cheered, and Milt pried Jerry's white-knuckled hand from his arm rest. "You okay, Jerry?"

"I'm not okay, but I'm better than I was a few minutes ago. How about you?"

"I'm fine. Believe it or not, I've walked away from rougher landings."

"And you still don't mind flying?" Jerry asked pale faced, eyes wide open.

"Army don't ask whether you mind."

"Good point. Can you see your family?" Jerry asked as the plane turned towards the awaiting crowd.

"Folks, if you'll keep you seats for a few minutes more it would be appreciated. We have a hero amongst our midst. The

Mayor of Peoria is waiting to greet Staff Sergeant McCoy, so please allow him and his escort, Under-Secretary Powell, to disembark first," the pilot announced.

Shaking the hands of well wishers as he walked down the aisle to the exit, Milt smiled and thanked them. *When is all this attention gonna go away?* As he approached the exit, Milt asked Jerry, "Should I go out first?"

"Of course. They want to see you, not me."

One step out of the plane and Milt smiled the smile of his lifetime as he saw Vi running towards the plane, waving and yelling, "Milt, Milt, welcome home, dear."

She made it! Thank God she made it! He rushed down the exit ladder and set off in a collision course that ended when Milt lifted Vi off her feet in an embrace that he hoped would never end. He kissed her then yelled to the cheering, whistling crowd, "I love my wife. Thank you for invitin' me to your town and lettin' my wife greet me first."

Milt embraced Vi once again, and murmured in her ear, "I missed you so. I promise we will never be apart again. Your love is all that kept me going."

"I know sweetheart, our love made these long days apart shorter."

As they broke their embrace, Milt gently grabbed her hand and said, "We still have a few more days to go before it is just our time. I still have to do this War Bond stuff and then we are free." Milt turned from her and prepared himself for the onslaught of the horde of Peoria well-wishers and dignitaries. "Before all the hand shakers get here, let me introduce you to someone." He pointed to the man now standing next to him. "Vi, this here is my boss, Under-Secretary of the War Department, Mr. Gerald Powell."

"Pleased to meet you, Mrs. McCoy."

"The pleasure is mine, sir. Thank you for bringing my husband home. Please do call me, Vi."

"You're welcome, Vi, but you give me too much credit. I only escorted your husband on this important War Bond tour. Your husband's heroics are why he is deservedly here. Oh, and please call me Jerry."

Before the tall, thin man wearing a European-style sash denoting him as the Mayor of Peoria could join them, Vi whispered to her husband, "I thought you said he was a stuffed-shirt? He seems nice."

"He changed my mind," Milt quickly whispered in response before the Mayor presented his hand.

"Sergeant McCoy, welcome to Peoria. We are honored by your presence." The Mayor shouted to ensure that all would hear above the airport and wind noise.

"Thank you, sir. I grew up less than fifty miles from here. I've always wanted to visit your beautiful city."

"Am I to take it that this is your first visit?"

"Yes, sir, but hopefully it's not my last visit."

"You are always welcome to our little river town. But for now, you can always tell everyone that you 'Played in Peoria'."

As the crowd laughed and cheered, the Mayor explained to Milt that the saying 'Played in Peoria' was an old vaudeville joke that the town had adopted and changed to mean that you can't fool the folks of Peoria.

Milt smiled politely. "Oh, well, I sure don't intend to fool 'em."

"Good for you son. Now please let me introduce some folks to you and your lovely bride."

Are they gonna run out of folks to introduce me too? Half of Peoria must be here.

Near the end of the line, Milt noticed a tall, pale soldier leaning on a cane and standing next to a pretty blonde who looked familiar. As Milt stretched his memory for a name of the young lady, the Mayor said as he gestured to the tall soldier, "This young man insisted, despite his injuries, to be here today. Please take a moment to ..."

Before the Mayor could finish the soldier said, "How ya doin' Sarge?"

"Real good, Private. Hold on, is that you Bill? Bill Wilder?"

"Sure is. Been awhile. Looks like you're doing fine."

"Now that I'm home, I'm doin' great! Last time I saw you we were still at Anzio. What you been up to?"

"Not much. Ever since Anzio, I've been in one hospital after another. After all those operations I feel like I'm held together by bailin' wire. They finally sent me home a couple of months ago. Guess they can't do much more for me."

"I'm sorry to hear that, Bill."

"Don't be, hell if it weren't for you I wouldn't even be standin' here. I'm just thankful I finally got a chance to thank you for savin' my butt. Sure would appreciate it if you'd let me and my family treat you and your bride to supper this evenin' at the Pere Marquette's restaurant."

"That would be great, but I don't know what they have planned for me. I still gotta sell them there War Bonds."

"You're free this evening," Jerry interjected.

"In that case, we'll be glad to take you up on your offer. But, you know you don't have to treat us. I was just doing my job."

"Don't be so humble, Sarge. You know that I know different." Bill stared off into another space in time. Slipping back into the present, Bill said, "Oh, my manners are a bit rusty. This young lady proppin' me up is my sister, Monica. I think you two met in Chicago."

Oh my God, it's her. She ain't all dolled up, so I didn't recognize her. From the look on Vi's face this is gonna be one hell of a supper.

Monica offered her hand. "Hello Milt. Good to see you again. Is the lady you're with your lovely wife?"

"Yes, I am!" Vi said in an air chilling tone.

Monica ignored Vi's cold reception. "Pleased to meet you, I'm looking forward to seeing you tonight."

"Likewise!" Vi muttered.

* * *

As they rode the elevator down to the lobby, Milt noticed that Vi was gripping her purse so tightly that her knuckles were white. "Relax, sweetheart, the Wilder's just want to thank me."

"Oh, I'm sure one of them wants to do more than that."

Damn! She is still steamin'. She hardly said two civil words to me all afternoon. I was hopin' for somethin' more, but right now I'd settle for her smile. Got a feelin' supper is gonna' hit my gut like a bomb. It could be the best meal ever and my gut would still be flip floppin' all over the place.

"Sweetheart, I told you, that girl was totally embarrassed and proper after she found out I was married. From the looks of her today she is still embarrassed. Please, don't cause a scene. We can talk about it later."

"I won't embarrass us any further, but, believe me, we still have some talking to do." Vi said as they exited the elevator.

"There they are. Come join us. Mom, Dad, and my sis are waiting for us at our table." Bill pointed to the table in the back of the restaurant.

"Thanks, Bill. Can I help you to the table?"

"Nah, thanks anyway. I think I can make it. I'm trying to learn how to walk with this cane. Walkin' with this thing takes some gettin' used to, but beats hell out of losin' a leg."

Crap, she's dolled up again. I guess when they are as good lookin' as her it don't take much to make 'em look temptin'. Who's that other fella with 'em?

"Mom, Dad, let me introduce you to Sergeant McCoy." Bill said. He started to seat himself, but paused and then pointed at the tall, dark, handsome young man standing next to his dad. "Oh, I almost forgot, this here is Monica's fiancé, Richard Peel."

Fiancé? That sure is a surprise. She sure didn't act like she was engaged when I met her in Chicago. Wonder what Vi thinks of that? This is gonna be a long, interestin' night.

"Pleased to meet you, Mr. and Mrs. Wilder. Allow me to introduce my wife, Vi."

Mrs. Wilder bubbled with enthusiasm as she hugged Milt, then Vi. "Oh I am so happy to finally meet the young man that delivered our boy safely home to us. We'll never forget what you've done for Bill and his family."

I don't know what to say. Never met the folks of any of the guys I helped out. They are makin' this a lot more than what I'm comfortable with. I was just tryin' to keep my butt in one piece.

Vi came to his rescue. "Thank you so much for asking us to share supper with you. The last few weeks have been quite a whirlwind for Milt, so a quiet supper with folks is quite a treat."

"Like Vi said, it has been kinda fast and furious lately, so I'm really glad to slow down. This restaurant looks like something out of a movie. You didn't have to do all this, but we appreciate it."

"Yes we did," Mr. Wilder said, "now let's be seated. Milt would you mind sitting over here between Bill and me?"

"No, not at all, it'll give me a chance for Bill and I to catch up."

"Great, and Vi, if you don't mind, you can sit between Mrs. Wilder and Monica."

Oh, great. I hope Monica doesn't end up wearin' her dinner. So far so good, Vi didn't say no, and she didn't chill the air saying okay.

As they started to take their seats, Milt, to his horror, heard Monica say, "I'm going to powder my nose before supper, would you like to join me?"

Milt let out a quiet sigh of relief as he heard Vi say, "That sounds like a good idea."

"Milt, Bill tells me that you're in town sellin' War Bonds. You must be glad to get away from the Army, but how did you manage getting home before the war is over?" Mr. Wilder asked.

With one eye on the departing Vi and Monica, Milt said, "I'm not certain how I managed, but I'm sure glad they picked me."

"Dad, don't believe a word the Sarge is sayin'. After you get to know him you'll figure out the Sarge doesn't like to toot his own horn. Army sends back the fellas who get their top medals to help sell the War Bonds. If Milt was wearin' his medals tonight he'd be clankin' when he walked."

"Did Bill tell stories at home? He was always tellin' us stories. I'll bet he has me walkin' on water when all I did was my job," Milt said with a smile.

Mr. Wilder chuckled and shook his head. "You two are something. Let's order some champagne before the young ladies return."

"None for me, sir, but I'll take a ginger ale."

"Sorry, Milt, I forgot. Bill said you didn't drink. I imagine you'll never drink if you got through that war without a nip," Mr. Wilder said as he signaled for a waiter.

"Waiter, please bring a bottle of champagne, with six glasses, and one ginger ale. Please hurry if you would. We'd like to surprise the ladies when they return."

I wonder if I'm being too hard nosed about booze. I can't even raise a glass of champagne to celebrate. One of these days I might try it, but not today. Got a hunch I'll have my hands full with Vi after this dinner. She sure left the table loaded for bear.

"The girls must be about done powdering their noses from sound of their giggles. They must have had a good chat," Mrs. Wilder said as the waiter appeared with their champagne.

Hope she's right. I can hear 'em giggling up a storm. Here they come, and I ain't believin' my eyes. Those two are arm-in-arm and giggling like school girls.

Standing as the ladies approached, Mr. Wilder lifted his glass, "Here is to heroes and young ladies. May they always be in abundance and shine as brightly as the ones at our table."

The fiancé finally contributed to the table banter, "Here, here."

* * *

"What a lovely evening." Vi said as she pushed her husband on to the bed. "Good company, great food, and finally we're alone. I love you so very much Mr. McCoy."

"I love you too, sweetheart."

"I know you do. I have proof and validation."

"Validation? What are you talking about?"

As she slowly disrobed for the evening, "Oh a certain young blonde vamp told me all about how much my gentlemanly war hero loves me."

"So that's why you two were so chummy after the visit to the powder room."

"Ho-hum." Vi said as she exaggerated her fake yawn. "Now you will get your reward, my hero." The last of her garments slid to the floor.

"This is one reward I'm really looking forward to! Sure is a whole lot better than all those medals the Army gave me!" Milt smiled as he struggled to rid himself, at a record pace, of all of his formal Army fabric encumbrances.

* * *

Following a vigorous rap on the door, Milt heard someone say, "Room service, may I come in?"

"Are you sure you have the right room? We didn't order breakfast." Milt said as he wiped the sleep from his eyes.

"Yes, sir. This is room 712. The order says to deliver this breakfast to room 712 compliments of the hotel. May I come in?"

"Give us a minute." Milt gently shook Vi. "Vi, sweetheart, are you awake?"

"Kinda," Vi mumbled from beneath the covers. "What time is it?"

"A little before eight. We need to get decent. There is a guy at the door who wants to deliver us breakfast."

Vi sat up straight. "We can't afford that!"

"I know, but he says the breakfast is on the house. Guess this hero stuff pays off."

"Would you rather I come back in a little while, sir?"

"No, no, just one more minute." Milt said as he leered at Vi as she slipped into a robe. *Wish that guy had showed up a little bit later. Nothing like exercise before breakfast, and I do need my exercise. Later! Guess I better open the door, or he'll keep knockin' loud enough to wake up the rest of the hotel.*

"Mornin', come on in," Milt said to the short, thin young man dressed in a Pere Marguette bellhop outfit.

"May I set the tray on the table, or would you prefer it in bed?"

Noting Vi's smile and slight giggle, Milt said, "I think we'll have it in bed."

With a wink, the bellhop nodded. "Okay, you folks get comfy in bed, and I'll set the tray between you."

"Come on Vi, we're gonna eat like a king and queen." Milt propped up the pillows.

"Here is a little something for having to wait so long," Milt said as he offered some of his fast dwindling pay.

"That's alright, sir." The bellhop said as he indicated that Milt should put his money away. "The manager said not to accept any gratuity. He said it's totally on the house."

"Yeah, but you oughta get something for your trouble."

"Don't worry, sir. They took care of me. You folks enjoy your breakfast. Call me when you want me to pick up the tray."

Milt toasted Vi with his orange juice. "Good morning, sweetheart. This isn't how I planned to start the day, but it'll do. I can still start the mornin' right a little later on."

Vi pulled Milt's face to her, and gave him a long lingering kiss. "Good morning, my dear husband. Don't eat too much, or we might have to wait a bit to start our day off right."

Milt suddenly put his fork down on his plate.

Vi laughed. "Don't be silly. Eat. We have a long day ahead of us. You'll need your energy."

"That's for sure. After last night, I don't know if I've got any more oomph."

"You better have! I didn't wait four long years for just one night." Vi looked down at the tray. "What is that envelope addressed to you all about?"

"I don't know. Let's take a look," Milt said as he opened the envelope. "We'll, I'll be darned."

"What is it, dear?"

"It's a note from Jerry wishin' us a good day. Says he will meet us at the rally. A car will be waiting for us at the front of the hotel at 11 AM."

"That's nice of him. I guess he's not such a bad guy after all."

"Yeah, he's loosened up a lot since I met him. But, I'm surprised he isn't gonna escort us to the rally."

"It sounds like he trusts you to show up."

"Guess so. Sure am glad he does. That gives us about three hours, and breakfast sure ain't gonna take that long," Milt smiled and gently rubbed his hand across Vi's breast.

"I'd say breakfast will be served cold," Vi cooed.

* * *

As Milt stepped on to the raised rally stage, Bill Wilder said, "Good morning, Sarge. Good morning, Mrs. McCoy."

Before Milt could answer, a sweet feminine voice from behind Bill said, "Good morning, Sergeant. Good morning, Vi."

"Good morning, Monica. How are you today?" Vi almost giggled.

"Good, but I'm sure I'm not doing as good as you," Monica said with a smile.

She clutched Milt's arm and smiled. "You're right!"

Milt reddened as he changed the subject. "Bill, have you seen my boss, Under-Secretary Powell?"

"No. He was here earlier. Said something to the Mayor, and then he took off right quick like. Last I saw him he was at the back of the Armory."

Struggling to focus on the back of the Peoria Armory, which was filled to capacity for today's War Bond rally, Milt thought he saw Jerry Powell. *I would swear I just saw Jerry, but it looked like he was with my dad. What in the hell is goin' on?*

"If you're lookin' for your boss, he isn't out there. Said to tell you he had some urgent War Department business to take care of. Why don't you and your lovely bride come sit with my family and me?" the Mayor of Peoria said.

Shocked by what he had just seen, Milt did not answer the mayor. Instead, Vi answered for him as she tugged on his sleeve. "Thank you, sir, we would love to."

"Yes, we would appreciate that. Sorry, I was distracted. I thought I saw someone I knew."

"That's all right. All those people cheerin' can be distracting. I remember how I lost my focus at many of my election rallies. We're sittin' just to the right of the podium," the Mayor said as he pointed to their seats.

The Mayor's introductions of Milt and Vi to his party seemed endless. Relieved that the handshakes and small talk were done for now, Vi whispered into Milt's ear, "Are you okay?"

"I'm fine. I was just a bit shocked to see Jerry and my dad together," Milt whispered.

"Oh no," Vi mumbled as she began to nervously wring her hands.

Milt placed his hand over hers. "Don't worry. I'm sure there is an explanation. Jerry knows about me and dad."

Suddenly the cheers and whistles of the crowd reached another ear splitting level as Bill Wilder, with the aid of Monica, hobbled towards the podium. "Thank you Mr. Mayor, and thank you my fellow citizens of Peoria. I appreciate the kind words, and the kindness of all of you." Bill waved his right hand to the crowd. "I especially want to thank the staff at Peoria Methodist Hospital. Without their help, and the help of my sister, Monica, I wouldn't be able to walk to this podium."

An obviously inebriated rally attendee yelled, "Will you marry me, Monica."

"Too late, fella she's already engaged," Bill yelled back.

After a brief pause for the crowds' laughter and cheers to subside, Bill turned to Milt. "Of course, one person here that I owe much more than a thank you to is the Sergeant sittin' in back of me. If it were not for his heroic acts, I would not be here. I will forever be in his debt, and I am honored to introduce to you the bravest man I've ever met in my life—Sergeant Milt McCoy."

Milt stepped forward as the crowds crescendo overwhelmed his emotions. He took a moment to survey the crowd as he collected himself. *This crowd may not be as large as the Chicago one, but it sure is louder. Maybe it's because we're inside an armory instead of out on a pier. The place is packed. I can't believe that my old man*

showed up again. Looks like he's drawing a crowd of cops, and some-
body is in his face, but I can't see who it is. Whoever it is sure has the
old man's attention.

"Good afternoon, Peoria. Like Private Bill Wilder said, I'm Sergeant Milt McCoy. Thanks for invitin' me to join y'all today. It's a fine day in Peoria, but somewhere out there in the Pacific there are some soldiers that don't think it's so fine. Our hearts are with them, but they need more than just our well wishes." Milt paused as he tried to remember the rest of what he was supposed to say.

Just as Milt was about to continue, he heard from the back of the crowd a lone voice say, "Yeah, but your thieving ass sure ain't there like it should be."

Oh crap, here we go again. Wait a minute, now I can see whose
chewing on the old man. Hell, it's Jerry, and he sure did just now land
a good right cross on the old man.

With jangled nerves, Milt continued, "That drunk in the back is right. I'm not there, but my thoughts are. But he is also wrong. I wasn't sent here by the War Department to steal from you folks. If I didn't believe that the fight we are fightin' was a righteous one, I'd agree that askin' folks to buy bonds would make me a thief. Now, I know I'm no genius, but, one thing I know for sure is that we are doin' the right thing. The world didn't need Hitler, and it's for darn sure it doesn't need any more of Tojo! Now, please folks, dig deep and buy the War Bonds that will give us the bombs and bullets we need to kick that Jap's butt all the way to hell!"

Milt waited for the crowd's roar to die down. *Where the hell*
did I come up with all those words? I better quit while I'm ahead.

"Thank you Peoria, and please buy as many War Bonds as you can afford. God bless, you," Milt yelled as he waved to the crowd and retreated to his seat.

Vi grabbed Milt's arm in a tender embrace and smiled, one of her special smiles that came from her twinkling eyes as well as her widening lips. "I'm so proud of you. You were wonderful. I was so scared for you when your dad started yelling, but you handled it so well."

"Thanks, sweetheart. You weren't the only one scared. My legs went weak. I have no idea where all those words came from. Did you see Jerry and my dad?"

"No, I couldn't see anyone but you. I love you so much, and I'm so proud to be Mrs. McCoy." She kissed him lightly on his cheek.

"I love you too sweetheart. Too bad you couldn't see them. The old man didn't surprise me, but Jerry sure did."

"Why?"

"Cuz, he was back there with Frank chompin' on his butt real good before the old man yelled his crap. After Frank spit out his crappy words, Jerry shut him up with a great right cross. The old man went down like a sack of potatoes."

"Is Jerry still out there?"

"I don't know. I was kinda busy trying to think of words, so I lost track of him."

Before Vi could respond, a young man silently approached Milt from the rear of the podium and handed a note to Milt. "Sergeant, Under-Secretary Powell asked me to deliver this to you."

"Thank you," Milt said to the departing message bearer.

"What does it say?"

"He apologized for my father's behavior, and asked us to join him for supper tonight at our hotel."

* * *

"Do you have a reservation, sir?" The thin, pencil-mustached man standing at the entrance of the Hotel Pere Marguette's dining room asked.

"Uh, no sir. We were invited to meet our friend Under-Secretary Jerry Powell for supper."

"Oh yes. He did tell me to expect you. Right this way, sir, madam," the formally attired man said as he subtly pointed towards the rear of the dining room.

As they made their way to the waiting Jerry Powell, Milt and Vi were stopped by numerous well wishers, all of them strangers, but all of them with words of praise for not only Milt's bravery, but also his words of earlier that day. *This being famous can be a pain. All I wanted to do was have supper with my wife and our friend.*

Jerry noted Milt's discomfort and came to his rescue. "There you are. I was starting to think we would have to start without you. If you would, please excuse us folks, Sergeant McCoy is on a rather tight schedule."

Approaching Jerry's table, Milt noticed another gentleman seated at the table. Milt extended his hand to the slender, full mustached man. "Good evening, I'm Staff Sergeant Milt McCoy, and this is my wife Vi."

Before the tall, distinguished looking man could reply, Jerry said, "Milt, I would like to introduce you to the Secretary of War, Mr. Henry Stimson."

Oh did I ever step in it this time. He's the big boss. "Pleased to meet you, sir."

"Likewise, young man, I've been looking forward to meeting you ever since I heard your inspiring words earlier today."

"Uh, thank you sir. We're pleased that you could join us for supper."

"I wish I could. I needed to chat with the Under-Secretary, and, unfortunately, the only time available to me was the brief period of time before you were to meet him for supper. I wish I could stay, but I have a plane to catch. Nice meeting you young man, and your lovely bride." The Secretary excused himself and left.

"That sure was a surprise. Hope my screwin' up Chicago wasn't why he was here for this rally. Did he see all of it? Including you deckin' my old man?"

"Afraid so, that's one of the reasons he insisted on meetin' with me."

"Oh. Did me and my old man get you in trouble?"

"No, not at all. He did mention the incident, but that is about all. Said something in passing about how I should have let the Peoria police handle your father."

"I gotta admit I was surprised you took care of the old man. Where did you get that wicked right cross from?"

"Some of my boxing skills finally paid off," Jerry said in a sheepish tone.

"Boxing? You were a boxer before you went to work for the War Department?"

"I wish I could share some pugilist exploits with you, but unfortunately, I can't."

"Why not? We won't tell anyone."

"I'm sure you won't. No, what I meant is, I never boxed."

"Jerry, you're really confusing me. I saw what you did to my old man."

"Yes, but that is the first time I ever landed a punch on something other then a heavy bag. You see, my father, who was a huge man and quite the brawler when he was younger, enrolled me in a boxing club when I was twelve. But, I never did box in the ring."

"How come? From the looks of what you did today, you woulda done just fine."

"Same reason I fought the war from the safety of a War Department desk. You see, much to my father's disappointment, I couldn't pass the physical. The doctor detected my heart murmur, so my life changed."

"Oh, I'm sorry to hear that, but believe me, you didn't miss a thing. Does your heart murmur make things hard for ya? I've been around you for about a month now, and you seem okay to me."

"I've learned to live with it. The only limitation I have is that I must not engage in prolonged physical activity. Consequently, I never was allowed to box or shoulder arms for my country."

Their table was suddenly besieged by a small, efficient staff of waiters bearing dishes that delighted the eye and filled the room with delicious aromas. "Sirs, madam, may we serve you?"

Before Milt could protest that they had not ordered, Jerry said, "Yes, please, the lady gets the Cordon Bleu, and the Sergeant and I, the steaks."

Vi smiled. "I've always wanted to try Cordon Bleu, but we never were in a restaurant that served it."

"Milt mentioned, in Chicago, that one day you'd like to try its unique taste. Tonight you will fulfill your culinary dream as my guest."

"Thank you, but you didn't need to do that."

"Yes, I did, Mrs. McCoy. This is a night to celebrate, and a night to thank my friend, your husband, for all he did for me."

"Uh, you might be makin' a bit too much out of me, Jerry. I can't recall doing much for you except trotting around the world tryin' not to forget the words you gave me to say at the rallies."

"What you did in Chicago, and your calming presence during the trip to Peoria did wonders for me," Jerry said as he placed his right hand on his chest.

"That wasn't much. I really don't understand. Chicago was really just doing what you said I should. I helped you on that plane just like I would do for anyone."

"I agree, but watching you and listening to you inspired me, and made me realize that we were more alike than not. Your father and mine were much more the same than perhaps you know."

"Oh come on, Jerry. My old man is just a drunken old sinner. From what you told me about your pa, I doubt they are the same."

"On the surface they are different, but they both are the same in one way. Both of them discounted their sons. Your father thought of you as a bum, and mine thought of me as a worthless physically deficient son. Both had a vision of how we should be, and when we didn't meet the vision, they had no use for us."

"Whoa," Milt said as a noticeable deep exhale escaped him.

Vi noticed both men lean back into their chairs. Hoping to lighten the night, Vi said, "This Cordon Blue is all I thought it would be and then some. The asparagus with its sauce is exquisite. Thank you, Jerry."

"I'm so glad you like it," Jerry said as he slowly recovered from his pensive mood.

"Jerry, you said that this was a night of celebration. Is there anything in particular we are celebratin'?"

Gesturing to the nearby waiter, Jerry said, "Yes, there certainly is! I almost forgot. Thank you for asking, Vi."

"May I be of further service?"

"Yes, bring me a bottle of your finest champagne and three glasses."

"Uh, Jerry, I appreciate you getting champagne for us, but I don't drink."

"I'm sorry. I forgot. When the waiter returns, I will ask him to bring something else for you and your lovely bride."

"Appreciate it. This must be some sort of extra special celebration if you're orderin' bubbly."

"You might say that," Jerry said as he smiled and handed Milt a folder.

"What's this?"

"Read it, and then tell me if it isn't a good reason to celebrate."

"Your champagne, sir," the waiter said as he presented it to Jerry for his inspection.

"Thank you, and would you please bring ..."

Milt interrupted Jerry, as his eyebrows lifted in jubilant disbelief. He pointed at the folder and said, "Its okay Jerry. Ya don't need to order anything else. For this I'll make an exception. This deserves one of them there bubbly toasts."

"Dear, what is it?" Vi said, "It must be really good news for you to finally partake."

Milt ignored Vi. "Jerry, is this the real deal? I can't believe it! Am I really done with the Army?"

"Oh my, God!" Vi blurted out as tears began to ruin her mascara.

"Milt, the document you are holding clearly states that under the authorization of Secretary of War Henry Stimson, you are, as of midnight tonight, honorably discharged from the Army."

"Is that what he was signing when we walked up?"

"Yes, it was."

"Jerry, did you have anything to do with this? I thought I was supposed to return to my unit when the rallies were over? I ain't complainin', but how come I'm not goin' back?"

"You were supposed to go back after the War Department released you back to the Army. The Secretary asked me my opinion of your pending orders. He asked me if we could use you for rallies in other sections of the country."

"Heck, I woulda done rallies till my smile was permanent if that's what it took to be close to my family. Anywhere in the good old U.S. of A. beats heck out of overseas."

"I know, but we don't have many more rallies scheduled. Eventually you would have returned to your unit."

"How come he changed his mind?"

"After I told him the cost of returning you to a unit that in all likelihood would not engage the Japanese would be better spent on ammunition and bombs, the Secretary asked me what he should do. Based on the discharge papers you are holding, I'd say he agreed with me."

"Jerry, I don't know what to say except thank you very much," Milt said as he picked up his champagne glass and raised his arm towards Jerry. "The only other thing I can say is cheers to the man that made me and my family very happy. Cheers, Jerry."

Raising her own glass, as tears moistened her face, Vi added, "I thank you Jerry from the bottom of my heart."

"Your welcome, and let me be the first to welcome you back to civilian life, Mr. McCoy."

21

I wonder if that bus driver can find any more holes in the road. Every time he hits one it sure makes me wonder why in the world my old man drinks. Two glasses of champagne and I was as happy as could be, but the headache I got now sure don't make me feel so good.

After another jolt of the bus forced Milt to softly moan, Vi asked, "Are you alright, dear? Do you want me to ask the driver to let us off? I'm sure he would stop for a minute or so."

"No. No need to stop. My headache will go away once we get off this rough road."

Overhearing Milt and Vi's conversation, the chubby older man sitting across the aisle from them said, "Sergeant, pardon me for interrupting, but I might be able to help you." The fellow traveler extended his hand, and said, "Allow me to introduce myself, I'm Doctor Merle Schuman. When we get to Pekin, I'm sure the bus station will have aspirin. Take two and I'm sure your headache will be gone by the time you get to your destination."

"Thank you, sir. That's a good idea," Milt said as he rested his head on the back of his seat. "Maybe if I can grab a few winks before Pekin I'll get to feelin' better."

Fifteen minutes later, Milt heard Vi say, "Sweetheart, sweety, we're pulling into the Pekin bus station. Do you still want to get off and get some aspirin tablets?"

"Oh, thanks dear. That nap did me some good, but I think I'd better get those aspirin tablets the doctor told us about."

"Pekin, folks, Pekin," the burly bus driver yelled out. "We'll only be here for a few minutes, so don't lollygag if you get off to stretch your legs."

"Sweetheart, if you want, I'll go get the aspirin. Running to the station and back might not do your headache any good."

"That's alright. Between my long legs and this Army hero suit, I can make it to and back a bit quicker then you. My headache is almost gone. I'll be fine."

Within seconds of the bus stopping, Milt was off the bus and loping towards the station intent on a quick purchase and swift return. Rounding the corner of the station, Milt's advance suddenly slowed to a crawl. *Crap where did he come from! I forgot he's livin' in Pekin now days. Hope he doesn't see me. His back is to me, so he must be just passin' by. Sure hope my old man doesn't turn around.*

As he approached the bus station's outdoor counter Milt looked over his shoulder and noticed that Frank was still ambling along in a path directly away from the station. *Thank God, but I better keep my voice down. Last I knew, the old man still had pretty good hearin'.* In a soft voice, Milt asked, "Do you have aspirins for sale?"

"Sure enough do. But, I can't imagine a big strapping Army hero like you needin' 'em. How many do you want, son?" the bus station attendant asked in a booming voice.

Milt cringed. "Two, please. How much do I owe ya?"

"For heroes like you, ya don't owe me a thing. You need some water for 'em?"

"Thank, you. I'll take you up on the water," Milt murmured.

As the attendant got his water, Milt turned his head to see if Frank was still walking away from the station. *Crap, he's stopped. I'll bet he heard this old coot carryin' on about me bein' a hero. I hope the old fat ass keeps his voice down when he comes back.*

"Here you are, Sergeant. Hope this aspirin works for ya," the returning attendant said in a robust voice.

Before Milt could thank the attendant, the bus driver yelled, "All aboard folks, next stop is Canton and after that Farmington."

"Thanks for the aspirin," Milt said as he quickly turned and dashed for the awaiting bus.

Just as Milt arrived at the door of the bus, he heard an old familiar, but un-welcome voice yell, "By God, it is that bum of a son!"

As Milt took his seat, he heard the bus driver say to someone attempting to board, "Sir, if you don't have a ticket, you will have to leave."

"No, I won't! I'm gonna get that no good son of mine off this here bus! The Army ain't gonna protect him now," Frank said as he pointed to Milt.

"Sir, all I know is you ain't got a ticket, but he does." The bus driver screamed and pointed at Milt. "Now get off my bus, or I'll make sure you do!"

"Like hell you will," Frank yelled as he attempted to get past the bus driver.

"Yeah, I will," the bus driver said as he pushed Frank.

After Frank stumbled out the door of the bus, the bus driver shut the door and started the bus' exit from the bus station stall. Despite Frank pounding on the bus door and yelling every obscenity that he could think of, the bus began its trek to Canton without Frank.

"Sorry about that folks. Next stop is Canton. This road is a bit smoother, so sit back and relax and I'll get you into Canton in about forty five minutes," the bus driver yelled.

"Whew, that was quite a stop. I swear that old man seems to know where I'll be at before I do," Milt told Vi.

"I sure hope that is the last time he finds us," Vi said as her face turned an angry red.

"Me too! But we can't do much about it right now, so I think I'll take a nap and let the aspirins get a chance to work."

"Good idea. While you're napping, I'll read the pamphlet Jerry gave us."

"Huh! What pamphlet?"

"The one Jerry gave you at supper last night."

"I don't remember him giving me anything but those discharge papers."

"Of course you don't. He gave it to you after your second, and, thank God, your last drink of champagne," Vi said with a sigh.

"Oh, I'm sorry. Did I act like a damn fool? Did I embarrass you?" Milt's face dropped while it turned red.

"No, you didn't embarrass me. You just got very happy.' She smiled and kissed him on the cheek.

"Was Jerry upset with me?"

"Didn't seem to be. He helped me get you back to our room. I think Jerry was more upset with himself than he was with you. He apologized over and over again for giving you alcohol for the first time."

"Was I that bad? After the way I behaved and this headache, I'm more convinced then ever that I shouldn't drink. I thought my old man was a damn fool! Sounds like I was actin' like a fool myself!"

Vi drew Milt in close. "Quit beating yourself up! You were just very happy. You didn't make a fool of yourself, and I am still proud to be your wife. Now, get some rest, and I'll tell you what's in the pamphlet when you wake."

What a lucky guy I am. I ain't never touchin' that crap again! No wonder my old man is such an asshole. Booze definitely brings the devil out in a person. How the hell does he git through his days' bein' hung over all the time?

Milt stirred from his nap when he heard the bus driver bellow, "Canton, folks, Canton. For you folks stoppin' here, make sure you take all your things with ya. We'll be here for about ten minutes if the rest of you folks want to stretch your legs."

As their fellow travelers seated across the aisle departed, the window on the other side was now visible. "Oh my God, Vi, you will never believe what is right across the street!"

"Don't tell me it's your dad!"

"No, it's the Walgreens where you used to work." He hugged Vi as much as the confinement of the seats allowed.

"Oh, do you think we have time to go there?" Vi said, her face contorted with pure joy.

"I don't know, lets ask."

Rushing towards the exit of the bus, Vi yelled, "Yoohoo, Mr. Bus Driver, do we have enough time to visit Walgreens?"

The driver grinned at the excited pretty young lady rushing towards him. "Only if you and your boyfriend hurry. I got a tight schedule so I can't wait."

An indignant Vi blushed as she rushed past the driver, "He's not my boyfriend, he's my husband. We'll hurry."

As they scurried towards the Walgreens, Vi asked, "Why are they all laughing?"

"Because you said I'm not your boyfriend. All I can say is, I better be. I sure wouldn't want some other guy to be."

"Oh, don't be silly, of course you are. Forever! Just like I'm your wife and girlfriend, forever!" Vi giggled as she stepped through the Walgreens front door.

With a gentle squeeze of her hand, Milt said, "Bring back memories?"

"Yes, all of them good, especially the day you walked through that door."

"Wish we could stay longer, but I think all we got time for is gettin' a soda."

"That's a great idea." She tugged Milt along the aisles to get to the soda fountain.

A very skinny, tall, coke-bottle-thick bespectacled young man stopped them. "Oh my goodness, Vi. What are you doing here? I thought you were over in Farmington."

"We're just passing through on the bus to Farmington. We thought we'd stop in for old times' sake. Jimmy. This is my husband, Milt McCoy."

"Wow! Are you the famous Sergeant McCoy I've been reading about?" Jimmy said as he grabbed Milt's hand and vigorously shook it.

"Don't know about the famous part, but I am the fella they plastered all over the paper. Pleased to meet you, Jimmy."

"Jimmy, our bus leaves in about five minutes so we're in a bit of a rush. Do you think you could serve us a soda real quick like?"

"Sure thing. Coming right up." He rushed to the other end of the soda fountain counter.

"Nice, kid, but he sure does like to pump a fella's hand," Milt said as he shook his hand in the air and faked a wince. "Has he always been the easy-to-excite type of fella?"

"Yeah, he's a sweetie-pie. All the customers love him. He was probably a bit more excited today because of your uniform. Army wouldn't take him because of his bad eyesight, so he just idolizes Army heroes."

"Here you go. You might have to drink 'em real quick. It looks like the bus is startin' to load back up. Sorry, I hurried as fast I could."

Milt put a half dollar on the counter. "You did fine, Jimmy. Wish some of my soldiers would of snapped to like you did."

"It was only twenty cents. I'll get your change real quick like," Jimmy said as he turned towards the cash register.

"Gotta run, Jimmy, keep the change," Milt said as he swallowed half of the soda in one gulp.

Oh crud, the bus is starting to roll. We better get a move on. "Come on Vi, they're gonna leave without us if we don't hurry."

"Good to see you Vi. Come back when you and your husband got more time to visit," Jimmy yelled as he waved to the departing McCoys.

"Nice seeing you, too."

What in the hell is that bus driver doin'? He's makin' a U-turn. Farmington is the other way. Well I'll be damned. He's pullin' up in front of the Walgreens and openin' his doors.

They boarded the bus. "Thank ya, sir. That was mighty kind of you."

"Think nothing of it, Sarge. Us Big Red One vets have to look out for each other," the bus driver gruffly said.

"You served in 1st Division?" Milt said.

"Yep, I was too old for this go-around, but I was in the 1st under General "Blackjack" Pershing durin' the Great War. Glad I could help you out, Sarge. Now get comfy, and I'll try to miss the potholes," the driver said as he closed the door.

"What a small world," Milt said as he sat down. "In ten minutes we met an old friend of yours, and found out our bus driver is a vet from my outfit."

"It certainly is. It was so good to see Jimmy. That was sweet of you to give him such a big tip."

"Couldn't resist myself, I always had a soft spot for well meanin' folks that work hard."

"Yeah, he's a good egg. Speaking of good eggs, I'm sure glad our bus driver made a special stop for us. Waiting for the next bus would have been awful. I so want to get home."

"Me too, this has been quite a day. Started with a pain in the head, and then we got a Frank pain in the tail. I sure hope the rest of the trip doesn't have any pain."

"I'm sure it won't. How's your headache?"

"Much better. Those two aspirins and a nap did the trick. Did you finish readin' that pamphlet while I was nappin'?"

"Yes, and I'm sure glad Jerry gave it to us. I had no idea what the Veterans Administration was planning for us."

"Is that what the pamphlet was all about?"

"Yes, Jerry said he's going to be working for the Veterans Administration when the war is over. He said all of you veterans will get this pamphlet when they're discharged. I'm sure glad he gave us one," Vi's eyes widened with excitement.

"Why?"

"The way Jerry told it, the government doesn't want another veterans uprising like they had in '32, so they decided to make sure the vets are treated right this time. If the V.A., that's what Jerry called it, does what this pamphlet promises, then we are sitting pretty."

"Now you got me all excited. What the heck are they promising?"

"You can get $20 a week for a year or until you find a job. If you want to go to school, they'll pay for it, and the one I like a lot is that they will give us a loan for a house with nothing down. Honey, now we can buy our own place! And, you can get a chance to finish your education. Isn't that great news?" She squirmed in her seat and grinned.

"Sure is, sounds like they don't want another Coxy's Army. Who do we have to see about getting all those promises filled?"

"Jerry gave us his phone number, and he said to give him a call when we get ready to take the VA up on their promises. Look, we finally made it to Farmington."

"Good old, Jerry. Gettin' back into civilian life sure got a whole lot less scary. Right now though, from the looks of that crowd at the bus station raisin' those welcome home signs, you and I had better get spruced up and ready to hug some folks."

22

"**M**ilt, Milt, welcome home," the large crowd roared discordantly.

At the left of the crowd came well wishes in Italian accented English from Mrs. Prozini, who held a bewildered Butch up above the crowd. At the sight of his son, Milt couldn't help but notice how much his boy had grown since the last photo Vi had sent. Wading into the crowd with the intent of hugging his son, Milt was overcome by the cheering folks in the middle that he couldn't believe were at the gathering. Stately Judge Wilson, the distinguished Professor, the bear of a man Punch, and even Pastor Brown, competed with the town reprobates, Earl and Ed, to gain access to Milt's hand.

With strained patience, he endured the jubilant crowd's demands for hand shakes and their back slaps as he made headway toward his goal of hugging his son for the first time in four years. Within a few feet of his goal, Milt heard Vi say, "Sweetheart, Butch looks a bit scared. Be patient with him."

Before Milt could answer, he heard a familiar, and welcome, voice say, "Welcome home, Milt. I'm glad you're home. Butch needs a dad, and I'm too old for that job."

His handshake turned into a back-slapping hug. "Thanks, Denny. I'm ready to take on the job, but I'm real thankful you stepped into my shoes while I was gone."

Denny smiled and pointed to an advancing Mrs. Procini. "Looks like ready or not, you're about to put those shoes back on."

"Butchy, Butchy, your poppa he is a home!" Mrs Procini told Butch in her bubbly broken English. Handing Butch to Milt, she said, "Giva you poppa a bigga huggy!"

Holding his son, the inexperienced father softly said, "How you doing Butch? Remember me? I missed you so ..."

Seconds after Milt's first words to his son after a four year absence were spoken, Butch's eyes began to frantically roam the crowd. Finding his safe haven, Butch interrupted his father and lunged towards Vi as he bawled, "Mommy, Mommy!"

Vi stroked Butch's head as he squirmed in his father's arms. "It's okay, sweetheart. This is your daddy. Be a good boy and give him a hug."

"I don't want to! I want Mommy!" Butch screeched and wildly flailed his arms and legs.

"Maybe you'd better take him, honey. Let's let him get a chance to know me," Milt said, even though his face couldn't hide his disappointment.

As Vi hugged Butch and wiped away his tears, Milt turned to the crowd and said, "Thanks for the welcome home, folks. I'm so happy to be back in Farmington with friends and family.

Hope Vi and I can visit with all of you real soon. But right now, I hope you understand us skidaddlin' home so quick like. Looks like me and my family need a chance to get to know each other again."

* * *

Watching his wife fix breakfast for her family, Milt still felt like he was in a dream. It was barely a few weeks ago he was at the mercy of the Army. Sitting down with a cup of coffee at this time of day was a pleasant, almost forgotten, experience. The demands of the war, or the Army preparing for the next battle, usually blunted his desire for a peaceful cup of early morning coffee. Well rested for the first time in months, Milt felt like a new man.

Denny interrupted Milt's quiet contemplation of the joys of peaceful coffee when he joined Milt at the kitchen table. "Good morning, how are you today?"

Vi brought a cup of coffee for Denny and refilled her husband's cup. "Good morning. I'm doing great. Got one of the best nights of sleep I've got in a long time. Butch finally decided it was okay to sleep in his new bed. Our bed is just too small for all three of us."

Denny chuckled. "Yeah, it looks like the little fella is finally rememberin' who you are."

"Sure am glad he got his memory back. I was startin' to wonder if he'd ever take to me."

Balancing three full plates and a coffee pot in her hands, Vi cautiously walked towards the table and said, "Gentlemen, your breakfast is served."

Man, am I ever lucky. A beautiful lady waitin' on me hand and foot, and she can cook up a storm. This breakfast has everything any man could ask for, eggs sunny-side up, fried potatoes, and a slice of cured ham. Milt, I think you didn't get out the Army, you just died and went to heaven.

"Sweetheart, this is the kind of breakfast me and my Army buddies dreamed about. If they could see me now, they'd be green with envy. I'm sure glad your mom taught you her cookin' secrets."

"Thank you sweetheart, now let's say the blessing and eat while it's still warm," Vi said as lowered her head in prayer.

Without the usual prompting, Milt said, "Lord, thank you for this bounty, and bless the hands that prepared it. Amen."

A food devouring silence followed that was finally broken by a little voice. "Mommy, Daddy, I'm hungry."

Breaking her attention from her half finished breakfast, Vi patted the seat of the chair next to her. "I'll get you some milk and make your breakfast. Hop up into your chair, and I'll be back with your breakfast real quick like. Be a good boy while I get it."

"No! I wanna sit next to Daddy!"

Vi shot an amazed look at Milt. "Okay, you sit with Daddy."

Assisting his son's climb to his lap, Milt said, "Good morning Cyrus. I mean Butch."

Confused, his son pointed to his little chest and said, "Daddy, me not Cyrus. Me Butch!"

Milt chuckled at his son's insistence on being called by his nickname. "Sorry. You're right. You are Butch, but you also have another name."

Before her confused son could ask another question, Vi gave Butch his milk. "Here's your milk. Mommy is making your eggs." Leaning in close to Milt's ear opposite from Butch, Vi whispered, "It's okay sweetheart. He's got so used to being called Butch, I decided not to teach him his real name until he's ready for school."

He nodded as he watched Butch helping himself to some of his breakfast. "Do you like Mommy's fried potatoes? You can have some of mine if I can have some of yours when Mommy brings your breakfast."

Butch cocked his little head and said, "I like Mommy's tatoes. They're mine!"

He is full of himself this mornin'. Looks like we've got to teach him about sharin' as well as what his real name is.

Vi placed Butch's breakfast in front of the empty chair and said, "Here's your breakfast, sweetheart. Hop up in your chair."

"No! I want to eat with Daddy," Butch said as he vehemently pointed to the area next to Milt's plate.

"Today you can eat with me, but tomorrow you eat in your chair. Okay?" Milt said.

"Okay," Butch said.

The looks between the adults conveyed their relief that Butch was showing signs of accepting Milt as his father. Milt and Vi smiled at each other as if finally the family was again a family.

"Looks like someone has a new little buddy," Denny whispered to Milt.

"Yeah, he sure surprised me. I thought he might be a bit upset with me this mornin'. He wasn't too thrilled last night about sleepin' in his bed. Kids sure can be a mystery."

"Yep, speakin' of mysteries, you give any more thought about coming to work for me? I had to let that last fella go about a month before you got home. He kept takin' naps in the grease pit. Sure could use your help."

Milt reached for Vi's hand. "We were talkin' about that last night. We're a little bit afraid of us stayin' here and workin' for ya."

Before Milt could finish his explanation of their decision, Denny suddenly sat up ram-rod straight. "Oh? I don't understand. Why are you two afraid?"

"Frank. He knows where your station is and probably knows where you live. We can't let him come around raisin' cane with you and Barb."

"You got a good point, but let me worry about him."

"Wish it was that simple. Anyway, we decided that I'll work for ya just long enough to train someone to do a good job for ya. We're also gonna rent that place next to Mrs. Procini. We'd still be nearby, but we wouldn't be makin' you and Barb a target of Frank's crap. Butch is a bit attached to Mrs. Pozini, and the Signorelli boys living with her might help scare away Frank."

"As much as I hate to admit it, you two have a good plan. What you gonna do after you move on?"

"Haven't quite figured that out yet, but the biggest thing we want is for Butch to be safe from Frank."

* * *

A convertible rumbled up to Denny's station, with a series of loud, bass varoom and bam sounds that Milt couldn't identify, but the driver was one of the unforgettable characters he'd recently met.

Milt scratched his head and greeted him. "Wow, Jimmy, that's quite a car you're drivin'. It's got a Hudson hood ornament, but what kind of a Hudson is it?"

With a jump over the driver's side open window, Jimmy exited the car with the grace of a gymnast and began to profusely pump Milt's hand. Jimmy grinned. "Sarge, it's a six cylinder, hundred horse, '35 Hudson Terraplane Coupe."

"That's a new one for me. I've never heard of such a car. By the way, my name is Milt. I ain't in the Army no more, so just make it Milt."

"Okay, Sarge, I mean, Milt. Until I saw it last year at an estate sale in Canton I'd never heard of it either. Couldn't tell how good it might be cuz it was really in bad shape. I bid fifty dollars. I had a hundred dollars I'd saved. I was willin' to go to seventy five, but nobody else bid on it. So, it's my baby now."

"Looks pretty good, and sounds great. Don't mind me asking, how much it cost ya to get it fixed up?"

"Not much, I had to buy a few parts and a new top. Parts ran about $50. I did all the work myself, so I got a car that was $725 when it was new for about $100. Not bad, huh?"

"Not bad at all, in fact pretty darn good. I didn't know you were a mechanic."

"I'm just a shade-tree mechanic. Always liked tinkering with cars. I rebuilt my dads old 1930 Model A Roadster when I was a junior at Farmington High School. I was one of the few kids with a car."

"Oh, I didn't know you were from Farmington. I thought you were from Canton."

"Walgreens was the only place I could find a job when I graduated in '40. They don't pay good enough for me to live on my own in Canton, so I still live with my folks here in Farmington."

"Vi was in the class of '38. Did you know her then?"

"I knew who she was, but I didn't know her. Seniors didn't hang around with twerpy sophomores."

Milt chuckled as his thoughts wandered back to high school. "I know what you mean. I knew a few pretty seniors when I was a sophomore, but they sure didn't want to know me. Guess I should be glad she didn't know ya, or she might not of ended up with me."

Jimmy blushed and shuffled his feet. "I doubt that Sarge."

Milt sensed Jimmy's discomfort. "Anyway, what can I do for ya today?"

"Filler up, and let me check my oil."

"I'll fill your car up, but I can't be lettin' you check the oil. That's my job."

"Oh, okay."

"Gas must get a bit expensive runnin' back and forth to Canton every day."

"Not really. I use my dad's old Model A for work. It's only a forty horse four cylinder, so I don't need to fill it up to much." Pointing at the convertible, Jimmy continued. "Besides the extra gas this baby would eat, I think I'd freeze if I drove this back and forth in the winter."

"Why don't you find yourself a job here in Farmington? Sure would save you a lot of time and money if you worked close to home. Ever think of workin' as a mechanic?"

"I'd like too, but you got one of the mechanic jobs in town, and the other mechanic job belongs to an old fella that's been fixin' cars ever since Henry Ford made the first one."

"Well this might be your lucky day. Vi and I've been thinkin' of movin' on. My boss, who just happens to be Vi's dad and a darn good boss, is gonna need a good mechanic to replace me. Would you like for me to put in a good word for ya with him?"

"Wow. Would I ever! I've always wanted to be a mechanic. You think he'd be interested in takin' a chance on me?"

"I can't say for certain, but with your shade-tree experience, I've got a hunch he'll at least consider ya."

Jimmy jumped back into his car. "When will ya know if he'll take me on?"

"Tell you what, Jimmy, come back next week about the same time, and I'll introduce you to him. Meanwhile, I'll put in some good words for ya. Okay?"

As he sped away in a screech of rubber, Jimmy yelled, "Thanks, Sarge, see ya next week!"

* * *

The quiet of a not very busy day had evolved into a day of cleaning and inventorying stock. Jimmy's dull tasks were interrupted when he heard a voice repeatedly yell, "Goddammit Milt, get your ass out here."

Jimmy approached the profane, drunken old man who could barely stand, and politely said, "Milt isn't here, may I help you?"

Frank closed the gap between them, and with spittle flying said, "The only way you can help me four-eyes is to get that asshole Milt out here right now!"

Jimmy stood rigid with shock as he marveled at Frank's lack of grooming and his language. *This old fella sure is something! In five years of working at Walgreens I never ran across anyone like him. He stinks like a Peoria brewery. I'll bet he hasn't had a bath in months. He's got a mouth on him I know Pastor Brown wouldn't approve of. Wonder who this old guy is, and why does he want to see Milt?*

"I'm afraid I can't fetch Milt for you. He's not here. Maybe I can help you. By the way, I'm Jerry. What did you say your name is?" Jimmy extended his hand to Frank.

Frank swatted Jimmy's hand aside, and yelled, "Shit, four-eyes you must be deaf as well as blind. You can't help me! Got it?" Frank paused to right his balance, and grabbed Jimmy by the shirt and pressed his face into Jimmy's. "Now, goddamnit, git that no-good son of mine out here!"

Jimmy tumbled from Frank's sudden release. "Sir, I can't get him. He's not here right now, but he'll be back soon."

Frank charged Jimmy and bellowed, "Bullshit, he's hiding out in that grease pit!" Pushing Jimmy aside, Frank careened towards the entrance to the station. "I don't need any help from you. I know where his rabbit hole is!"

Jimmy regained his balance and raced ahead of Frank to block the station's garage door. "Sorry sir, I can't let you in the garage. Boss doesn't want customers in the garage."

"I'll bet he don't. That pit could hide Milt and all sorts of crap. Now get out of my way!" Frank said as he attempted to roughly push Jerry aside.

Standing his ground in spite of the push, Jimmy said, "It ain't like that sir! We just don't want customers fallin' in the pit and gettin' hurt."

"You are so full of shit, four-eyes. Move your ass out of my way!" Frank grappled with Jimmy in an attempt to clear his gateway to the garage.

"My glasses, my glasses, you knocked off my glasses! Please sir, I need my glasses. Do you see them?"

"Are these your glasses?" Frank asked in a sarcastic slurred voice as he stepped on Jimmy's glasses.

Jimmy moaned at the sound of his glasses being crushed. "Oh no, not my glasses! I'm almost blind without them."

"Too bad! Now where you hidin' Milt?" Frank said and sneered at Jimmy, who was blindly searching for a pathway out of the garage.

"I swear mister, I ain't hidin' him!" *Oh please God help me find the garage door. I can't see it so please Lord, guide me.* "Owwww, oh that hurts," Jimmy moaned moments after he fell into the grease pit. " Help me mister, I think I broke my leg. Oh God, it hurts."

Jimmy's moans of pain were overcome by Milt shouting, "What the hell have you done, dad?"

"I ain't done shit! That blind-ass four-eyes, fell into the pit."

"Yeah, after he knocked off my glasses and stepped on 'em. He didn't believe me that you weren't here," Jimmy yelled from the bottom of the pit in a painful angry voice.

"Dammit Dad, you've went too far this time! I'm calling the cops!"

"No you ain't!" Frank grunted as he attempted to land a wild punch on Milt's jaw.

"Oh yeah, I am!" Milt ducked Frank's punch and kicked his feet out from under him. "Jimmy, are you all right? After I get the Sheriff over here to take my dad in, I'll take you to the Canton hospital."

Jimmy moaned. "I'm hurtin', but I can wait. Do what you have to do."

"Sheriff, this is Milt down at the Sinclair Station. Could you come over as soon as possible?" Milt yelled into the station's phone.

"Sure thing, you sound a bit upset," Sheriff Deputy Clark said.

"Yeah, my dad showed up, and busted Jimmy's leg while I was over at the post office. He took a swing at me, but I knocked him out cold. I sure could use your help."

"Be there in two shakes of a lamb's tail," Deputy Clark said as he hung up.

"Okay Jimmy. Let's get you out of the pit," Milt said as he walked back into the garage. Looking over where he had left his unconscious father, Milt said, "Jimmy, where did my old man go?"

"He came to a few minutes ago, and said something about he knows where you live. Then he stumbled out the back door."

"Oh crap! Jimmy, Deputy Clark is on his way over. Tell the Deputy to load you into his car, and meet me at Mr. Stewart's house. Lock the front door when ya leave."

"Okay, don't worry about me."

Milt ran to the station phone and called the Stewart residence. Before Denny could greet him, Milt in a quick, but calm, voice said, "Denny, Frank was at the station while I was at the post office. He didn't find me so he's headed your way. I'll be there in a jiff."

"Yeah, I know. He's out front screamin' his head off."

"Sorry about that, I'm on my way," Milt shouted and hung up.

Please God, don't let Frank hurt them. This ain't worth it. I oughta just pay that old bastard off with my musterin' out money. Don't know if it would get him off my ass, but I'm tempted.

"Mine Inspector, open this here door, you chicken shit!" Frank yelled.

As he approached the Stewart residence, Milt collected himself. "Get away from that door, Frank! They ain't done anything to you. You wanted me, so here I am."

"Damn right, I want you!" Frank said as he lurched towards Milt. "Now, pay up you no good bum."

"Let's get something straight Dad, I ain't no bum! If anyone is one you sure as hell are." Milt said, hoping his father would react. *Keep flapping your gums you old reprobate. Longer I can keep him talkin' the more time Deputy Clark's got so he can get here before the old man gets completely out of control. Screw paying him off. Even if he is my dad, I'm chargin' this old bastard.*

Frank raised his fist and shook it at Milt. "You gotta be shittin' me! I ain't the one that stole CCC money."

"Maybe not, but I didn't either. I don't owe you a damn dime!"

Lunging towards Milt in an attempt to grab Milt's throat, Frank hissed, "You owe me plenty, and I'm gonna choke it right out of ya!"

"No you won't sir, now take your hands off of Milt," Deputy Clark's voice of authority boomed.

Startled, Frank sheepishly said, "Afternoon, Deputy. This ain't what it looks like. Ya see, we were just funnin'. Weren't we Milt?"

Milt glared at Frank. "Maybe you were having fun, but me, and Jerry, and my family, sure as hell weren't." Milt turned towards the deputy. "Afternoon Deputy, I'm sure glad to see ya. Appreciate it if you'd arrest this old drunk that's got the nerve enough to call me a bum of a son."

"Milt, I'm your father! This ain't right! You can't ask the law to lock me up."

"Maybe he can't, but I can!" Denny boomed as he joined Milt and patted him on the back.

"Me too!" Jimmy yelled from the front seat of the Deputy's patrol car.

"Guess what Dad, so can I!"

* * *

Staring at the departing patrol car and its noisy occupants, Milt and his extended family were speechless. Jimmy moaned in pain with every abrupt move of the car, Frank continued his drunken, profane outbursts, and Deputy Clark altered between words of compassion for Jimmy and blunt commands for silence directed at Frank.

Some of the key players in the day's drama were gone, but Denny's little patch of Farmington still felt the chill that Frank's disturbance had brought over the day.

My old man sure showed his ass this time. Milt marveled as he hugged Vi. *He shook everybody. Vi sure is upset, I can feel her shakin'. She even has goose bumps. Denny looks like he's so angry he's about to shake apart. Little Barb's eyes couldn't get much bigger. She's only fifteen. She doesn't need to see this kinda crap. I've got to do somethin' about this! None of us needs to keep puttin' up with this. As long as I'm handy, Frank will keep coming back for another piece of me.*

"Daddy, is it okay if I go to Bev's house? She asked me to spend the night," Barb asked.

"Is her mom and dad gonna be home tonight?"

"Yes, Daddy. Her mom is making something special for dinner. Bev says they're celebrating her brother coming home."

"Okay, but instead of coming home tomorrow morning, go over to Vi's. Spend the day with her. I don't want you home by yourself until the Sheriff tells me what they're gonna do with Frank. Understand?"

"Yes, Daddy, I'll come home after you close the station," Barb said.

Milt watched Barb depart. "I'm sorry about this Denny. We sure didn't need this, and Barb's too young to have to see Frank show his butt."

"It's not your fault. But, I agree, she's too young for such goings on. I'm havin' a hard enough time raisin' her without Sarah. Folks like Frank sure don't make it easier"

"I know, and that's one of the reasons why me and Vi need to clear out of here."

"I don't know that your leavin' would solve things."

"Kinda agree with you. But at least Frank wouldn't be coming over to Farmington lookin' for me."

"Maybe I could help you get him that CCC money. That's the only reason he keeps comin' around."

"I thought about payin' Frank my CCC money, but I got a hunch he'd still keep showin' up and raisin' cane. It ain't just the CCC money. Him and I never got along. Every time he'd get a snoot full he'd be over here. We just can't stay and put you and Barb through any more of his shenanigans."

"As much as I'll miss Vi and that little rascal Butch, I think ya might be right. But where ya gonna go?"

"Vi and I were talkin' about it just yesterday. We're thinkin' about headin' over to Galesburg after Jimmy's ready to take my job at the station."

"What's waitin' for ya over in Galesburg?"

"Nothin' really, but I do know some folks over there."

"I forgot you went to school over there. Do you know folks that can help ya?"

"Not really. None of 'em got any work for me, but they might know folks that do. The biggest reason we're thinkin' of goin' there is that it's in Knox County."

"Oh, I get it. Frank's not about to come near Knox County, or Sheriff Foster would make sure that his next stop would be the Federal pen."

"Yep! I'll find work over there and Frank won't be botherin' us. Looks like I'll win more ways then one."

"Hate to see ya go. I'll miss all of you. But I know it's best. Galesburg ain't that far away, so I expect y'all to visit every so often," Denny said as he hugged Milt and Vi.

"We will, Daddy. Butch will be lost without you to pester."

"Our home will always be open for ya. We'll miss you too. If it wasn't for my dad we wouldn't even be thinkin' about movin'."

"I know. When you fixin' to leave?"

"Hard to say, but we sure won't be going until Jimmy's leg is mended and I can find work. I'm guessin' some time close to Halloween."

"That's not that far off. You'll need to get crackin' on findin' a job. If you'd like, Judge Wilson and I could ask a few folks we know over in Galesburg to keep their eyes open for ya."

"That would be great. Thanks."

* * *

Vi opened the kitchen door and looked at the bare kitchen table. "Are we too early?"

"Come on in, Sis, you can help me. I've never made this much food before," a worried looking Barb stirred one of the pots then adjusted the temperature of the oven. "I don't know how Mom cooked so much on that old wood stove. This new gas stove is wonderful, but it doesn't make cookin' a snap."

Poor Barb looks like she's about to fly apart. I hope she ain't nervous cuz of us joinin' them for dinner. Maybe we can cheer her up. "From the smell of things, you're doing fine, Barb. And the way Butch is droolin', I'd say he's likin' the idea of diggin' into your home cookin'. Butch, are you ready for your Aunt Barb's supper?" Milt said.

"Yummy, yummy, I'm hungry. I want to eat," Butch said as he climbed into the kitchen table chair he had claimed as his own over the past few years.

"See, nothing to worry about. Butch likes it already."

"Your meal will be fine. Mom showed both of us plenty of her cooking secrets. You probably learned better then I did," Vi hugged her sister and brushed a wisp of hair away from Barb's eyes.

"I doubt that! Besides, I haven't cooked big meals before."

"That doesn't make you a bad cook. It just means you haven't had the chance to practice all that Mom taught you."

"Grampa, Grampa, I'm here." Butch screamed as he climbed down from his chair. In a flash, the rushing Butch collided with Denny's legs.

"Evenin' everyone." Denny grinned and picked up Butch. "You know it's sure a good thing this boy ain't six inches taller. How you doin', ya little rascal?"

"I'm not a rascal! I'm a boy!" Butch protested as he beat his little fists on Denny's chest.

"Yeah, but I love you anyway. Now give me a big hug," Denny hugged his grandson. Freeing one of his arms, Denny extended his hand to Milt. "Glad you McCoys' could join us for supper, and, maybe, a celebration."

"I'm glad you invited us. How did you know we might have something to celebrate?" Vi asked and hugged her father. "You and Milt keep Butch entertained while I help Barb."

"Okay, but now you got me wondering who's gonna kick off the celebration – you or me? Mine can wait till supper if yours can," Denny said but his face betrayed his anxiousness. He started for the back door, "Come on Butch, I heard you learned how to do a summersault. Why don't ya show me and Daddy your new trick?"

Butch ran for the back yard, and attempted a summersault. "Look at me!" he squealed.

Watching Butch laugh and repeatedly do his latest tumbling discovery, Milt wondered, *how will Butch take the move? He loves that old man so much. Reminds me of how much I loved my grandpa.*

"How's Jimmy workin' out?" Denny asked as he applauded Butch's umpteenth summersault. "Milt, Milt, did ya hear me, or were you somewhere else just now?"

"Sorry, I was thinking about you and Butch and my grandpa. Jimmy's doin' fine. He surprised me after he got out of the hospital. His broken leg doesn't slow him down a bit. We got him a new pair of glasses too."

"Yeah, I was kinda amazed myself at how fast he recovered. But, I guess what I'm asking is— is he ready to take over for ya?"

"He was ready a few days after he came to work for ya. Kid knows his way around cars, and the customers seem to really like him. Why ya askin'?"

Vi stuck her head out the back door and said, "Supper's ready. Get washed up, and get ready for Barb's wonderful meal."

Leading the stampede, Butch brusquely pushed the screen door and yelled, "Chicken, chicken, yum. I like chicken."

"Well at least someone likes my cooking." Barb smiled as she anxiously smoothed out her apron.

"Butch! You know better. Now you get yourself down from your seat and wash your hands." Vi sternly corrected Butch even though her eyes were smiling at Butch's enthusiasm. "And, you wash that pout off your face. Aunt Barb's meal won't go anywhere while you're washing up."

Protests from Butch resolved, everyone sat in front of a spread that rivaled any meal that Barb's mother used to offer. "If everyone will bow their head in prayer, today I would like to give the blessing." After a few moments to allow Vi the time to instruct Butch as to the proper manners of prayer, Denny said, "Thank you, Lord, for this bounty that you have provided, and bless the hands that lovingly, and carefully, prepared it. Please watch over us in the days to come. Especially watch over the McCoy family as they start their journey. In Jesus' name we pray. Amen."

"Amen."

"Denny, ya stumped me when ya asked the Lord to especially watch over my family. What journey ya talkin' about?"

Denny grinned. "I often wondered if hungry folks paid attention to the blessing. Sounds like I didn't sneak that one past ya."

"You didn't sneak it past me either, Dad. What journey?"

"The move to Galesburg, which might come sooner then you think. Milt tells me Jerry is ready to take over, and I think Pastor Brown might have found Milt a job."

"Oh, well that is a surprise. When are we moving?" Vi asked.

Before Denny could answer, Milt asked, "What kind of a job?"

"Tell you what. I'll tell you all about it right after supper. Barb worked too hard for us to let her meal get cold while we chat. Okay?"

"Okay. But then you'll get your BIG surprise," Vi said as she smiled.

"What is it?"

"Not fair, Dad, if we've got to wait, so do you," Vi said wagging her finger at Denny.

"Fair enough. Pass the chicken, please," Denny reached for the passing plate of Barb's fried chicken.

What kind of a job could Pastor Brown dig up for me that would provide for my family? I hope it's a good one. If it ain't, I sure will need Vi's help to figure out how to turn it down.

"Barb, that sure was good. Looks like Butch approves," Denny said pointing at his grandson who was licking his plate.

"Oh, good Lord, Butch, you know better then that. Stop licking your plate, this instant. If you want more, just ask like a civilized little boy."

Butch held up his plate and sheepishly pleaded, "Can I have more, Aunt Barb?"

"How do you, ask?" Barb said in imitation of Vi's childrearing standards.

"Please, can I have more?"

While Barb and Vi settled Butch into his second helping, Denny turned to Milt. "While we're waiting for the growing boy to finish up, I might as well tell you about your new job."

"From the sounds of it, I'd say you're pretty sure I'll be taking it."

"Nope, but it is right up your alley."

"Dad, please, before we die of suspense, what is it?"

"Well, Pastor Brown asked the Presbyterian pastor in Galesburg if he knew of any jobs open for a mechanic. Turned out he not only knew of one, but he was the boss lookin' for someone."

"What in the heck does a Presbyterian pastor need a mechanic for?"

"Funny, I asked the same question. Seems this here pastor owns a dairy, and his fella that keeps the machines runnin' has one foot in the grave and the other on a banana peel."

"What kinda machines? I got a hunch keepin' 'em runnin' isn't all the fella does. I ain't milkin' no cows for a livin'."

"Can't blame you there, but this dairy ain't the farm kind. It's the Heavenly Dairy, where they pasteurize the milk and turn it into all sorts of dairy stuff. You know, like butter and ice cream."

"Ice cream, oh boy, Ice cream. I want some," said Butch.

"We'll see, but first eat your chicken, and let me talk to your daddy. Okay?"

"Okay," Butch said as a slight pout began to appear on his lower lip.

"Heavenly Dairy. I've heard of it. I'd heard it's owned by a pastor. If I remember right it's on the east side of the CB&Q tracks up near the north edge of town. Wonder, what in the heck kinda mechanic work I'd be doing."

"Don't rightly know, but I imagine you'll find out when ya go talk to Pastor Swenson next week. Should I tell Pastor Brown to set the meetin' up?"

"Sounds good. If it gets us away from Frank and pays good, I'll take it. I don't much care what I'm doing as long as I'm not in Farmington. We really need to get out of here!"

Leaning back in his chair Denny rubbed his chin. "I understand wantin' to get out of town, but not needin' to right away. What's the big rush?"

Vi smiled and blurted out her BIG surprise, "The rabbit died. We want to move before I get too far along."

Before everyone could congratulate Vi and Milt, all of the adults at the table burst into laughter when Butch vehemently pointed out the window towards the garden and said, "No, Mommy. The rabbit isn't dead. He ate Grandpa's peas."

23

"**D**addy's home, Mommy, Daddy's home," Butch squealed as he pointed out the window towards a tall man loping along the shaded lane that led to the McCoys second story apartment.

Vi peered through the window and softly patted her son's shoulder. "He's almost here. Let's surprise Daddy at the door."

The door opened just as Milt reached for the door knob. His balance disturbed, Milt stumbled forward into his smiling son's arms. "Daddy sure is glad ya grabbed me, or I'd been down flat on my face," Milt said as regained his balance.

Vi laughed at the two loves of her life. "Welcome home, dear. I guess we almost were a little too glad to see you. How was your first day?"

"Good. The Pastor showed me around, and the guys all seemed to be a good bunch. The old fella I'm takin' over for was good about it. Poor old guy looks like he's on his last leg."

Vi hugged Milt and ruffled Butch's hair. "I'm glad you had a good day, but now you are all ours. Do you want some coffee before supper?"

"No, thanks, I think I'll take this little guy out and let him blow off some steam. Butch, you want to go for a walk with Daddy?"

"Yes, Daddy!" Butch tugged his father towards the door.

"Supper will be in about thirty minutes." Vi smiled and waved as her family rapidly descended the stairs.

* * *

Milt gazed fondly at the abundant, lush green canopy that made the hot, humid summers of mid-state Illinois tolerable *One thing about Galesburg I missed are these beautiful elm trees.* Distracted by the overhead sight, Milt stubbed his foot and stumbled. *I sure didn't miss these damn brick sidewalks. Bricks keep lifting as the elm tree roots grow. Damn walks are never even. Teach me to be gawkin' at the tree tops instead of watchin' my step.*

"You're funny Daddy," Butch giggled.

"Why's Daddy so funny?" Milt smiled at his son.

"You walk funny." Butch said, as he imitated his father's stumbling gait.

Before Milt could answer him, he heard a voice from the past say, "You sure do, Soapy."

Milt looked towards the bubbly female voice who had just reminded him of his high school nickname. "Oh my Lord, it's Betty Hartmann! I haven't seen you in ages. How are you, and who is that little fella holdin' your hand?"

Betty smiled, and giggled, as she often used to do in high school, and said, "Actually it's Betty Howard now, and I'm doin' great. It is so nice to see you after all these years." Pointing down to a slightly chubby young boy who was trying to hide behind her, she said, "This is my son, Roger. He's a little shy."

Before Milt could say hello to Roger, Butch tugged at Milt's pant legs and asked, "Who's Soapy?"

"I am. Mrs. Howard used to call me that a long time ago." Quickly changing the subject before his son's inquiries would monopolize conversation, Milt asked Betty, "How old is your son? He looks about the same age as Butch."

"He's four, and from the looks of it they are going to get along just fine," Betty said as they watched their sons bolt away from them in a game of chase.

"Yeah, it looks like your son can be a ball of fire, just like Butch."

"You'll have to bring him over some time and let them play. We live over on South Street. Tell your wife I'm always home."

"I'll tell Vi. I'm sure she would love to bring Butch over. We're livin' in an apartment until work sorts out, so I'm sure any excuse for her to get out and about would be welcome. Where abouts on South Street do you live?"

"We're at 724 South Street. If you folks aren't doin' anything Saturday, why don't you drop over for supper? I'd love to meet your wife, and introduce the rest of my family."

"That would be great. What time? Anything we can bring?"

"Supper will be about 5:30, okay? Come early for coffee. You don't need to bring anything."

"Great, we'll be over a little before five. Now, I better grab that young'n of mine. Supper's in about five minutes, so we better skedaddle. See you Saturday."

* * *

Butch burst through their apartment door and yelled, "I'm home. The lady said Daddy was Soapy."

"Well hello to you too, Butch. Soapy?"

"Daddy, Soapy," Butch said as he climbed into his chair.

"Dear, I thought you were Milt. Is there some old secret I should know?" Vi teased as she hugged Milt. "Why don't you men get ready for dinner, and then you can tell me about your day and your secret name."

"Come on Butch, we need to wash up." Milt turned towards Vi and whispered, "Before my dear wife knows all my secrets."

"Get out of here, and come back ready for explainin'," Vi said as she flicked her kitchen towel towards Milt's departing backside.

After two minutes of squirming around the water faucet, the wet handed Butch escaped the bathroom in a mad dash for the supper table. "I'm hungry," a determined Butch commanded.

"That was quick," she said to Milt as he took his chair at the head of the table.

"Yeah, I guess dryin' his hands ain't something he thought necessary." Milt shook his head and grinned. "You might bring that towel you know how to use on my tail."

Butch leaned over and looked intently at the back of Milt's chair, and said, "You don't have a tail, Daddy."

"Sit up, Butch, and get ready for supper." Vi set the pot roast on the table.

"Looks good, dear, and smells even better. I was hoping for pot roast, but I thought we were out of beef ration coupons."

Vi served her husband, then cut Butch's meat for him. "That's the last of the coupons. Enjoy. We won't get any more beef for a week."

"Sure will be glad when Truman stops the rationing. War's over, so why do we still have to ration?"

"That's beyond me, dear. Anyway, tell me about your day."

"Not much to tell. Didn't do a whole lot today, except get the skinny on the machines I'll need to keep runnin'. Not like car machinery, but most of it is easy to figure out."

"What's the boss like?"

"You mean the Pastor. He doesn't like being called boss. Says we only got one boss, and he's in heaven. Didn't chat with him much today, but he said he wanted to talk to me later on about education I can get at night."

"Oh, I heard the business college and Knox College will be offering night school that the GI Bill will pay. That's nice of the Pastor to think of that for you."

"Yeah, but I just started on the job. He might be gettin' ahead of himself. Oh, by the way, I met an old high school friend while Butch and I were out and about. She's got a cute little four year old that Butch took to right away."

"That's nice. Do they live nearby?"

"About two blocks away on South Street. She invited us to supper Saturday night. I hope it's okay, I told her we would be there at five."

"It's fine, but I don't have anything to wear. Our baby is growing so fast. Nothing that's nice fits anymore."

"Don't worry about that. You look fine in what you have on. Betty is salt of the earth, and has a heart of gold. You'll like her. Besides, I know you're dying to find out why she called me Soapy."

* * *

"I'm hungry, let's eat!" Butch commanded.

"In a few minutes, my dear son. But, first change out of your church clothes."

"Why? I'm hungry now!"

"Do what your mother said and quit askin' why. You don't want to get your Sunday suit that Grandpa bought you dirty, do you?"

Milt smiled as he watched his disappointed son depart for his bedroom. "That boy sure is full of himself today. He hasn't wound down since we visited the Howards last night. It was a miracle we got him and Roger calmed down long enough to eat Betty's delicious supper."

"I'm glad he's made a friend. The Howards seem like such nice folks."

"I change my clothes. Can I eat now?" Butch said as he ran for his chair.

Vi smiled. "Okay, you two men get seated, and I'll get our dinner."

As she returned, the aroma of their now uncovered Sunday dinner filled their home. "Oh boy, Butch, smells like we're gonna eat real good today."

"Not until we say our blessings. Would you lead us in our thanks, dear?" She said as she prompted Butch to lower his head and clasp his hands.

"Thank ya Lord for guidin' us through this busy week, and the Sunday feast we are about to enjoy. Bless the hands that prepared this bounty, and watch over us in the days to come. In Jesus' name we pray. Amen."

"Thank you, dear. Now, we can partake in the Lord's bounty," Vi said.

"It sure is good to have our first Sunday dinner in our new home. I can't believe ya made such a fine meal so soon after church. Butch barely had time to get out of his Sunday best."

"I love you both so much. I wanted our first Sunday dinner to be a good one we didn't have to wait for. Both of you this past week have made me proud of you, so I used one of my mom's old cooking tricks. Mom always had a Sunday dinner waiting on us when we got home."

Milt reached for her hand. "I love you too, sweetheart. You have no idea how much I appreciate all you do for us."

Butch squirmed. "I'm hungry, Mommy. I want to eat!"

She served Butch some of the left over pot roast she had converted into a hearty stew. "That sure was a nice evening we had yesterday. I really like the Howard's. Betty has an infectious laugh, and her husband Wayne seems like her pleasant, quick-witted perfect match. Butch sure took to their sons Roger and Paul."

"Gotta admit, I enjoyed it too, even if I did have to listen to Betty tell about one of my most embarrassin' times. I knew you'd like her. When we were in school together, you could always count on her to make ya laugh."

"Betty sure got a kick out of telling us about your nickname. She was laughing so hard when she told us I thought she was going to cry. I can just see you on-stage saying your lines and blowing bubbles out of your pipe. Couldn't you see that some-one had put soapy water in the pipe?"

Milt blushed, after all these years, at the embarrassment. "If I hadn't been scared out of my mind I mighta noticed. Only reason I got in that play was to get the attention of a girl. I kinda enjoyin' play actin' till I saw all the folks in the audience. Got scared, and the next thing I knew I was blowing bubbles every time I spoke."

Vi teased. "Well did you get her attention?"

"Yep, but the wrong kind. She's the one that started cal-lin' me Soapy. Nicknames like that aren't exactly the kind that make girls swoon. Oh well, just as well. I might never have met you if I'd had a high school sweetheart."

Vi smiled. "Then I guess I owe whoever put that soap in your pipe a big thank you. Anyway, eat your stew before it gets cold."

"Mommy, can I have some more please?" Butch held his bowl up.

"We don't have anymore, sweetheart. But, Mommy is bak-ing an apple pie for dessert."

"Oh boy, pie and ice cream," Butch squealed.

"Apple pie sure sounds good. I know it smells great. Do we have any coffee left from breakfast?"

"I'll get you a cup, and then you can tell me more about what the boss, I mean the Pastor, talked to you about."

"Here you are," Vi said handing Milt his coffee. "Not certain, how good it is. You might need to add some cream."

"Its fine sweetheart, why don't ..."

"Can I go now?" Butch said as he scooted out of his chair. "I wanna go play."

"You're excused, sweetheart, but next time don't interrupt." After she was sure he was out of range, Vi softly said, "I swear that boy is getting cuter and cuter every day. Now that we are free of his little inquisitive mind for a moment, tell me about that education idea the Pastor talked to you about."

Stalling, Milt sipped his coffee — *Where's that little rascal when I need him. I could use one of his interruptions* — and then sipped it again. "The Pastor is a good man. He keeps talkin' about how the country owes so much to her brave soldiers. He seems to think that he owes me the chance to go to school."

"So, what are your thoughts about it?"

"For starters, I don't think he owes me anything. I appreciate him wantin' to help me, but I ain't so certain that goin' to school is a good idea."

She sat up straight with a look of disbelief. "Why not? Education never hurts, and besides the government's paying for it."

"I know, but I'm too old for schoolin'! It's been so long since I went to school. I'd probably flunk out."

She moved her chair closer to Milt, and kissed him gently. "Sweetheart, you're never too old for education. Besides, with me helping you it won't be hard at all."

"Yeah, I know. Every once in awhile I read about folks gradu-atin' that are a lot older then me. But you're forgettin' I didn't graduate from high school, so no college would take me."

"Maybe Knox won't take you, but I know you don't need a high school diploma for the business college."

"What good would graduating from a business college do me? I don't think that's what the Pastor had in mind."

"You don't know that. Promise me you'll talk to the Pastor about it."

"If it'll make you happy, and get my dessert faster, I promise."

* * *

Milt's sudden entrance surprised Vi. *He's home early, and he doesn't look very happy. This isn't like Milt. He always seems so happy with work. I'll bet it's about school.* She noted his firm grip on a paper noticeably smeared with red ink. "How was school, dear?" Pointing to the letter he was starting to wad up, Vi asked, "Is that your business writing class assignment?"

"Yeah, and the teacher bled all over it. I'm starting to think I ain't cut out for this schoolin' crap!"

"Language, dear, Butch might still be awake! I put him down early tonight. He played so hard with Roger, he almost fell asleep at supper."

"Sorry, I forgot myself. I'm just fed up with this writin' class. My accountin' class is fine. I always was good with figurin' numbers. But my writin' teacher makes me wonder if I'm some kinda idiot."

"That's okay. I know you're frustrated, but don't start doubting yourself. You've never been one to run away from challenges. Sit down, and I'll get your supper for you. While you're eating I'll look over the teacher's marks. Maybe I can help. I always did well in my English classes."

As she removed his supper from the warming oven, Milt smoothed his scrunched assignment and placed it in front of Vi's chair. "Hope you can still read this. I kinda took my temper out on it. Miracle I didn't tear it up on the way home."

"It might be a little difficult to read, but I can probably read enough of it."

"Thanks, sweetheart, these pork chops, baked with apples, smell delicious. If it's all the same to you, I'm gonna forget all about that paper, and concentrate on something I know I can still do right," Milt said with a smile as he picked up his knife and fork.

Vi smiled. "You're welcome. Don't mind me while I read this."

A quick read of Milt's first paragraph, Vi's smile faded. *How do I tell him he can't write the way he speaks? I've lost count of how many improper contractions and conjunctions he used. Numerous misspelled words, incorrect verb tenses, dangling participles, and even a few aint's sprinkled in his first four sentences. I know he didn't finish high school, but his English composition is like that of a fifth grader.*

"You made quick work of your supper, dear. Did you like your pork chops? Would you like a cup of coffee and your pipe?"

He smiled and patted his bulging tummy. "You keep feeding me like that, and folks will start wonderin' which one of us

313

is gonna have a baby. Coffee sounds great. I'd love a smoke if it won't bother you and that little bun in the oven."

"I'm far enough along now that your smoking doesn't bother us. I'll be right back with your coffee and pipe. Then I'll tell you how I might be able to help you."

She gave him a chance to get his pipe loaded and lit. "Sweetheart, I hope I don't hurt your feelings. But, I must be honest with you."

"That bad, huh?"

"Yes and no. You got your point across, but your grammar needs to improve."

Milt scrunched his face and peered through half closed eyes. "How the heck do I do that? I'm durn near twenty seven years old. If I ain't learned grammar by now . . . . when am I ever gonna learn it?"

"I have a couple of suggestions, if you want to hear them."

"Sure, but I hope you aren't gonna tell me I gotta change into some fancy pants."

"No, I like you just the way you are. All man and all mine!"

"I'm all yours, but if I can't get this here college stuff I might not be enough man to provide for the family. So what ya gonna suggest?"

"First thing, start telling yourself you can, and then use good grammar when you speak. I'll help with reminders when you don't, if you'd like me too."

"What do you mean? I don't recall folks not understandin' what I'm sayin'," Milt said in a defensive tone.

"Yes, I do understand you, but the way you speak is not proper for writing. When you write you have to pay attention to not only your point, but the words you use to make your point. It's late, so let's talk about this more tomorrow. Just remember, Milt, I love you, and I'm only trying to help."

Milt pulled her closer and gave her a slow gentle kiss. "I know you're tryin' to help me, and I love you even more cuz you're tryin' so hard for me and our family." Pulling her in a little closer, Milt grinned one of his devilish grins while rubbing noses with her and said, "Now let's get to bed."

She giggled as she broke free from him. "Let me clean the dishes first." Turning towards the awaiting kitchen disorder, Vi said over her shoulder, "Oh, I almost forgot, you got a letter from Indiana. It was sent a couple weeks ago to Dad's house. He got the mailman to forward it to us. It's on top of the Philco."

As she washed the dishes, Vi questioned whether she was hearing sobbing. Stopping to dry some of the dishes, Vi became convinced that Butch had awoken from a bad dream. She peeked into Butch's room, and was surprised to find Butch snuggled up next to his teddy bear and purring a slow, shallow snore. *That's strange. I would have swore he was crying. Must have been my imagination. No, there it is again. Oh my, it's coming from the living room.*

Entering the living room, Vi asked the red-eyed Milt, "Are you alright, sweetheart?"

"The letter is from Grandma. She's failing and wants me to come home one last time," Milt said as he struggled to hold back tears.

Vi kneeled next to him, and took Milt's hand away from his brow. "Oh, I'm so sorry. If you want, I'll make arrangements tomorrow. You must go home."

"I want to, but we can't go," Milt blubbered.

"Nonsense! It hurt you dearly that you didn't make it home in time to see your grandpa before his passing. You are going home!"

"You can't make the trip, and if you aren't goin' it's for darn sure I'm not!" Milt patted her protruding stomach.

Vi stared into his eyes. "Milt McCoy don't you worry about me! I'll be fine. I'm not due for another four months. If you like, I'll check with Doctor Alterman before we go."

"Even if the Doc says okay, I still got work and school to answer to."

"From what you've told me of him, the Pastor will give you time off. School can wait. If they give you a hard time then so be it."

With silent tears falling down his cheeks, Milt said, "I love you so much. Thanks for peppin' me up. First thing tomorrow, I'll ask the Pastor for a week and a half off. Don't want to just drive over and back. I need some time with Grandma. On the way home, I'll tell the school I'm gonna miss next week. If they got a problem with me being out, that's their problem. Let's plan on headin' out the day after tomorrow. Okay?"

"I'm sure we can start then. I'll see the doctor tomorrow."

* * *

"Indiana is beautiful! No wonder you liked it here. Seems like it has a lot more trees then Illinois, and the fall colors are gorgeous. What is that red one?"

Milt smiled, but didn't answer Vi. Instead he focused on another of Indiana's speed breaks—farm tractor that would lose a race with a turtle— that frequently clog Indiana's dusty narrow rural roads. Re-entering his lane after carefully passing the tractor and courteously waving to the farmer, Milt said, "Yeah, Indiana is really something in the fall. That Red Maple you pointed at is beautiful no matter what time of the year. You think it looks red now, you oughta see it in the summer."

Vi corrected Milt's grammar "You meant to say should, not oughta, right dear?"

"You're right, but do me a favor, please don't correct my grammar while we're visiting Grandma, okay?" Before Vi could answer, Milt's eyes widened as he broke into a big smile. "See, your lessons are working. I just said visiting, not visitin', and instead of saying workin' I said working."

"I understand. I'll wait, and, yes, I did notice." Vi said as she smiled and lightly touched Milt's forearm.

"Cows, Mommy, cows. Look, look!" Butch squealed as he pointed at the milk cows grazing in the pasture.

"Yes dear. Maybe, later on, Grandma will let you pet them."

"That's surprising," Milt said as he glanced at the cows. "I woulda bet that Grandma got rid of the milk cows after Grandpa passed."

"Are we almost there?" Vi said as she withdrew her compact from her purse.

"Almost, we turn at that next right up ahead. It's about five minutes from the turn."

Finished with her make-up, Vi said, "Butch, come up here with Mommy now, so I can comb your hair before we get to Grandma's."

"I don't want to!" Butch said in a tone that reflected his growing pout.

Milt quietly chuckled at his son's obstinance then whispered to Vi, "It's okay, sweetheart, he looks fine. If you get him up here, no tellin' how much cane he'll raise."

"I just want him to look nice for your grandma," she said as she twisted a lock of her hair.

Milt smiled and said, "You both look just fine for Grandma. Now, quit fiddlin' with your hair and relax. We're almost there."

Milt turned into the long entrance to his grandparent's place, and was struck by how orderly the farm appeared. *Wow, what a surprise! Cows in the field, clean pig sty, chickens scratchin', and the barn has even been recently painted. I'll bet that fella and young gal standin' next to Grandma had something to do with how good the old homestead looks.*

Opening the door of his '38 Hudson, which thanks to his and Jimmy's renovations ran just like new, Milt waved, and shouted, "Grandma, I'm home!" Rushing towards Grandma, he suddenly stopped and remembered his family. Embarrassed, Milt returned to the passenger side of the car, and opened Vi's door. "Sorry honey, I almost forgot ya. I didn't mean to, I'm just happy to be home."

Vi straightened her dress and smiled. "It's okay sweetie, I understand." She opened Butch's door, and noticed her son's eyes had widened and the corners of his mouth drooped. "You might need to help me with Butch. He looks a little bit scared."

"Come on Butch. You want Daddy to carry you?"

A very thin, weather-beaten older lady asked Butch, "Come on out and see Grandma. Do you like cookies?"

"I like cookies!" yelled Butch as the prospect of cookies prompted him to jump from the car before anyone was prepared to catch him. As he scrunched his face up, he let out an eardrum-piercing cry. "Daddy, I fall! I fall down!" Before Milt could respond, Butch tugged on Milt's pant leg and yelled, "Daddy, Daddy, pick me up!"

"Sorry, son, you surprised me," Milt said as he picked up his son.

Truth be told, I wasn't paying attention to him at all. I was just tryin' to figure out what happened to Grandma. She's a shadow of herself. That gingham dress hangs on her. It used to fit mighty snug. Can't believe her hair is snow white. Before I left for the Army she hardly had any gray in it. Still got that smile that can sooth the beast, but her face looks tired. I can't ever remember seeing her with dark pouches under her eyes.

Vi sensed that her husband was distracted by the obvious ill health of his grandmother, so she extended her hand and said, "Hello, I'm Milt's wife, Vi, and that young man is your great-grandson Cyrus, but everyone calls him Butch."

Grandma ignored Vi's outstretched hand, but instead closed the gap between them and hugged Vi. "Pleased to meet you, Vi. I feel like I already know you. Milt told me so much about you in his letters."

Vi blushed. "All good things, I hope?"

"Oh heavens yes, if you don't get a chance to read his letters before you go home, I'll send 'em home with you."

"Grandma! You didn't keep all of them did ya? Vi reads them she might never think the same of me," Milt said in a half-concerned, half-kidding tone.

"Yep all of 'em!" Grandma said as she defiantly crossed her arms in front of her. "Oh, my manners are slippin'. This here young man standing next to me is Warren McKenney, and the beautiful young lady by his side is his wife Fiona."

Milt extended his hand to the tall, sturdy-looking young man, and said, "Long time no see, Cousin Warren. We were just kids messing up the hay loft the last time I saw you. Good to see you again." Turning his attention to the small, barely-old-enough-to-be-wed young lady, Milt said, "Nice to meet you, Fiona, looks like Warren got a prettier wife than he had any right to expect."

The red-headed Warren shook Milt's hand and gave him a tight, one-arm hug. "Good to see ya again, Milt. Looks like ya landed a prettier gal then ya ever thought ya would, yourself."

"Warren and Fiona came to live with me after Grandpa passed. They've done wonders with the farm, and kept good care of me too." Looking down at Butch squirming in anticipation of the cookies that were offered so long ago, or at least long ago by four year old standards, Grandma offered her arms and said, "Butch, are you ready for those cookies?"

Butch leaped into Grandma's offered arms. "Yes, please."

"Okay everybody, let's go get this boy some cookies," Grandma said as she nodded towards the back door of her house.

Grandma looked towards the entrance of her driveway, as she assured Butch that cookies and milk were waiting just beyond the kitchen door. Opening the door, she motioned with her head for Warren to join her.

"Are you okay, Grandma? Do you want me to take Butch?" Warren said as he noticed a pained look in Grandma's eyes.

"I'm fine, but we got company. Get in the house before the rest of us, and get yourself out the front door with the shotgun. See if you can persuade my daughter and her sorry excuse for a husband to leave before they get everyone all worked up," she whispered into Warren's ear.

Milt looked up from chatting with the much shorter Fiona and caught a glimpse of movement inside the house. *Why the hell is Warren headin' for the front door with Grandpa's shotgun in hand?* "Excuse me folks, I'll join you in a minute. I left my pipe in the car," Milt said. *That's a bit of a lie, but I need to get my tail to the front of the house. Warren ain't the type to all of a sudden, for no reason at all, grab a gun and head for the door.*

A ninety degree turn towards his car, and Warren's behavior was no longer a mystery. In one instant, Milt's day changed. *Oh crap, that's the old man's truck heading for the house. What in the hell is he doing here? How did he know I was visiting Grandma? I swear that man has Milt radar.*

Closing on the wide-legged standing Warren, Milt pointed to the incoming truck. "Is that why you high-tailed it out here with that squirrel gun?"

Through clenched teeth, square-jawed Warren said, "Sure is." Bringing the gun up to take aim, Warren yelled, "Git your tails outta here! Grandma don't want to talk to ya'll."

Bess leaned out of the passenger window and yelled in her tobacco-ravaged voice, "You tell that ma of mine, I ain't leavin' till I get what's mine!"

"Sounds like this ain't the first time they've been pesterin' Grandma. What the hell's my ma mean about gettin' what's hers?"

"I'll tell ya about it as soon I get these two outta here. Grandma wants me to do it quiet-like. She don't want them to disturb the boy and your missus. Let's go talk to these two heathens," Warren said as he lowered his gun to port-arms and commenced his determined short journey to Frank's truck.

"What the hell you doing here, Milt?" a disheveled, but, from the sounds of it, surprisingly sober, Frank asked.

"Paying my respects to Grandma before she passes. Now why don't you turn that truck around and git till you're ready to pay her respect?"

"Payin'? 'Fore we talk about us payin', how about you tell us when you're payin' us that CCC money." Bess yelled at Milt. "And when you're done payin', then that Ma of mine can pay up."

Milt ignored their umpteenth attempt to get his CCC money. He struggled to contain his rising anger. "Look, Grandma is dying! Now is not the time for feuding over money. Besides, Grandma doesn't owe you a thing!"

Bess' face turned even redder then her graying-red hair as she exited the truck. "She sure as hell does! Don't ya play stupid with me! Ya know what's in her will as well as I do."

"Ma, git back in the truck, and let your mom die in peace. I don't know what's in the will, but now ain't the time to be squabblin' over it. You don't like what's in it, you can fight it when the judge reads it." He shifted his focus to a sudden downward movement of Frank's right hand. "Frank, if you're fixin' to pull out a gun, ya better think twice! You pull one, and you'll find out what the Army taught me. It won't be nice, but it will be painful!"

"Son, you'd do that to your pa?" Frank said with an incredulous look on his face.

"Damn right I would! I've got a family in there to think of," Milt pointed at the house. "Now, for once in your life, do the right thing and leave peacefully while you can."

"Who the hell you think . . . .," Bess exploded.

Frank yelled. "Shut up, woman, and get your tail back in the truck." Frank remained quiet as Bess murmured profanities. Frank stared at Warren's gun, and then suddenly shifted the truck into reverse. "Alright Milt, we'll do it your way. Don't want no shoot out. Besides, you two have the drop on me."

"Glad you came to your senses. Do yourself a favor, and stay away from Grandma. You two can feud over the money after she's gone," Milt said as Frank began to turn his truck around.

"I'm leaving, but I ain't staying away. You won't be here the next time we come callin'."

Raising his shotgun to the aim position, Warren growled, "Yeah, but me and this 12 gauge will be. Next time I ain't warnin' ya. Two shots of double-ought sure as hell will take care of that rattle-trap of yours, and if that don't stop ya, I know one double-ought to your knees will."

The departing Frank thrust his left fist high out of the driver's window, and raised his middle finger. "See ya soon, ya shit heads!"

"Sorry you had to see that," Warren said as they watched Frank's truck depart.

"Don't worry about it. I'm used to their crap. I just hope Butch didn't get an ear- full. What got those two all lathered up?"

"They've been coming around ever since the sale of the farm was in the newspaper, and somehow they found out about what's in Grandma's will. Ever since then, those two show up every now and again raising cane and wantin' money." Warren walked back to the front door of the house with a slight limp.

"Who did Grandma sell the farm to? If she sold it, how come she's still here?"

"Her stayin' here till she passes was one of the reasons she sold it to me."

"How long have ya'll lived with Grandma?"

"She took us in right after I was discharged from the Marines in '43. I guess about three months after your grandpa died." He pointed to his right foot. "We were so thankful she took a chance on me. Veteran or not, with this foot, I wasn't gonna find work."

"I didn't know you were a vet. You got out early because of your foot?"

"Yeah, I was at Pearl when the Japs hit it. Shrapnel tore up the tendons in my ankle real bad. Docs couldn't fix it, so the Marines gave me a medical discharge in early '43. Your grandma said you were in the Army. Did you just get out?"

"Yeah, I got out about five months ago."

"What you been doing?"

"Right now, I'm working in a dairy as a mechanic, and, thanks to the GI Bill, I'm going to business school at night," They reached for the front door. "Warren, would you leave that shotgun in the front room. No need to concern the ladies and Butch."

"That's what I was plannin' on doin'." Pausing before opening the door, Warren said, "Glad you're using that GI Bill too. Roosevelt sure did take care of us vets. Thanks to that law, I was able to buy this farm. Actually, they loaned me the money for the house, and your grandma persuaded the bank to loan me the rest."

While Warren hid the gun in the front room, Milt entered the kitchen to distract his son. "How are the cookies, Butch?"

"Yummy," Butch mumbled through his chocolate-chip-smeared mouth.

"Grandma, from the looks of it, I'd say Butch loves your cookies as much as I did." He smiled at the sight of his son, who at the moment looked like a choclate-chip- cookie-stuffed chipmunk.

* * *

"Fiona, that chicken and home made egg noodles were delicious. I always loved it when Grandma made that meal." He leaned back in his chair to give relief to his stuffed stomach. "I'd say Grandma approved. That's the most I've seen her eat all week."

"Yes it is, and now I need a little time in my rocker. Milt, would you help me out to the back porch?" Grandma asked in a weak voice. "Ladies, I hope you'll excuse me. I'm a bit too tuckered out to help with the dishes."

"It's okay. Fiona and I will have them done in no time." Vi looked at Butch, who was already exiting his chair before being excused, and said, "Of course dishes would go faster if some-one kept Butch entertained."

Warren smiled. "I'll keep him out from underfoot." Warren turned to the little fella that he and Fiona had become attached to. "Butch, you want to help me drive the tractor?"

"Oh boy, oh boy, can I drive it?" Butch said as he darted past his mom on his way to the door. Three quick steps out the door, Butch turned and said, "Come on Wareen, Wareen come on!"

"That boy sure does like Warren," Grandma chuckled as Milt carefully assisted her to her back porch rocker. "Maybe some day he and Fiona will have a little boy. I know they want one, but the Lord hasn't blessed them just yet."

Milt sat down next to Grandma. "Yeah, Warren has sure grown up to be a fine young man. You must think pretty highly of him seeing how you sold the farm to him."

"Yes, I do Milt. I wanted the farm to be left with someone who was worthy of it." Pausing to catch her breath, she contin-ued, "I knew you weren't a farmer, but Warren is. Don't worry I haven't forgotten you," Grandma said as she laid her nearly lifeless hand on his forearm.

"Sorry Grandma, I didn't mean you shouldn't of sold it to him. I'm glad he's got it instead of Mom and Dad. They woulda ruined it in nothing flat." Noticing her tears, he said, "Grandma what you do with the farm and your will is up to you. You could cut me out, and I'd still love you from now until kingdom come."

Patting Milt's cheek, Grandma stared into Milt's eyes. "Grandpa and I always loved you like a son, and we will look down upon you and your family from heaven every day and smile." Grandma reached into her apron pocket, and removed a bulging envelope. "Here, Grandpa and I want you to have this."

Not reaching for the envelope, Milt said, "Grandma you don't have to do this."

She pushed the envelope into his hands. "No you take this. It will help you and your family."

He opened envelope, and was stunned. "Grandma, this is a lot of money."

"Yes, it is. It's about $5,000 dollars."

"Wow, where did you get all this money? I can't take all your money. You still got some time left. Enjoy yourself."

"Some of it's your CCC money, which Grandpa invested for ya, and some of it is from the sell of the farm." Grandma paused, and her face changed from the joy of giving, to the sorrow of her life changing without her consent. "Don't worry, I have plenty left. Besides, the doctor says the cancer won't give me much longer on this earth."

Tears streamed in a steady trickle down his cheeks. "Don't say that Grandma, you still have lots of time to watch your great-grandson grow."

She wiped his tears away. "Hush now, don't you cry. I've had a good sixty-five years, and now it's my time. I'm so glad ya came and let me meet your lovely wife and precious little son. It pained me to write ya, but I so wanted to see ya one more time, and to meet your family."

"Have Warren call me when you get closer. I'll break all the speed limits to get here before you join Grandpa. I promise, Grandma!" Milt said as he tenderly squeezed his grandmother's hand.

With difficulty, Grandma turned her frail body towards Milt, and kissed him lightly on his cheek. "No, I wrote you when I did because I wanted Vi to be able to travel. She'll be about seven or eight months when my time comes to once again be with your grandpa. She shouldn't travel then, and your place is with her. I am so glad I met her. She is a wonderful young lady. Take care of her and your children, and always keep my love in your hearts."

24

To an outsider, Milt's nightly ritual game of catch with Butch looked boring. It wasn't, but it may have appeared as such because the enjoyment of catch had been superceded by Milt's distracted mind skipping from one pleasant thought to another.

Sure am glad that Butch is taking to baseball. I was about seven, just like Butch, when I got coordinated enough to make playing catch with my grandpa fun. Thank God for Grandpa and Grandma. Never thought, I'd own a home. We put that money they left me a couple of years ago to good use. Paid for this house in full, no damn bank's ever going to take away our home! Couldn't have asked for a better place. Just down the street from the Howards. Butch is over at Roger's almost as much as he is home. Vi and Betty get along great. Good company for Vi while I'm at work and school. Can't wait for school to be done, I need to spend some more time with Butch and his brothers. That damn stork needs to quit coming. I love those boys, but all the Lord's blessings are sure getting expensive. I was tickled pink when his brother Eddie joined our family in February of '46, but boy were we surprised when another rabbit died three months later. Wouldn't trade little Wally—actually, Walter, as Vi insists I call him, for the world, but that stork sure had crappy timing. Watching those two playing is better then watching any old damn movie. Those boys can get into more damn mischief then I ever dreamed of. Butch is a good older brother, but I know at times he's just putting up with them. I imagine it's hard for a seven year old to put up with toddlers. Hard enough for me at times to handle the three year old and his two year old brother.

"I'm sorry Dad, are you okay?" Butch yelled at his distracted father who had just caught the ball with his chest instead of his glove.

"I'm fine, son. Not your fault. I should've been paying better attention."

"No, it was my fault. I didn't throw it very good." Butch looked down and shuffled his feet.

"Don't beat yourself up, Butch. Wasn't a thing wrong with your throw. I must be getting tired, I shoulda had it. Why don't we go see if Mom has supper ready, okay?"

As they walked towards the kitchen door, Butch said, "Okay. Can we listen to the White Sox game after supper?"

I'd say I've turned him into a Sox fan for life. Just like Grandpa did me. "If Mom says it's okay, we'll see if we can tune it in. Storms this time of the year sometimes interfere with the radio."

"Hope we can. I want to hear them beat those durn Yankees. I don't like 'em!"

Milt chuckled. "You got lots of company. Most folks, except those in New York, can't stand 'em. Don't get your hopes up though. Yankees are hard to beat."

"Dad, you think they'll win the pennant?"

"Hope not. The only team that might beat them out is the Red Sox. That Ted Williams is really something. We'll see."

"What about the White Sox?"

He put his arm around his son's shoulder as they walked up the back porch steps. "Sorry son. We aren't gonna take it this year. We'll be lucky if we can stay out of the cellar. Only teams worse than us this year are the Browns and Senators." He opened the screen door.

"There are my two favorite ballplayers. You two get washed up. Supper's about ready," She hugged Milt and patted Milt on the shoulder.

"Are we having chicken and noodles for supper, Mom?"

"Silly, you know we are. You saw me make the noodles this morning. Now get to going or there won't be any supper left for you." She smiled as her son dashed for the upstairs bathroom.

"That boy sure is growing up fast. Can't get over how he can throw for a seven year old. He can really hum it."

"I must admit, I was a little worried. I looked out the window just in time to see you miss his last throw. You said you were okay, but you looked like it hurt."

"I wasn't about to tell Butch it did. He already felt bad enough. Tried to blame himself, but truth is my mind was wandering so much I just out-and-out missed it."

"Are you alright?" Vi asked as a look of concern came across her.

"I'm fine. It smarted. Probably wouldn't have hurt at all if I hadn't already been feeling so crummy. I've had a bad headache and a slight fever all darn day. My back and neck really feel stiff."

"Maybe you should get yourself to bed after supper. You've got a busy day tomorrow. Remember, we have to visit Butch's teacher tomorrow before you head off to your accounting class."

"Can't turn in right away, I promised Butch we'd listen to the Sox game. Almost forgot about that teacher visit. From the sounds of it she's not too happy with Butch's story about the stork," Milt chuckled.

She wagged her index finger at him. "It's not funny, Mr. McCoy. You must watch your language around the children." Despite herself, she also began to laugh. "Even though you shouldn't have said it in front of him, I do agree, the stork's neck might need to be busted. Two kids in one year was a bit much for me."

"I would have loved to have seen his teacher's face when Butch told her about our visit to the zoo. Wish I could have seen her face when Butch told her that I was going to wring that stork's damn neck if it didn't quit coming to our house." He laughed at the image of the flustered teacher, and slapped his knee. "Bet she'll think twice in the future about asking kids to explain their picture."

"What picture, Daddy?" a suddenly present Butch asked.

"Oh, ah, oh, ah a picture show that Mommy and I saw a long time ago," Milt said as he looked sheepishly at Vi for her support.

"Yes, it was a very funny movie. Now get yourself seated and let's eat."

* * *

Damn, it's 5AM already! Some mornings I hate that friggin' alarm clock. This is one of 'em. That headache kept me up all night. I couldn't get comfortable. Back and neck hurt so much that sleeping on my back was impossible. Tried to roll over, but for some reason I just couldn't. Oh well, time to roll out and get some of that delicious smelling coffee Vi's brewing. What the hell is going on, I can't move my legs? I must have pinched a nerve or something. Nerve must also be connected to my arms, I can't move them either.

"Vi, Vi, would you . . ." Milt attempted to call her but lacked the breath. Confused, Milt took a deep breath and yelled, "Vi, I need your . . . help, I . . . can't move"

Damn, she probably can't hear me over the radio. It ain't loud, but I can't seem to get enough breath to yell loud enough for her to hear me. Trying one more time, he yelled, "Vi, help!"

"Honey, did you call me?" Vi said as she entered their bedroom. "I've got your morning cup of coffee for you."

Milt struggled to tell her. "Thanks . . . don't think I can . . . drink it."

Concern and confusion began to register on her face. "What's the matter sweetheart? Are you, okay?"

"I can't move . . . and can't breathe . . . very good," he breathlessly said as worry and tears began to appear in his eyes.

"Oh my! I'm calling Doctor Alterman," she said.

"No . . . it's too . . . early. Call . . . later," he said with what little breath he had.

"I don't care what time it is. You need a doctor right away," she yelled from the kitchen.

"Doctor Alderman, I'm sorry to bother you so early, but Milt has a very peculiar problem I'm worried about. He can hardly breathe, and he can't move his arms or legs." As she listened to the doctor's soothing assurance that all would be well with Milt; she stretched the phone cord and her neck to check on her husband. "How soon can you get here? Is there anything I can do right now? I am very concerned!"

Hanging up from the far from comforting phone call, Vi said, "The doctor is on his way. Is there anything I can get you?"

"Cold wash . . . cloth . . . I'm burning up," he said as his slow head rolls made Vi wonder if he was becoming delirious.

"Be back in a jiff," Vi said as she scampered to the kitchen.

Before she could return with the cold damp wash cloth, Wally's loud, screeching cries from the nearby crib shattered the silence of the house. Rushing to her husband's side, she tenderly placed the wash cloth on his forehead and said, "Here you are, sweetheart. Hope this helps. I'll get Walter taken care of, and be right back, okay?"

He attempted to smile as he breathlessly responded, "Okay."

Cooing to her toddler, Vi nervously peeked out the front door window until she heard little footsteps from above. Turning to tell Butch and Edward to go back to bed, her attention was diverted by a soft knock at the front door.

She opened the door, and said to the short, distinguished-looking older man, "Thank you for coming so quickly, doctor. I'm so sorry to bother you so early."

"Think nothing of it, no need to apologize. Now, show me to your husband." Looking up at the bewildered young McCoy boys sitting on the top step of the stairs, the doctor turned to Vi and whispered in her ear, "After you escort me to your husband, I advise you to get you sons back to bed. I might be doing some tests that could frighten young children."

"Yes, of course, my husband is in our bedroom. Please follow me. You boys go back to bed until the doctor leaves."

Standing up, Butch tugged at his brother's hand, and asked, "Why is the doctor here, Mom?"

"Daddy asked me to get him to visit us. He isn't feeling well. Now go back to bed. Stay put till I call you. Be good, and I'll make pancakes for breakfast, okay?

"Yum, yum, pancakes," Eddie squealed.

"Come on Eddie, Mom will call us when the pancakes are ready."

"Thanks for your patience, doctor. We don't get many visitors this time of day. They're curious, bright little boys, thank goodness. Now, if you'll follow me."

The doctor entered the bedroom. "Good morning, Milt, your missus tells me you're having difficulty breathing and moving you arms and legs. How are you feeling now? Any better?"

Milt struggled to catch his breath, and shook his head. He attempted to say no, but, despite his best efforts, not a word left his lips. *God, this sure is scary. Why the hell can't I even get breath enough to say no? Damn! What the hell is happening to me?*

The doctor noted Milt's difficult response, and asked Vi, "May I use your telephone?"

"Of course, it's right around the corner." The color in her face began to drain.

"Thank you. While I'm calling the ambulance and the hospital, I would advise you to pack a small overnight bag for Milt," the doctor said over his shoulder as he hastened to the phone.

"Oh no, this sounds serious! What's wrong with Milt?" she said as tears began to appear in her eyes.

"I haven't done any of my tests, so I can not say for certain. However, I don't want to delay in getting Milt to the hospital to confirm my suspicion. Hopefully, the hospital will tell me I am wrong."

Milt struggled to talk. "Sweet . . . Vi, it's . . . gonna . . . be . . . okay."

In spite of her tears, Vi held his hand and smiled. "I know sweetheart. The doctor will take good care of you."

Upon his return to the bedroom, Doctor Alderman said, "The ambulance is on its way, and the hospital is standing by for Milt's arrival." Extracting his stethoscope and some long needles from his bag, he said, "Milt, I'm going to listen to your lungs and perform a couple of tests before the ambulance arrives. The tests might, if all goes well, be a little bit painful. Nod your head if you grant your permission for me to test you."

Slowly nodding his head, Milt again attempted to speak, and again, failed.

The doctor carefully turned Milt for access to his back and said, "It's okay, Milt, now relax. I want you to take some deep breaths while I listen to your lungs."

After several minutes of listening to Milt's lungs, the doctor said, "Milt, I'm going to ask you some questions. Answer them by nodding or shaking you head. Do you understand?"

Milt gave a slight nod.

"Have you had a continuous bad headache for over 24 hours?"

The doctor noted Milts nod, and asked, "Have you experienced a slight fever within the last 24 hours?"

Milt slowly nodded as he grimaced with pain.

"Now the last question, have you experienced stiffness in your back or neck in the last 24 hours?"

Milt's sweating head slowly once again responded to the affirmative. An increasingly nervous Vi asked, "Why are you asking these questions?"

He turned to face Vi, and whispered, "I will tell you, but please for your childrens' and Milt's sake, I implore to you to keep your reaction to what I am about to tell you silent, okay?"

With wide eyes a suddenly scared Vi murmured, "Okay, doctor, but please tell me. I would rather know than stand here with my fear running wild."

"I understand. I am asking him questions that I ask all of my patients that I suspect may have been exposed to polio."

She slumped towards the doctor, and softly said, "Oh my God! Please God, spare my Milt. He's a good man, he doesn't deserve this."

"Are you alright, Vi? Would you like some salts before I proceed with the rest of my tests. I will warn you, the tests may be disconcerting."

"I'm fine. It was just such a shock. Please continue with your tests."

Picking up the long needles he had earlier removed from his medical bag, the doctor told Milt, "I am going to poke you with this needle in several areas of your extremities and your back. I will cease to poke if you show any sign of pain."

After several pokes of the needle without any responses, the early morning silence of the neighborhood was shattered by the wailing of an ambulance siren. The silence of the house was further damaged by the patter of little feet, and a seven year old yelling, "Mom, mom, there's an ambulance in our driveway."

Before she could stop the inquisitive Butch, he rushed into his parents' bedroom. "Stop hurting my Daddy!"

Grabbing Butch before he could close the gap between himself and the doctor, Vi hugged her son and said, "He's not hurting Daddy. Doctor Alderman's trying to help Daddy. Now go back to bed."

"No, I want to stay here! He better not hurt my Daddy!"

"Young man . . ." Vi began to correct Butch's behavior but the pounding on the front door interrupted her.

"Did anyone call for an ambulance?" a heavy set, short young man yelled from the front door.

"Yes, coming," she answered. "Just a moment, please."

Granting entrance to her house, Vi pointed to the rear of the house and said, "The doctor is in our master bedroom. He ordered the ambulance. Follow me please."

"Morning, Doc, you ordered the ambulance?" the older of the two ambulance crewmembers asked.

"Yes, please take Mr. McCoy to Cottage Hospital. They are expecting him. I will follow in my car."

"Why is Daddy going to the hospital?" Butch asked.

"Your daddy is sick, son. I will do everything I can to make him better as fast as we can. Now be a good boy and help your mommy while Daddy is in the hospital, okay?" Doctor Alderman said.

"Okay, can I tell Daddy goodbye?"

"Of course."

A confused Butch rushed to his dad's bed and said, "I love you Daddy. You, okay?"

"I'm okay," Milt blurted out and then collapsed into the arms of the ambulance attendant who was loading him onto a stretcher. As the stretcher was carried past Butch, Milt haltingly said, "I . . . love . . . you . . . too . . .be good."

* * *

"May I help you Miss?" the young nurse behind the nurses' station asked.

"Yes, I'm Vi McCoy, and I would like to visit my husband, Milt. Would you please direct me to him?" She struggled to maintain her composure.

The tall, slender nurse handed Vi a cloth facial mask and said, "If you will please put on this sterile mask, I will be more than glad to escort you to him."

Oh my goodness, whatever Milt has must have them worried if they are making me wear a mask. I wonder where he is. All I see in this ward is a bunch of long, shiny, horizontal things that look like small boilers with heads sticking out of them.

As they approached one of the cylindrical stainless steel devices, the nurse said to the head sticking out of the end of the tube, "Mr. McCoy, your wife is here to visit you."

Vi's eyes widened as the color drained from her face. "Good morning, sweetheart."

Before she could continue, the nurse offered her a chair near Milt's head, and whispered into her ear. "He is rather weak, so keep your visit short and don't be surprised if he struggles to answer your questions. When you're done visiting, please return to the nurses' station."

She nodded as she seated herself. Vi lowered her head to within inches of Milt and said, "How are you, dear? I love you. Butch said to tell you he misses you and loves you too."

He looked at Vi with sad, confused eyes, and haltingly gasped, "Fine . . . hard time breathing . . . breathe better in this thing . . . got headache but . . . fever gone . . . love you . . . where kids?"

She calmly stroked his forehead. "Glad your fever is gone. I left the kids with Betty because the hospital said not to bring them. Did the doctor say how long you'd be in the hospital?"

Weakly shaking his head, Milt said, "No . . . depends on . . . how long I . . . need to be in . . . this here . . . iron lung."

"Is that what they call the shiny thing you're lying in? Why do they have you in it?"

He nodded. "It helps me . . . breathe. I almost . . . stopped breathing . . . before they . . . put me in it."

As she adjusted her chair for a better view of Milt's face, Vi noticed the nurse, who was standing next to Doctor Alderman, gesture for her to return to the nurses' station. "Sweetheart, I can't stay very long. I'm sorry, but the doctor wants to talk to me. I'll come back as soon as I can, okay? I love you."

"Love . . . you . . . too. Come soon . . .okay?" Milt said with pleading eyes.

As she walked towards the nurses' station, Vi dabbed her eyes with her handkerchief while her mind repeatedly asked God why this was happening to Milt. Sniffling, she approached the nurse and the doctor and said, "Good morning, Doctor Alderman. You wished to see me? I hope you have good news."

The doctor gently took Vi's arm. "Good morning, Vi. Please come with me, and I'll share with you what we know about Milt's condition." Turning towards the nurse, he said, "Would you be so kind to bring a cup of coffee for me and Mrs. McCoy? We will be in the residents' lounge."

"My pleasure, sir," the smiling nurse said. "How do you like your coffee, Mrs. McCoy?"

"Cream and sugar, please."

"Vi, from the short few years I've had the opportunity to know you, I believe you are the kind of woman who appreciates a direct explanation." At a table in the far corner of the residents' lounge, the doctor gestured for Vi to be seated. "Am I correct?"

"Yes, and the quicker your answer, the more I would appreciate it."

He thanked the nurse for the coffee, and then told Vi, "Mrs. McCoy, your husband has contacted the polio virus. There are three types of polio, and my tests show that he may have what is known as bulbospinal polio, which causes paralysis not only in the extremities but also in parts of the respiratory system. We won't know for —"

"Oh my God! Oh my God! No, no . . . please don't tell me he will forever live in that horrible thing," Her tears began to drench her cheeks.

Handing Vi his handkerchief, he continued, "Based on his progress since he went in the lung a few hours ago, I doubt that he will be in the iron lung for much more than a week or two weeks at the most. As soon as we see that he can breathe on his own without difficulty, we will remove him from the iron lung."

"What happens after he gets out of it? Will he be cured?"

"I wish I could tell you he will be as good as new, but unfortunately there is no cure for polio. I'm so sorry. I will elaborate if you wish."

In a serious, almost solemn tone, she said, "Please do, I want to know what my family can expect."

He patted Vi's hand and looked directly into her eyes. "The affects of polio depends on the type of polio, age of the patient, and level of physical activity engaged in during initial exposure to the poliovirus."

"What about Milt?"

"I can't tell you with certainty. Based on available research, I can say that older victims of polio are hit harder. Milt is already showing signs of regaining his respiratory functions, but because of his age and his physically demanding job, I'm not certain as to how much his extremities will be permanently damaged by polio."

"When will you know?"

"Shortly after he's able to be removed from the iron lung, I will recommend that he be transferred to Methodist Hospital in Peoria. The polio specialists there will be better able to tell you Milt's long term recovery expectations. I wish I could do more, but I am only a general practitioner. Milt needs the treatment of specialists if there is any hope of minimizing the affects of his polio."

"I want Milt to get better, but we can't afford specialists all the way over in Peoria. We can hardly afford to pay you. Isn't there any way he can stay here?"

"Now, now, Mrs. McCoy, let's not be worrying about the cost. Your husband was a veteran, so I believe he can get help from the Veterans' Administration."

"Milt has a friend, Jerry Powell, from his war years who's a big shot in the V.A. I'll call him as soon as I can. How long do you think Milt will be in the hospital?"

"It depends on his progress in the next few weeks. If he gets out of the iron lung with only minor paralysis in his arms and legs, then I would say anywhere from a year to two years."

"Why so long? He just can't be down for that long! We have some savings, but not enough for that long. We own our home, but we still have to make taxes. How are we going to eat? Oh Lord, why us?" Vi said in a torrent of words of worry.

"If you expect Milt to have some ability to perform necessary physical functions, such as walking, he will need to be in their care for an extended period of time. I don't have all the answers for your financial worries, but if Milt's recovery is important, you will find the answers."

"Yes, of course. I'd move heaven and earth if it would get him well, but I don't know how to find the money it's going to take. Milt and I overcame the Depression, but at least we were physically able to work and we didn't have little kids depending on us," Vi intently said as she gripped the doctor's forearm.

"Mrs. McCoy, like I said, I don't have all the answers. But, trusting in God and the kindness of others is a good start for finding solutions to your financial worries. I have a lawyer friend you can see that might be able to assist you with obtaining a deferment of taxes until Milt gets out of the hospital."

"We can't afford a lawyer, we can barely afford to pay you," she slumped into her chair.

"You don't need to concern yourself. My friend, Barry, won't charge you. If he does, his next doctor bill will be astronomical. As far as my bill goes, let's worry about that once Milt gets back to work."

Wiping a tear from her eye, she smiled. "Thank you. Rest assured we will make your bill the first we pay once he's back on his feet."

"I know you'll take care of me. In the meantime, I would also advise you to consult with Milt's employer. The Pastor is a very fine man who I'm sure won't hesitate to help. Also, talk to your family. Some of them may be in a position to help."

Vi sat up tall. "Those are all good ideas. We made it through the Depression and the War, so we'll get through this. But tell me, why as much as two years in the hospital?"

"If they feel there is any hope of restoring muscular function to the affected limbs they will perform tendon lengthening and nerve graft operations. After those heal, Milt will be subjected to extensive physical therapy that will be quite lengthy, as well as painful. That process might take as long as two years."

"As much as it worries me as to how we will make ends meet, I hope he's well enough to get all those operations and therapy. What if he isn't well enough?"

"In that event, he will be given physical therapy only, and released after he has been fitted with braces and special corrective shoes. Even though it is a less extensive process, it still will take about a year."

Vi looked down at her lap and became quiet. She took several deep breaths. "Thank you for being honest with me, and also for all your good advice. If you would be so kind to answer a couple more questions, I would appreciate it."

"Of course."

"The questions I have are about the kids. Are they in danger of getting polio from Milt?" Vi asked with worried lines across her forehead.

"I can't give you a definitive answer, but there are some precautions you can take. The consensus of recent medical literature regarding polio is that the polio virus is borne through the exchange of liquids. Therefore, as soon as you get home, remove the children from the kitchen and then scrub all of your dishes, glasses and cups in hot soapy water. Also, launder all towels and linens."

"Okay. Last question, when can the children visit their dad?"

"In about two weeks. By that time you and the children will be out of quarantine, and Milt will no longer be infectious."

"What! Why will we be in quarantine?"

"Sorry, but health department regulations demand a quarantine of two weeks for any household that polio is reported in.

Technically, you shouldn't even be here at this moment, but I delayed notifying the health department."

"That is not going to go over well with Butch. He's a typical rambunctious boy, and he's dying to see his daddy. How are we going to get groceries?"

"Stop at the store on the way home, and get all that you can think of what you will need for the next two weeks. When the health department comes out later today, or early tomorrow, they will assign a person to you from the Red Cross who will do your shopping for you while you are in quarantine. Also, if you need anything besides groceries, here is my card. Don't hesitate to call. My wife and I will be glad to help."

"Thank you Doctor, may I see Milt again for a short while before I go?"

"Of course, of course, let me escort you to him."

Approaching Milt's steel cocoon, Vi's mind quickly raced through a succession of what-ifs and necessary tasks she needed to address to survive the upcoming long absence of Milt. *Please God, give me strength. I can't fail Milt and the boys.* "Sweetheart, I hope you'll understand what I'm about to tell you. I don't like it, but the doctor just told me that the health department is quarantining the boys and me for two weeks. I'll visit —"

Milt shook his head violently, and tried to yell as loud as his depleted breath would allow. "No . . .no . . ."

Doctor Alderman gently placed his hand on Milt's forehead. "Milt, it's for the best. It will protect your children and others against this horrible virus. They will be able to call you anytime during visiting hours. The nurse can bring the phone to you and hold it for you. Now, if you want to get better, please calm yourself and rest."

"Okay. I . . .love . . . you . . . Vi. Tell kids . . . I love . . . them too," Milt said and then closed his eyes in exhaustion.

"I love you too, sweetheart. I'll call you tonight, and every chance we get. Rest now, and remember how much your family loves you."

* * *

"Daddy, Daddy," yelled Butch as he ran far out in front of his brothers Eddie and Wally, towards his father's hospital bed. Reaching his dad's bed, Butch leaped as high as he could but fell short of the landing he hoped for. "Daddy, help me up. I want to hug you. We miss you," Butch pleaded with his eyes as well as his mouth.

Milt reached his arm down and touched his son. "I missed you too, but I can't lift you up here, son."

"Why?" Butch said as his brothers joined him and began to chime in with their own demands for their father's attention.

Vi interrupted the commotion. "Calm down, boys. Daddy can't lift you into his bed because the doctor wouldn't like it if he did. Now quit pestering your father, and stop yelling or the doctor will send us home. You don't want to go home do you?"

"No, Mom, but why can't —"

"And no more why questions, young man! Now give your father a hug and a kiss. You're tall enough to reach him," Vi said. "Edward and Walter, come here and I'll boost you up so you can hug your Daddy."

Wiping away the slobber of Walter's kiss, Milt looked down at Butch and said, "I'll bet you're glad to go outside again. Are you playing catch with the neighbor kids?"

"Nah, all the other kids have that Red Cross sign on their door like we used to have on ours. I can go outside, but nobody else can. Be glad when they can come out. Not as much fun playing catch by myself."

"Sorry to hear that, son," he said as he mussed up his son's meticulously combed hair. He looked at Vi. "How many houses are quarantined?"

"Four. The Swenson's boy came down with it about a week ago, and so did the McCall's youngest son and the Yeager's little girl. I feel so bad for them, but I really feel bad for the McGuire family. All three of their kids were struck by that terrible bug two days after it got you. Their mother cried and screamed so much when they loaded them into the ambulances that they had to give her a shot to calm her down."

He reached out to take his wife's hand. "I kinda know how Mrs. McGuire must have felt. Watching the nurses putting kids into the iron lungs really tugged at my heart." He waved his other hand in a large sweeping arc. "Look around this ward. I'm the only adult in it. What a nasty bug this polio is! Mostly picks on the young, but from what I hear, the young ones usually recover but adults don't."

"Speaking of recovery, not needing that iron lung and having use of your arms, I'd say you are on the road to recovery." Vi smiled. "Has the doctor said anything about your progress?"

"Doc Alderman was in earlier, and he told me that he was real pleased with how I'm doing," His smile faded. "Said getting out of that steel coffin with arms that worked was a good sign."

"I get the feeling you aren't telling me everything. What did he say about your legs?"

Milt looked away and mumbled, "He said he wasn't certain about whether my legs would beat polio. Told me I needed to transfer to Methodist Hospital in Peoria where they have doctors that know more about fixing polio then he does."

"When I last visited, he told me you might need to go to Peoria."

"I don't know what to do, hon. I want to beat this damn bug, but we can't afford staying in the hospital much more. Even if we could, I'd never get to see my family if I'm all the way over in Peoria." His worry lines deepened on his forehead.

"The most important thing is to get you better. Your getting well is worth a lot more than seeing each other as much as we'd like."

"I know you're right. Being apart from all of you isn't something I want to do, but the War proved to me that I can. But, I have no idea how we're gonna pay the hospital."

"Believe it or not, the hospital is not going to cost us a penny. I called Jerry, and he is sending me the forms to fill out for the V.A. to pick up the hospital bill."

"Thank God! Good old, Jerry. He said he'd be there for us if we ever needed him. Wish I could have got more time to really get to know him. How's he doing in his new job?"

"He sounded real happy. Already got a promotion, now he's in charge of all of the V.A. offices in the Midwest. Oh, and I almost forgot, he's getting married."

The head nurse for the day shift picked up a squirming Walter. "Sorry to interrupt your visit folks. Would you like us to assist you with your visit? We have an extra nurse on duty that would be glad to watch the children for a short while so you two can chat."

"Um, is that okay with you, dear?" Vi asked.

"Appreciate it. We've got a few family things we need to discuss, and it would be easier to do if these little rascals weren't under foot."

"Me no rassel!" Edward insisted.

"Yes you are son, and I love you. Now go play with this nice nurse. Daddy will see you after Mommy and I talk, okay?"

With a loving smile, Vi and Milt watched their sons leave. "Sure was nice of her to watch the boys for us. I've got a hunch she doesn't know what she got herself into." Almost in unison, they broke into a devilish chuckle. "Anyway, so Jerry has the hospital covered for us. That's a big worry off our shoulders, but we got a lot of other places our savings need to stretch. If I go to Peoria, our savings will fly away in a hurry."

"I know, but if there is any hope that you can walk again I will find a way to make ends meet."

"Unless you got a rich uncle I don't know about, I don't see how we can do it."

"Sorry, no rich uncle, or aunt, or cousin, or anyone else, but I have been doing some checking on things. Doctor Alderman's lawyer friend helped me —"

He reared his head back as his eyes widened. "Lawyer, lawyer, we ain't got no money for no damn shyster! What the heck were you thinking?"

"Calm down, sweetheart. The lawyer got us out of our house taxes until one year after you get out of the hospital and are back working. The doctor asked his lawyer friend, Mr. Barry Brush, to do it for free, and he did."

"A lawyer doing something for nothing. That oughta be in Ripley's Believe it or Not. I thought I'd heard it all. One thing's for certain though, he's a pretty good lawyer if he got us out of our taxes."

"I think you'd like him. It's nice to know we won't lose our home to taxes while you're getting well."

"Yeah, it's good to know you don't have to worry about having a roof over your head, but what about the other stuff? You and the boys still gotta eat."

"Thanks to the Pastor, I got some of our eating figured out. Since I told him you were in the hospital, I haven't cooked a supper. Every day someone shows up from his congregation with a supper."

"That sounds like the Pastor. He's a good man. If you ain't cooked supper in three weeks, I'll bet he thumped the pulpit real good."

"As generous as he and his flock have been, I'd say the Pastor really takes Luke 6:38 of the Good Book serious. I almost fainted when one of his milkmen showed up with all sorts of milk, cheese, butter, and even ice cream. I told the fella we didn't order it, but he said the Pastor said to give it to us."

"You're kidding me, right? Next thing you'll tell me is that he offered me another job and dairy for the kids until I get out of here."

"How did you know? He said he'll be by later this week to talk to you about work once you get back on your feet."

"Well, I'll be darn. Boy did we luck out, but you can't just live on dairy stuff. What about meat and potatoes?"

"Thanks to Doctor Alderman and lawyer Brush, we won't lack for food on the table. They talked to a grocer over on Broad Street who attends Synagogue with them. I met the grocer yesterday, and my heart went out to him. He looked like life had not been kind to him."

"Why so?"

"He couldn't stand up straight. I thought at first it was because he was old, but when I looked closer I realized he wasn't as old as he looked. For a grocer, I was shocked by how thin he was. When he shook my hand his shirt sleeve rose up, and I saw some numbers on his wrist. Don't know what they were, but he must have been embarrassed by them because he quickly covered them."

"From the sounds of it they were identification numbers that the Nazi's tattooed on Jews in the concentration camps."

"Oh my! Maybe that explains why he got so excited when I introduced myself. His English wasn't all that good, but I did understand him when he said if you could fight Hitler for his people then giving you groceries was the least he could do."

Milt nestled both of her hands into his. "I love you so much, Mrs. McCoy. Always knew that I could count on you. With what you've done I can sleep a whole lot better. Gotta admit I was really worried about how my family would be provided for."

Vi kissed her husband and whispered into his ear, "I love you too, Mr. McCoy, and I hope you know I'll always be there for you. Don't worry about us, you just get well. We will be fine and Dad will help get us to Peoria as much as we can."

Despite the interference of the hospital bed, they hugged while they cried soft tears of gratefulness for the kindness of others. Milt squeezed her one last time before releasing her. "I wish I could hold you forever, but I think we better give that poor nurse a break. Sounds like Eddie and Wally are teaming up on her. They stay much longer and she won't want any of her own."

* * *

Milt sat up in the hospital bed. "You sure are a welcome sight. Someone up there must have heard me wish to see you."

"Sorry it took so long to get here. I had to get the boys to agree to stay with Dad and Barb while I visited you. Butch was excited to see his Grandpa, but he really wanted to come with me. I slipped away when Dad distracted them with ice cream."

"I'll bet that worked. Those boys do love their ice cream. How was your dad?"

"Doing pretty good, but Barb sure is trying his patience."

"Denny still has a full time job scaring Barb's boyfriends off?"

"Yeah, but that's not why she's been so difficult lately. Dad's seeing the widow Harrington, and Barb isn't too happy about it."

"Barb was pretty close to her mom, so I can understand it."

"Dad says the same thing, but he also feels like seven years after Mom's passing it's alright to see other ladies. Anyway, enough of that gossip. How did your first day at your new home away from home go?"

"Not too bad, except for that head nurse. I got a hunch her and I aren't gonna always see eye-to-eye," Milt pointed out his room door, at a quarter angle, towards the partially visible nurses' station.

Tilting her head to the right to follow the direction of his point, she asked, "Are you talking about Nurse Helga, the tall, middle aged lady who has her hair in a bun? She seemed nice to me."

"Don't let her fool you. She says she was a nurse in the Army, but the way she acts, I'd say she was the one in charge of the German Army nurses."

"I'm sure you're just tired from the trip to Peoria. Give her another chance after you get some rest," Vi said as her eyes glanced around the room. "At least you have a nice sunny room instead of being in a ward. From what I've seen so far, Methodist is a much more modern hospital."

He glared towards the offending nurse. "Yeah, sharing a room beats the heck out of a ward, but I wish that Nazi nurse would take it a little easy on me. I wasn't here five minutes, and she started making me do exercises that wore me out."

"I'm sure she was just following doctor's orders." Vi removed a large folder from her purse. "Maybe this will cheer you up."

"What is it?"

"It's a surprise," she said as she handed it to him.

"Sure is a surprise. What am I supposed to do with this here accounting book?"

"Read it, you silly man."

He frowned. "Why should I do that? Oh, I get it. If I can't go to sleep, I read it."

"No, it's not to put you to sleep, even though it might." She chuckled and pointed to the rest of the folders' contents. "You're going to read it and then complete the workbook and homework."

"What?"

"Last week, the Pastor and I spoke with your teacher, and we got him to agree to let you finish your Accounting courses by correspondence."

"Why did you do that?"

"It will give you something to do besides laying around thinking about things you can't do anything about. Also, when you finish your courses you'll be ready for the new job the Pastor told you about."

"Thanks, sweetheart, but you know I'm not too keen on working behind a desk for the rest of my life. I'm gonna walk out of this place in a year or so, and all I want to do is go right back to my old job. I like fixin' things a whole lot more then pushin' numbers around a ledger."

"Good for you, Mr. McCoy." Nurse Helga interjected as she joined them. "A good positive attitude will help you get better much faster. Now are you ready for your afternoon therapy?"

"Vi, this is Nurse Helga I was telling you about." Shifting his focus to the stocky nurse, he said, "Nurse Helga, this is my wife, Vi. She just got here a few minutes ago. Could we start therapy in about thirty minutes?"

"Nice to meet you, Mrs. McCoy. I'm sorry to interrupt your visit, but if we wait much longer to start his afternoon session his supper will be cold by the time we finish."

"Okay, okay. Can ya give us ten more minutes?" Milt struggled to be civil.

"Ten minutes, but no more," she said as she turned and left the room.

The nurse now out of range, Milt sneered and said, "See what I mean? That old babe is a pushy old battle-axe. Before I get outta here, I'll bet her and I just might tangle."

* * *

My legs are killing me! I hope Nurse Helga leaves me alone for awhile. Since that last operation, her therapy exercises are gettin', harder and harder on me. Doc says his strechin' the tendons operations will help my muscles recover. Hope that happens soon. After two of those operations I'm starting to wonder. Only thing I've got out of 'em so far are legs that can't do what that Nazi nurse wants me to do. I've been here almost a year and I still can't stand by myself. The Doc's carving on me gave me a few muscles in my legs that seem to be startin' to work. When I first got here I couldn't move my legs at all. Now, I can move my legs some, but not enough to walk. Wish to hell I could stand up on my own. Movin' my legs don't mean squat if I can't stand!

"Are you ready for your lunch, Sergeant McCoy? The way you were dragging through the morning exercises, I'd say you need something to pick you up," Nurse Helga said as she placed Milt's lunch tray on his hospital bed table.

"Yeah, I could use some coffee, but if that lunch isn't any better than yesterday's it ain't gonna give me anything besides a belly ache." During his examination of the offered lunch of overcooked vegetables nestled against gravy drenched mystery meat, it dawned on him that Nurse Helga had referred to him by his military rank. "What did you just call me?"

"Sergeant McCoy, which is your rank, isn't it?

"Nope, that's what it was a long time ago! How did you find out about my Army rank?"

She handed him the current edition of the Peoria daily newspaper. "Read about your Army adventures in today's newspaper. Quite an article, it makes you out to be a real hero. Afternoon therapy starts in an hour. Enjoy your lunch," she said with a smile that could have been mistaken for a smirk.

Damn, I need that newspaper article like I need a hole in the head. They must have needed to sell some papers. That hero stuff is old news. I wish they wouldn't have told everyone I'm here in the Peoria Methodist Hospital. I don't much look like a hero laying here. Hell, I look more like an old used up wet dish rag. Sure hope I don't start getting' a bunch of visitors because of this damn paper.

"Could I get some more coffee?" Milt yelled towards the nurses' station. *Gotta have something to wash down that crappy lunch! Hell, it was barely better then K-Rats.*

"Room service," Nurse Helga answered in an insincere at-your-service tone. "Drink up soldier, afternoon therapy starts in fifteen minutes."

"Crap! Didn't you torture me enough this morning?"

"From the looks of how comfy you are, I'd say you need at least a couple more hours before we're done for the day."

"You might think so, but my legs and arms feel like they're gonna drop off."

"Buck up soldier! If you plan on walking out of here you'll need all the therapy I have time to give you. Now drink up! I'll see you shortly."

I know that old Nazi is right, but I damn sure don't have to like it. So far the only thing that's gotten stronger is my arms. I thought the Army made me pretty strong, but holding myself up on those walking bars for most of the day puts quite a strain on my arms. Wish my damn legs would get better. Gotta admit, I got more strength in 'em since I got here, but I know they still are useless to me. Coffee cup is empty, so I might as well get this over with.

"Nurse, let's get your afternoon fun started. I'm ready if you are," Milt lifted his legs over the side of his bed.

"Well look at you, sir. You even got your legs over the side without me helpin' ya," the muscular nurse's assistant said as he entered Milt's room. "I guess ya can't hold a good old Army Sergeant down forever."

"Nah, I'm still down. But one of these days, Ben, if I can help it, I won't need your help anymore. How'd you know I was an Army Sergeant? Did you read today's paper, too?"

"Yes, sir, and it made me feel real good to know I've been helping a hero. Us Army vets gotta stick together, you know."

"You were in the War?"

"Yes sir. I served with the 92nd Infantry Division in Italy. After I read the paper this morning, I got to thinkin', and I'm pretty sure the 92nd and the 1st Division were in some of the same battles. Never ran into ya, but we were on the same battlegrounds."

"Ninety Second, huh? Didn't you fellas have a buffalo for a mascot? We were at parade at the same time as the 92nd, and we damn near got run over when that woolly monster broke free of his reins. If I remember right, it took about five of you fellers to get him calmed down."

Ben laughed and shook his large black head. "Yep that was us. They called us the Buffalo Soldiers. I remember that parade. The General was so proud of us he had our mascot, who we called Bull, flown over for the parade. Good idea, but I think Bull didn't like flying cuz he was in a nasty mood that day."

"Alright you two, strolling down memory lane will have to wait." Nurse Helga ordered as she shot a stern look at Milt and Ben. "Sergeant McCoy, you are to report to the therapy room in five minutes. Ben, please assist the Sergeant, but only when he absolutely can't do it himself."

"Wait a minute, I'm not a Sergeant any more, and I ain't still in the United States Army."

She frowned and pointed her wagging index finger. "No, you're not. But you are in mine, and I am in charge! Now move it soldier!"

Muttering his disdain for her, Milt grasped Ben's shoulders and pulled himself upright. Twisting his body to align it with the waiting wheelchair, he said, "You know, Ben, I think that old battle-axe enjoys bossing me around."

"Nah, she's hard on all the patients. She's just pushin' you to get better," he said as he helped Milt lower himself into the wheelchair seat.

"If that's true, then I oughta be runnin' the bases for the Soxs' by now," Ben pushed the wheelchair towards another therapy session in what Milt had come to believe was, in truth, Nurse Helga's torture chamber.

* * *

After a soft knock on his door, a pleasant voice said, "Mr. McCoy, you have a visitor. Should I send him in?"

Thank God for an interruption! This damn accounting book was about to turn my exhausted mind out like a light bulb. "Thank you, nurse. Who is it?"

"I'm sorry, he didn't say, and I didn't think to ask him. Should I find out who it is before I escort him to your room?"

"No, that's alright. Send him on in. I was hoping for something to take me away from my homework," Milt said.

Wonder who it is? I'll bet it's my old Army buddy Bill Wilder. Or better then him, maybe it's his sister Monica. I could go for another look at that sexy babe. One look at her and I'd make a tent in a hurry. Milt, what the hell are you thinking? You're married to a fine woman, so put your dirty, straying mind back on the straight path. Two years in this hospital bed without the warmth of my Vi's sweet body pressed against me sure has screwed up my mind.

"Evenin' son, long time no see," Frank said as he shuffled into Milt's room.

Pausing to let his emotions digest the disappointment of his father standing in front of him, Milt noticed that Frank didn't quite look like himself. Clean shaven and, for the first time he could remember, the old man was wearing clean, not-wrinkled clothes. *Wonder what the hell got into him.* "Yeah, but not long enough! What the hell are you doing here? If you're after money, I ain't worked since I got polio. Two years of being in here didn't do my fortunes any good. So if you're still trying to get money I don't owe ya, you oughta try gettin' blood out of a turnip. You'd have a hell of lot more luck with the turnip."

A slight frown appeared as he said with an almost notice-able edge, "Good to see you too son."

"Wish I could say the same. Like I said, what the hell are you here for? And what's with that cross you're wearin'? Must of stole it off a priest."

"I know we got a few things between us, but I was hopin' you might be glad to see me. If you ain't noticed, I'm sober and . . ."

"I noticed. Usually I can smell you before I see ya. Probably because you're broke. If you're here to panhandle forget it!"

"Tain't here for money, son, I saw the paper today, and I thought the Christian thing to do would be to visit ya."

"Christian? You got a lot of nerve! What do you know about being a Christian? You gonna ask for a donation that'll go straight to your pocket?"

"I ain't gonna ask ya for a dime. When your Ma died the preacher that planted her helped me find Christ. That's why I'm wearin' the cross of our Lord."

Milt raised his upper torso and his voice. "Ma died? When was that? How come nobody told me?"

"Tried to son, but I couldn't find ya. Good many times I called that old Sinclair station you used to work at but old man Stewart kept hanging up on me shortly after I said hello."

"Can't hardly blame him, can ya? When did Ma pass away? How come her passing wasn't in the paper?"

"About a year ago, she didn't make the paper cuz I still need her government check. Sorry it took so long to tell ya. Maybe the Lord wouldn't let me find you till now."

Bewildered by his father's incredible logic, he asked, "How do you figure the Lord had anything to do with it?"

"Cuz I wasn't much in a forgivin' mood till now. Figured we'd just hiss and piss at each other. Don't think the Lord wants that."

Milt raised his voice. "What the hell do you mean you weren't in the mood for forgivin'? Seems to me, if any forgivin' oughta be owed it's me forgivin' you and Ma. I ain't the one that lived my life in violation of God's commandments!"

Frank leaned in close to Milt's face. "Don't you give me any preachin'! I ain't the one that forgot to honor his parents, and you're the one that forgot about the Lord said thou shall not steal."

"How many times do you have to be told that I didn't steal from you and Ma. I sent the money to the ones who really raised me—Grandma and Grandpa. How the hell do you have the guts enough to call me a thief while you're still gettin' Ma's check even after she died? You are one disgusting piece of shit! Now git the hell out of here!"

"I'll git when I'm ready, and I ain't ready just yet!"

"Nurse, nurse! Come and get this old reprobate out of my room," Milt yelled as loud as he could.

"Should of listened to that preacher. He said you probably weren't ready to hear the teachin' of the Lord. But he was right, you don't owe me any money cuz the Lord brought polio down upon ya to punish you for your thievin' ways."

"What? What kind of stupid idiot of a preacher would say such a thing! The Lord doesn't strike down folks who are trying to do right. If I could walk, I'd kick the shit out of both of you heathens!"

"You can't, but I can! So if anybody is gonna do any shit kickin' it's gonna be me."

Nurse Helga calmly said as she entered the room, "You're wrong, sir. It will be me unless you leave my patient alone. Please leave, as Mr. McCoy requested you to."

"Like hell you will, little missy. I'll leave when I'm damn good and ready," Frank said as he launched himself towards her shaking his fist at her.

In a swift motion she grabbed his outstretched arm and twisted it around towards the small of his back while she slammed him face first into the wall. "You're ready!"

After a forceful escort of Frank to Nurse Assistant Ben, she returned to Milt's room. "Are you okay, Sergeant?"

Over the loud profane protests of his father's forced departure, Milt said, "Thanks to you, I'm fine. Where did you learn that nifty little trick?"

"Army nurses went through about the same basic training as you did."

"Glad you paid attention that day. Stuck in this bed I was kinda at the mercy of the old man. Like I said, thanks a lot."

"Think nothing of it Sergeant. Us Sergeants have to stick together. Now get some rest. You've had quite a day." She departed with a smile.

Well I'll be damn, she was a Sergeant. Kinda figured she might be. She's tough as nails in therapy, and thank God she was tough enough to handle my old man.

* * *

"Morning, Mrs. McCoy, how are you and Butch today?" Nurse Helga said as she shook Butch's hand. "If you don't mind, I'd like a few moments with you before you visit your husband."

"Why? Is something wrong?"

"No, but I think before you chat with Milt you need to know about Doctor Phillip's visit of earlier today. Perhaps you'll let one of my nurses escort your boys to the cafeteria. A clown is performing there for our children in residence, and they are serving ice cream and cake."

How do I say no? The mention of ice cream set all three of the boys into a pleading frenzy. She's trying not to show it, but I get the feeling what she wants to discuss with me is important. "Okay boys, calm down, and behave for the nurse. Have fun, and please don't get ice cream all over your shirts."

Led by Butch, they all promised to be on their best behavior and skipped away holding onto the smiling nurse.

"Thanks for giving me some time with you, Mrs. McCoy. I've been accused of not being the most diplomatic—just ask your husband and his father—so forgive me if what I have to tell you sounds a bit blunt."

"You're welcome. After all this time I feel like you are a part of our family, so please call me Vi. Milt told me about how you handled Frank, and all I can say is if that's what you mean by not being diplomatic, then Milt and I approve. I can be a bit of a straight-to-the-point person myself, so please do not mince words on my behalf."

"Well, Vi—and please call me Helga—today was not a good news day for Milt. Doctor Phillips changed Milt's therapy treatment to permanent non-ambulatory. I'm afraid it was quite a blow to Milt, and he is still quite upset."

"What does permanent non-ambulatory mean?"

"It means he will never walk again unassisted."

"Oh no! Oh God please no," Vi said as the color drained from her face.

"I know it's not what any of us hoped for, but we still can help him to return to a life that is somewhat as it was before."

"I don't understand. If he can't walk, how will his life be the same?"

"Tomorrow we will fit Milt for braces, special orthopedic shoes, and custom fitted crutches. Once these devices arrive, he will resume his physical therapy, but now the physical therapy will focus on teaching Milt how to walk with the aid of the braces and crutches." She gently laid her hand on Vi's shoulder and handed her a tissue. "I am so sorry. But, the good news is he will at least be able to walk with crutches, and he will be discharged from the hospital in about one month."

Through her tears and body tremors, Vi said, "Oh my God! He must be devastated. Milt was so certain he could beat polio. Should I come back another day?"

"No, I believe he heard the children. If you go home without first seeing him he will wonder why. If you want, I'll stay with you while you visit. But please, let Milt tell you about the news. Probably would be best if you don't let on that I told you. I'm not certain what I can do to soften the blow, but I am willing to try if you want."

"Thank you. Your presence might help me find the strength I'm not sure I have right this moment. Before I pop in on him I think I had better use the ladies' room." She turned towards the ladies' room as tears fell down her cheeks.

"I'm available for as long as you need me to be. Stop at the nurses' station when you are ready to see Milt."

After crying tears that seemed endless, Vi looked at her red eyes in the ladies'room mirror and silently prayed, *Oh God, please give me the strength to help my husband. Help me find answers that may give him solace.*

After one final check of her mascara, she closed her compact and tapped Helga on the back. "If you're free, I'm finally ready to see Milt."

"Don't worry about my schedule, I'm ready and available for as long as you want me to be," Helga softly said as they neared Milt's room.

"Milt, you have a visitor. Are you ready for visitors?"

"Yeah, as long as it's not that damn Doctor Phillips! He's visited enough for one day. Matter of fact I don't care if I ever see that s.o.b. again."

"It's me, sweetheart," Vi said as she peeked around the corner of the door frame.

"Finally, a friendly face, hope you've got good news. Your news has gotta be a whole lot better then the crap they dropped on me this morning."

"I don't understand, dear. Sounds like you got some disturbing news today?"

"Yeah, I guess you could call tellin' a man he ain't never gonna walk again disturbing. Two goddamn years of gettin' cut on and pushed and pulled every which way ain't got me squat."

"Did the doctor say you'll never walk or just have to walk with crutches?"

As he slapped his hand violently down on the hospital table, he yelled, "Walking with crutches ain't walkin'!"

"Milt, please don't hurt yourself, or the table." Nurse Helga calmly requested. "I agree that walking with the aid of braces and crutches is not as easy as without, but you will be able to get around on your own. You will have limitations, but . . ."

Smacking the table again, he yelled, "Damn right I'll have limitations—like holdin' down a job!"

"Sweetheart, please calm down. I'm sure the doctors didn't want to give up on your dream, but they aren't God. They can only do so much. Good thing is that they haven't given up completely, and you'll still be able to work."

"How do you figure? You heard what they told me! Did I miss something? Sounded like to me they said—tough luck Milt. Get use to bein' crippled!"

"From what I just heard, that isn't what they said. You're just disappointed and taking it hard."

"Damn right I'm disappointed! If that ain't what they said, then what did I miss?"

"I think you were so hurt you didn't want to hear about walking with crutches. Sweetheart, you'll still be able to get around, and the Pastor still has work for you."

"How do you figure? I might be able to walk like Frankenstein, but that won't do me much good when I'm tryin' to fix his damn dairy machinery."

"Don't be silly. You're a lot more handsome then Frankenstein." Vi smiled and ran her fingers through his hair. "Fixing machinery might be hard for someone on crutches, but don't forget the Pastor offered you an office job."

"Vi, you know I don't want to work behind a desk," He looked down and his eyes began to tear up.

"I know. But you know that sometimes we don't have choices. Working as a bookkeeper may not be what you want, but at least it supports the family."

"You're right, and if I have to I will." He paused, then lifted his head up and jutted his jaw forward in defiance. "But first, if the Pastor will let me, I'm gonna take a crack at my old job."

"I understand, sweetheart. If you want, I'll talk to the Pastor. Promise me though that you will think about taking the book-keeping job if your old job doesn't work out."

"You know I will, sweetheart. I won't let the family down." He cocked his head towards the sounds of his loud, jubilant boys who appeared to be testing the nurses, and said, "Sweetheart, why don't you rescue that young nurse before she swears off having kids of her own?"

"Good idea. I'll be right back." She giggled at the sight of Edward and Walter befuddling the young nurses' attempt to keep their young, excited voices to a hospital ward level.

"Nurse Helga, while my wife is gone, I'd like to apologize for all the crap I gave you today. You've done fine by me and my family, and you didn't deserve my harsh words," Milt said as he reached his arm towards her.

Shaking his hand, she said, "No need to apologize. The news you got today would try the soul of anyone. I didn't take offense. Anyway, rest assured I'll help you as much as I can in the next month or so to help you master walking with braces and crutches."

"Thanks. I'll try my best." Breaking into a smile he continued, "I won't even call you a Nazi when you order me around, Sarge."

Dodging the boys' charge towards their father's bed, she said, "That will be a welcome change, Sarge. Now, enjoy your boys, and get rested up for tomorrow's session in the torture chamber."

25

"See you tomorrow, Milt. Ya sure ya don't want me to help ya get up those steps?" his apprentice, Erick, asked.

"Nah, I can manage. Thanks for giving me a ride home," Milt said as he locked his braces and adjusted his crutches in preparation for his nightly Mt.Everest-like assault on the back porch steps.

Vi pushed open the back porch screen door. "Evenin' sweetheart. Evenin' Erick. Appreciate you giving Milt a ride home. I'm getting so big with this child," she said as she lightly patted her pregnant stomach, "it has become quite a job to fetch Milt after work. Takes almost all I can do to just herd all my boys into the car."

"Think nothin' of it, Mrs. McCoy. Glad I can help. See you tomorrow, Milt," he yelled from the delivery truck's window as he backed out of the McCoy driveway.

Before Milt could attempt his stiff-legged, crutch-leaning climb up the stairs, she said, "How was your day, sweetheart? Do you want me to give you a hand?"

With his customary response to offers of help, he said, "How many times do I have to tell you? If I can't do it myself then I ain't worth spit!"

"Sorry, dear. I just wanted to make it easier for you. You look tired."

"Damn right, I'm tired. Picking myself up almost every hour and walking stiff legged all day can wear a body out." *Crap, I did it again. Ain't been home five minutes and I'm already takin' my day out on her.* "Sorry, hon. I shouldn't be taking it out on you. Go on in and get the boys taken care of. Don't worry about me."

"The boys are fine. They're playing over at Roger's house. Would you like to sit with me on the steps while we have the house to ourselves and enjoy a cold iced tea?"

In as graceful of a sitting that his brace-stiff legs permitted, Milt landed with a detectable thud on the third porch step from the bottom. Milt released the lock on his braces so that he could bend his legs, and said, "Iced tea, sounds great. It's been a tough day, and some quiet time with you before I have to conquer these steps sounds good."

"Be back in a jif. Would you like me to bring your pipe?"

"That would be great. Thanks, hon."

God am I ever glad she stuck with me. Lots of women would have given up. Two years without any help from me and wondering where the next dime is gonna come from must have been hell. I gotta do right by her. Can't keep coming home and taking it out on her. This job is tough to do without legs. The Pastor has been patient, but with all the falling I'm doing I don't know for how much longer. Erick is a smart fella, but I don't know if he's ready to take over.

"Here you go dear. One iced tea, and Prince Albert, still in the can," Vi said with a giggle.

"Huh," Milt said as he ascended out of his consuming deep thoughts. He smiled at Vi's resurrection of the old joke that opened the door of their relationship, and said, "Oh, thanks, dear. I guess I had better let the prince out."

"Sorry for startling you. You looked really deep in thought." She struggled to lower her heavily laden pregnant body to a step near him.

"Like they say, it was pretty deep for a shallow mind." He chuckled as he prepared his pipe for smoking. "I was just thinking about the day."

"Anything in particular?"

"Just trying to answer the same old question."

"You must have fallen down a few times today. Every time that happens, I notice you have moments at night that your mind is far away." She embraced him with her right arm and lowered her head onto his shoulder.

"More than a few times. The Pastor and Erick were good about it, but it embarrassed me to no end. Nurse Helga said it might take awhile to get used to walking like this, but I'm starting to wonder."

"Speaking of Helga, she called today."

"Still checkin' up on me?"

"No, don't be silly, she just wanted to say hello and see how you were doing. The more I got to know her the more I liked her. She may have pushed you a bit, but I know she did it because she cared."

"Yeah, I know, but she sure did her pushin' real good. What's she up to now days?"

"She's thinking about moving to Galesburg. Now that the polio epidemic is over and Dr. Salk invented the polio vaccine, they might be closing down her ward at Peoria Methodist. She said Cottage Hospital might have a spot for her so she wanted to ask about Galesburg. I hope you don't mind, but I asked her over for supper next Thursday."

"No, I don't mind. Wish they'd had that vaccine a few years earlier," he said as his smile faded.

"I do too, sweetheart. But at least our kids are safe. Before you tell me more about your day, do you want some more iced tea?" she said as she started to awkwardly get up from her step.

Tugging on her dress, he said, "Sit down. I'm fine, besides we don't need two of us tuckered out. Save your energy for supper." He rubbed her swollen belly tenderly and said, "You might also save your energy for our baby. Sounds like little Josie is wearin' you out."

"She's trying to." Vi said as she sat back down. "The way that baby is kicking, I'm starting to wonder if Mrs. Procini knows what she's talking about."

"You know her better then I do, but your dad says her ring test is always right. So, we're gonna have a baby girl. One thing I know for certain—after this one the stork is out of business. Four tries and no girl ain't gonna talk us into a fifth try."

"Sweetheart, I hope it's a girl for you to turn into a spoiled daddy's girl, but even if it is a girl—Vi's oven is closed!"

"Speaking of kids, when are they coming home?"

"Betty said to give her a jingle when we want them home. Before I do though, tell me more about your job. Are you going to stick with it, or change to be the bookkeeper?"

"That is kinda what I was thinking about when you brought out my iced tea. I knew a couple days after I started back up that I'd end up as the bookkeeper. Can't fight facts—a man with stiff legs and crutches can't do this job. It's hard to fix machinery while you're falling on your can all the time."

"Then quit making yourself miserable and take the book-keeping job."

"I know you're right, but I can't."

She frowned and sat up straight. "Milt McCoy, you aren't making any sense at all! You just said performing your job from your backside wasn't working! You may not prefer to be behind a desk, but for the sake of yours and your family's happiness take the bookkeeping job!"

Startled by her vehement feelings, he said, "Sweetheart it's not just me not wanting to be chained to a desk. The book-keeping job pays less. We need all we can get."

"Oh, I didn't know that. Have you talked to the Pastor about the pay? Maybe you could get a little extra if you did something besides just bookkeeping."

"Like what? All I know how to do is stuff I can't do with these bum legs."

"Didn't you say Erick wasn't as good a mechanic as you? Maybe you could advise Erick when he's stumped. Or maybe the Pastor could let you help with sales. I know you don't like to brag, but people like to buy things that heroes like."

She's got me. Don't know what the Pastor will think, but like some fella once said: "nothing ventured, nothing gained".

"You're awfully quiet. What are you thinking?"

"Thinkin' you're right! I'll talk to the Pastor tomorrow. Also thinking we ought to get those boys home," he said as he locked his braces in preparation to rise up into his stiff legged, brace-supported stance.

*   *   *

Exiting his car, which he now could drive thanks to modifications the local chapter of the VFW contributions bought, Milt locked his braces in place and adjusted his crutches to his armpits. Instead of his wife smiling down from the back porch, the stoop was empty. *Where's Vi? She's always waitin' for me. What is that whimpering? Sounds like Vi's crying. God, I wish could run to her.*

Calling for her as he climbed the newly built back porch ramp the Pastor's church had donated, his mind raced even though his legs couldn't. *Is she alright? She's almost due. Hope it isn't the baby coming early. I better get my tail in the house. I can't do much, but I can always call someone.*

He opened the kitchen door and saw Vi sitting at the kitchen table with her head resting on her arms as she loudly sobbed. "Vi are you alright? What's wrong? Is it the baby? Should I call the doctor?"

Vi raised her head and wiped away her tears, and said, "Don't call the doctor, I'm fine."

"Then why are you crying?"

"Butch broke . . .," she started to explain but once again tears erupted.

"What did he do? Do I need to have a talk with him, or should I break out the belt?"

Vi held up her index finger, and after Milt silently acknowledged her request for a moment she made one more attempt to collect herself. "I took care of it. Butch didn't really do anything bad, he just broke my heart."

"What do you mean? Breaking his mother's heart ain't exactly nothin' good. What's he done?"

"After you went in the hospital, Butch started mowing lawns, raking leaves, and shoveling snow for neighbors. Then he would turn over the money they paid him to me. He told me he wanted to help. After you got out of the hospital, he stopped giving me the money. But, today he gave me this," she showed him five dollars. "That makes me proud, but also breaks my heart."

"Why would he do that? I thought we agreed to keep the money problems just between us," he said with a slight frown.

"I thought I had kept it away from him, but I forgot he could hear all our late night conversations."

"Huh? How's that?"

"He just lays on his bed and hears everything said in our room. Our heating register is right below his. So he just kept his ears open and heard everything when we were talking about money last night."

"Oh my God, what else did he hear? I better put something over our register, or our son will be telling us about the birds and the bees."

"That's why I've kept kinda quiet when I enjoy the pleasure of my husband's company," Vi's cheeks glowed with a blush.

* * *

With a white-knuckled grip on the railing of the back door ramp, Milt seethed as he pulled himself up from his fall to the floor of the icy slick ramp. *God, I hate this damn winter! It's cold enough to freeze the balls off a brass monkey. Where the hell is everybody? I could freeze to death and no one would be the wiser.*

"Vi, Vi!" he yelled. Catching his breath, which the cold prairie wind gusts had robbed from him, Milt tried one more time to get someone's attention. "Vi, Butch, one of you come give me a hand. I fell and I'm havin' a hell time getting up."

What a welcome home—wind, snow, and a deserted house! Where the hell is everyone? They better hope like hell they have a good explanation. Don't much like fallin' on ice! And, no one around to help really ticks me off! One of my damn crutches went slidin' down the ramp when I fell. Gonna be rough getting up this slicker then owl shit ramp without both of my crutches.

Ten minutes later, Milt struggled to the top of the ramp. He opened the back door, and slipped on a patch of ice just as he started to enter into the kitchen. While he pushed himself away from the kitchen floor he yelled, "Goddamn it is anyone home?"

From the downstairs bedroom, Milt heard Vi yell, "Coming dear, I didn't know you were home. I was changing Josie's diaper. Sorry I didn't hear you. Josie has the runs, so she was screaming her head off. I'd be screaming too, if my butt was beet red." She bent over to help him up and asked, "Are you alright?"

Brushing her offered hand aside with an angry burst of force, he shouted, "Yeah, but no thanks to you! How come the house is so damn cold? It's almost as cold in here as it is outside. You trying to grow icicles or just hoping to cool my-mad-as-hell mood down?"

"Don't be silly, we won't need icicles until we get the Christmas tree," she said with a contrived lilt and forced smile. She slid a chair towards Milt. "Sorry you had such a bad day. If you'll hold the baby after you get seated, I'll get some coffee started for you. Stove will heat the kitchen up. Coffee and your pipe might cheer you up."

Milt pulled himself up on to the chair. "Coffee and a smoke sounds good." After he released the lock on his braces so he could bend his legs, he squirmed into a comfortable seat position and reached for the baby. Softened by the cooing of Josie, Milt's civility and his concern for his family finally returned. "Is the furnace working? Doesn't sound like it."

"Something's wrong with it, but I haven't had time to check it. Josie took up all my time. If you want, I'll go down and look at it while you play with Josie. Or, as soon as Butch gets home I'll have him check it. Probably just out of coal."

"I'm freezin', but the way Josie's fussin' I think we'll wait till Butch gets home," he said as he handed the baby back to Vi. "Where the hell is he? He should have been home from school hours ago."

"He came straight home. You should have seen him. You'd think he'd never seen snow before. It's the first snow of winter, so I let him go play in it with Roger. Furnace stopped about twenty minutes after he tore out the back door. I expect him home any minute now," she said as she reverted to her childhood nervous tick of twirling her hair around her index finger.

As if waiting in the wings for his cue, an excited Butch burst through the back door and yelled, "Dad, look out the kitchen window. Ain't, our snowman neat?"

Before Milt could answer, Vi corrected Butch. "The word is, isn't, not ain't. Please watch your language, son."

"Yeah, and while your minding your grammar, you get your tail down in the basement and get the furnace going again. Mom and I can't do everything around here."

"Ah, geez Dad, the guys are waitin' for me. Can't I . . ."

"I don't give a damn who is waiting! Now get your skinny little tail down there and get that damn furnace going!" he yelled as he swung his crutch at Butch's head.

"Sorry Dad," Butch meekly said as he ducked beneath his father's wild swing.

"Don't wanna hear no goddamn sorry! Get that son-of-a-bitching furnace working before we all turn blue!" Milt yelled in a crazed voice as he shuffled closer to his son for another wild swing.

"Yes Dad," Butch murmured while he ran towards the basement stairs.

"Milt, he's only. . ."

"I don't want to hear it!" He clamped his mouth shut with vehemence as his body struck a rigid crutch-aided stance.

Hoping that the silence of the past few minutes meant that Milt's unusual anger had dissipated, Vi asked in a soft tone,

"Sweetheart, I know coming home to a cold house and me not being able to help you disturbed you, but don't you think you might have been a bit to hard on Butch?"

Jerking his head towards her, he yelled, "No, I wasn't! He needs to learn that taking care of his family comes first! I won't have my son runnin' around having fun when he's got work to do. I ain't gonna raise no goddamn bum! He's actin' like a no good . . ."

Vi slapped Milt across the face as hard as her short, one hundred forty pound frame could muster. Vi shook her finger at him and yelled, "Don't you ever call him that! He's only nine, but for the past two years he's worked harder than most men would!"

"You hit me! I can't believe you did that!" he said as he struggled to regain his feet.

Shaking with anger, Vi continued. "Yes, I did. I didn't mean to knock you down, but if you ever call him that again—I'll leave you. Your dad almost ruined you with that kind of talk, and I'll be damned if you'll do it to our son!"

Staring at her with anger in his eyes, he said, "You have a good point, but we don't need to be hitting each other."

"You're right, but I can't believe you said that. Did you see what you almost did to Butch? My heart skipped a beat when I saw you swing at him."

Milt hung his head as his anger drained from his face. "I'm sorry. I got carried away. It won't happen again."

"It better not. I won't tolerate my children or me being beaten upon just because you're angry. I'm sorry I slapped you. I heard that horrible name, and it brought to mind all the pain I've seen it cause you. Our son deserves better."

"Yeah, he is a good boy." Rubbing his jaw, he smiled in hopes of changing the tone of the evening. "You sure surprised me. I didn't know you could pack such a wallop, and I think that is the first time I ever heard you cuss."

"Surprised me too, I guess that phone call from your dad today upset me more than I realized."

He rolled his eyes to the ceiling, and asked, "What the heck did he want? I thought this day couldn't get any worse."

"Believe it or not, he wants you to come see him."

"Yeah sure, like that's gonna happen."

She sighed. "Actually, after what just happened, I think you need to go see him."

"Huh, you gotta be kiddin'! Why would I go see him?"

"Because he's dying, and it is the Christian thing to do. It might be a waste of time, but at least you will have done your duty."

"Will you go with me?"

"No, I think you need an opportunity to close things out between you two. If I was there you two might not get honest with each other."

"You gonna be okay with me if I don't go?"

"No I won't, because you're a bigger and better man than that."

26

Milt labored to swing his heavy iron-braced legs towards a visit, possibly a last one—or so he hoped. *How the hell did I let her talk me into this?*

What the hell does the old bastard want that Vi thinks is so damn important? I don't know, but I'll be damned if I'll let him see me in that wheelchair the nurse keeps trying to force me into. But I gotta admit that these slippery floors sure make a ride in a wheelchair tempting.

Fighting to maintain his balance, he pushed the heavy hospital ward door open, and in a gruff voice spoke. "Anyone here by the name of Frank McCoy?"

"Sir, may I help you?" a short, plump, middle aged woman clad in a stiff white nurse's uniform asked with a disarming smile.

Milt remembered it was his dad that he held in contempt, so he smiled and said, "I hope so ma'am. I understand my father, Frank McCoy, asked me to visit him. If you would be so kind to point out his bed, I'd appreciate it."

She noted the visitor's struggle to maintain his balance and said, "Mr. McCoy's bed is at the end of the room on the left side. The floor was just washed, so it is rather slippery. Let me get you a wheelchair, and I'll take you right to him."

"I can manage ma'am. If you don't mind, I'd rather not have him see me in a wheelchair."

Having worked with many polio victims during her career, the nurse understood. Although not in keeping with hospital regulations, she consented to allow Milt to walk with her to his father's bed.

After what seemed to be a marathon event, Milt finally reached Frank's bed. "If I can be of any further assistance, please let me know," the nurse said and departed.

One quick look at his father confirmed what Vi had told him. *Christ he looks worse then I did right after I got out of the iron lung. I guess all those years of boozing and floosies finally caught up with him. About goddamn time!*

Before Milt could greet him, Frank lifted his arm with a grimace of pain, and pointed to the other side of the bed. "Glad you made it Milt, say hello to your new Ma."

Ma? Christ, that girl is hardly old enough to be out of pigtails. She sure as hell ain't old enough to be out of school, and way too damn young to be married to that old fool let alone some young'n. I wonder if that's the Richards girl. I heard she ran off with some older fella, but I can't believe it was with my old man!

Milt reeled from his father's startling revelation, but hid his feelings as he said, "Ma'am, if it's all the same to you, I'd like a few private moments with my Dad."

"Surely sir, I'll just go get me a soda and be back in awhile," she replied in a girlish voice.

Frank coughed a prolonged painful cough. "What is this sir shit, girl? You remind this here boy that you are Ma not ma'am. Now git, so I can set this boy straight. While you're at it, fetch me some of that corn liquor from my truck."

Before Frank could spew any more of his venom, Milt leaned over to be closer to Frank but lost his balance and landed on top of him. *Crap! That oughta draw nurses to us like flies to shit. I might as well make the best of it before they get here.* He bluntly tapped Frank's chest with his rigid index finger and said through clenched teeth, "If anybody's setting anybody straight it's gonna be me setting your pathetic old ass straight! Got it?"

Frank's eyes widened while color drained from his alcohol ravaged face. Stunned, he said, "Bullshit, it's you that needs the straightenin'."

Milt shook with anger. "Listen old man, I'm only here because Vi talked me into it. Said you were in a pretty poor way, and it might be the last time I see you. After that crap about a 'new Ma' I hope to hell it is."

After a short pause to catch his breath, Milt realized he hadn't finished. "What is this shit about a new ma? Hell, I didn't have a first one. Ain't no way in hell you can say Bess and you were Mom and Dad. You two were just pathetic pieces of shit that got together and somehow God screwed up and gave you losers a kid to screw up."

With what little strength he had left, Frank pushed Milt off of him. Surprised, Milt fought for balance but his stiff, braced legs failed him. Frank looked down at Milt, and in a raised voice that hardly caught the attention of anyone beyond his bedside, he spoke. "You fuckin' bum! If I was able, I'd take you right out of this life, just like I brought you in it! I asked you to visit so I could apologize for misjudging you all these years, but now I see I was right all along."

"Bum! Bum! I got news for you. It used to make my blood boil when you called me that, but after all I got put through, and all that I came through, I just flat don't care. If anyone's a bum it's you, goddamn it! You ain't done shit with your life besides drink, beat on folks, and screw anything in a skirt that's dumb enough to get near you!"

The nurse arrived and insisted on helping him to his feet. "What happened here? Are you two okay?"

Not wanting the interference of an outsider, both men were quick to assure her that all was well, and that Milt's fall was only because of the slick floor. Having seen more than one last-one-before-they-die family conversations during her career, the nurse reluctantly accepted their false assurances, but insisted that Milt be seated in a wheelchair during the rest of his visit.

Milt hated the thought of his old man seeing him in a wheelchair instead of proudly standing in spite of his polio, but, for the sake of getting the nurse to leave, he gave in to her demand.

As she assisted Milt in getting settled into the wheelchair, he glared at his dad. After the nurse departed, Milt decided to attempt to bring their last visit to some degree of civility. "I guess we both got a bit carried away. We both have lots of things between us, so I probably should've let you go in peace instead of coming to see you one last time."

After an awkward pause, Frank tried his own stumbling attempt at conciliation. "I should never of asked you here. If that fella you were in the war with hadn't visited, thinkin' I was you cuz he saw in the paper that a McCoy was in the hospital, I would still of thought you were a bum, and I don't need a bum visitin' me."

There he goes again with that damn bum crap. Gotta ignore it this time or I might forever live with regret. "What guy? I didn't know that any of my war buddies lived in this area."

"Said his name was Bill Wilder. I think he was from Peoria. At least he said he saw in the Peoria Journal Star that a McCoy was in the hospital. He sure carried on about you at some place called Anzio. Even said you saved his life, and you got some sort of medal for it? How come you never told us?"

"I remember Bill. Nice fella, but I wouldn't say that I saved his life."

"Well that's what him, and the Army seems to think."

"Think all they want, I was just trying to keep myself in one piece. I never told anyone about any battles because I didn't want anyone to worry."

"Anyway, boy, after he visited and told me all about how you damned near got your own self killed savin' him and a couple of other fellas, I got to thinkin' about me and you. Then the nurse in charge, Nurse Helga, visited me, and after the kind words she had to say about ya, I really got to thinkin'."

"I'm sure you did," Milt said with a look of disbelief.

Frank struggled to find his breath. "Nah, I didn't mean it that way. Like you said awhile ago, I know I wasn't always much of a dad to ya, and I know that over the years I called you some mean things. I could tell ya it was just the liquor talkin', but we both know it wasn't."

Weakened by the effort of his confession, Frank's body was racked by deep and ragged coughing. While he struggled to find strength, he signaled a request for Milt's patience. After a few more body contorting coughs, Frank once again continued, but in a much softer, hard-to-hear, voice. "Plain truth is, I've been thinkin' about you ever since that polio got ya. Lot of fellas woulda just quit, but not you. Findin' a way to walk and feed your family was really somethin'. After I heard from that Wilder fella and Nurse Helga, I knew I'd misjudged you. It's a bit late to say I'm sorry, but I can tell ya that I'm convinced you're not a bum. Now get outta here and let me die in peace," Frank said as he offered his hand to Milt.

Milt hesitated for a brief moment before he shook his father's weak, limp hand, and called to the nearby nurse as he fought back tears. "Please come and get this wheelchair. I'm walking out of here! It's for certain I won't be wheeling out of here like some lazy bum. You heard my dad, I ain't no bum! Matter of fact, my son ain't either!"